Brutal Little Secrets

C.S. Berry

Author Note & Content List

Dear Reader,

Thank you for choosing Brutal Little Secrets. First thing, this is a continuation from Whisper Pretty Lies and will be completed in Dark Tangled Truths. Originally it was meant to be a duet, but this story grew too big for two books. There will be a cliffhanger at the end, but the next book is coming soon!

Hot guys playing hockey and riding motorcycles, check. Artistic girl with her own dreams and goals, check. Villains abound, check. Revenge on the cheating boyfriend... you'll have to read to find out.

This book contains darker themes, which can be found on my website csberry.com/lust-liars under content warnings. Your mental health is important. If you're concerned, you can always reach out to me.

Evan and her guys are determined to find their happily ever after!

XOXOXO
C.S. Berry

Content warning:

Dark themes including bullying, blackmail, chasing scenes, consensual somnophilia, and stalking. It also includes attempted sexual assault.

Chapter 1

Hawk

Leaving the party to go get Annie after her douchebag of a boyfriend stranded her is a no-brainer. I left Cam drunk with no keys and Damon to deal with Olivia. He wanted Olivia to leave Annie alone but paying her too much attention might make Olivia even more territorial.

I ride as fast as I can down the country road until I get to the pull off. Annie sits on one of the railroad ties they use as curbs. Her arms are wrapped around her knees, making her look small in the headlight of my motorcycle.

How could someone who cares about her abandon her out here? In the middle of nowhere? It's not even walkable back to town. Did Chase plan to leave her out here and then come back later? Hoping she'd be grateful to be rescued after he abandoned her?

Fuck him.

We're going to destroy Chase Chadwick.

I park and cut my engine. As I cross the lot to her, I shrug out of my leather jacket. It's not that cold out tonight, but the wind can be chilly when I ride. She doesn't look up as I approach.

Draping my jacket around her shoulders, I squat in front of her and lift her chin. Fuck. Her face is tear-streaked. Her blue eyes are watery. She won't meet my gaze.

I push down all the fury I feel toward Chase right now and focus on the girl before me.

"Hey there, Annie." I brush my thumb over a stray tear on her cheek.

She sniffles and whispers, "I'm sorry."

"For what?" I slide my hand to cup her jaw, and she leans into my touch. I don't know if she's aware she's doing it. The need to protect her at all costs flows through me.

"For making you leave the party." Her eyes remain downcast.

"You didn't make me do anything." I blow out a breath. "I was getting worried about you when I got your call."

She trembles and pulls my jacket around her tighter. "I didn't know who else to call. My mom's busy. Cam was drinking. Damon—" Tears slip free. "I don't have anyone else—"

She cuts herself off on a small sob with the back of her hand pressed against her mouth. Fuck. My chest aches to see her like this. I sit next to her on the railroad tie and wrap my arm around her shoulders, pulling her into my side.

"Did he hurt you?" I ask, quietly. We don't know much about their relationship except he cheats on her. It's an asshole move. He may have gotten rough if she didn't want to be with him. Right now, she doesn't seem hurt besides emotionally. But if he hurt her physically...

No one would stop me from tearing through him. Not Cam. Not Damon.

"He grabbed my arm, but mostly he scared me." She rubs her arm and sighs. "I told him I knew he was cheating on me. He wanted to..."

She turns into me and buries her face in my chest. Her shoulders shake as she cries softly against me. I'm going to kick Chase's ass. But I have to ask.

"Did he force you?" I try to keep my anger out of my voice. Not that we're much better, but at least we give her a fucking choice. And if he did, I'll encourage her to press charges, because fuck him.

She shakes her head and her eyes get this far off look. "I ran away before he could touch me, and he left me. Got in his truck and left me out here in the middle of nowhere. He didn't even know if I had my phone."

I glance around the area. There are a few low lights for the parking lot and there's moonlight, but otherwise it's dark out here. It's a few miles outside of town, and the nearest gas station or house isn't close. If this is the type of shit he pulls, we need to rethink letting her remain with Chase.

It may be part of the plan, but I'm not risking Annie.

Right now, I need to get her some place safe and warm.

"You ready to ride, baby girl?" I brush her hair off her cheek and behind her ear.

Her eyes lift to mine, searching. "Are we over?"

Fuck. The hurt and resignation in her eyes are almost my undoing. The party tonight. Cam is hopefully sleeping off his keg stands. The girls were all over me, but I didn't touch any of them. But Damon... Fucking Damon had Olivia all over him tonight.

He had a good reason. Mia thinks Damon is into Evan. Olivia was suspicious, and for our plan to work, we need to keep that a secret.

I sigh. "No, we're not over. We're playing the roles, so people don't suspect anything."

"Damon went into a room with Olivia." She sighs like she expected that. Like we'd be like Chase and cheat on her.

"He was probably angry at seeing Chase kiss you."

She makes a dismissive sound like that would be ridiculous, but I know Damon. We've been friends forever and I've never seen him react to a girl the way he reacts to Annie. I dismissed it at first. Figured he's fucking angry. Angry at his father. Angry at Chase. Angry at having his future ripped away.

But there's something else here. He doesn't have to sleep with

Annie to fuck with her. But I know that's where she spends her nights. In his arms. In his bed.

Maybe the first night was a control thing, but he just holds her now. He set us up with the feed to his cameras, figuring we deserve to have those pieces of Annie since she's ours. He takes care of her.

When it comes down to it, I don't know if he'll be able to drive her and her mom out of his life. Not if it means losing Annie.

"Come on, Annie. Let's head back into town."

She doesn't try to stand. "What for?"

This girl. Fuck. "To get warm and to find out what we do next."

Her gaze darts up to mine. "I don't want to be around Chase anymore."

I nod. Honestly, I'm not sure I'll be able to see him and not beat the living shit out of him.

Standing, I offer her my hands to pull her up. Once she's standing, she brushes off her ass. When she tries to offer my jacket back to me, I shake my head.

"You wear it."

She puts her arms in it while I get my helmet on. Then I help her with hers. When I get on the bike, she doesn't hesitate to climb on behind me. She still wraps around me like a koala bear, tucked in tight against me, but I like the way she feels.

I go slower on the way home. This is one of my favorite roads to ride on. And having Annie with me makes it even better.

Riding with a girl is a simple thing, but when everything else in my life screams at me to excel, riding is just joyful for me. I could ride with Annie wrapped around me for hours.

As we reach town, I could take her to my house, but she'll be more comfortable at hers and Damon's.

All the lights are out when we pull up. Their parents are probably out in the city for the weekend again. But I know how to get in. When I park in the garage and shut off my motorcycle, Annie climbs off and for a moment, I wish she still had issues.

I like taking care of her, which should make me hesitate, but I'm through hesitating when it comes to this girl. As soon as both helmets are secure, I take Annie's hand and lead her to the side door. The code unlocks the door, and I guide her in. While this may be where she lives now, this is where I grew up. I'm more familiar with the house.

As I lead her into the kitchen, she follows behind me. Her fingers tangled with mine. The fear I felt when she called to tell me she'd been abandoned in the woods still clings to me. When I stop and look into her blue eyes, I find it still clings to her as well.

Taking hold of her hips, I lift her onto the counter before turning and getting her a towel, wetting it with warm water. When I hand it to her, her smile is sad.

"Thank you."

I move over to the refrigerator and grab us bottles of water. "Are you hungry?"

"No, thank you." She wipes at her face with the towel as she peers around the kitchen. "I think this is the first time I've seen this kitchen without staff in it."

"Guess they can't afford a night kitchen employee." I grab a small tray of veggies just in case she changes her mind.

She hums in agreement.

When I walk back over to her, I set the items beside her on the island. I step between her knees and slide my hand beneath her hair and tip her chin, so she looks into my eyes.

I search her stormy blue eyes for a moment. "What do you need, Annie?"

She shrugs. Does no one take care of this girl? It seems like she expects nothing from any of us. Sure, we're essentially blackmailing her, but it doesn't seem like she expects anything from anyone in her family or friends.

"Damon should be home soon." I brush my thumb across her cheek.

She stiffens and looks away, biting her lip. She believes something happened between Olivia and Damon. But there's no way. Damon should be the one to tell her this, but I take her chin between my thumb and finger and make her look at me.

"He doesn't break promises or rules or whatever the fuck we have."

Her wide eyes blink. The hurt lingers. Another reason to fuck Chase up. His fucking around on her made her doubt her desirability. And then Damon goes and lets Olivia hang all over him like he's going to fuck her.

"Damon's not going to fuck anyone else." I blow out a breath. Her eyes search mine. "He might make it look like he's fucking someone else, but he wouldn't actually do it."

She swallows.

Fuck, I hope I'm right. He's been tense with the current condition of our agreement. He wants to fuck Annie. Who doesn't? He wanted to push her, and he got her to change the original agreement, but what if it wasn't enough?

What if he wanted to hurt Annie because he couldn't handle seeing Chase kiss her? Fuck. I have to trust he did the right thing, but it might set him back with Annie again.

"Let's get you cleaned up and in bed."

She nods. "It's been a long night."

I lift her down to her feet and give her a bottle of water. I take the other one and the vegetable tray and lead the way to the staircase.

When we get to her room, she walks in and hesitates. She doesn't look at me when she asks, "Are you going to leave?"

I set everything down on her desk and turn to look at her. The more time I spend with her, the more she captivates me.

She's always been as smart as me, maybe even smarter. Before her, I've never really sat down and discussed Shakespeare with a girl, or anyone else for that matter. Usually when I'm with a girl, I have other intentions. I lean back on the desk and cross my arms over my chest. I don't know which way she's headed with that question.

"Do you want me to?"

Her blue eyes meet mine before she lowers them again and shrugs.

I'm across the room with her face in my hands before she can gasp.

"Tell me what you want, baby girl. I'll give it to you."

Her hands come up and tentatively rest on my waist. Her stormy eyes search mine. "Stay."

I kiss her softly. "Always."

She leans into me. I take her into my arms and hold her. She's had a rough night and needs me to be gentle. I can give that to her.

"Do you want to talk about it?"

"Not really." She releases me and I step back, giving her space. "He didn't do more than kiss me. And I really didn't have time to stop him. I didn't want him to kiss me."

She drags in a rough breath, and her fingers play with the label on the water bottle. "I don't want to do this anymore, Hawk."

I arch an eyebrow when she lifts her gaze to mine.

"Date Chase," she clarifies. "He keeps pushing for more, and I don't even want to be alone with him. I never thought he'd... That he would..."

Her eyes well with tears again. I take her water and set it on the nightstand.

"It's been a long night." I thread my fingers with hers and pull her toward the bathroom. "Let's take a quick shower, and we'll crawl into bed. Things should be brighter in the morning."

She looks at me doubtfully but lets me bring her into the bathroom. She slips into the water closet while I start the shower. When she comes out, I've stripped down to my boxers.

"I wasn't sure if you wanted to share or take turns," I explain and step into her, lifting Damon's shirt off over her head.

Her blond hair falls around her shoulders as I drop the shirt on the floor. She works on her jeans as I move around her to unhook her bra. Unable to resist, I kiss her shoulder. Her skin is soft beneath my lips, and I inhale that woodsy scent that clings to her. She shivers but doesn't pull away.

When I rub my thumb across the mark Damon left on her shoulder, she trembles.

I don't touch her more. Not that I don't want to, but she's been through a lot tonight.

She turns to me, naked. My already semi-hard cock grows harder. It amazes me I dismissed her for so many years. Looked through her as if she was nothing more than another classmate. I've never had to try for a girl. None of us have.

But she makes me want to try.

She reaches for my boxers. "Take a shower with me, Hawk."

I nod and thread my fingers through her hair as she lowers my boxers. She lifts her eyes to mine, and I draw her against me to hug her. She sighs and rests her head against my chest. Something shifts inside me and falls into place.

This girl is mine.

Chapter 2

EvanAnn

I take Hawk's hand and lead him into the shower, letting the water flow over me and wash away the night. It's taken less than a week, but Damon has me trained to ignore nudity for the most part.

I almost wish I was more self-conscious. I'd rather think about anything except what happened tonight.

But I can't stop it. The whole night was too much.

My mind is still spinning about Chase and Jackson. For a moment, Chase scared me the way Jackson did two years ago. Seeing Jackson at the game had my nerves already shredded. I never told Mom why I was eager to move from the apartment building, but she seemed just as determined to get away.

Being left out there in the woods should have been the worst part of the night, but nothing was like seeing Damon with Olivia. My stomach churns and I squeeze my eyes shut, trying to stop the image from returning. Seeing him come out of that room with her begging him to come back in—it broke something in me. Maybe it was this fragile thing that was quietly growing between me and Damon.

It hurt like a bruise to my pride when I found out about Chase.

But Damon... It cuts so much deeper. I don't know if I can handle it if he cheated on me.

I wrap my arms around myself and look up into Hawk's green eyes. He studies me as he fills his hands with my shampoo and works it into my hair and scalp. I close my eyes at the sensation. It's sensual, but caring. Tears press at the back of my eyes.

What do you need? Hawk's words haunt me. When was the last time someone worried about what I needed?

That's not enough.

When's the next time you're going to be able to eat, Evan?

I like you in my bed, little devil.

Shaking my head, I try to banish Damon's voice from inside it. I thought I was strong enough to keep this relationship purely sexual. They're just using me, so I should be able to use them. It makes sense. But the walls I built feel shaky. And tonight has been rough.

Damon might have slipped beneath my walls when I wasn't looking. I glance up at Hawk. Maybe they all have.

"Are you sure he didn't sleep with Olivia?" I can't help it. It's like this sickness building inside me. I know what Hawk said. But I saw Damon come out of a room with her. My insides twist and die a little. If the guy who promised to be only mine was fucking around on me because I wasn't putting out, how can I blame Damon for doing the same thing?

"He didn't fuck Olivia." Hawk guides me into the water and tips my head back to rinse the shampoo out of my hair. "If he did, he'll tell you."

"You'd tell me if he did?" I hate that my voice sounds so small and hurt, but I can't let this go. No one came forward to tell me about Chase until Damon. I won't have someone I trust cheat on me. Swallowing, I know I'm technically cheating on Chase every minute I'm with these guys. I don't want the Devils to mess around with anyone else. If that makes me a hypocrite, I don't care.

"Of course, baby girl." Hawk pulls me into his body and holds me, our bodies slick from the water.

It feels good to be held. His hard cock rests against my stomach, but I don't feel any urgency from him. He's not pressing me down to my knees or asking me to suck him off. My skin buzzes like it always does around them, but I don't want release right now. I need something far more important. Peace of mind.

I rest my ear over his beating heart as he strokes his hand down my wet back.

He rests his hand on the back of my head. "This arrangement and the deal we made means we'll stand by our word. I don't know what his intentions were when he went up to that room with Olivia, but I don't think it was to have sex with her."

I nod, wanting to believe him, but the rot inside me persists. Hawk is guessing about Damon. Will I believe Damon if he tells me nothing happened? How many times did Chase lie to my face? Saying I was the only one for him while he was off fucking someone else?

"It feels like I should be honest about something." Hawk reaches for the conditioner.

"I don't know if I can take much more honesty tonight," I admit.

He smirks and combs the conditioner through my hair with his fingers. "I didn't really have to practice for my audition. I played Romeo during my stint in *Shakespeare in the Park*."

A huff of a laugh releases from me. He grins.

"I just wanted to put that out there."

"You were amazing." I shake my head.

"See? I was hoping for awe-inspiring." He rinses his hands and grabs my soap, giving me some and filling his hands. "I almost came in and did the balcony scene, but everyone expects the balcony scene."

I roll my eyes and let Hawk tell me about his experience. Theater is my first love after all, and it's easy to let the rest slip to the back of my mind while his hands glide over my body and he talks Shakespeare with me.

Cam

Damon sits across the station from me at another desk. I am so fucked. There are a dozen other teens still here. Most of the parents have already come by to pick up their partiers, but my father and Damon's haven't made it in yet.

"Since this is your first offense, you'll be charged a fine and possibly time." Officer Taggert types into his computer. He seems bored of all this. "You'll have a court date to appeal the decision, but the breathalyzer reading is on your record."

I wish I was more sober because I'm sure this would drill in the fact I need to drink less. Instead, fuck, is this a trip.

Officer Taggert slides a pamphlet my way. I glance down at the Teen AA meeting drivel he's trying to push on me.

"Sir, I only drink at parties." I don't mention that I party most nights, but I don't always drink, so it's a balance.

"Camden Lane Warwick."

I flinch at my father's voice. Officer Taggert stands and holds his hand out to my dad.

"Sorry to bother you, Mr. Warwick." Officer Taggert gestures to the other seat. "We're almost finished here."

Dad lowers into the chair beside me, sitting up straight while I'm slouched. I look almost exactly like him, Maybe that's why he expects me to act like him too. My hair is as long as my mom will let it get, which is definitely longer than Dad's. I run my hand through it and don't need to look at him to feel the disapproval in his eyes.

Even when I tried to be his little clone, it was only disapproval and nitpicking. So I decided to go another way. Life has been easier.

"What can we do to make this go away, Officer Taggert?" My dad is ready to donate to the fucking police fund if I can keep a pristine record for his school of choice.

"The court hearing is in a week." Taggert's tone doesn't change.

Dad's smile tightens. "Perfect."

I don't laugh, but Dad will take care of this before the hearing. That's his job as my father. To make shit like that go away so I can get into Yale. It takes another ten minutes before we're out of the station. Damon's dad arrives as we're leaving. My dad stops to talk.

"This shit needs to end. Won't be long before the boys will be off to college," my dad says.

"One can only hope." Adam sighs. "I can't seem to get it through Damon's head that hockey is a dream that could go away with one injury. He needs to focus on getting a degree while at college. Not go to a college for hockey."

"College will straighten them out." My dad's hand tightens on my shoulder.

Fuck them both. It's like they never had dreams beyond what they achieved. If I were as good at hockey as Damon, I wouldn't let my dad stand in the way. I'd go after it just as hard as Damon does. And yeah, maybe my dream for college is smaller than my dad's, but it's what I want.

"We should have you and Lisa over for dinner some time." Adam smiles. "Heather and I have been talking about having a small dinner party."

Small, like fifty guests. I chuckle before I can stop myself.

My dad's eyes narrow on me before he meets Adam's gaze. "We'd love to. I can't wait to meet your new girlfriend. I need to get Cam home and sober before his mother finds out."

Adam runs a hand through his hair. "Yeah, not looking forward to whatever excuse Damon has this time."

Fuck our fathers. It's like they forgot what it's like to be a teenager. Grandma told me about the shit they used to get up to. So fuck them.

They say their goodbyes and we head out to the car. My phone is in my pocket, but I don't dare take it out where Dad can decide to take it away from me. I'm sick of high school, of parties, of being on a leash.

College is just a longer leash. I'll still be tied to my father for his money unless I want to find a way to work through college, which sounds like hell.

Once we're in the car, he hands me a bottle of water. He's silent on the way home. He probably won't lay into me until I'm hungover and trying not to puke my brains out. This isn't the first time he's had to pick me up somewhere because I was too drunk. Though, it's the first time he's picked me up from the police station.

I would have scrambled out the back of the party with the rest of my friends if I knew where the fuck Evan or Hawk or Damon were. I didn't want to leave them behind. But Hawk and Evan weren't at the station. Hopefully, they jumped the fence.

Chase was at the station, though, holding an ice pack against his cheek and glaring daggers at Damon.

His father arrived earlier and took him home. Asshole was probably sober. Maybe Evan got out with Mia, who I didn't see.

When we get home, the kitchen light is on, but my mother stopped waiting up for me years ago. We walk in and I grab another bottle of water from the fridge.

"We're talking in the morning, Cam." Dad shakes his head as he passes me. "This shit has got to stop."

I acknowledge his statement with a grunt and head up to my room. I'm still not sober enough to go anywhere and my motorcycle is still at Fletcher's. When I get to my room, I lie back on my bed and stare at the ceiling with the glow in the dark stars stuck to it.

I check my phone and there are no messages from Hawk, Damon, or Evan. I don't even know where Evan is.

ME:

Where you at, goody two-shoes?

When I don't get an immediate response, I glance at the time. It's ten after three in the morning. I put my phone on the charger and wonder what fresh hell tomorrow morning will bring.

Chapter 3

EvanAnn

"I'm not finished talking to you!"

The muffled voice wakes me. The arms around my center tighten, pulling me back against a warm body. I almost slip back into sleep.

"I'm going to bed." Damon?

The night comes flooding back to me in technicolor detail. The party. Chase. Damon with Olivia. Being left. Hawk. Safe. I snuggle into Hawk and his breath huffs against my temple.

"Have you been drinking?" Adam asks. My room is pitch black. The door to the bathroom is closed, but the hallway light shines beneath my door. The voices come from the hallway.

"Of course not." Damon's voice moves down the hall.

"Then why would you get into a fight at a party? I thought I raised you to be smarter than that. Do I have to worry about your temper? Do you need to go back to therapy?"

"No."

Damon got into a fight at the party? Was that after I left? How did his father find out? I hold my breath, waiting to hear more.

"I don't know what to do with you." Adam's voice comes through the bathroom.

I give up on sleeping and sit up. What happened tonight? Hawk keeps his arm around my legs.

"What were you even fighting about?"

Nothing from Damon. I can imagine him standing there. The tic in his jaw when he doesn't want to say anything twitching.

"First the accident, riding at night on a winding road, and now this." Adam sounds almost sad. "I'm calling the therapist on Monday. You're going to start weekly sessions again."

"Whatever *you* want. It's not like I have a choice in my own life." Damon doesn't raise his voice.

"I don't know what to do with you. You need to take this seriously. You're both eighteen. He could have filed assault charges." Adam's voice turns my blood cold. What did Damon do?

"He didn't and he won't."

"Are you going to at least tell me why?" Adam sounds tired.

I hold my breath, waiting to hear the answer, but Damon remains silent.

"We'll talk in the morning." The door shuts and footsteps walk down the hallway away from us. A shiver goes through me, but I don't take my eyes off the bathroom door. My heart throbs in my throat while my insides shrivel. Part of me wants to confront Damon, knowing he probably won't tell me anything either. And the other part wants to sink into his arms and let him hold me.

Tonight was difficult.

He moves into the bathroom, and the shower turns on.

Damon

My jaw aches, and I just want to crash, but I turn on the water and see Evan's clothes in the hamper. Her door is shut. I didn't expect to find her in my bed, but when I opened the door and Dad followed me, I was worried she would be.

Soft and warm, waiting in my bed, because that's where she belongs. My empty bed is a stark reminder that I fucked up. She never would have left with him if I hadn't wanted to hurt her like she hurt me. Even though Evan wasn't trying to hurt me, it didn't sting any less.

My dad wasn't happy to pick me up at the police station. He remained quiet until we came up here.

If it were only my father at home, he'd have kept me up to talk to me—or rather, at me. But now that he has Heather, he's eager to return to bed. He's not paying attention to what's happening in his own house. They haven't noticed Evan sleeps in my bed, and there are no locks on the doors to the bathroom.

Maybe my dad's actually in love this time. Maybe she could be it for him, but she's nothing like my mom. My mom was smart, beautiful, and kind. She was the partner my father needed. No woman could ever take her place, and I'll see to it Heather never does.

I strip down but glance at Evan's door. Is she awake still? Did she hear all that? I burn with the need to go in and claim her. Need to make sure that asshole didn't do anything to her.

But Olivia wears this cloying perfume that clings to me. I need it off me. Fuck, I fucked up. What if Evan is done with me after tonight?

Will the blackmail hold her to me?

I step into the shower and long for her soft skin brushing mine. Those wide eyes looking up at me as she sinks to her knees for me. Fuck, I stroke my cock a few times, but I don't want to come to my memory of her.

Instead, I wash my body. I didn't notice the soft click of the bathroom door, but when I turn, I meet Evan's stormy eyes. She's in a nightgown, sitting on the counter watching me. Her face is expressionless.

Her legs dangle with her bare feet tucked together. I turn off the shower and grab a towel, never dropping her gaze. When I step out, I hang my towel and glance toward the open door. Hawk's asleep in Evan's bed.

He rescued her. She wouldn't have been out there if it wasn't for me.

Of course, he's her hero. He's lucky he wasn't at the party when it got busted. He's the straight-A student, the fucking golden boy, heading to Ivy League in the fall. The guy my dad wishes I was. Hawk is good at hockey. Might even be able to land a deal by playing in college, but he's not me.

I live hockey. Before Evan. Before that fucking accident. I could have been signing a deal right now to start playing professionally. Instead, I'm here, starting fights and trying to get into this girl's pussy.

My cock twitches. It's hard for her, and I'm not about to hide it. This girl has me.

I walk over to my sink and turn on the faucet, grabbing my toothbrush. She releases her breath, but remains quiet, watching me as I brush my teeth. There are bruises forming on her arm that I didn't put there. My grip tightens on my toothbrush. I should have broken his nose.

After I wipe my mouth, she brushes the backs of her fingers over the bruise forming on my jaw. Her gaze lingers on it. I want to ask her what happened, but I'm afraid her answer will have me flying out of here to find Chase and put him in the ground. If he hurt her...

"Explain tonight, please?" Her voice is quiet and steady.

I lean into her touch for a moment, savoring it. "I had to prove a point to Olivia."

Her hand drops into her lap. "What point was that?"

Fuck. I lower to my knees in front of her and rest my head on her lap. Her fingers thread through my hair.

"That you being on the back of my bike meant nothing." I turn my head and kiss the inside of her knee.

Her fingers pause. "Why would it mean anything?"

"I don't let girls ride on my bike." I release my breath and massage her calves.

"You have a helmet." She sounds confused.

"That never gets used." I lift my gaze to meet hers. "I couldn't let her decide you were competition. Olivia has been cruel to girls who liked me before."

"Did you—" she cuts herself off and swallows.

"Never."

She searches my eyes. "You were in a room with her."

Her voice is steady, but her breath hitches.

"To prove a point." I don't drop my gaze.

"Did you?"

The only thing I proved was this girl has a hold on me I've never felt before. "We went into that room, and the only girl I could think about was you."

She searches my eyes, confused.

"Did you kiss her?" Her fingers hesitate in my hair.

"No, little devil."

"Did you touch her?" Her fingers sink into the strands and tighten.

"No."

"Did she touch you or kiss you?"

A wary smile crosses my lips. "No, little devil."

She breathes out, and some of the tension eases from her.

I slide my hands up to the backs of her knees and massage. Her breath catches and her eyes widen.

"Tell me what happened, Evan." I need to know.

She blows out a breath and looks away from me, taking those eyes, shutting me out. "Chase was aggressive tonight. You saw the kiss I couldn't stop if I tried. I don't know why he was like that."

"We've been circling you." It makes sense. "He wanted to stake his claim."

"Who did you fight?" Her fingers trail down to my jaw. Her gaze follows her fingertips.

I don't answer, instead I rest my head in her lap. "Did he hurt you?"

"No." Her fingers stroke through my hair, and some of that tension inside unwinds. "He scared me, and I ran into the woods. He didn't chase me because he was afraid of injuring his knee."

I inhale her woodsy scent and kiss the soft skin on the inside of her thigh.

"What do we do now?" she asks.

I stand and lift her against me. "We go to sleep and figure out our plan in the morning."

When I move toward my bed, she pulls on my hair.

"Hawk," she says.

I glance over my shoulder at him sleeping in her bed. I say his name louder, and he jerks awake. His sleepy eyes meet mine. I nod my head toward my room, and he pushes up.

I don't bother with boxers but lay Evan down and crawl into bed next to her, gathering her against me. She curls into me. So much shit happened tonight. I just want to hold her and know she's safe in my arms, in my bed.

Hawk climbs in beside Evan. "What happened?"

"Party got busted. Cops took us to the station. Cam's dad picked him up before my dad arrived."

Hawk puts his hand on Evan's hip and slides up next to her. "He was drunk when I left."

"He was still drunk at the station." I slide my hand on Evan's waist and meet Hawk's eyes. "There will be consequences from tonight."

Evan's gaze tips up to me. "I didn't—"

"Not you, little devil." I brush my lips against hers. That longing to sink into her and claim her presses on the back of my mind. But she's been through a lot, and tonight isn't the night to push. "We'll all have consequences from our actions."

She rests her head against my chest, and her breath blows across my skin.

"Annie doesn't want to be alone with Chase," Hawk says. "She told him she knows about his cheating."

"I broke up with him." She trembles in my arms. I wish I'd fucking killed him.

"We need to talk tomorrow. Figure out how to handle all this, but for now, we need to sleep. We have a scrimmage in the morning."

Chapter 4

EvanAnn

An alarm goes off, and Damon kisses me before getting out of bed. Hawk kisses my temple and leaves too. I'm too tired to move and snuggle back into the warmth Damon and Hawk left behind.

A hand shaking my hip wakes me. "Evan."

I open my eyes and squint at Damon. "What?"

"You need to go to your own bed." He rubs my hip under his covers. "I'm leaving for hockey."

I nod and snuggle with his pillow. I don't want to move an inch. His pillow smells like him. He chuckles and lifts me into his arms, dragging me from the warmth.

"But the bed will be cold." I burrow my nose into his shirt as he walks into my room.

He lays me down and pulls the covers over me. I release an exasperated sigh at the cold bed and narrow my eyes on him. His jaw is bruised and my fingers itch to touch him there.

He didn't answer me about who he got into a fight with. Was it Chase? Wasn't the whole point of using me for revenge to prevent them from fighting Chase directly?

Smirking at my disgruntlement, Damon dips his head and kisses me like we have all day until I want to drag him into bed. When he stands, I sigh in disappointment.

"Are you coming to the game today?" He runs his hand through his hair.

"I don't think so." I never checked in with Mia. When I texted her from the bathroom at the party, she was busy with a guy. When Chase left me, I didn't want to interrupt her to have her try to find me in the middle of nowhere. She's new to the area. And what if she was with Jackson Riordan? And she brought him with her?

Maybe he's changed and maybe he hasn't. I didn't want to risk it.

Hawk was the right call last night.

Damon kisses my neck and a little shiver races through me. I bite my lip, hoping for more.

He straightens. "We'll talk later."

When he shuts my door, I roll over and close my eyes, but now I can't go back to sleep. The bed doesn't smell like him and it's cold. It makes sense for him to move me in here in case someone comes upstairs and finds me in Damon's bed, but I don't like it. It's not where I sleep.

I roll over and grab my phone from the charger.

There are messages from Mia, an unknown number, Chase, and another unknown number. The unknowns could be cast members. I gave everyone my number the first day. I just haven't had the time to put all their numbers into my phone.

My cheeks flush at *what* or rather *who* I've been busy with.

MIA:

Where are you!?

Party got busted! Hope you weren't here.

Made it over the fence before they got to the backyard

Are you busted?

Do you need me to come bail you out?

Except for the first text which was when I found out about Damon and Olivia, they're all from last night after I was already back here. Maybe I should have called Mia to come get me. It felt like a lot to put on a new friendship.

ME:
Wasn't at the party
Didn't feel well. Went home

MIA:

Oh, thank god, I felt like the worst friend for leaving you

ME:
No worries

MIA:

Hockey scrimmage today. Wanna go?

Do I want to watch Damon, Cam, and Hawk on the ice? Yes. But I need to start prioritizing my own life again. And my priority is school and the play. I glance toward Damon's bedroom. I can't let them take over my life.

No matter how tempting they are.

ME:
I can't *sad face emoji*
Have to work on homework and the play

MIA:

Coffee later?

But I want to have good friendships too, and coffee should take less time than the scrimmage. Besides, I need to tell her about Chase.

ME:
Yes, please

MIA:

I'll text

I close her message. Taking a deep breath to prepare myself, I open the one from Chase. Will he be hateful or will he be remorseful? And would I really believe him if he was remorseful?

CHASE:

Fuck, babe, got busted

Coming to get you now. Sorry I was a dick

Where r u? Fuck.

Are you home already?

Drove past your place. It's being torn down?

Please let me know you're okay

I feel like shit

I shouldn't have left you

I look at the time stamps. He would have left me out there for three hours before he came looking for me. It also meant he went back to the party after ditching me. He did say he was going to find someone to fuck.

Why did he even bother texting me? I release my breath and focus on what he said about our house.

Our house is getting torn down. That gives me pause. I really did like living there and it was a good little house for us.

As for Chase, I need to be cordial to him since he's a principle in my play. But that doesn't mean I need to be nice to him.

ME:

I'm safe

No thanks to him. And then I silence the conversation, because I don't really want to listen to whatever excuse he has for his behavior. I'm done.

I run a hand over my face, and my chest lightens. Done.

Rehearsal will be awkward for a while, but he'll get over it. And I know better for the future than to get involved with a self-absorbed actor like him ever again. Not that the Devil's trio aren't full of red flags, but they aren't asking me to date them. Just fuck them, which the more they make me come, the more curious I am about the actual fucking part.

And after last night, I want to be the one who decides when I'm ready. Not someone pressuring me to fuck him to keep him. Like it's my fault Chase cheated. Though I am curious what he gets out of our relationship because why would he ever think I'd take him back?

How desperate does he think I am?

And speaking of cheating, I need to talk to the Devil's trio about letting other girls hang on them. Even at parties. Yes, I understand they don't want our relationship to come out into the open, but that doesn't mean they have to be so... *giving* to the female students.

I open one of the anonymous text conversations.

UNKNOWN NUMBER:

Where u at, goody two-shoes?

Got busted last night

You coming to our game today?

This is Cam BTW

ME:

Sorry you got busted

No gotta catch up on homework

UNKNOWN NUMBER:

Such a goody

I smile and shake my head. I save Cam's number. Is it weird to want Cam, Hawk, and Damon? All three of them? Any girl would kill to have just one of them, but I have all of their attention.

Hawk thought it was all about Damon, and I would have taken his deal if it'd only been him. I'm not sure that's true. Without Cam and Hawk, I might have fought harder. Damon can be a bully when he wants something. But Hawk seduces, and Cam flirts. I don't think I would have let Damon steamroll over me without them wearing me down.

We didn't talk about it, but I guess we're still good. They know I broke up with Chase. But what happens next? If I'm not being used to get info on Chase, does that mean they don't want to play with me anymore? Did I miss my opportunity with the Devil's trio?

They talked about exploring their darker desires. A shiver goes through me. So maybe that's still on the table. Everything they've done only makes me want more. More of them.

They aren't acting like it's over. Hawk and Damon slept with me. Damon may not have said he was sorry, but the way he knelt before me last night made my heart race and thump so fucking hard.

Besides, Damon mentioned taking all three of their cocks inside me. At the same time. That hasn't happened yet.

My body heats now just thinking about it. I squirm as my pussy pulses with need. Maybe they'll keep me for that. Though Mia would probably do it right now, if they asked. Probably a lot of girls would jump at the chance. But most girls wouldn't keep it to themselves.

I don't know how long our arrangement will last. With Chase out of the picture, they could cut me off at any time. Maybe I should start taking advantage of the guys while I have their attention. I want to have sex with them, though I still worry about trusting them.

However, that night, with the butt plug, fingers in my pussy, and a cock in my mouth was epic. What will it feel like with three hot bodies pressing into me? I cross my legs against the needy ache forming.

I open the final text thread that came in after Chase's texts.

UNKNOWN NUMBER:

I thought I lost you

My heart stops and chills race down my spine.

My first thought is Jackson. But how would he have my number? We changed phone carriers and got new numbers when we moved to the house. I look at the number the text came from, but the area code is from this area. It could be a misdial or maybe someone in the cast trying to get ahold of me.

Actors can be pretty dramatic at times. I try to shake off the chill. That's probably it.

Just because Jackson scared me when I was younger doesn't mean he's actively trying to find me. The football game was probably coincidence. It was summer when we hung out. I didn't want to talk about Anteros with him. For just that summer, I wanted to be Evan-Ann, a girl. Not a talented director and actor. I take in a cleansing breath and release it.

It's probably not Jackson. I probably overinflated that moment in my mind. To him it might have just been a kiss.

Don't make assumptions.

ME:

Hi, not sure if you're trying to reach me, but check the number again

That's a pretty non-threatening and nice way to say you might have the wrong number—if it's a wrong number—without giving away information.

UNKNOWN NUMBER:

I'm never losing you again, Evan

My heart thumps hard. It still might not be Jackson. It could be someone fucking with me. Like Chase. Or even someone like Olivia if she thinks I have a thing for Damon—or worse, Damon has a thing for me. That's what he was worried about and why he let her hang all over him.

I block the number. If it's a misunderstanding with one of the actors, they'll have to tell me at rehearsal. But I'm not playing this game right now.

———

Damon

I can focus on the ice and the way it feels under my skates without having to worry about Evan in the stands with Chase. Hawk pointed out Mia was here solo before the game began. She sits closer this time. We haven't heard if she got with anyone else on the team last night.

I skate circles around the defense and score three goals during the first two periods.

With our team comfortably ahead, I hang back and let the others take the lead, assisting on goals and helping keep the way clear for some of the newer members of our varsity team. My leg, even though it's healed, could use the break. It doesn't hurt as much as it did when I first got back on the ice.

Even with my leg, it's an easy day on the ice, which is another reason I wanted to move up this year.

If I can get four hours of sleep and still skate circles around the competition, I need more of a challenge. I'm glad to be playing this year at all, but I still shouldn't be here. Having Evan is a good distraction from everything that's happening.

We win our scrimmage and lineup for handshakes with the other team before going down to the locker room. Cam looks green as he lowers to the bench to take off his skates.

"What's the damage?" Hawk asks as he works on his skates.

"Dad's pissed. No more going out on school nights. Had to give him access to my location on my phone." Cam shakes his head. "It's fucked."

I blow out a breath. We're both fucked. "Not sure what my dad's going to say, but it won't be good."

"You beat up Chase Chadwick." Hawk laughs. "Man, if you knew you were going to end up doing that, we could have finished this whole thing before it started."

"I'm sure I'll get the talk about how I'm not mature enough to head off to the big leagues." I shake my head. I don't have to remind them we wouldn't have Evan if we'd fucked up Chase in the beginning. She'd probably still be in the dark about him fucking around on her too. "We need to talk to her."

"She broke up with him last night before he ditched her in the forest." Hawk runs a hand through his hair.

"Good." Cam shakes his head. He barely contained his anger when he found out she was left out there alone. I don't know if it's really sunk in for Cam that she knew he was drunk and couldn't come rescue her. "We should return the favor. Scare the shit out of him."

"I'm game," I say. Chase deserves what's coming to him after the way he left her out there. Alone, afraid. I rub the corner of my mouth. "What if he wants her back?"

"Then we tell him to fuck off." Cam stands and removes his gear to head to the showers.

"He may be useful." I don't know why I'm pulling at this thread. I don't want Chase touching her or kissing her, but if she's free and we're free, what the fuck are we doing?

Hawk narrows his eyes like he doesn't like where I'm driving this. "We'll talk it over with her."

It's late afternoon as we head to our own homes with a plan to meet up before we go to Olivia's party tonight. She texted me to say it was going to be low key since Fletcher's party got busted. The problem is, if Evan isn't there with Chase, why would Olivia invite her?

Chase doesn't deserve to share the same air Evan breathes. If he touches her, I'm not sure any of us will hold back. When I picture the bruises on her arm, I want to bury him for hurting her.

If I bring her to the party, all hell will break loose. Part of me likes the idea of the chaos.

After I dump my gear in the mudroom, I go to my room the back way to avoid running into my dad. When I walk through the bathroom, I find Evan curled up on top of her covers asleep with a book open in front of her.

I lean against the doorframe and look her over. Things have changed since that first day.

Last night during the game, when I dragged her under the bleachers, she was scared, but when she realized it was me, she relaxed. It couldn't have been Chase she was afraid of because he was out on the field. So who did she think I was?

It swam around my mind the rest of the game and last night while Olivia was talking my ear off. But it got pushed to the background after what Chase did to her.

I blow out a breath and sit on the edge of her bed. Her woodsy scent makes my cock twitch like it's trained on the smell of her now. She's wearing her usual clothes. Not the high-end clothes her mother bought her.

Maybe I read Evan wrong.

She's lived here for a week and known about it for two. No one at school knows she lives here with me. Not even her friend or boyfriend. She hasn't tried to fit herself into the Haves.

She's worn the skirts she asked her mother for, but the ones she had were dangerously short. I smirk. Not that I minded. I actually prefer the old skirts.

She's continuing on like she always has. Like nothing's changed in her life. Like I haven't taken it over. If she wanted popularity, she could have seized it. If she wanted material goods, all she has to do is ask, and my father would give her mother anything she wants.

Evan stays with her people. I don't trust Mia, but she doesn't know about Evan's relationship with the three of us. Relationship. I scoff. I guess that's what we have if she's not dating Chase. It's not like I'll let Evan start dating other people.

Not until I'm finished with her.

Fuck, what are we doing? I run my hand through my hair.

She startles awake and looks up at me with wide, terrified eyes. She relaxes when she realizes it's me. What the fuck? Who did she think it was creeping into her bedroom? I better be the only one doing that. Or Cam or Hawk.

She stretches and sits up. "Must have fallen asleep."

"Must have."

She blinks those pretty eyes and smiles like she's happy to see me. "Where are the others?"

"Home, getting ready for tonight. We need to talk."

She nods, and her fingers reach for the bruise on my jaw. I grab them before she can touch it again.

Her eyes search mine. We're in weird territory here. I should demand she suck my cock or drive her wild with my mouth on her clit and sink my finger into her wet cunt, but instead, we're just sitting here. And while I'd be happy to fuck around, I just need to be close to her. Something shifted last night.

Once I can fuck her, I'll get her out of my system.

"What's the plan for tonight?" she asks.

"Olivia's party." I release her hand.

She nods. "I was supposed to go with Chase."

She glances at her phone but doesn't reach for it.

"Do you want to go with us?" The words slip from my lips.

Her gaze darts to mine in confusion. "What?"

The fuck am I doing?

"Damon!" There's a sharp knock at my door. My dad. I stand and go face the music.

Chapter 5

EvanAnn

Damon goes through the bathroom and barely closes his bathroom door. When he lets his father into his room, I hold my breath. My door to the bathroom is still open.

"Let's hear it then," Damon says.

"A fight?" Adam sounds disappointed. I heard that part last night. What I'm curious about is with who? Was it something because of Olivia? Or... I don't even want to think it, because I don't understand what that would mean.

Damon doesn't answer his dad, but I'm not surprised.

For a second, I'm locked in place. Should I leave my room? Or stay and listen?

I shouldn't listen. But I'm so fucking curious. He wouldn't tell me who he fought with. Does his dad know?

My cheeks warm as I flatten against the wall next to the bathroom door. I shouldn't be doing this, but I can't seem to help myself. I want to know why, and maybe his father will help me understand Damon better.

"You can't keep fucking around like this. Not if you want to be a professional." Adam's tone is strong. "You're far too reckless. If I can't control you, how would anyone else be able to? Fuck, Damon, you're old enough to get charged for assault."

"If you knew what he did—"

"I can't go around decking every guy I disagree with. That's not how the world works. You need time to learn to control your anger."

"You mean bury it inside."

"No, I mean learn some control. Hockey will be there—"

"You've already cost me my shot."

"There will be other shots."

"Not like this. They talked to us about this. This was my best chance. I can get time to go to college. They encourage that. But if I wanted in, this was my opportunity, and you took it from me."

My heart pounds. If I could chase my dream right now, would I? If someone said you can mentor under this director, but you'll miss your senior year, could I pass that up?

"You could have died, Damon. How am I supposed to protect you when you risk your life? You need college, structure. You need something to fall back on if you get injured. Your temper is an issue if you can't control it. For fucks' sake, you punched Chase Chadwick."

I cover my mouth as I gasp. Damon punched Chase? I considered it, but it doesn't track. That's not how Damon wanted to take Chase down.

I'm not surprised Chase returned to the party after abandoning me out in the middle of nowhere. My stomach churns. Maybe I should be, but I'm not. How long would he have waited before coming back for me? Would he have? How many girls would he have fucked while I was out there, cold, alone, and afraid?

How am I going to face him without kneeing him in the fucking balls?

"They aren't pressing charges, but this is your wake-up call. You need to get your act together. You need to figure out what you want out of life."

"Are you finished?" The rumble of rage in Damon's voice has me worried, bringing me back to the present.

Maybe I should leave my room. Go somewhere other people are until he cools down. My body shivers with anticipation as I remember the last time he was angry.

"I need you to think about what you want, Damon. And what you need to do to achieve it. I can't sit back and watch you self-destruct. It's not what your mother would have wanted." Adam lets out a sigh before Damon's door opens. "You're too old for me to ground. I can't take away anything, but I hope this makes you reevaluate your situation. You can't keep steering your life into a brick wall and expect to come out unscathed. If you won't try for me, try for your mother. She wanted the world for you."

Damon is silent as Adam's footsteps walk past my door. For a second, I just breathe. I shouldn't have stayed. That wasn't for me to hear. Our lives are more entwined than they should be already.

Damon walks through the bathroom, and I don't move away from the wall fast enough. His angry eyes meet mine when he finds me. Obviously eavesdropping. Fuck. What do I even say?

He glances over his shoulder before he shoves me toward my closet.

"Damon?" I say, unsure of his mood. Angry, yes, but there's a coldness too. The coldness makes me worried more than the anger.

He strides over to the door and locks it. "Get changed for the party."

"What? I can't go." I look at my closet like something might pop out of it. "I'm not with Chase anymore."

His gaze narrows on mine. "You need to look the part, Evan."

The part? He sweeps into my closet and I can hear the hangers sliding against each other. I swallow. Is he mad I was eavesdropping? Or just mad in general? I can't even say I'm sorry I overheard.

"Look the part of what?" I wrap my arms around myself.

"Our whore." Damon walks back out and throws a short skirt and a crop top on the bed. Things my mother bought.

I'm ignoring the *whore* part, but my eyes widen at the outfit. What was my mom thinking? I mean, they're cute, but these aren't clothes I would ever wear. Maybe she thought I might want a different style for this new life, but this isn't my life. I haven't changed.

My eyes meet Damon's. Except he, Cam, and Hawk have taken over my life.

But what was my life before? A boyfriend who cheated on me. Being left alone all the time at the house because my mom was busy with her boyfriend. The only thing I had was school and theater. It was enough, but would I be happy with that now?

Would I always regret not exploring this attraction with the Devil's trio?

"Don't you want to make your ex jealous, little devil?" Damon closes in on me. He reaches for my shirt before I realize what he's planning.

He pulls it off over my head. And spins me around to face the wall, pressing me against it with his body. My breath catches as heat rushes through me. I rest my forehead on the wall.

"Chase will want you back. Won't he? Do you want to go back to your manwhore?"

"No," I whisper as he releases my bra and reaches around me to undo my jeans. I don't fight him as he undresses me. Maybe I should. Maybe I shouldn't let them have any more control over my life.

What's the worst that happens? Damon shows everyone the videos? It's not like most will care except that it's salacious. But I'm not a blip on anyone's radar, so it might be a few uncomfortable weeks, and then they'll find something new to fixate on.

He shoves my jeans and panties down over my hips. They fall to my knees. He's breathing heavily and for a second, he rests his head against mine. My breath stutters as desire floods me. His hands come up and hold my bare hips. The heat of him warms me. Anticipation buzzes beneath my skin.

The worst thing that would happen is they'd stop touching me like this. My heart thumps as I silently acknowledge I don't want out of this twisted thing we have. I want to dive deeper.

"Why did you hit Chase?" My voice is small like it's a secret, but I need to know.

"He left you like garbage, Evan. You." Damon slips his hands around my stomach, drawing me back against his body. "He couldn't just walk in and have fun when he abandoned you in the middle of nowhere."

I'm trying not to read into anything, but fuck, am I confused. "I thought he was untouchable?"

"He is." Damon's hand slides between my legs and cups my pussy.

I let out a shuddering breath at the ache pulsing there. He makes me ache.

"I shouldn't have hit him, but..."

I want him to continue talking. I want him to touch me more. My mind melts in the heat that comes off his body and stirs mine. I try to part my legs for him, to give him access, but my jeans bind my knees together. When he slips his finger into me, we both groan.

"So fucking wet, little devil."

"Damon," I whimper as he begins to finger fuck me slowly, pressed against the wall. It's not enough. It feels fucking amazing, and I'll get off, but this revenge will end. I don't want this to end without feeling them inside me.

I'm already addicted to their touch.

"Fuck, you make me forget myself." He draws his finger out of me, and I whimper at the loss. He finishes lowering my jeans and makes me step out of them. "We don't have long."

"Why?" I drop my bra as I turn around.

He growls as he takes in my naked body and then his mouth is on mine. He pushes me back against the wall. His hand tilts my head, so I'll open my mouth more for him. I surrender. Anything for him. He devours me, consumes me. I want to climb up him and wrap myself around him.

I want to burn for him until I'm nothing more than ashes.

"Get dressed." He steps away and goes into his room.

My heart pounds as I try to catch my bearings. I hear his drawers open and shut. Fuck.

I walk to the bed on shaky legs and look at the clothes he picked out for me, including a set of red lace panties and bra. The clothes aren't what I would pick for a party. I put on the bra and panties, but I hesitate on the red top and black skirt.

On weekends, I wear jeans and sweatshirts to these parties, even in the summer. I don't want anyone to see me. I prefer to watch life happen, rather than participate. This is the kind of outfit Mia would wear, but she's comfortable being the center of attention.

Chase will want you back. Those words echo in my head as I sit on the edge of the bed without putting on the clothes and lift my phone. Is that what Damon wants? For me to go back to Chase?

I glance at Damon's and my shared bathroom. Chase has to know I won't forgive him for what he's done. He can't be stupid enough to think I'll take him back. I open the text messages Chase sent me today that I haven't read.

CHASE:

I'm so sorry

I don't want to lose you

I swear I can change

I'll be better

Come to the party with me tonight

I'll show you how much I want to be with you

Only you

I toss my phone to the side and bury my head in my hands, torn between frustration, confusion, and anger. Why? Why would I ever go back to him after what he did? Does he think I'm that desperate?

I think of the girl I was before he asked me out, before he noticed me.

Yeah, I was desperate enough to say yes to dating him. Even knowing he was a fuck boy.

Damon comes to the bathroom door, straightening his cuffs. He's dressed in jeans and sneakers with a dress shirt in black. My mouth goes dry. He's gorgeous. His blue eyes lift to mine, but not before he looks me over, dressed only in my underwear.

He smirks. "I thought you might like a little more coverage, but I can definitely get behind that look. Or under."

Slightly amused, I shake my head and offer him my phone to look at the messages. "I told him I knew he was cheating on me. He didn't deny it. He probably went back to the party to fuck someone before coming back to get me."

Damon glances over the texts. "He wants you, Evan. You can get revenge. You can own him. It's the way to break him."

I run my hand over the skirt fabric on the bed next to me, avoiding his gaze. Do I want Chase to pay for what he did to Damon? For using me? "What if I'm the one who gets broken?"

"Then we'll put you back together." He nudges my chin up to look into my eyes. I wish I knew what he's thinking. What's going on behind those blue eyes? "Just a little while longer and then we'll pull the rug out from under him. Make him give up his whoring ways for you, but tell him he can't touch you until you know he's been faithful."

Will that work? Will it stop all the touching? What will everyone think? What have they already been thinking? Most people have to realize Chase cheats on me. But no one told me. I don't want him back for real, but there's got to be more to him dating me. Some reason.

"He knows I'm not at my old house anymore." I bite my lip. "I don't want people to know about this."

He smirks. "What? Living in the lap of luxury? Fucking your future stepbrother? What's there to hide, little devil?"

I draw in a breath and release it.

"They're going to find out." Damon slides his hand over my neck and moves in closer. "It's bound to happen, but if you want it to be a controlled release, we can do that."

"I don't want things to change," I say softly. It's a vulnerability I'm offering him. Too many things changed after my dad's death. The longest we lived anywhere was two years. I got comfortable, and I thought letting Chase into my life wouldn't be a bad thing.

I thought I could have change, and it wouldn't blow up my life. I almost laugh bitterly at that thought now.

"Tonight, I want you to shine so that asshole knows exactly what he's lost." Damon leans down so his breath touches my lips. His blue eyes hold me captive. "Then you can give him conditions on how you'll take him back. We'll decide whether we need to push it further. You may be his to everyone else. But at night, you'll be mine, and I'll make you come so hard you scream."

I swallow and his fingers tighten on the sides of my neck. Not tight enough to cut off my breath, but enough I can feel the power he holds over me. He doesn't have to show me. I feel it in my bones. I'm his.

"Let's get you dressed, little devil. It's time to raise the stakes."

Chapter 6

Damon

We ride to Hawk's house, the only place guaranteed safe from parental interference. He lives a few blocks from me in an old Victorian his mother updated and restored. One of the original houses in the neighborhood.

Evan slides off my bike and tugs at her skirt. I set my helmet down. I should just take her somewhere and fuck her tonight. To hell with everyone else. No Chase. No Olivia.

Just her curled around me as I fuck that perfect little cunt.

Her gaze lifts to mine and her eyes darken. Just thinking about watching her take the others into her body has me rock hard and ready to change our plans. Hawk's parents aren't home. We could just spend the night getting each other off.

Fuck the party.

"Fuck, goody." Cam takes her into his arms, breaking our stare down. He hugs her tight. "If anything had happened to you…"

I shake it off. This girl fucks with my head. This isn't about Evan. It's about revenge. It's about taking everything away from Chase the way he took everything from me.

"I'm never getting wasted again." He kisses her temple before he holds her at arm's length and looks her over. He lets out a low whistle at her outfit before searching her eyes. "Are you okay? Hawk said you were okay, but are you?"

Her cheeks flush and she looks down at the ground. "I'm good, Cam."

He smirks. "You're better than good. You're fucking gorgeous in red."

He glances at me with a look that says, *have you seen this?*

"Thank you." Evan's blue-gray eyes find mine. "Should we..."

I nod. "Let's go inside. We need to discuss our plan."

"If the plan includes fucking Evan in front of that asshole, I'm in." Cam grins, but Evan gives him a look that's a mix of horror and intrigue. She won't be a good girl for long after we get our cocks in her. She just never had a guy who would push at her boundaries.

Fuck. I'll fuck the girl on stage in front of the whole school if that's what she wants. I don't mind an audience. I don't care as long as I get to fuck Evan.

Cam stops and plucks a flower from the flower bed next to the driveway. He holds it out to Evan. "For you."

"Thank you." She takes it, and her cheeks flush pink. She brings it to her nose and sniffs it. "No one's ever given me flowers before."

"Never? Not even a dandelion?" Grinning, Cam wraps his arm around her shoulders and draws her into Hawk's house. His eyes are soft and focused only on her.

"Not even." Her eyes widen as she takes in the décor in the house. That vase in the corner with erotic images on it or maybe the painting above the sitting room couch of a tastefully naked woman being fed grapes by a man. Part of me wants to ask what she thinks, but I need to stay focused. We all need to be on board with the plan.

My problem isn't getting Evan on board. She'll want her own revenge on Chase after the shit he's pulled. It's getting the guys to agree. They're protective.

Hawk meets us in the hallway and leads us to the rec room in the basement. Cam walks with Evan over to the couch and draws her down onto his lap. She twirls the little flower in her fingers as she rests her head back against his shoulder.

His hand slides up her thigh to rest next to those red panties. Fuck, short skirts and lacy panties are all Evan should be allowed to wear.

I sit across from them where I can enjoy the show while we strategize. Hawk sits next to Cam on the couch and pulls Evan in for a kiss.

I wait a minute before clearing my throat. "We have things to discuss before we can play tonight."

Evan's lips are a little swollen as she leans against Cam's chest and meets my eyes.

"What's the damage?" I look at Cam, knowing his parents will punish him.

He blows out a breath. "Lockdown on weeknights. He's tracking my fucking phone like I'm a toddler. And he won't be happy until my grades go up."

"What courses are you struggling with? Maybe I can help?" Evan turns to look up at him.

"You want to tutor me, goody?" Cam's fingers stroke her through her panties.

Her lips part. I'm going to have to buy her more short skirts.

"If it will help." Her gaze flicks to me. When she notices where I'm looking, she opens her legs more, giving me more of a show. Such a good fucking slut.

"Next time we do this, I want my cock buried in your cunt while we discuss our plan," I say.

Her eyes meet mine and hold them, but her lips remain closed. I tip my head to the side. I expected a protest or not for another two weeks. But she doesn't say no. Who knows how many planning sessions we'll have before this all ends. This might be the only one. But if I get her on my dick, I'll make sure there are more.

"How are we moving forward with this?" she asks.

Cam moves his hand back to her thigh and meets my gaze. Hawk looks at me too. This is my revenge plot after all. But I know this part won't sit well with either of them.

"He wants her back." My gaze locks on Evan's. We've talked and she knows what she needs to do.

"Fuck, no." Hawk stands and runs his hand through his hair. "You didn't see where he left her. He threatened her. If he gets her alone, next time she might not be able to get away. I'm not risking her."

"Who in their right mind goes back to a guy like that?" Cam shakes his head and wraps his arm around her waist, holding her tight against him. Like he can save her now. "He can't honestly believe she'd go back to him."

Evan's voice is calm when she says, "Why didn't you tell your dad Chase was the one who caused your accident?"

"People like us get away with shit like this." I lean forward with my elbows on my knees. "Chase might have received a fine and maybe a sentence that would have been commuted at best. He wouldn't really pay at all. If we'd told the authorities who we saw, we wouldn't be able to go after him. People would know it's us. He may know it's us, but the motive wouldn't be there. Not without him admitting guilt."

"Why don't you tell your dad?"

I chuckle. "He'd make it go away too. That's his business partner's son. He wouldn't let me exact my vengeance."

"I think Chase knows it's you he hit." Evan's voice is soft.

I nod. "Probably. But he also thinks I don't know it was him."

Evan absorbs that and takes a deep breath. "What do you want me to do?"

"Damon, she can't go back to that asshole." Hawk steps forward like he can stop any of this. The time to stop it would have been before we ever went after Evan. Now we're in too deep, and Chase hasn't paid nearly enough. I want him ruined.

"I play him the way he's been playing me." Evan's stormy eyes turn hard as she nods at me. She might want revenge for herself. Did he even crack the surface with Evan? I thought it was odd he was with her. But now that I have her, I understand the appeal.

Not the fucking around bit, but the need to keep her.

"I'm not saying she agrees to be his girlfriend again." I rub the corner of my mouth and meet Evan's eyes. "But if he wants her, he can work for it. She can make his life hell with the hope he can win her back."

"He can't get her alone again." Hawk sits on the edge of the couch and looks at Evan. "You need to go somewhere. You go with one of us. He doesn't get you."

Evan reaches over and takes his hand, squeezing it. "I don't want to go anywhere with him alone."

"She'll give him rules," I say.

Evan arches an eyebrow my way, and I smile.

"If he wants you back so badly, he can pay the price. You'll talk to him at the party and then you'll come home with us."

"What if he wants to go somewhere else to talk?" Evan asks.

"Absolutely not." I need her in my sights at all times. Hawk's right about that. He doesn't get her alone anymore. Ever.

"Are you going to tell everyone I'm living with you?" Evan leans back against Cam. She hasn't closed her legs even though Cam isn't touching her. She's showing me her panties. Later I'm going to rip those panties off her and make her scream with pleasure.

"Do you want me to?" I lift my gaze to hers.

"Not yet." She shakes her head and stands. Cam helps her.

"It's going to come out eventually, little devil. You can't hide forever."

"But not yet." Her face is determined as she paces between us.

With Olivia circling me, it's best for Evan to remain our secret. If Olivia even considers something is happening between me and Evan, she might blow everything up. But just because Evan lives with me doesn't mean anything is happening.

"I need to clarify something." Evan stops to meet my eyes.

"What, little devil?"

"When does this end?" She cocks her head a little. "With us?"

"Why? Do you want to find a new boyfriend?" I remain cocky, but even if she tries to get someone else, I won't let her go.

"No. I just..." She takes a deep breath. "Never mind."

"You're ours for as long as I want you to be ours."

She presses her lips together at my non-answer. The reality is I'm not sure I'll ever let her go. This year she'll be mine and Cam's and Hawk's. But my plan is to get rid of the gold-digger, and doing that might lose me Evan.

I don't like how that thought makes me feel.

"Fine. One more question." She doesn't look happy, but she's not going to push it. Maybe she doesn't want it to end either. She looks at Cam and Hawk and wets her lips. "You mentioned darker desires as something you want to explore with me."

"Not hearing a question." I arch an eyebrow.

She huffs out a breath and gives me a look. "What exactly do you want to do to me that you can't get from other girls? I'm not going to let you fist me, if that's what you're hoping."

I chuckle and stand. She holds her ground as I close in on her and cup her jaw to lift her gaze to mine.

"Part of it is curiosity." I stroke my thumb over her lower lip. "I want to watch you take the others and know that afterwards I'll sink into your warm cunt and start all over again. I want to hold you down while I fuck you hard and not have you go tell other girls I'm too rough. I want to slip into your tight asshole while Hawk fucks your pussy and Cam fucks your mouth." I slide my thumb between her lips, and she darts her tongue out to taste it. My hard cock jerks. "I want to hunt you down and fuck you where I find you. So many things I want to do to your tight little body."

She sucks on the tip of my thumb, and her eyes darken. The silver is more prominent. Her eyes fascinate me. She wants me, and it's fucking intoxicating.

I draw my wet thumb down the pulse in her neck. She shivers beneath my touch.

"I want to make you beg me for it." Hawk steps beside us and tips her chin his way. "I want to make you crawl for me. To punish you when you do something wrong and reward you when you do something right. I want power over you, baby girl."

A little whimper whines in her throat.

Cam moves in so we're surrounding her. She turns to him.

"What do you want?" she asks.

"Fuck, goody." Cam smirks. "I want to fuck you any way I can get. Definitely want to do anal and double penetration. I want to fuck you at a party where your ex can see and he knows it's my cock buried inside you, driving you crazy. I like the idea of fucking you right under everyone else's nose like it's our secret."

She swallows.

"When you're ready to fuck us, little devil."

Her eyes shift up to mine.

"I want to fall sleep with my cock buried in your cunt. Fuck you while you're asleep." I grab her hair and pull it to arch her neck. "Make you my toy. My little cum slut. I want to own you."

Her eyes hold mine, and I'm tempted to kiss her, but if I start now, I won't want to quit until I have her naked beneath me. We have things to accomplish tonight.

"What about you, little devil?" I drag my thumb over her lip.

Her eyebrows knot in confusion. "What about me?"

I stroke my fingers down her throat and wrap my hand around it loosely. "Is there anything you want to try with us?"

Her cheeks flush, and she looks down, taking her gaze from me. I tighten my hand around her throat, and her eyes flash back to mine.

"There must be something." I stroke my thumb along her jaw. My cock aches to fulfill her fantasies.

Her lips part. "I just want all of you."

Chapter 7

EvanAnn

I tug at my skirt as I walk up the sidewalk to Mia's house. Damon dropped me off so she can give me a ride to the party. We decided it would be a bad idea for me to show up with them.

Especially at Olivia's house. She's obsessed with Damon. My stomach twists. And, while we want to get under Chase's skin, it's too soon for me to be seen with other guys. He and I just broke up last night.

I texted Chase and told him while I was willing to talk, I'd meet him at the party.

The breeze tickles my skin as I reach Mia's door and knock. This skirt is shorter than my old uniform skirts and the crop top leaves my midriff bare. The whole outfit barely covers me. I don't know how comfortable I'll be at the party, but the heat in the Devil's trio's gazes when they looked at me boosted my confidence. I just need to be careful how I sit.

I don't mind flashing my panties at my guys, but I don't need to be the talk of the school.

When Mia's aunt answers the door and lets me in, she shows me to Mia's bedroom. Mia's told me she needs to decorate it still, but I'm surprised at how barren it is. A blank slate and completely lacking a personality, unlike the girl occupying it.

"I'm almost ready." She leans close to the mirror, putting on her eyeliner. "Finishing touches."

"Sorry I wasn't able to get coffee with you earlier. I fell asleep." I didn't do much makeup. Just a little concealer to hide the darkness under my eyes.

She turns and her eyes widen as they take in my outfit. Her smile morphs into a grin. "Where have you been hiding, Miss Evan?"

My cheeks heat as I slide a hand down the black skirt. "Chase has been cheating on me, and he tried to leave me in the woods last night."

"Fuck. So we're after revenge then." She purses her lips and nods. "I like it. But we'll definitely need to work on your makeup and hair first."

She turns and begins to pull stuff out of her makeup kit. "Sit and tell me all about it. I'm so sorry. He's an asshole, and we hate him. Do you know who he's been with?"

"Abby, his old girlfriend. Another girl at a different party, but I don't know who. For all I know, he's been through the whole school while we've been dating." Anger chases through my words. I look down at my hands, because if I'm going to sell this, I need to be willing to take him back.

Damon wants me to get back with Chase, but that's going to make me look like a fool. What will Mia think of me?

He's been cheating this whole time. What would make me think he's going to change now? Except I'm not going to let him back easily and I'm not really taking him back.

"What an asshole." She tips my chin up and considers me for a moment. Her blue eyes roaming over my face. "I know just the thing that will get back at him."

"Makeup?"

She chuckles. "Yes, looking fabulous will make him regret ever stepping out on you, but you should totally treat him with his own medicine."

She begins to apply the makeup.

"His own medicine?"

"Find a guy and fuck his brains out. That will show Chase exactly how it feels." Mia smirks. "I'd suggest cutting his balls off, but he is one of your leads for the play, so probably not the best timing."

"I don't know if I'm that kind of girl." Though there's a part of me that is. I've enjoyed what I've been doing with the Devil's trio. Every minute of it just makes me want more. Frankly, the anticipation of what might happen after the party is more of an incentive than the actual party.

She tips my face to the side. "We're all that kind of girl deep down." She meets my eyes. "I know you're sweet, or you wouldn't put up with me. But I think you deserve better than some asshole who fucks anything that moves."

Which is exactly why I wanted to break up with him last weekend when I found him cheating on me. Maybe I need to prepare Mia for me going back to Chase. "We did have fun together occasionally."

Her lips flatten and she gives me a look that says *really?* I keep my expression hopeful.

"Close your eyes." She works on my eyeliner. "I mean, it's up to you if you want to take him back but make him work for it. Don't give him an easy way to reclaim you. Let's make him see he's not the only one you could be with. Give you some leverage if you really want to forgive him."

I open my eyes, and she checks her work.

"One more thing." She turns and rummages in her makeup. She faces me twisting open a lipstick tube in red. "*Don't Stop* red. Guaranteed to make men crawl after you."

I shake my head and give her a wry smile. "Men don't crawl after me."

"They will tonight because you look hot." Mia applies the color to my lips and sighs. "If I ever decide to go gay, I'd knock on your door first. You're a fucking catch."

I laugh, and some of the tightness that's been crushing me all day loosens. I grab her hand. "Thank you for being my friend."

When I stand, she turns me to look in the mirror. Between Damon's outfit and Mia's makeup, I hardly recognize myself.

Tonight I'm baiting my ex, but I'll be going home with the Devil's trio. Fear won't hold me back anymore.

Cam

We ride up to Olivia's house. Most people who got taken to the police station last night won't be here. Fletcher is definitely in trouble with his parents. But there's a lot of parents who don't push hard on their kids, and a bunch of people scattered before the police could get them.

That means the party is still lit.

Damon, Hawk, and I walk in. This time I'm sticking with them. And Damon won't put his hands anywhere on Olivia. Though someone will have to hold me back when Chase gets here. I've been wanting to pound that fucker since he ran Damon off the road. But what he did to Evan can't stand.

Damon wants Evan to go back to the asshole and figure out why he wants her so much. She can make him grovel for it, which I'll enjoy laughing about while I eat her pussy.

Olivia walks up to us as soon as we come through the door. "Hey, guys. Drinks are in the kitchen. If you're going to vape or smoke pot, please go outside. Music is in the house. Pool is open for business. Damon?"

She closes the distance between the two of them and puts her hand on his chest. Her fingers trace over his muscles as she looks up at him through her lashes.

"We need to finish what we started last night." She gives him a smile that says she's all his for the taking. "I've made sure to make my bedroom off limits."

"I'm here to hang with my boys tonight." He takes her hand off him and drops it. "Maybe next weekend."

She pouts, but we walk past her. There's the usual crowd and a group of Anteros girls and guys off to the side. Chase doesn't seem to be here yet, and neither is Evan. We find a few chairs in a corner and take our seats to enjoy the show.

Hawk goes to the kitchen and returns with some sodas. I half-hoped he'd at least bring one beer, but I get it. I can't afford another ticket. Dad's made it clear if anything else happens or my grades drop further, I'll be on probation at home and have to drop hockey.

That's not happening. Fortunately, hockey is good on my application for colleges or he would have taken it away already.

We watch the other students. The party is less chaotic than Fletcher's was last night.

The girls next to us start whispering and pointing toward the door. I glance over, curious what's got them in a tizzy.

Two blonds have walked in, both in short skirts and crop tops. Evan. Fuck. Mia must have done her hair and makeup because she was a smoke show earlier, but now she's straight fire. And we're not the only ones who've noticed.

"T-shirt and jeans next time. These fuckers shouldn't get to see what's mine." It bursts out of me, knowing that all these other guys at the party are staring at Evan's hot little body. I want to punch them all. And then turn her over my knee and make sure she knows that body is mine.

"Payback." Damon tips his bottle up and drinks his soda, setting the empty bottle on the floor. He rises to his feet, but Hawk and I stay seated. "I've got this one."

He stands, and we sit back to watch the sparks fly. He stops in front of Mia and Evan. It's a calculated risk with Olivia. But she's probably off pouting. They talk for maybe a minute before he smirks and heads to get more drinks.

Mia grabs Evan's arm and shakes it, but Evan's gaze falls on me. She has this tease of a smile on those red lips.

I lean into Hawk. "Think it'll smear?"

"Fuck, I hope so." He adjusts himself. Probably wondering what her lipstick will look like on his dick. I'm bound to find out what it will look like on mine.

I chuckle. "We're going to have competition if we're not careful. She's not in a relationship right now."

Mia leads Evan toward the area where a bunch of girls are dancing to the music. I chuckle as I watch her. Fuck, our girl can't dance for shit, but she looks cute trying to dance like Mia.

When Damon hands me another soda, I scoff.

"You want me to have to piss all night?"

"Better than not being able to ride." Hawk glances around to make sure no one's paying attention to us. "You need to cool it with the drinking. Seriously, you were shit on the ice today."

I blow out a breath. He's not wrong, but he's got the grades and the reputation my dad wishes I had. "I just needed to blow off some steam."

"We have a girl you can blow off steam with." Hawk tips his drink toward Evan.

Less than two weeks and we'll be in pussy heaven. I still haven't figured out how inexperienced our girl is. Someone has to have fucked her. Maybe it's the trust issue or maybe she's worried about performing. We're a lot, but I'm willing to help teach her how to move.

Liam walks over to Mia and Evan on the dance floor. Mia bites her lip as she flirts with him. Evan hasn't seemed to notice her dance partner isn't paying attention anymore. When she finally does, she moves to stand with Mia.

Liam says something, and Evan laughs. My gut twists and I start to stand.

"Cool it." Damon shakes his head. "Just watch the play happen."

Chase walks in. His gaze finds Mia, and he heads toward her. His eyes nearly pop out of his head when he realizes Evan is the hot little thing next to Mia.

"Now?" I ask, aching to be let loose on this asshole.

"No." Damon looks casual, but he's on edge too.

He may think he's ready for Evan to play with Chase, but she's still the girl I had to give instructions to the first time she gave him head. I don't know if she's ready for this.

Chapter 8

EvanAnn

Liam tells a joke and I laugh. He eyes me with a lot more interest than he did last weekend or ever before. But I don't want any of these guys. I just have to keep my gaze from slipping to the ones I do want. The ones I've decided to have.

I just have to get through this part of the evening. And then I'll let them be my reward. I won't be doing this for them, but I'm definitely doing it for me.

"Hey, Mia, have you seen—" Chase cuts off when I turn to look at him. "EvanAnn?"

Mia was right. Seeing him look me over like he doesn't know me is fucking powerful. His jaw is more bruised than Damon's. I wish I'd been there to see the fight. Part of me wants to deck him right now for abandoning me out there.

"Can we talk?" He reaches out to take my arm, but I pull it away before he can touch me. "Please, babe, I want to explain."

Like any explanation will take away what he did. Or what he might have done. What would have happened if I hadn't run off? Would he have forced himself on me? I shudder internally. Maybe he thinks I owe him for the months we were together.

Fuck him. I don't owe him anything.

Mia rolls her eyes, but this is what I've been waiting for.

I touch her arm. "I'll be back."

"You need me, I'm here." She leans back against Liam and wiggles to the music.

I smile and let it fall when I return my gaze to Chase. *Find somewhere relatively away from everyone but not completely private.* Damon's words ring in my head. That's not a problem. I never want to be alone with Chase ever again.

I'm not familiar with Olivia's house, but Damon mentioned there were usually areas around the pool. The guys are here and will intervene if I need them.

Nodding to Chase, I lead the way outside and away from the water's edge. His friends call to him from the beer pong table, but he raises his hand and smiles before following me to a couple of chairs next to an unlit fire.

I sit down and cross my legs, leaning back to wait for his explanation.

"I never should have left you out there." He leans forward and puts his hand on my bare knee. "When you weren't there, I went nuts, thinking I really fucked up."

I glare at his hand, and he pulls it back. *Let him do all the talking.*

"Fuck, babe." He runs his hand through his hair. I focus on the bruise on his jaw. Part of me wishes I could have seen his face when Damon hit him. "I was so angry and worked up. I didn't want to accidentally hurt you. We needed to cool off."

Then drop me off at my house, you wanker.

"I've been going through some shit at home, so I needed release. I didn't want to push you, so I thought it wouldn't hurt to be with other girls until you were ready. I only want you, though." Chase runs his hand through his hair again. Then drops it to his lap. "I've fucked up so bad, but I don't want to lose you, EvanAnn. I really do think we can go the distance."

He starts again on his vision of our future. But I know what the reality would be like. I'll be working on location, and he'll be fucking anything that moves. We'll have our children and then the children of his other women. But it won't matter because we'll be a power couple.

I sit back with my arms crossed as he goes on about his fantasy future and really look at the guy who was my first boyfriend. On the outside and on paper, he's a catch. He's popular, attractive, knows how to be sensitive—or at least knows how to act sensitive. And he noticed me.

I'd like to say that wasn't the biggest draw, but I've gone through almost three years of school without making a close friend or finding a boyfriend. It was lonely, and Mom was just beginning to see another new guy.

I didn't want to get left alone again. And he was interested in me.

Maybe I thought it would be over before the end of the school year. But then we made it through the summer, and I thought everything would be golden this year. Instead, I find out I'm not as attracted to him as I thought. Or whatever I felt for him wasn't physical.

Suddenly three guys who are completely out of my league wanted me. Want me. It's not even a competition between what they make me feel and what Chase made me feel. And even if I'm just a passing phase for them, it doesn't matter because I'll remember what they gave me all my life.

But Chase? Chase will just be the asshole I almost gave my virginity to who cheated on me.

"What happened to your jaw?" My tone is steady, like I'm asking about the weather.

He rubs his jaw and glances toward the house. "Damon Storm sucker punched me. I don't know why he's messing with us, babe. But I'll figure it out. He was all over Olivia. I think she has a thing for me."

I narrow my gaze, because Damon couldn't possibly have a thing for me.

He holds his hands up. "Not that I'm interested in her. Or anyone else."

How much longer do I need to listen to this shit? I'd rather be watching him get torn apart by wild dogs.

"I really don't want to lose you, EvanAnn." Chase drags in a breath and releases it. His gaze rakes over me. "I'll do anything to get you back. Just consider it? Please. We're so good together, babe."

I lean forward and brush my hair over the shoulder that's bare. "Look, Chase. You hurt me. I'm going to need time to get over that and see if I can really trust you again."

"Anything, babe. You tell me what I can do, and I'll make it happen."

This part is up to me. I can give him my terms now or make him suffer until Monday, a holiday for most schools, but because we're private, we don't get the day off. Oh, I'm definitely going to make him suffer.

"I have to think about it." Even though I've been mentally broken up with Chase for a while, I don't want to have him back at all. But if I'm doing this for show, he's really going to commit this time. Even if I'm never going to let him touch me again.

"Can we go somewhere?" he asks. His eyes drop to my bare thighs.

Does he think I'm an idiot? Fuck this guy. I narrow my eyes, and he holds his hands up.

"Like coffee or maybe a late dinner and talk about it." He gives me this hopeful look. That's the problem with actors. Is this real or is it an act?

I may never know. What I do know is the guys in there who want to fuck me aren't playing a part. And what I get from them is so much more than Chase has given me.

"Not tonight." I smooth my skirt down. "We can talk at lunch on Monday."

"Monday? Babe, we could talk more tonight." He seems disheartened as I stand. I wish I could say that didn't make me happy to make him grovel.

"Monday. Don't fuck anyone between now and then, and maybe I'll be willing to hear you out." I shrug like I'm not sure. When I walk away, it feels really fucking good. It would have felt even better to tell him about the Devil's trio, but that's not part of the plan. Yet.

Someone turned down all the lights in the house except for the strobe lights on the dance floor. I walk in and know where I want to go. But I need to hang out a while longer.

Mia dances with Liam. They're pretty much all over each other, so I lean against the wall nearby. On the outside again. Besides, I'm not much of a dancer.

"Hey, you're EvanAnn, right?" A guy who looks vaguely familiar sidles up beside me and smiles. "Wayne Anderson. We had history together last year."

"Aren't you on the hockey team?" I'm pretty sure I remember Mia listing off his stats with all the others. The names and numbers are all jumbled in my head. I'm not sure how she keeps it straight.

He grins and leans into me so he doesn't have to yell that loud. "Yeah, thought with Liam hitting on your friend, you might appreciate some company."

My cheeks grow hot. This is definitely not typical. But before I was dating Chase, I never came to the parties. Maybe if I'd branched out, I would have had more options. If I'd gone to parties *and* had Mia do my makeup *and* Damon to dress me.

"Find someone else to hit on." Hawk steps up and gives Wayne a look. Wayne holds his hands up and walks away.

"He didn't even fight for me." I sigh and shake my head, like I'm disappointed.

Hawk puts his hand next to my head on the wall and smirks down at me. "Did you want me to fight for you, baby girl?"

Shivers dance down my spine. It may be too soon to be flirting with guys, but it's no longer off limits.

"So, were you sent over because you're the one and done type of guy? Non-threatening to the other girls because they'll get their turn when you finish with me?" I arch an eyebrow as I search his green eyes.

"Cam probably would have worked too, but I volunteered." Hawk leans in to say in my ear. "Damon was going to tear poor Wayne a new asshole if someone didn't get him to fuck off."

I glance toward the dark corner I know Damon watches me from. Shivers work through me. "I guess he doesn't want Olivia to go feral on my ass by coming over himself."

"She's got no right to be so territorial over him." Hawk brushes my hair behind my ear, and sparks shimmer through me, making my panties damp and my insides heat.

"Do I have that right?" I'm aching to find out.

"You want to claim us, Annie? Show these other girls and all these guys that we're yours?" His green eyes twinkle, and I wonder if he wants me to claim them. It's not the game we're playing, though.

"Can we leave yet?" I bite my lip.

He growls low enough that the sound rumbles through me. My insides are liquid fire.

He reaches for my hand and drags me deeper into the house instead of out the front door like I'd hoped. We pass through a room where the music is low and slow and there are couples making out on almost every surface.

Hawk chuckles and pulls me against him. "Wanna stop and watch for a while?"

I shake my head. Even though I'm curious, I want the others too. I want us to be alone with no one else watching or listening.

He keeps walking, and I struggle to keep up. This low buzz of energy flows through me at his rushing to get me alone. No one is in this part of the house as he takes me down to a lower level.

"Where are we going?" I whisper, afraid to get in trouble for being somewhere we shouldn't.

"Out, without causing a scene." His other hand holds his phone and he thumbs a message to someone. "Text Mia. Tell her you're catching a ride."

I think of what she told me earlier about fucking someone as revenge. Maybe it's somewhat revenge, but I'm definitely all in on these guys. I fire off a text, and she sends me a devil emoji. She has no idea.

When we finally pass through an exterior door, their motorcycles are parked here. Hawk gives me his jacket to put on.

"She rides with me tonight." Damon's voice sends shivers through me.

I turn to watch them approach. Sparks dance through my system.

Cam sweeps me into his arms and kisses me thoroughly. "Please tell me you have that lipstick with you, goody."

"I do." Mia gave me the tube to keep in case I needed to reapply.

He smirks. "I'm going to need you to freshen it often for me."

I arch an eyebrow, but Hawk puts my helmet on.

Damon's already straddling his bike, and I climb on behind him and slide close so my lacy-covered pussy is against his denim ass, squeezing my thighs on the outside of his. His motorcycle rumbles beneath us as he pulls out from behind the house.

"Want a taste of our darkness, little devil?"

I rest my head against Damon's back and just enjoy the feeling of being close to him. Anticipation buzzes through me. "Are you going to spank me?"

Cam chuckles.

Hawk's voice comes through the Bluetooth. "No, baby girl. We're saving that for something special."

"So what do you want to do to me?" I ask, noticing we're not heading toward the houses.

"Are you afraid of the woods, goody?" Cam's voice sends shivers through me.

"Is it too soon?" Hawk's voice is low and concerned.

I consider last night. It wasn't the woods I was afraid of. "I'm not afraid of the woods, but I don't want to be left in them again."

"No one's leaving you, baby girl."

I trust them not to. My insides warm. They may not be boyfriend material, but I trust what they say and that they'll take care of me if something goes wrong.

The bikes hit the town limit and burst with speed as we hit the highway. We go about five minutes down some country roads and pull off into a different parking space than the one Chase took me to. This one doesn't have lights, and the pavement is cracked with grass growing between it. Abandoned. It would make a great apocalyptic film background.

After they park, the others get off the bikes, so I follow. Damon helps me take my helmet off.

"Can you see in there?" Damon asks, gesturing to the forest.

I turn to look into the trees. There's enough moonlight to make it shadowy.

"Yes." Unease and tension wind inside me. "What's the plan?"

Damon grabs my hair and tips my head back, making me gasp as his lips claim mine. His hand slides up my side under the crop top to squeeze my breast. Leaning into his touch, I whimper into his mouth as awareness explodes through me.

"We're going to give you a head start." He rests his forehead on mine. "If we catch you, we're going to fuck your mouth, little devil."

My cheeks heat as I look at the others. It's dark and with how wet my panties are, it might be the perfect time to push through one of the boundaries. Plus, I won't have to choose who goes first and it's dark. So hopefully less noticeable.

I want them all to fuck me. I'm ready.

When I turn back to Damon, I raise up on my toes to get near his ear. "Only my mouth?"

"Yes." His hand tightens in my hair, pulling slightly. He releases a low growl that makes my pussy ache. Our bodies are pressed tight against each other.

I wet my lips next to his ear. "Ask me again."

I drop back down and look into his eyes.

They narrow on me before widening. He grabs the back of my neck. "Can I fuck you, little devil?"

My breath catches. "If you can catch me."

His mouth crashes down on mine. His hand slides under my skirt and grabs my panties. My heart pounds at my decision.

Against my mouth, he says, "Are you sure, Evan?"

"Yes."

A rip breaks into the quiet night, and I gasp at the touch of pain as Damon rips my panties from my body. Damon slides the remnants in his pocket.

My insides are burning with need.

"You wet for us, little devil?" He doesn't wait for me to answer. His hand cups my pussy and presses a finger inside, sliding in easily. I bite back my moan. "You want our cum inside you?"

I hum my answer, barely able to think. I'm wound so tight.

"You get a safe word this time, baby girl." Hawk closes in on my back. "If something is wrong or you get hurt, call out red. Like a stop sign. Do you understand?"

I nod.

Hawk slides his hand along my thigh and when Damon removes his finger, Hawk slides his deep inside me. I gasp as he fucks me with his finger. Damon circles my clit as I lean back against Hawk to watch Damon's eyes in the dark. I can't see the color, but the need for me is so fucking obvious.

I want to fuck them all tonight.

Cam's hand slides over my breast and teases my nipple into a hard peak. "We need you soaking wet for us, goody."

I gasp in Damon's breath as his mouth covers mine. Their hands work me as I cling to Damon's shirt.

I cry out into Damon's mouth as my release gushes around Hawk's fingers, leaving my thighs wet. They all withdraw as I'm catching my breath.

I look up into Damon's eyes. He sucks his finger in his mouth, and his grin is almost feral.

"Ten... Nine... Eight..."

I pull away from him and stagger off on weak knees into the woods. Adrenaline pumps through my system as I hurry away from them and the numbers keep counting down. Yelling *wait* won't stop them. For a moment, real fear creeps through my system. Did I really give them permission to fuck me like this?

In the woods, after they catch me? Am I supposed to struggle? Try to get away?

My pussy throbs. I don't hate the idea.

My heart races and I'm almost dizzy trying to figure out where to hide. It seemed logical. I don't have to decide who goes first. Someone will catch me and fuck me, and it will be done. I won't be a virgin anymore.

No need to think more about it.

It doesn't always hurt the first time. I'm sure I read that somewhere. Besides, anything could break a hymen. Even a finger fuck.

"Two."

Fuck, fuck, fuck. My pulse catapults. I duck behind a tree, trying to catch my breath. The wind cools the wetness between my legs. Any number of things can stretch or tear a hymen. I doubt there's much there at this point as often as the guys have had their fingers between my legs. A fresh wave of arousal flows through me.

"One." Branches crack as they enter the woods. They aren't rushing, which is almost more terrifying. Because the closer they get, the more the urge to run presses on me. As soon as I move, they'll know where I am. My heartbeat is loud in my ears.

It's possible they'll decide to fuck my mouth. Just because I gave them permission doesn't mean they'll slam into me at the first opportunity. And it's not like they'll come at me all at once. Right?

Fuck.

I could yell the safe word. *Red.* It would stop them, but I don't want to stop. Even though my heart feels like it's going to pound out of my chest, I want this. Honestly, I want to be out of my head. I don't want to worry about two weeks from now when the decision is finally taken out of my hands.

Maybe they'll find out I'm a virgin or maybe they won't even notice. I've read that guys can't really tell. But I'll know it's gone. Finally.

A branch cracks to my left, and I cover my mouth to stop from screaming. It's darker in the woods than it appeared from the road. The canopy provides cover and instead of the guys I know, all I see are shadows shifting through the night.

A crack directly behind me makes me bolt. I can't handle it. It doesn't matter that I'm giving away my position, I need to run. Footsteps fall after mine. I'm not going to outrun him. I can't outrun any of them, but I can try.

Arms wrap around me, and we go falling toward the ground. Holding in my shriek, I brace for impact, but he turns us so I fall on him. His chest and arms are bare. I scramble to get off him, to get away, but he comes with me and I'm kneeling on the dirt with him behind me.

His hands grab my hips and fear chases through me. The word *red* lingers on my tongue, but then a warm mouth is on my pussy. My body melts, programmed to ache for their tongues on any part of my body. My fingers dig into the leaves on the ground.

When he sucks on my clit, I forget to run. I forget what I've offered. The heat curls inside me and I open my legs for him. The flood gates open and I shatter.

A belt clinks and a zipper unzips as my release chases through me. It registers somewhere in my mind as I try to come back down. Something much bigger than a finger thrusts into my pussy, ripping me open. I scream at the pain.

"Fuck, fuck, fuck, fuck." Oh fuck, it burns. Fuck. Every inch of me is clenched around him.

He's huge, and it feels like he's tearing me to pieces, like I'm way too small for something that big, but he's not moving.

"Are you okay?"

Damon. I pant through the pain. Tears flow down my cheeks. Lies. It was all lies. Fuck, this hurts.

"What's wrong?" His body covers me, but he's still inside me and my pussy is throbbing, but not necessarily in a good way. "Talk to me, little devil."

He brushes my hair away from my face and feels the wetness of my tears. He begins to withdraw.

"Ow, ow, nope." I grab his hip to hold him still. "It'll pass."

Fuck, I hope it does. Unless that's a lie too. I whimper. Maybe if we just stay like this for a while. If he never moves again.

"What will pass?" Damon's voice is suspicious, but he can't see anything in this darkness either.

"What the fuck is happening?" Hawk.

"I just need a moment," I whisper.

"Fuck, goody. Please tell me you're not a virgin." Cam sounds stressed.

"What?" Damon says.

I laugh a little. "Not anymore."

"You didn't think to mention that, little devil?" Damon rocks his hips gently and presses his fingers, slick with something, on my clit.

The pain is receding as pleasure rolls through me. His fingers are working some sort of magic. My core tightens around him inside me, and I release a little moan. That didn't feel so bad.

"You thought I was a whore." I blow out a breath. "I didn't want to disappoint you."

Damon's head rests against the center of my back. "Fuck."

My hips begin to rock with his fingers, and the pain is mostly gone. He begins to draw out, and I panic.

"No, it's feeling better, please."

He slowly eases back in. "I'm not saying I would have fucked you on a bed of roses for your first time, little devil, but I probably wouldn't have thrust in so deep on the first go."

He does it again, pulling out and sliding back in, while his finger rubs my clit in tiny circles. My insides hum with pleasure.

"I don't like roses. They're too garish." My words are breathy.

His fingers are working their magic, and I grow wetter as he drags his cock along my walls. "You're so fucking tight. Fuck. Come for me, little devil. Come on my cock so I can come so deep in your cunt you'll never get me out."

My fingers dig into the leaves as he moves a little faster, snapping his hips into mine. I can't focus on anything but his finger on my clit and his cock thrusting inside me. Oh, fuck, why did I wait?

Catching my breath, I tumble over the edge. My pussy milks his cock as he thrusts a couple more times. One final thrust and I can feel the pulse of his cum through his cock as he pumps it into me. This is the most erotic thing I've ever felt in my life.

For a moment, we stay connected, breathing deep to slow our hearts. When he pulls out, Hawk lifts me into his arms. I bury my head into his neck, knowing I'll have to face all three of them in the light.

So much for them not noticing.

Chapter 9

Hawk

As we walk out of the woods to the bikes, I cradle Annie against me. I wish I had a car to lay her down in the backseat to check to make sure she's all right. Her face is buried in my neck, and I don't miss the irony of me finding her teary-eyed in the woods two nights in a row.

This parking lot doesn't even have railroad ties to sit on. We just need to get her home.

Once we're at the bikes, Damon turns on his headlight. Cam walks up to us and brushes off Annie's hands, checking them in the light for any wounds. He does the same for her knees. When he finishes, he rests his hand on her hair. She keeps her face buried in my neck.

"You knew?" Damon accuses Cam.

Cam shakes his head. "I guessed she wasn't as experienced as you thought she might be, but I didn't think she was a virgin."

Damon looks like he wants to rip her out of my arms. I readjust how I'm carrying her. If he tries to claim her as his own, we're going to have issues. Just because he fucked her first doesn't give him different rights. She's all of ours.

"We should head back." I nod toward the motorcycles, then meet

Damon's eyes as he shrugs on his shirt. Damon tore her panties. Maybe they're salvageable and she can get some coverage from them. "She'll be more comfortable with panties on."

"Fuck that." Cam kicks off his shoes and takes his jeans and boxer briefs off before pulling his pants back on. "Here, goody, these will have a little more absorbency than the slivers of lace Damon buys for you anyway."

"I'm sorry I ruined your night," she whispers into my neck.

I arch an eyebrow at Damon. She hid this from us because we labeled her a whore.

He narrows his eyes on me, but then his eyes soften on Annie. "Come on, little devil. Let's get you home. We can discuss this there."

I lower her to her feet, and Cam hands her his boxers. She pulls them on under her skirt and looks up at us with tear-streaked cheeks. But those blue eyes are determined.

"What's there to discuss?" She tosses her hair over her shoulder and straightens. "I agreed to your terms, and you agreed to mine. I'm open for business."

"Tomorrow." I grab her and draw her into my arms, kissing her softly on her lips. "After you've had a bath tonight."

I meet Cam's and Damon's eyes, and we all agree. I help her put her helmet on, but she heads to Damon's bike. She climbs on behind him and wraps her arms around his waist. He pauses and puts his hand over hers for a moment.

"Yours or mine," I ask. I don't know how much privacy we'll get at Damon's since the party bust yesterday. But if that's where he wants to take her, I won't argue. I want Annie comfortable.

"Yours." Damon clears his throat. "You have the better tub and no parents who might think Sunday morning is a great time to discuss our shortcomings."

We take off back the way we came. But as we approach Damon's house, I say, "Go on, get the bath started. I'll grab Annie some clothes."

"Thank you," she says softly through the Bluetooth.

Is she still hurting? "There's some ibuprofen in the medicine cabinet."

I pull into Damon's house and leave my bike at the side of the house. Not bothering to take off my helmet, I enter through the back door, head up to Damon's room, and cross through the bathroom to Annie's. I grab her some things from her closet and put them into a bag.

I make sure no one is in the hallway before sneaking out. By the time I get home, Cam sits on the closed toilet while Annie is in the bathtub alone. Her face is scrubbed clean of the makeup. I put her clothes on the counter for her and return to the bedroom. Damon sits on the bed with his head in his hands.

When I sit next to him, I run a hand through my hair. "I would have been just as rough."

"I should have known." It's almost like he's reexamining every interaction with Annie, looking for what he missed. I've been doing the same thing. But she didn't want us to know.

"How?" I bump his shoulder. "She didn't have a freshness-sealed label. I know, I looked everywhere."

He grins and shakes his head. "Did you suspect?"

"Not really. Now that I know, it explains some things." I rub my jaw. "It also explains why Chase wasn't at her place that week."

"Evan wasn't giving him anything." Damon runs his hand through his hair and stares at the door to the bathroom like he has x-ray vision. "She didn't know how to give a blow job. She's definitely masturbated though."

"You still haven't shared that video with me." I know the real question both of us need to examine. The one that's tearing me up inside. "Would you have believed her if she told you?"

He doesn't answer. The truth is, neither of us would have wanted to believe her. She was a whore for us to use as a tool to get revenge on Chase. The other question is...

"Would it have changed our plan if we had known?" She's the key to getting Damon's revenge. Take the thing Chase wants. Take his future. We still don't know why he wants her so badly, or maybe we do.

"Fuck." He scrubs his hand down his face. "What do we do now?"

"Talk with her." I lead the way into the bathroom. I lean against the counter, and when Damon comes in, he joins me. Cam has his elbows on his knees with his hands clasped between his legs while Annie sits with her knees up and her arms wrapped around them protectively. Her hair is piled on top of her head in a bun.

She rests her head on her knees and looks at the three of us. Her cheeks glow pink, but she doesn't say anything. She looks so young and innocent. Fuck.

"Are you okay?" I keep asking it, but when she screamed in pain, I panicked. Whatever hurt her, I was prepared to fight.

She drags in a breath and runs her fingertips through the surface of the water. "A little sore, but I've been told that's typical."

"You still want to do this, goody?" Cam lifts his eyes to hers.

Her gaze drops to her fingers in the water. "I don't see what the big deal is."

"You let me rip you apart, Evan." Damon stands and paces a few steps. His anger is at himself, and I hope Annie knows that.

"I mean, you're big, so it probably would have torn either way." She shrugs but doesn't look at any of us. Like losing her virginity in a forest as if she's our fucking prey isn't most girl's nightmares.

"There's a difference between riding a bike for the first time on a sidewalk versus down the side of a mountain," Damon snaps at her.

"I thought you two fucking would help matters." I shake my head. This isn't working. I grab a towel, holding it up. "Time to get out before you prune, baby girl."

When she stands, I wrap the towel around her body and lift her out of the tub. Her blue-gray eyes lift to mine. I still want her. We all do. And from the look in her eyes, she still wants us.

"We should play truth or dare." Cam looks at all of us as we turn to him. "Look, neither of you would have believed Evan if she told you she was a virgin because you convinced yourselves she was a whore. Maybe it's time to get some of the misconceptions out of the way. If you don't want to tell the truth, take the dare."

I rub the towel over Annie's body. "What do you think?"

She glances at Damon before shrugging.

I have to offer. "If you just want to go to sleep—"

"I don't." She wets her lips. "I'll play."

EvanAnn

I'm dressed and sitting on the bed with three guys. Damon refused to do this sober and got a bottle of vodka and four shot glasses from somewhere in the house.

He pours one for each of us and passes them out. As he hands me mine, he says, "Only one for you, little devil."

I grow warm. That first night, it loosened my lips. Maybe not telling them I was a virgin was a bad idea, but I don't regret it. It's one moment of pain for me to be able to explore everything with them.

"Rules." Cam leans back on his hands. "Everyone answers the question. You don't answer, you get a dare."

"What kind of dares are you proposing?" I ask.

"Depends on who the player is." Cam winks. "Like if I had to dare Damon, I might make him suck on your breast for a minute without popping a boner."

"Fuck off," Damon says, pouring another round for the guys only. Part of me wants another shot, but I know I'll be too drunk to make decisions, or maybe even sense.

"Or I might make him take a body shot off you." Cam arches an eyebrow as his brown eyes flow over my body.

Everywhere he looks heats. Part of me hopes I get to play with Cam. We haven't gotten time together lately. Though we had a quickie in the closet at school on Friday.

Hawk grabbed me comfortable leggings and panties to wear, but for my top, he gave me one of his shirts. No bra. I'm used to being naked around these guys, but right now, I feel so vulnerable, like they've seen inside me and found me lacking.

"Any more rules?" I ask as they down their shot.

Cam smirks. "Come sit on my lap, goody."

It's one of my rules to follow their orders. I crawl across the bed, and he guides me to sit in his lap. My head rests against his shoulder. His warmth surrounds me. In his arms, I feel safe and protected. I inhale his sandalwood and leather scent and let it draw me in.

"Whoever is holding Evan goes first." Cam says with a laugh.

Hawk rolls his eyes. "How about Annie moves between turns?"

"Fine." Cam concedes. "Evan gets to sit on the person asking the truth, and then she gets to ask her own truth."

He squeezes my waist, and I realize he's giving me more opportunities to learn about them.

I lift my gaze to Damon as he downs another shot. His eyes lower to my lips. My pussy pulses, empty, achy. It wasn't all bad. Yes, it hurt, but not toward the end. He made me come, but they always make me come. I squirm a little.

"Ask your question." Damon lifts his gaze to Cam.

Cam squeezes me. "How old were you when you got your first kiss? And with who?"

I almost spin around. That's the truth he wants to know? Not why did I hide my virginity? I mean, I didn't hide it so much as not mention it.

"Nine," Cam says. "Mary."

"Nine." Hawk smirks and runs his hand through his hair. "Also, Mary."

My mouth opens and closes. *Go, Mary.*

"Eleven." Damon meets my eyes. "Gwen."

They both look at me. I swallow.

"Sixteen." A tremor goes through me, remembering how he cornered me. I couldn't escape. Do they know him? He plays hockey. Should I tell them?

"Who with?" Cam asks. "Chase?"

"Not Chase, but..." I look down at my hands. It's not like he has a common name, and I don't want to start this out by lying. "I'd rather not say."

Damon's eyes narrow on me like he's going to push it.

"So you want a dare, goody?"

I bite my lip and turn to look up into Cam's dark eyes. "I guess."

"Give me a shot."

My brows pull together. That's it? Damon pours a shot glass and hands it to me. I turn to hand it to Cam, but he shakes his head.

"Not from a glass. I want it from your mouth." Cam smirks. "Pour it into your mouth and don't swallow. Put your lips on mine and give me the shot."

I take a breath and dump the shot into my mouth, careful not to swallow. I lean into Cam and press my mouth to his before opening and giving him the shot. He catches the back of my neck and swallows the vodka before kissing me, dragging me onto his lap to straddle him.

He tastes of the vodka and something richer, that taste that is all Cam. Heady, rich, tempting. He slides his hand over my ass and squeezes. When he lifts his head from mine, I'm aching for more.

"Your turn." He nods to the others.

What do I want to know about the Devil's trio? So many things, but Cam didn't start with the hard stuff. So maybe I shouldn't either. But what I really want to know is if it would have made a difference to them if they'd known I was a virgin.

"How old were you when you lost your virginity?"

Cam chuckles. "Fifteen."

Hawk's green eyes spark. "I haven't yet. Wanna help me out, baby girl?"

"I really don't believe you." I shake my head.

He winks. "Fourteen."

I turn to Damon. "Thirteen."

My mouth opens and closes. Just because I didn't have the opportunity didn't mean they didn't, but thirteen? I probably could have lost mine at sixteen if I hadn't been terrified of Jackson. If he'd made me feel half of what these guys do, I would have.

"Come on, Annie. Time to rotate." Hawk sits against the headboard and I crawl on the bed to his lap, relaxing back into him. He takes a minute. His fingers run up and down my arm, sending little sparks through me.

"When's the first time you masturbated?" Hawk's hand rests low on my stomach. "Eleven."

I inhale sharply.

"Ten," Damon says, looking at me.

"Twelve," Cam says with a smirk.

I swallow. "Fourteen."

"Want to show us, baby girl?" Hawk dips to kiss my neck. I tip my head to give him better access. The delicious shivers of pleasure from his lips flood me with desire.

"You can save that for a dare." I bite my lip as my gaze collides with Damon's.

"What's your next question, little devil?"

My mind goes to Mia and something that's been niggling at me this whole time. "Have any of you had a threesome or more?"

"Not until you, goody." Cam throws me a kissy face. My cheeks heat.

"Only with you, Annie." Hawk scrapes his teeth on my neck, ripping a sigh from my lips.

Damon's eyes capture mine. "You. And hoping to do more."

There's this part of me that worried they wouldn't want to play with me if they found out I was a virgin. Not that I am anymore. But Cam's kiss, Hawk's lips, and Damon's heated eyes make that worry vanish. My pussy clenches.

They want more, and so do I.

Chapter 10

EvanAnn

Damon doesn't say anything, but I crawl across the bed to him. He draws me down onto his lap. I shouldn't feel safe with him, but when I inhale that earthy, dark scent, it makes me crave being close to him and reminds me of nights tangled in his sheets naked with him.

I shouldn't feel anything but attraction to him, but there's something about him that draws me in and makes me long to be in his arms.

"Tell me what you did with Chase, little devil." His words are soft and for once not accusatory.

I blow out a breath and look down at my hands in my lap. "We kissed. He grazed my breast once. He wanted more, but he knew I was a virgin and was okay with waiting."

"Obviously not." Cam shakes his head. "That's on him. Not you."

I pick at the comforter next to my legs. "Yeah, well. It didn't exactly spark confidence that telling a guy about my virginity would make him want to fuck me."

"Did you do anything more than kiss before us?" Damon asks.

I drag in a breath and hold it, looking down at my hands. "No."

"Fuck," Cam whispers. That first night they took turns in my mouth and going down on me. It was amazing.

Damon's fingers tighten on my waist. "Would you have believed Evan if she said she was a virgin?"

"Yeah," Cam says. "I knew there was something off from what we were being told. And if I had a girlfriend all alone at her house, I wouldn't have been getting some on a couch at a pool party."

"Oddly specific," I grumble, knowing he's talking about Chase. But I appreciate that Cam didn't let others color his view of me.

"I don't know." Hawk runs a hand over his hair. "I might have questioned it, especially at first. But I don't know if I would have believed you. Sorry, Annie."

I shrug, but it hurts a little knowing he wouldn't have trusted me.

"I wouldn't have." Damon slides his hand between my legs and rubs me through my leggings. "You were dating a guy who I saw getting head by a blond when he ran me off the road. Guys generally don't wait for their girlfriends to be ready. They push. Maybe you were bad at it, and he didn't want to take the time to train you."

I try to shift away, but he holds me in place.

"I'm being honest, Evan. I'm not trying to sugarcoat this. Everything around me was telling me you were a whore acting like a good girl."

Fuck this. I try to pull away again. He tightens his hold, pressing his fingers against my clit, which apparently doesn't have any compulsion against wanting him even when he's being an asshole.

He continues, "I didn't know you. We weren't in the same circles. I only knew what I saw and what other people told me."

"What other people?" I turn to look into his eyes.

"Olivia."

My insides chill. "Stop touching me."

"No. Fuck that. You want the truth? She's an evil bitch who spreads rumors. I didn't trust what she said. But it fed into the story I told myself. Chase and his whore of a girlfriend were the reason I didn't go off to live my fucking dream. That accident cost me my future. So yeah, I wanted to believe that the tight little fuck toy who had moved into my house was a whore."

His eyes search mine and I don't know what to say to that. What to say to him. It burns something inside me, but at least he's not trying to lie to me.

"What tears me up inside is, I knew." He grabs the back of my neck. His fingers squeeze the tight muscles. "Little things didn't add up. That week I watched you every fucking day."

My breath catches in my throat.

"Cam's right. If I knew my girl was home alone, I'd be in that tiny twin bed with my cock buried deep inside her, making her scream. I couldn't make sense of it, because it didn't fit the story. *You* didn't fit the story. And if that was the truth, then I was blackmailing the wrong girl. I was forcing some innocent to play my games."

He takes in a breath and narrows his eyes on me. "It would mean I should do the right thing and let her go."

My heart crashes. My fingers dig into his shirt. I don't want that. Not now. Can he see my panic?

"But I can't." He brings his mouth to mine and stops, holding me in sweet anticipation of his lips on me. "Because you're mine."

He captures my mouth, and I surrender. I'm not mad he thought I was a whore. I knew that from the beginning. I don't care that he blackmailed me into this twisted relationship. All I care about is the way it felt when he was moving inside me, so much better than his fingers.

"Ask a question, goody, before he forgets and fucks you again." Cam's voice pulls me out of it as Damon lifts his head. Cam chuckles. "Ask something I won't answer so I can get a dare."

I pull away from Damon, searching his blue eyes for something. I'm not sure what. Maybe assurance that what I'm feeling he's feeling too.

He draws me back to him. "You're ours, Evan. Every inch of you. I can't wait to watch the others fuck you while I take your mouth."

I'm heated again, almost aching with the need for release. Dragging in a breath, I try to focus on something I want to know about all of them. We're definitely leaning more sexual, but what do I want to know?

"Who do you think about when you masturbate?" I look at Cam first.

"You and those tiny skirts you wore to school before the new ones." Cam wets his lips. "During literature, I want to slide my hand between your legs, slip beneath those cotton panties, and see how wet I can make you."

"That's not—"

"Fair? The right answer?" Cam chuckles and grabs my ankle dragging me across the bed toward him. "What isn't fair is that Damon gets you to himself during the week. That I have to compete for time with you on the weekends. I'm pretty sure it's after midnight, which means it's tomorrow."

He grabs the waistband of my leggings and drags them off my legs. I rise up on my elbows and watch him, biting my lip. I want him. His gaze focuses on my cotton panties Hawk brought.

"Fuck, goody. Why are these panties so sexy on you?" He slides his hand along my clit through the panties and I hiss in a breath. His dark gaze collides with mine, holding me, giving me an out if I need it. "Dare me to eat your pussy, Evan."

I could say no right now. They'd let me take the out. But I don't want that. I want to feel him buried deep inside me. I want Hawk inside me. And Damon. Fuck, I never want this to end.

"Eat my pussy," Damon says with a smirk.

"Not cool, man." Hawk shakes his head.

"I'll take it." Cam drags my panties off and shoves them in his pocket. "Bend your legs, up and out."

I do as he asks and flatten myself on the bed. He licks my clit and slides a finger into my pussy. I hold my breath, waiting for the burning pain. But there isn't any. His lips close over my pussy, and he sucks on my clit. Electricity shimmers through me, and my back arches.

My shirt lifts, and I open my eyes to see Damon over me, taking my shirt off. Hawk bends down and takes my breast into his mouth as Damon takes my other. They're all sucking on me, hands exploring my naked skin, feeding the fire that always rages out of control with them.

I can barely breathe, waiting for the eruption.

Cam presses in another finger, stretching me, making me full, but not as full as Damon's cock had been. I slide my hand into Damon's hair and grab onto Hawk's shirt as the waves threaten to drag me under.

My hips rock with every thrust of Cam's fingers and the slide of his tongue against my clit. Damon bites gently on my nipple as Hawk does something with his tongue that makes me see stars. Gasping, I shatter all around them.

Cam's mouth and fingers leave me, and he thrusts his cock inside me. I moan at the thickness of him, but there's only a small burn of pain that quickly gets overwhelmed by the pleasure. He holds my hips up as he gently rocks inside me. Every nerve is sensitive from my orgasm, and they spark to life again.

"Fuck, you feel so good on my cock, goody."

Damon kisses up my neck until his mouth captures mine. Cam thrusts a little harder and I moan as it winds me even tighter, pushing me closer and closer to the edge, building me even higher than before.

"Do you like his cock in your pussy, baby girl?" Hawk kisses me behind my ear. Hands tease my nipples. "I can't wait to feel that pussy squeezing my dick."

I whimper. Fingers tease my clit, making everything inside me tighten. With a cry, I explode around Cam's cock.

"Fuck. You're so fucking tight." Cam groans as he comes inside me for the first time. So warm and deep.

He pulls out and slides his fingers in his cum to push it deeper inside me. An aftershock trembles through me as Damon pulls away.

Hawk rubs my hip. Cam leans over me and takes my mouth. I wrap my arms around his neck. My body feels like it's fucking glowing.

"You okay?" Cam asks, between kisses to my ear.

"So good." I turn and find his lips again, needing to feel him, taste him, breathe him.

"I could fuck you all night, Evan," he whispers.

When I open my eyes to his dark ones, my pussy clenches. I want that. I want all of it.

"I wanna watch you take Hawk's cock." Cam kisses me and moves to sit up next to the headboard. "Take that thick cock into your tight little pussy."

"Hands and knees, baby girl." Hawk's green eyes capture mine.

Damon stands next to the bed, stroking his dick. Fuck, that was inside me. I still haven't caught my breath from Cam, but I want more. So much more.

Damon smirks down at me. "Crawl over here, little devil. Show me how much you love our cum."

Grateful I'm back to his cum slut, I shift to my hands and knees and crawl over to Damon. His hand sinks into my hair and holds me where he wants me.

"An orgasm will help her take it." Cam gives Hawk a thumbs up as I feel him kneel behind me.

"I know how to fuck a girl, Cam." Hawk rubs his fingers over my swollen clit, slowly building me up. I moan as the rush of pleasure pours through me. Damon looks at my face as he strokes his cock right in front of it. I wet my lips, needing to taste him, to suck on him while the others take me.

When Hawk slides a finger inside my pussy and fucks me with it, I moan. Fuck, it glides against my walls, lighting me up inside and out. He works his finger in deep.

He chuckles. "Feel good, baby girl? Don't worry. I'll make you feel even better."

He pulls out of my pussy and rubs my wetness over my puckered hole before he slides his finger inside my ass. I relax as he pushes through my tight ring.

"Ah." I almost buckle as he begins to fuck my ass with his finger.

"Such a good girl, letting us fuck you." Hawk's words make me glow. "Fuck her mouth. Open up, baby girl."

I part my lips and taste Damon's precum on his tip as he pushes inside. He begins to thrust in time with Hawk's finger in my ass. Hawk notches his cock at my entrance and my hips long to rock to take him in. His fingers strum my clit until my climax has me moaning around Damon's cock in my mouth.

Hawk eases his cock inside me with his finger still in my ass. He takes his time moving in and pulling out, then pushing in farther before pulling almost all the way out, stretching me slowly and letting me get accustomed to his size. When he fully seats his cock inside me, I swear I can feel him touching my womb in this position.

I feel so full and stretched. Nothing has ever felt like fucking them before.

"Fuck, baby girl, you take my cock so fucking good. Do you want my cum in your pussy?" He holds still with his cock buried deep and fucks his finger in my ass a few times. I shiver, ready for more. "I need to hear you beg for it."

Damon pulls me off his cock and I gasp in a breath. "Tell him what you want, little devil."

"Mmm, fuck me, please. Fill me up with your cum." My eyes meet Damon's darkened ones. "Both of you."

Hawk chuckles and squeezes my ass. "Such a good little fuck toy."

My pussy squeezes around his cock and I part my lips to take Damon back inside. They begin to use me, fucking my mouth and pussy. Claiming me.

I come apart at the seams as my orgasm rips through me. They're not done using me though, and it feels so good. Damon buries himself in my throat and comes in a rush as I swallow around his tip. When Damon pulls out, he pushes my head to the bed, making me take

Hawk even deeper. I close my eyes, trying to memorize this feeling. Every thrust kisses my womb and my release gushes around his dick.

"That's it. Milk my cock. Take it all." Hawk thrusts a few more times and stills as his warmth floods me.

When he pulls out, I know he's staring at my pussy. Suddenly Cam is behind me, and I feel him press the head of his cock to my asshole. He strokes his cock, and warmth floods my ass as he comes in and on it.

He drags his fingers through his cum and pushes it into my puckered hole until he's fucking my ass with two fingers. I'm so tired, but it feels so good. Keening, I shatter around his fingers one last time. Damon rubs his thumb along my jaw as I try to catch my breath.

"You're going to be a fantastic fuck toy, little devil."

His words fill me with warmth. I smile, because isn't that what every girl wants to hear? Okay, maybe only me.

Damon lifts me off the bed, and I wrap around him as he carries me into the shower. Hawk's already in there washing himself off. Cam closes the door as he joins us.

I laugh.

"What's funny?" Cam smirks.

"My shower at home wouldn't even fit two of us. It barely fit me." I glance at the multiple shower heads and enough space for all four of us to stand comfortably.

Damon lowers me to my feet. I sway a little, not sure my knees will support me. My legs feel like rubber. Hawk draws me back against him as the others wash me and themselves. I'm turned in Hawk's arms, and they do a thorough job of cleaning between my legs until I'm tempted to ask for more. To start over and do it all over again. Instead, I yawn.

Hawk passes me to Cam, who holds a towel open for me and engulfs me in it. I use a toothbrush Hawk gives me to brush my teeth as Cam dries me off. The guys pull on their boxers. But when I look for my panties, they're nowhere to be found.

Damon lifts me into the bed and tucks me under the sheets

without my panties. I snuggle into the warmth of two bodies before drifting off to sleep.

Satisfaction flows through me. I'm no one's trophy anymore.

Chapter 11

EvanAnn

I may not have been that sore last night, but now as I sit in a plastic chair listening to my cast butcher Shakespeare, I'm decidedly uncomfortable. Maybe fucking three guys on the night I lost my virginity was too much.

My lips curve into a smile. No, I can't regret what I did last night. And I definitely can't wait for the next time. I clue back into my cast and wonder if most of them are hungover.

"Okay." I stand and draw the attention of the actors. "Let's take ten, get something to drink, and then reset."

Sunday afternoon rehearsals are vital to my plan. It's the only time that doesn't conflict with sports or other extracurriculars. It's a great time for a full run through, but right now, the cast is still learning their lines.

I lower into my seat as everyone steps away to use the bathroom or get a drink or go fuck in a closet. I don't care as long as they're back in ten minutes. My fingers toy with my pen as I read through the notes I made on this scene.

"Hey."

I look up into Chase's blue eyes, slightly annoyed he disrupted my concentration. Did he ever make my heart flutter or was it just the idea of him that made me feel something? Popular, hot, interested in me.

He lowers to a squat in front of my table with a smile. "How are you holding up?"

"I'm good. What do you need, Chase?" It feels like he's expecting something from me. I clearly told him we'd talk on Monday.

"I was hoping we could talk some more. About us." He looks hopeful.

I guess I should be acting more broken up over our breakup. Instead, I have a sex hangover from fucking three guys last night. Not to mention coming on Hawk's tongue this morning. I smile a little and that must encourage Chase.

"Maybe after practice we can go grab a coffee and talk it out."

I arch an eyebrow. What's there to talk about really? He's a lying cheater, and I'm boning three guys, so I think we're just over at this point. Right? Damon wants me to continue using Chase, but what if I didn't? What if I just told him he could go fuck himself?

But I want to understand why, which is annoying. But fuck, why date me at all? He clearly wasn't serious about a relationship, but he stayed with me. Why? I want to know his motive. I need to understand.

But not today. Today I want to bask in my after-sex glow. And that definitely doesn't include talking to Chase.

"Tonight isn't a good idea. I have a lot of homework and need to work on the play." I run a hand over my hair, which I pulled up into a bun. "I told you we'd talk at lunch on Monday. Right now, I don't really want to get into it with you. I need to focus."

"Oh." He straightens like he really thought I'd be like *I forgive you and take you back.* "Yeah. I'm sorry, babe. I just really want us to be okay. I miss you."

And I really want to scream at him, how could we be okay with him fucking every other girl in this school? He left me out in the middle of nowhere at night. What would ever make me good with that?

"Hey."

I look up as Hawk walks past Chase and hands me a Diet Coke.

"You looked like you could use a pick me up." Hawk's green eyes are only on me, and something stirs inside me. It helps calm the fire raging within that wants me to tear my ex a new asshole.

Chase's eyes narrow suspiciously on Hawk.

"Thanks." I smile at Hawk and wonder if the rumor mill picked up on our leaving the party together. Or at least sneaking off. The room was pretty dark, so maybe no one thought anything of it.

Mia walks over and looks at the guys. "How's it going, girl boss?"

I blow out a breath and open my Diet Coke.

She glances at me and Chase and Hawk. And then lifts her eyebrows. I'm sure that's some sort of girl communication technique, but I've got nothing. She must figure out something because she turns with a smile.

"Hey, Chase, do you want to run my lines with me over here?" Mia grabs his arm and pulls him away.

Hawk chuckles and sits in Keira's seat. "Are you back together with the fucker yet?"

"Nope." I take a drink. "I'm making him sweat."

"You know there's enough time left to find somewhere to be alone." Hawk's voice is quiet.

A shiver goes through me. "Not during practice."

"Thought I'd offer to take the edge off." Hawk starts to stand but leans over me. "You need me, I'm yours."

He walks off, taking with him that scent of citrus and leaving me a little needy. I cross my legs.

I drink the soda, which I did need, and curse my work ethic before returning to reviewing my notes.

Keira returns to the table and claps her hands to get everyone's attention. "Two minute warning."

She sinks into the chair beside me at the table. "How's it going?"

I smile. "Pretty good, actually."

"Didn't you and Chase break up Friday night?" She taps her pen on the table.

"Oh, yeah." Maybe I should act more broken up, but honestly. "I think it was for the best. He wanted something I wasn't willing to give him."

"Guys can be dicks sometimes. I didn't want to say anything, but he hit on me last week." Keira shudders like it wasn't a good time. "I was going to talk to you this weekend about it, privately. I thought you should know he was trying to get with other girls."

He definitely succeeded on other girls.

"I appreciate you saying something." I blow out a breath. No one else did. "Yeah, apparently he had a different idea of what our relationship meant."

"For what it's worth, Hawk seems really into you." Keira blushes and looks down at her paper. "Not that I'm the best judge of things like that, but..." She shrugs.

I glance over to where Hawk is working with Sophia on their parts in the play. She giggles every time he speaks. Hopefully she gets over that by the time we go off book.

I'm home in time for dinner. When I walk into the dining room, Adam and my mom sit at the table.

"Hi, honey." Mom stands and gives me a hug. "I feel like I never get to see you anymore."

We sit down, and Mom turns to Adam.

"Play rehearsal takes all her time. It's hard to find moments to reconnect." She reaches over and takes my hand, squeezing it. "The occasional meal."

Normally, I'd get her attention post-breakup. Her staying with a guy this long and moving in is definitely new. I missed our couple weeks of binging romcoms and breakup movies. We always find time for dinners during plays, though. Right now, we're definitely seeing less of each other than usual.

I glance toward the rest of the house. I haven't seen Damon today. Not since this morning. I don't really want to ask where he's at. What would they do if they knew we were sleeping together?

"Hockey takes up all of Damon's time." Adam smiles as he looks at my mom. "He's always doing extra training, but fortunately most of it he can do in our home gym. I've probably seen him at more dinners since you two moved in than I did last year."

"He seems very devoted to the game." Mom nods and picks up her fork.

I wish I knew more about where he was supposed to go this year. But I don't want to seem too interested and arouse suspicion with my interest. They have to know it's not normal to put two teens together like this.

But I'll be sleeping in his bed tonight and maybe doing more. Anticipation buzzes through my veins.

I'm lifting a forkful of food to my mouth when Mom says, "I'm surprised he doesn't have a girlfriend."

"That's one thing I've been grateful for over the years." Adam leans back in his chair. "No girl drama." He glances at me. "No offense, but relationships at your age tend to go sideways quickly."

Now would be the perfect time for me to tell Mom about my breakup. But what if part of the reason they feel comfortable putting Damon and me so close together is because I have a boyfriend?

"I don't know," Mom says with a smile. "Evan really didn't have a boyfriend until last spring, and he's been a good guy. No trouble at all. Isn't that right, Evan?"

I clear my throat. "No trouble."

Adam chuckles. "That's good then. Hopefully when Damon goes to college, he'll meet a good girl. That's how I met his mother. Beth was a pre-law student."

I don't know a lot about Damon's mom, but my curiosity is definitely piqued. I want to ask questions. Questions I shouldn't ask.

What kind of woman was she? What kind of cancer did she have? Was it slow or fast? Did they find it too late? Did she get treatment? What happened? How did Damon deal with it? Has he dealt with it? Is that why he's so angry?

Mom reaches over and squeezes Adam's hand. When he lifts his gaze, it's like he comes out of a trance. He smiles softly at her.

That smile stays with me as I finish dinner and head up to my room. It was a smile of understanding. Like they both went through something horrible and they get that part of each other. Maybe this relationship is good for my mom.

I walk to my desk and review my homework schedule for the week.

The door opens in Damon's room. I turn in my desk chair to see if he's going to come to me. The bathroom light and the fan come on. Then the shower starts. He doesn't close the door.

We never really talked about what happens after we have sex. If I want to get off, will he fuck me or just make me come with his fingers and/or mouth? Do I need to be specific?

If I want to fuck, do I just ask them to fuck me and they do it? I could text Hawk and ask him. Or maybe Cam would tell me. Damon isn't big on talking, though.

Urgh. I can't do this. No more focus on sex. I have shit to do.

I turn back to my desk and work on my homework. The shower shuts off and then the sink runs for a little while. That earthy scent wafts toward me. I shiver when I hear my door lock engage.

Anticipation slices through me and my panties are already damp.

I don't turn around when he stops behind me. His hair is damp from his shower.

He rolls my chair back, taking my hands from my keyboard and spinning my office chair around so I face him. Not that I was typing because I knew he was here. "How's your pussy?"

I let my gaze linger on the bulge behind his towel before sliding up over his abs and chest to his strong jaw, surprisingly soft lips, and those eyes. So fucking blue. His blonde hair is sticking every which way.

"My pussy is fine. How's your dick?" I raise an eyebrow. Maybe he'll realize the absurdity of his question.

Smirking, he lifts me out of the chair. My hands touch his warm muscles before he tosses me on my bed and comes down over me. My breath catches right before he takes my mouth.

Fuck it. My hands slide into his hair as he pulls my sleep shorts down along with my panties. He lifts from me to take off my sleep tank, leaving me naked beneath him. The towel hits the floor.

"Much better." He lowers his mouth to mine, and every inch of us touches. Skin to skin. The fire blazes inside me. He talks against my lips. "If I'd known you hadn't done this before, I would have been completely naked with you. Bodies sliding against each other. It's intoxicating."

"Yeah?" I'm more than a little breathless and on fire at the same time. It's like the overwhelm of having them all touch me at once, but just with Damon.

"Yeah." He kisses down my jaw and neck. He pauses in one spot to suck on me while spreading my legs wide and settling between them. His cock pulses against my pussy. Sparks dance across my skin where we touch.

He kisses lower, sucking and nipping my skin, making the fire within burn brighter. He takes his time tormenting my breasts, kissing, sucking, scraping his teeth against my nipple. I can barely breathe. The need for more pulses through me. My hips squirm beneath him, searching for more, aching for more.

He kisses my stomach and slides lower on the bed before pressing my thighs out to the sides and kissing my pussy. I almost come off the bed. The fire burns so hot I'm afraid I'll combust. He uses his tongue to fuck me before sucking on my clit and then sliding his tongue back inside me.

I move restlessly beneath him, wanting. Afraid to ask for it, but knowing he'll give it to me.

He hits a spot with his tongue that makes me gasp as pleasure floods me. He must be paying attention because he hits it again and again and again. My breath stalls and I arch up against nothing as my release drags me under.

He rises over me and takes my mouth. I taste myself on his lips as he notches his cock at my entrance and pushes inside. Instead of coming down from the high, I'm tipping right back over, moaning into his mouth as he fucks me slow and easy.

"Damon," I whisper as he kisses down to my neck, sucking on a place that feels like it's connected to my pussy, pushing me even higher. His hips don't stop.

"Yes, little devil?" He rises over me, resting his forearms on either side of my head as he continues to fuck into me over and over again. His hooded eyes search mine. Fuck, this is intense.

I've never been this connected to someone before.

"I need..." Fuck, I can't think. I can't seem to come down. I can barely breathe. How am I supposed to tell this god what I need?

He shifts and slides a hand between us, hitting the button that makes me spiral out of control. I cry out as I fly over the edge into the abyss. Freefalling into ecstasy.

He chuckles and presses a kiss to my open mouth, sliding his tongue against mine. "That's it, little devil. Come all over my cock. Fuck, you're so fucking tight and wet."

I wrap around him as it becomes almost too much. I whimper, "Damon."

"Don't worry. I've got you." He reaches up to the headboard and begins to fuck me harder.

"Oh, fuck," I moan as he touches me so deep inside the fire spreads like ripples on a pond, spiraling out farther and farther until my entire being burns.

He captures my mouth as I cry out the release that drags me under. He drives in hard and shudders over me as he comes.

I'm still trying to catch my breath when he rolls us onto our sides with his cock still hard inside me. I expected sex to be good with them, but nothing like this. His hand brushes my damp hair away from my temple. My eyes open to meet his. Our foreheads nearly touch as we both breathe heavily.

"Did I make up for last night?" He leans in and brushes his lips against mine.

I drag my finger across his chest and lift my gaze to his. "Why would you have to make up for last night?"

"This would have been a better first time." He slides his hand down to cup my breast and tease my nipple. My body trembles with the anticipation of more.

"I liked the way it happened. Maybe it wouldn't have been quite as painful."

He makes a scoffing noise.

"Okay, a lot less painful, but I chose that moment." I brush his hair back away from his face. "I didn't know who would catch me. Or who would take my first time. Honestly, I was hoping for one of those *I didn't even feel it* first times."

He chuckles and rolls me on top of him. His cock slides in deeper, and I release a little moan.

He sits up and wraps my legs around his waist before he stands with his cock still buried in my pussy. His dick twitches. That felt weird and arousing at the same time.

"Shower and sleep. I'm not planning on leaving this pussy tonight."

I squeeze around him.

He groans. "For that, I'm fucking you in the shower."

Threaten me with a good time. I giggle and he looks down at me with a cocky smile as he turns on the shower.

"Don't test me, little devil. I'm an athlete. I can go all night." He steps us into the warm water to rinse off the sweat.

Then he backs me against the wall and pins me there while he fucks me. I'm too sensitive and tumble into orgasm quickly. He fucks me until I feel him come inside me again. Only then does he lift me off him and actually let us wash each other.

After rinsing and drying off, he chases me into his bedroom and tosses me onto the bed. I feel lighter than I have in years. Giddy in a way that is contrary to anything I thought I'd feel with Damon.

He comes down after me and kisses me before thrusting inside me deep again. I moan at the stretch of him inside me. He rolls us so I'm draped over him with my legs on either side and his cock buried deep. It's a new and odd feeling.

"I'm never going to fall asleep like this," I murmur. It seems impossible. Every twitch of his cock sets me on fire.

He strokes his hand down my back. "Yes, you will, little devil. And I'll fuck you when I need to during the night."

Chapter 12

EvanAnn

I wake up, sticky and hot on top of Damon, our skin practically fused together. My hips are rolling against his and his cock is hard inside me. I'm aroused and restless. Normally, I would slip my hand down my stomach, over my clit, and make myself come.

I press up with my hands on his chest and look down at his sleeping face. He's out. I begin to lift off him, but the slide of his cock inside me makes me gasp with need. Tingles chase through my blood. Watching his face for signs he's waking, I lower back down and my insides shimmer.

He wants to fuck me when I sleep. I should be able to do the same, right? Besides, I'm supposed to use them if I want to get off. My fingers curl into the hard muscles of his chest. It's only fair.

My hips roll of their own accord against him. My body craving friction. Without the distraction of his eyes, I can take in his body more. He has a really great body—all hard muscles, clean lines. He's beautiful.

I rise up and lower onto him, biting back the moan of pleasure. I readjust for more leverage with my thighs. His face twitches. His lips part on a release of breath, but his eyes remain closed. I slowly work up to fucking him.

My eyes close at the sensations flowing through me as I ride his hard cock. The position allows me to angle just right to hit certain spots. His skin is hot and muscles firm beneath my hands. Part of me wants him to wake up and take control and the other part wants to keep experimenting and find what feels good for me without him showing me.

I've been getting myself off with my fingers for years. I know what will push me over the edge, but I've never been able to get this deep inside me before. My eyes open to see if he's still asleep. I bite my lip. I'm so fucking close it will only take a little push to go over the edge. Just a flick.

Does it count as masturbating if I'm using his cock and my fingers? Technically, he's right here. What's the worse that happens? I get off and he punishes me?

I slide my hand down his abs and that V-muscle, keeping my gaze on his face as I reach between my legs. My clit is wet, hard, and slippery. I rub it in circles as I fuck myself on his cock, hitting an angle that makes me whimper with pleasure. I tip my head back, feeling the pressure of my orgasm building.

My release washes over me. Trembling, I stop my movements, trying to catch my breath. My clit pulses against my finger and my pussy clutches at his hard cock. I look down at him and meet his darkened blue eyes.

He smirks and grabs my hands before rolling me onto my back. I gasp at the sudden movement. His hands press mine into the mattress near my head. When I bring my legs up, he sinks in a little deeper. I groan at the pleasure humming through me. He bends down and kisses my neck as he thrusts his cock inside me.

Already sensitive from the first orgasm, I suck in a harsh breath.

"I should have known you'd take advantage of me, little devil," he whispers in my ear.

I shiver beneath him. My hands held captive by his. He pushes up to hover over me, holding himself up with one arm, and with his other hand, lifts my wet fingers to his lips. He sucks on them as he strokes his cock in and out of me. My breath catches at the longing on his face. The muscles in his arm flex.

"It's within the rules to use me for your pleasure. I just didn't think you'd be bold enough to do it while I slept." He punctuates each word with a snap of his hips against mine. He presses my hand back into the mattress.

"You would have done the same in my position," I pant, getting closer to another orgasm. Him holding me down makes the fire inside me burn brighter. I've always been helpless to him.

He chuckles. "Wrap your legs around my waist."

I do as he says, and he presses in deeper. A moan escapes me.

"That's it, little devil. Can you feel the tip of my cock kissing your womb? I'm going to come so deep inside you, you're going to have me between your legs all day at school. When you talk to your boyfriend about his new rules, you'll drip me into those sweet cotton panties and think of how you rode my cock this morning. When you're sitting in class, trying to focus on the lecture, you'll feel my wetness and remember me thrusting my cock deep inside you, making you come."

I meet his cocky eyes, knowing I will. "Will you think of me?"

He groans softly, and it's the sexiest thing I've ever heard. "This hot, tight cunt trying to strangle every last drop of cum out of me? Fuck, I'm going to be hard all day until I can come home and sink back into you. Kiss these breasts, fuck your mouth, work that asshole up to take me, Cam, and Hawk. You want me to bring them home to you, my little cum slut? Make sure you're leaking with cum so you can sleep filled up?"

I tip over the edge, clinging to his hips with my legs as he pounds into me, our bodies colliding. When he groans, his face twists as his cum floods me. His forehead drops to mine and we breathe each other in. I expect him to release me and pull out. Instead, he lifts my slack body against him, staying buried inside me, and takes me into the bathroom.

He starts the shower and then fucks me against the wall until we both come again while we wait for the water to warm up. He pulls out so we can wash in the shower. Before he gets a chance to pin me and fuck me again, I hurry into my room to get ready for school.

I'm dressed with my hair up when I return to the bathroom to brush my teeth.

Damon chuckles and moves behind me, dressed for school. His lips brush against the nape of my neck. Fuck, that feels good. He pulls my hips back against his and pushes me down to lean against the sink. I meet his eyes in the mirror, already anticipating what he's about to do.

He flips up the back of my skirt and pulls my panties down. He releases his cock and slides it against my clit. "Make sure to get the back of your teeth too, Evan."

He draws his hips back until his cock notches at my entrance before he thrusts into me. I gasp in a breath. So fucking deep.

"Don't mind me. I'll be done by the time you finish brushing your teeth." He spreads my ass cheeks.

My face heats as the mirror shows him looking at my asshole and watching his cock slide into my pussy. I've never felt like a sex object before. I'm not the kind of actress you hire for bombshell. But the way he looks at me makes me wonder why not?

Because he looks at me like I'm everything he ever wanted. It's intoxicating. He slides his thumb into his mouth and sucks on it for a moment. Our gazes collide in the mirror. I pause in brushing my teeth, wondering what his plan is.

His grin is wicked as he presses his thumb into my asshole. I gasp.

"Only have two weeks before I can take this asshole."

I spit out my toothpaste and rinse my mouth with some water, trying to focus when all my attention is being dragged between my legs. To his cock and his thumb driving me out of my mind. "I still get to decide when you fuck my ass for the first time."

He slides his thumb along the sensitive nerves of my ass and my pussy clenches around his cock. He chuckles. "You want it, Evan. I bet you can come from having your ass fucked."

He alternates thrusting his thumb in my ass and his cock in my pussy until I'm clenching onto the sink and coming hard around him. I bite back the scream welling inside me. He thrusts in deep and his warm release fills me.

"Fuck." He pulls his thumb out, but leaves his cock inside me as he leans over me to wash his hands. His body surrounds mine and I press back into him. His blue eyes glint in the mirror as he meets my gaze. "You're going to make us late, little devil."

What? "I'm not the one—"

"Who woke me up fucking?" He pulls out and grabs a washcloth to clean his dick before putting it away. His cum runs down my thigh. "You set the tone for the morning."

I roll my eyes and turn to go to the bathroom. He catches the back of my neck and pulls me in for a kiss. My toes curl as my hands grab onto his arms to ground me in reality. Because he's doing something wicked to my body and my mind is getting the wrong ideas.

When he draws away, he takes a breath. "Need me to help you work up an appetite for breakfast?"

My laugh is husky as I push him away. "I need to clean up. I doubt I'll have time for breakfast."

He leaves me, and I hurry to finish getting ready after cleaning up. I don't have time to hit the kitchen, so I rush to the garage. When I sit behind the wheel, I notice a banana and a couple of egg bites wrapped in aluminum foil on the car seat next to me.

There's a note on the steering wheel.

Can't skip breakfast, little devil. -D

The day is normal. No one's looking at me or even calling me a slut. Maybe no one saw me take off with Hawk at the party. No one knows

I lost my virginity to the Devil's trio this weekend except for the four of us.

Even though it feels like it's written all over my face.

Mia talks to me in first period about how Liam is acting possessive of her. And how that's not her vibe. Everything that's happened wells inside me like pressure needing to be released, but I can't tell her I fucked the Devil's trio. Instead, I hold it inside and ask if she wouldn't mind sitting with Abby out in the courtyard for lunch so I can talk to Chase. She gives me a hug and tells me to give him hell.

Second period, I try to ignore Damon's grin at his phone as he snapchats the obscene things he wants to do to me from an account called Sex God. I also didn't know he installed Snapchat on my phone.

My cheeks are burning with the heat his words stir.

When Cam sits down, he turns to talk to me, while Hawk stares at the back of my neck with this little smirk. I'm hyperaware of all three of them and can't help thinking about the three of them on Hawk's bed with me, making me theirs.

Is it even possible to see them tonight? They have hockey. I have play rehearsal. Cam is effectively on lockdown during the week. The tutoring idea should make it so he can come over, or I can go to him, and we can spend time together.

I'll see Hawk at rehearsal, but usually with Chase, which is kind of a killjoy.

Chase has texted me all morning. Just random shit. Saying I look pretty today. That he can't wait until lunch. He misses me. At least he's respecting my boundaries today.

At the end of third, I make my way to the cafeteria. I kind of wish Hawk would sweep in and offer to buy my lunch and want me to sit with him. But I have to face Chase.

I have to give him my rules if he wants another chance with me. Part of me hopes he'll say fuck that and ride off into the sunset, fucking whoever he wants for the rest of the year. I'm sure Damon will find another way to get his revenge, and I won't have to pretend to be the sad sack willing to take back her cheating boyfriend.

Though I do relish making Chase grovel for me.

I grab my salad and sit at my table. For a second, it feels like last year and nothing has changed. I nod to the other Anteros students at my table, but we all keep to ourselves. If it weren't for the delicious ache between my legs, I could believe nothing is different. That I'm still the same.

My phone buzzes and I unlock the screen.

CAM:

Give him hell, gorgeous

ME:

Thanks

CAM:

Let me know if you need cheering up after

My cheeks heat thinking of what Cam would do to cheer me up.

"Babe!" Chase sits down next to me and I scoot a little to give him room, flipping my phone over. "I've been waiting to talk to you all day."

Setting my fork down, I turn to meet his winsome smile. No more playing games. "I don't know if I can do this anymore, Chase. I thought I could trust you, but I was wrong."

His smile falls. "Give me a chance to prove it to you, EvanAnn. I can be the guy you need. I swear. I'll do anything."

When I search his eyes, he seems sincere. But why? Maybe he really thinks that. It doesn't matter because I'll never trust him again. Maybe he could pretend to be the guy I thought he was, but that isn't the guy I want. I don't think it ever was. But for now, I have to pretend it is.

I clear my throat. "If you want to prove it to me, I need to go slow."

I blow out a breath and he reaches for my hand, setting his on top.

"Anything." He seems so fucking sincere. Let's see how he feels about my demands.

I lift my gaze to his. "You can't have sex with anyone else. But I don't think I can even kiss you right now. You hurt me too deeply."

Forget hurt. I'm fucking enraged. He left me stranded in the middle of nowhere. At night. He's not someone I would ever trust again. He deserves a swift kick to his junk, not forgiveness. But for now, I'll let him believe what he wants to believe. That I'd be naive enough to take him back.

He bobs his head. "That's fair. I never should have fucked other girls. I just didn't want to make you feel like you had to fuck me, so I took care of the need."

Resisting the urge to roll my eyes, I arch an eyebrow. "If you need release, you can masturbate."

He smirks. "It's not the same. I know you haven't had sex, but it feels different with someone else."

I cross my legs. If he only knew. Clearing my thoughts of Damon, Cam, and Hawk, I breathe out.

"I'll only meet you on dates. I can't trust you to drive me anywhere." I glance at him like I'm afraid.

"That's on me, babe. I never should have left you. I was coming back when the police took me in."

More lies. Damon told me Chase was coming back to the party without me. He would have gotten fucked and then maybe came back to find me. Part of me is curious what his excuse would have been if he hadn't gotten taken to the police station.

I raise my gaze to his. "I have to know, Chase. Do you think maybe you have a sexual addiction? If so, there's help for that."

He laughs. "No, I'm just a healthy teenage guy who likes to have sex."

"Did you use condoms?" I ask.

He rubs the back of his neck and looks away from me. Obviously not.

"I can't even think of being with you until you have an exam and your tests come back STI free. It's a few months after your last sexual partner. So..." Is he going to be honest with me or will he say it's been a month, so he won't have to wait as long? Not that I'd be willing to go shorter.

"I can do that. We can schedule it from today so you can be confident in the results." He reaches out to try to tuck my hair behind my ear, but I draw away from him. He frowns at his hand as he lowers it.

Good. He needs to feel this.

"I don't know if this will work." I exhale, pretending to be a girl who wants this man more than her own self-respect. Fuck, if he believes me, maybe I'm a better actress than I thought. "Maybe this is too difficult."

"I'm willing to try if you'll let me." He rests his hand over mine again since I didn't pull away last time. "I'm serious about making this work. You're the best thing that ever happened to me."

My brow furrows as I look down at my food. We've only been dating a few months. How can I be the best thing that's happened to him? What exactly is he getting from this relationship? There has to be something.

He clears his throat as he takes a bite of his sandwich. "Are we good to have lunch together?"

I look toward the outside where I know Damon, Hawk, and Cam are. I wish I could eat with them, but that's not part of this. They're the kings of the popular students. I'm nowhere near their level. I don't know if I would ever be welcomed out there.

Hawk walks into view of the windows talking with some girl I don't recognize. She's in a Deimos uniform. Maybe she's in one of his afternoon classes. I blow out a breath.

"Yeah, we can have lunch together," I say, playing my part.

We sit beside each other as we eat our food. After a few minutes, Chase asks, "What's happening with your house?"

I swallow my food hard and take a drink from my water bottle. Giving myself a minute to figure out my thoughts. Stick as close to the truth as possible.

I lift my gaze to his. "The rental was sold before Mom signed a lease. She moved us in with her new boyfriend."

"How are you coping with that?" He seems genuinely interested.

"It's not bad. I don't feel comfortable having anyone over because it's not really my house. You know?" I pick at my salad.

What would have happened if I'd let Chase in from the beginning? If he'd been there at the beginning of the year and I told him about my mom moving us in with Damon's dad? Would things have been different? Or was this always the path I would have walked?

Of course, if Chase had been faithful, he never would have run Damon off the road. Damon would have gone off to whatever hockey thing he had, and I would have been alone in that huge house. Alone in that massive bed.

Lonely enough to stay with a boyfriend I kind of liked.

"That makes sense." He looks around. "I want you to know I won't do anything to jeopardize the play. I know you didn't cast me because I'm your boyfriend. I can keep things professional if the worst happens and you don't forgive me."

"I appreciate that." I may not believe it because of how he acted when he left me in the woods, but I can appreciate the sentiment. It's the correct thing to say, but it's just part of his script.

He nods and begins a story about football practice like it's old times and I want to sit and listen to his prattle. I give him about thirty seconds, but I'm not his girlfriend. And I'm not obligated to listen to him.

"I need to work on some things for the play now." I rise, and Chase stands with me. "Alone, Chase."

I resist the urge to smile when his eyebrows dive together like he doesn't understand.

He lowers back into the chair. "I'll support you however I can. Can we meet for dinner on Wednesday?"

"No. I have dinner with my mom. I'm not seeing her as much with the play."

"I'll figure something out to spend some time together." He gives me a smile. "Go do your work. Be brilliant."

Chapter 13

EvanAnn

I stop at my locker to swap out my books. It feels like I'm being watched, but there's no one else in the hallway. Nothing makes a sound except my own heartbeat.

I shake it off and head toward the drama wing. I have my notes from Sunday's rehearsal open on my phone and read them as I walk.

"Careful, Miss Ward." Mr. Watson's voice jolts me out of my thoughts. "You'll run into walls if you fall too deep into your Shakespeare."

I smile as he joins me on the way to the black box theater. He opens the door for me, and we walk in. I breathe in the space, and it settles my heart.

"How's the cast coming together?" he asks and picks up chairs to move them to the center of the room. He's not setting them in a circle today. Each pair of chairs face each other.

"A little rough around the edges still, but I'm sure I can make them smoother." I take a seat in the audience to continue to work.

"As your advisor, if you need me to come to any practices, all you need to do is ask. I'll be at tomorrow afternoon's rehearsal to see how far you've progressed." Mr. Watson sets a chair at the end centered between the rows and looks over his configuration.

"What happens if two cast members get involved romantically and then they break up?" I lean my elbows on my knees, curious what his answer is.

"One of the core ideas we try to instill in all the actors who come through our program is professionalism. The job always comes first. Your private lives have no room on stage. If you need to talk to someone, get a therapist and work on yourself." He crosses the room and sits backwards on a chair in front of me.

"That's of course the standard answer." He rubs at his jaw. "The reality is it can be rough to get the actors to focus on their work. Especially if it's not an amicable split. Do you think you're going to have any issues?"

I draw in a breath and release it. "Teenage relationships tend to be a flash in the pan. I'm worried someone will get their feelings hurt and want to quit."

"Fortunately, like real theater work, if they quit, they lose something. Pay, prestige, their reputation. But here, they lose their grade. If you need someone to focus, you can always ask me to talk to them, or we can get them down to the counselor if it's outside of my comfort zone. You don't have to do this alone, EvanAnn. I know it feels like a huge weight right now, but you've got a team of teachers and staff ready to support you."

I smile. "Thanks, Mr. Watson."

A few girls come into the room talking. He glances at them and flashes me another smile.

"Anytime."

Between schoolwork, rehearsals, and hockey practices this week, it's been hard to find time with the guys. I don't know if Cam and Hawk told Damon to give my pussy a rest or what, but the last couple nights, we've just slept together.

I might have let slip that I was still a little sore to Damon Monday night. It wasn't anything I couldn't handle. I would have let him fuck me all night long. But that was Monday. It's Wednesday. I'm definitely feeling neglected. Not that I have the time to do anything about it.

Chase is acting like the best boyfriend ever, as if it's his job. He's brought me chocolate and has been super attentive, which means nothing can happen during the school day, except for brief touches and text messages.

Tonight is my night off, but that also means dinner with the family.

My mom texted me to meet them in the living room before dinner. After school, I sit in my room doing homework. I'm almost through with what I need to work on when my door opens and closes, and Damon walks into my room.

"Hey." I don't get up or do anything but wait for him to let me know what the plan is because I need to go down to dinner in about fifteen minutes.

"I need to change, but are you going to dinner tonight?" He runs a hand through his hair that still looks damp. He probably just got home from practice.

I nod and glance at my phone. "I planned to meet my mom in the living room."

His eyes narrow. "They're up to something, because my dad asked me to meet early there too."

I bite my lip and heat floods my cheeks. "Do you think they've figured it out?"

He smirks and shakes his head. "Nah, they would have demanded to see us right away. Not give me time to fuck you before dinner."

The fire bursts into flames inside me. I arch an eyebrow. "Now?"

He chuckles. "No, but your reaction was priceless. Give me five and I'll head down with you."

Five minutes later, we walk down the stairs quietly. We won't know what they want until we get to that room. I'm behind Damon as he opens the door.

"There he is," Adam says proudly.

"What the fuck?" Damon's words should have been a warning as I cross the threshold and see Tom and Jessica sitting across from my mom and Adam on the couch with my mother. Chase turns from where he's looking out the window.

His gaze meets mine, and my stomach roils. His eyes widen before he masks his expression behind a pleasant smile. But there are questions in his eyes. Fuck, I hope he doesn't put anything together.

"We figured it would be best to talk with you boys over dinner. So we can clear up this mess." Adam stands.

Tom grins. "EvanAnn, dear, I'm so glad you're here. With the play, you two are so busy I barely see my own son. Let alone the girl who makes it all happen."

I mask the panic I'm feeling and move into the room. Jessica pulls me in and kisses me on both cheeks. Chase acts like this isn't news to him, but I saw it on his face. He wasn't aware I lived here. He hasn't really met my mother.

"I imagine EvanAnn wasn't anywhere near that fight." Jessica holds me at arm's length and puts her hand on my hair. "She's a smart girl to not be at that party."

My insides chill. Of course, Chase didn't tell his parents the reason I wasn't at the party. He left me in the woods in the middle of nowhere. I didn't tell mine either. When I turn to Mom, she smiles.

"I've been meaning to call and set up a tea with you, Jessica." Mom leans into Adam's side. "Adam talks so much about you and Tom, I feel like I already know you. Plus, with the kids dating..."

I don't dare look at Damon. This is a fucking disaster in the making.

"We should sit down and have a conversation." Adam indicates the chairs. He and Mom sit on the sofa, and I quickly sit next to my mom as there's only a loveseat and another sofa. I'm not sitting next to Chase. And I don't know that I wouldn't cave and lean into Damon if I sat near him.

Damon sits in the center of the loveseat while Chase sits next to his parents on the other sofa. My chest crawls with unease, but I keep my smile pleasant.

"Do you want to explain what happened on Friday night?" Adam asks. His attention is on Damon, but he glances at Chase too. "Who started it?"

If I thought the times he yelled at Damon were uncomfortable, this is that times one hundred. It's made worse since Chase didn't know I was living here. And I need to be extra careful not to give away there's anything between me and Damon.

Tom chuckles when neither of them says anything. "This couldn't be over a girl. Chase has been with EvanAnn for months now. They see each other almost every night."

I want to laugh. No he doesn't. He's been whoring around instead. I meet Chase's blue eyes. He doesn't let his mask slip, and neither will I. If he wants to pretend everything is wonderful in our relationship, I can use that to my advantage.

Of course, now he knows where I live. And who I live with. He'll be keeping a closer eye on both of us, I would assume.

"I was worried with his previous girlfriend. He was just partying all the time. We even found drugs in his room she left behind." Tom shakes his head. "No, EvanAnn has been a real blessing."

Drugs? Are they talking about Abby? Is that why Chase wanted to date me? He needed a good girl to use as an excuse to go fuck around because he got in trouble?

"I threw the first punch." Damon glances at me when my gaze flicks to his. His words hit me in the gut. *He left you like garbage, Evan. You.*

"The police tested all the kids. You weren't drinking." Adam says. He turns to Tom. "Had Chase been drinking?"

"Not enough to be significant." Tom takes a breath and looks between Damon and Chase. That's not what Chase said. "Is whatever happened resolved? Or is this something that's going to continue to be an issue?"

Chase sits forward. "It was my fault."

I raise my eyebrows. That's unexpected. Is he going to say he left me to come back to the party to get some? Probably not, but Chase has to have a reason for claiming that.

Chase glances at Damon and then at me. "I said something about the blond that was clinging to him."

Damon looks down at his hands. Chase must be talking about Olivia.

Tom shakes his head. "Have you apologized?"

I feel like we're in kindergarten and the teacher is going to make them hug it out. If I weren't so horrified about this whole thing, I would laugh at the thought of Damon and Chase hugging. Is that what they would have done if the parents knew about the accident?

"Sorry for the misunderstanding." Chase has a nice smile on his face, but his eyes burn into Damon. "I didn't mean to make you think I wanted your girl."

I swallow as I wait for the explosion from Damon. That anger that boils just below the surface.

"No worries, man. We're cool." Damon leans forward and offers his hand to Chase and they shake. I'm sure this is all for show for the parents. I'm impressed by Damon's skill.

"I'm glad that's over." Mom stands and gestures to the dining room. "Shall we go eat? I'm sure the cooks won't let the food get cold, but I'm definitely ready to move on to something more pleasant."

Tom and Jessica rise and walk with Mom and Adam into the dining room without looking back at the three of us.

"This is your mother's new boyfriend?" Chase stands. His gaze is steady on me.

"Obviously." I glance toward the adults, but they're already in the dining room.

Chase looks me up and down before he turns to Damon. "Why did you really punch me that night?"

I hold my breath as Damon stands. He claps Chase on the shoulder and says, "You insulted my girl, remember?"

Chapter 14

Damon

I should have known my father would pull some shit like this. It would have been worse if it had been right after the accident. I wouldn't have been able to control myself. Evan sits next to her mother, and I take the chair on her other side.

It's not like I'm going to sit next to Chase's parents.

Evan's being so careful to not pay me too much attention. I understand why. It's part of the game. She plays it well, but she's got tells. They're so subtle I don't think Chase will ever notice because he doesn't know her.

Did he ever bother to get to know her? What's the point of clinging to her when she's given him the rules?

"So I wasn't aware you two finally moved in together." Jessica smiles at the server as they set a salad in front of her but then turns back to wait for Heather to answer.

Heather's cheeks flush with color as she glances at my dad. "Our rental house was sold, and with nowhere else to go, Adam was kind enough to let us move in with him."

Jessica nods, but there's a knowing gleam in her eyes.

"How's the team this year, Damon?" Tom asks, drawing me into a conversation as the women continue to discuss Heather moving in.

I've had enough dinners with Tom to know he doesn't want details or stats like some guys. He's not a fan. He's just making conversation.

"We have some new members on varsity who should help make this season a good one." I pick at my salad, keeping my hands above the table. I don't need Chase to realize I'm all over his girl. Not yet.

The fear of it is going to be there. That I'll seduce her away from him. His little director. But he still sees Evan as the scared little theater nerd and not the sex kitten she is for me. She's been faithful to him. Mostly. Until we let her know what he was up to and she was done with him.

We both want revenge for what he's done.

I'm done giving her pussy a break. Tonight, I'm fucking what's mine.

"Having any issues from the accident?" Tom asks. Doesn't he know his son was the reason for my accident or is he covering up for Chase?

"My leg has been healing with the right PT." I rub my jaw where the road rash is still healing. "Might have a few new scars, but I'm not planning on modeling, so..."

Jessica grins and leans her elbows on the table, putting her chin on her folded hands. Her eyes rake over me. "You could be, you know? A model."

I give her a half-smile. "You think?"

She puts her hand on Chase's jaw. "You both could be. I know hockey is your calling. Beth always talked about your talent, but you could go another way." Her eyes sparkle when she looks at me. "Even with a scar. It makes you more interesting."

Fuck, I think Chase's mom wants to fuck me. That was a route I wouldn't have taken even if it had been offered prior to Evan. Maybe I do have a few limits. Besides, Evan is ours. I wouldn't ruin that for a quick lay.

"I keep telling Evan to keep her options open." Heather leans back in her chair, looking over her daughter like she's a commodity. "She's so set on directing, but she's a talented actress. And so pretty."

Heather brushes Evan's hair behind her ear, and Evan blushes.

"She can go far in whatever she chooses to do." Chase smiles at Evan like he's halfway in love with her. It's such fucking bullshit, but both Jessica and Heather buy into it. Their eyes soften.

Evan takes a bite of her salad to avoid saying anything. I want to crawl into her thoughts and know what she's thinking. It's easy to watch her, but I want to see inside her mind. I still play back the footage of her day or catch the live show while I'm doing cardio or lifting.

There's something soothing about her going through her day-to-day, knowing she's waiting for me to come and pluck her up. I've watched her when I come into her room. She tenses in anticipation, waiting for me to touch her.

The disappointment of her shoulders falling when I don't. The way she gives in when I do.

I took it too far the morning she rode me. She flinched when she sat in class. Though it gave me a rush knowing I was the reason she was sore. The guys and I talked about it and decided to give her a break until tonight.

They're coming over after dinner. We'll make sure she comes multiple times. And see how she likes fucking with something in all her holes.

Chase narrows his eyes on me like he knows what I'm thinking. I meet his gaze with a smirk. I have the taste of Evan memorized. The feel of her skin beneath my fingertips. The places that make her gasp. The ones that make her squirm. The tightness of her cunt when she comes on my cock, milking me. The way she snuggles into me in her sleep and fits perfectly in my arms.

Chase doesn't have any of that because she's mine. Every. Fucking. Inch.

"Damon?" Dad says.

I turn to meet his gaze. "Yeah?"

"Tom was talking about colleges." My dad smiles like I should just jump into the conversation that buzzed around me while I was thinking about Evan.

"Okay."

Tom chuckles. "The boy is probably dreaming of hockey. Evan plans to go big. Somewhere like New York. Chase is bound to find something for film or go straight to Hollywood. Last time we talked, Damon, you were talking about some school in Boston."

I swallow and set my fork down. My appetite gone. "That school is no longer an option."

Evan's hand slides over my thigh under the table. It's subtle enough no one will notice, but her touch centers me, keeps me from exploding.

"You've got decent grades. They'd have to let you play hockey." Tom smiles like all it takes is a little money to grease the wheels. And in some cases, it does, but not this time.

"They only take players who are draft-ready." I lean back in my chair and meet Chase's gaze. "The accident fucked that up for me."

Chase has the decency to flinch. Has he figured it out yet? That I know and I'll do anything to make his life hell? Taking Evan is only one piece to the puzzle. Chase wasn't smart enough to get into Deimos so maybe he hasn't put the pieces together.

"Surely there's another school that's just as good." Tom seems determined.

They'll keep harping on this until I give them something.

"Crowne Mawr has a new coach. They're working on becoming a feeder into the NHL," I say with no emotion. What else can I do? I don't have a lot of choices unless I want to wait a year to go to college or try to do both Juniors at the same time as my first year of college and then transfer.

No matter which way I look at it, I'm fucked.

"Crowne Mawr is a good school." My dad nods at me. He doesn't understand it might be my only choice because he held me back this year. That pit of rage boils in my center, threatening to explode. "It's not that far away and if you can play and get an education—"

"I've actually considered Crowne Mawr for college," Evan interrupts. Her hand rubs my tense thigh.

My father pauses with his mouth open. I'm usually the one who interrupts.

"It makes sense." She smiles and looks at the adults, but not Chase or me. "It's close to home. Their directing program hosts a lot of famous directors. It's a program that will help me get noticed if I choose not to go to New York or don't get the scholarship I need."

The server comes around and takes plates. When she comes back with the main course, she sets the ratatouille in front of me and my steak in front of Evan. Before the adults notice and can say anything, I switch our plates. She smiles softly and squeezes my thigh before taking her hand away.

Chase studies the two of us closely. Does he suspect I've got her wrapped around my finger? And tonight I'll have her wrapped around me and fill her so full of my cum he'll smell it on her at school.

"My birthday is coming up in a few weeks." Tom tucks into his steak like a man on a mission. "I know EvanAnn is planning on attending, but I'd love for your whole family to come."

Heather smiles and glances at my father, taking his hand on the table. "That sounds amazing. We'd love to."

Evan glances at me, but I don't look back.

"We're taking a trip this weekend to celebrate on our own," Jessica says. She smiles and winks my way. "It's good to reconnect every so often. Chase has play practice, or we would have brought him with us."

Chase leans back in his chair. Wonder what or who Chase will do this weekend. It won't be Evan, but maybe this is something we can use.

EvanAnn

When dinner ends, Chase hangs back while the adults walk outside to have a drink next to the pool. Damon glances at the two of us and rolls his eyes before heading upstairs.

I'm tempted to look in the corners for more of his cameras, but I doubt he has the whole house bugged. And even though I know they're there, I haven't found any in my room or the bathroom.

I draw in a breath, bracing myself for what Chase has to say.

"Is *he* why you didn't tell me about this move?" Chase steps toward me, but I shift behind the couch, putting the furniture between us. He changes his aggressive expression to something more like hurt.

"It's not like I had a choice in the matter." I take in a breath and keep my tone light. Damon wouldn't really leave me alone with Chase. He'll be close enough that if I need him, he'll be here. "She didn't tell me until the last minute, and by then I didn't want to create more animosity between you and Damon and his friends."

"Is that why they always seem to be around now?" Chase studies me like he can see if something's changed.

He can't. I'm not any different. Just had my eyes opened to his cheating.

Besides, he has some nerve blaming me when he's the one who was cheating the whole time. I didn't create this mess. He did. He made me think I was special and worth waiting for by someone like him. Instead, he used me to keep up his lifestyle under his father's nose.

It's time to go on the attack. "What your dad said... Is that the reason why you're dating me? To help repair your image in your father's eyes? To have someone to say you're spending all your time with?"

Chase runs his hand through his hair, and his face softens as he comes to a decision. "Honestly, maybe at first, but you've been good for me, EvanAnn. I like you and think together we can make it."

I want to scoff, but I hold it in. I can't say the same about him.

Though in ways, he got me out of my shell and pushed me past my comfort zone. I needed a shakeup. At least I didn't give him my heart or anything of me.

"I'm going to have a few people over to the house this weekend." He smiles like we're on the same page again. "I'd love for you to come over. We can talk and hang out. You could bring Mia."

"How many is a few people?" I arch my eyebrow suspiciously, thinking he's going to try to seduce me.

"The guys on the team. A few of their girlfriends. Nothing major." Chase smiles. "My dad would kill me if I threw a party like Fletcher does."

"We're not okay, Chase," I remind him. I don't want him to think this weekend will be his opportunity to get me into bed.

"I know." He looks down, and when he looks up, he smiles. "We have to start somewhere if we want to move forward. What my dad said is true. You've been good for me. Just because I went into this for the wrong reasons, I still asked you out because I like you and find you attractive. I can see us having a real future together."

My skin crawls at the idea of giving him any kind of hope, but this is the part I'm playing right now. I'm the wronged girlfriend who's willing to take back her cheating boyfriend. I still can't figure out my motive for the scene, but I guess it doesn't matter. My real motive is revenge.

Maybe it started as Damon's revenge, but Chase shouldn't have thought I was an easy target. A plan is beginning to form. "Yeah, I'll see if Mia wants to come with me."

Chapter 15

Cam

Damon sits at his desk working on his homework while Hawk reads something on his phone. I left my phone at home and snuck out. It feels weird being without, but I'm not missing time with our girl just because I'm on lockdown.

"Got the burner phone to her." Hawk lowers his phone.

"I've got someone setting up a dummy number to use for texting." I rub my knees. "We could go either way."

Hawk nods and glances at his screen. "We need to make sure it's not too obvious."

I chuckle. "Even obvious will work on him."

When Evan's bedroom door opens and closes, both of the others lift their gazes to the bathroom door. She comes through and smiles when she sees us.

"That was fucking awkward." She breathes out and looks at Damon. "Are you okay?"

He shakes his head like she's trying to read too much into the situation. But he told us what happened. His dad decided to make a play-date for him with Chase. Fucking dads, always thinking they know how to fix shit.

"Did they leave?" he asks.

She nods and leans against the doorframe. "Chase is planning a party for when his parents are away this weekend. Lowkey, some football players and their girls. Wants me to bring Mia and join them."

Damon rubs his fingers over his lips, considering. But this one is totally in my domain.

"Let's make it the party of the year." I lean my hands back on the bed and wink at Evan.

"He did say he couldn't get away with a party like Fletcher's." She smiles at me. Those blue eyes sparkle.

I grin. "Do you know how fast a party can spiral out of control? Who am I asking? Of course, you don't."

I straighten and make my way over to her. Her heated eyes take me in. Fuck, am I ready to play with her. My cock twitches. One time in that tight pussy and I'm already addicted.

"You done with your homework?" I ask and stop in front of her.

She lifts her gaze to mine and nods.

"We should discuss strategy." Damon hasn't left his desk.

I put my knuckle under Evan's chin and search her eyes. "Do you want to talk strategy, goody?"

She wets her lips. "No."

"Good answer." I run my knuckle down the throbbing pulse in her neck, watching her swallow. My gaze follows my path. "I've missed you."

"I saw you today in class." She shivers but doesn't pull away.

"Let me clarify. I've missed fucking your pussy, sucking your breasts, kissing your lips." When I close the distance between us, she inhales. "Let me fuck you, goody."

"Please."

That word could bring me to my knees for this girl. "Is your door locked? Your mom isn't going to come looking for you?"

"Yes, my door is locked." She glances back toward her room. "My light is off, so she'll think I'm asleep."

I lift my gaze to hers and smirk. "Lights off sounds like a good plan."

Hawk tosses his phone on the nightstand and goes to shut the light off. Damon opens and closes a drawer. I can see Evan's shadow in front of me.

"What do you want me to do?" she asks.

"Get naked with me." I pull off my shirt and toss it to the side.

I prefer to see her pretty skin and curves. But we also need to make sure mommy and daddy don't interrupt our play. After my pants are off, I reach for her hips. Touching her bare skin lights me on fire.

She sucks in a breath as I pull her into my body.

Her hands flatten on my chest, burning an imprint of them against me. My cock rests against her soft stomach as I lower my head to take her mouth. She parts her lips for me and slides her hands around my neck, pressing her hard nipples against my chest. Fuck, I need this. I lift her in my arms and walk her to the bed as we rediscover each other's mouths.

When I sit with her in my lap, she straddles my legs. Damon turns on a dim lamp, and I pull away to look over her body.

"So fucking gorgeous," I say and cup her breast.

Her darkened eyes meet mine. When I take her nipple into my mouth, sucking on her, her fingers tangle in my hair, tugging me closer. I take more of her breast into my mouth, greedy for the feel and taste of her. My hand goes to her other breast and rubs her hardened tip before pinching it. Her pussy grinds against my lap.

"Pull her down with you," Damon says.

I lie down on the bed with my legs off the edge and keep sucking on her breast. She inhales sharply and something drips on my dick. When I pull off her breast and cup her jaw, I search her eyes.

"Tell me what's happening, goody."

Her darkened eyes meet mine. "Damon's fingers are in my ass, fucking me."

She lets out a little whimper and closes her eyes. Fuck, this is what I've never had with a partner before. Watching her take her pleasure from someone else while being a part of that pleasure. I didn't know it was missing until Evan.

I trace my thumb over her lower lip. "Do you like that?"

"Mm-hmm." Her hips move.

"What do you need, Evan?"

Her eyes focus on me, and she leans down to capture my lips in a carnal kiss. I thread my fingers in her hair and tip her head how I want it, swallowing her little moans. This girl may have been a virgin when we trapped her, but she's a fucking fast learner.

Everything she does is because she wants it as badly as we do.

I pull her back, and her lips are still parted.

"Tell me."

She wets her lips and meets my eyes. Fuck, I could fall into those blue eyes of hers and never come up for air. There's this part of me that wants to drown in her. I want to stay in this moment with her forever.

Forget school, hockey, and the future. This girl is all I need.

"I'm going to come." She whimpers.

I tug on her hair, and she focuses on me. "Tell me what they're doing, goody."

"He's fucking his fingers faster." She moans. "Sliding against my nerves, lighting me up."

"How many fingers?"

"Two." She parts her lips on a silent scream as her body tenses over mine. I've never seen anything more beautiful than Evan coming. It doesn't matter if it's for me or for one of my friends. She's all in on us and takes what she needs. Damon was brilliant, because this girl was meant for all of us.

"Get your dick wet, Cam."

I bring Evan's face down to mine. "Put my cock in your tight, little cunt, goody."

"Cam," she whispers as her hand trails down my abs to find my cock. Her fingers close over me, and she makes this noise of desire that makes my balls tighten. No girl has driven me this mad with need.

"Fuck me, Evan."

She lifts up, putting a hand on my chest to balance herself as she rubs her clit with the head of my cock before notching it at her entrance. Our eyes lock as she lowers slightly onto my cock.

"How does that feel?" I ask.

"Stretch. Full, so fucking good." She sinks down, taking more of me, deeper.

I let her have control without thrusting into her like I want to. "You want more, goody. Take it all. Take my cock all the way into that wet pussy."

She puts both hands on my chest and lifts a little before she slams her hips down against mine. Fuck. It's like an electric jolt of pleasure flooding through me. Her head tips back, baring her neck, thrusting those breasts out. I bite my lip as a groan rumbles from my chest.

"Cam." Her voice trembles.

"Pain?"

She shakes her head and meets my eyes. "No, it's good."

"So fucking sexy." I put my hands on her hips, but not to control her. I want her to find her pleasure. The video of her fucking Damon like this, while he slept, her finding her pleasure, runs on repeat in my mind.

Hawk moves behind her and cups her breasts, pulling her back against his naked body. "Damon told us you rode him. Show us, baby girl."

I smirk. Maybe Hawk hasn't had time to watch the video or maybe he doesn't want her to know we're watching her sleep with Damon. I just want her to do it to me.

She rolls her hips. Biting my lip, I resist the urge to buck up into her. Letting her take control is going to kill me.

"I want to see her take Cam's cock in her ass."

I turn to Damon's voice. He stands against the wall stroking his cock, watching us with her. There's no jealousy, which we worried about with how possessive he's become over Evan. Especially when he found out she was a virgin.

But he likes watching her with us. Seeing her take her pleasure while he's removed a little, but knowing he orchestrated this.

We're all here because he wanted this. When any of us gives her pleasure, all of us give her pleasure.

"Think of how good that cock will feel in your ass, little devil." Damon smiles and rubs his lips. "You came on my fingers. Think how much better it will be on Cam's cock. Hawk can suck your pretty little clit while Cam fucks your ass."

She groans, but her cunt clenches around my cock and she's getting wetter. She wants it.

He walks toward her and she doesn't drop her gaze from his. Her hips rock on me, restless, needy moves. Keeping one hand on her breast, Hawk runs the other down her stomach and rubs her clit. Her head falls back against Hawk's chest.

"Let us in, little devil." Damon takes her chin. "You know you'll love it. And then this weekend, we can fuck you all at the same time. Filling you up completely with our cum."

Hawk pinches her nipple, and she shatters on a low moan, her cunt clutching so hard around my cock. I bite my lip to keep from coming with her.

I'm not going to be the one to push her. If she wants me to fuck her ass, she needs to ask. But fuck, I want to be the first to slide into that tight, little asshole.

Her eyes flick down to mine.

"It's up to you, goody." I groan as her cunt pulses around me and hold back the need to come.

She bites her lip and nods. "I want to."

"Yeah?" I grab her chin before she can turn to Damon. He has a way of making her want to do everything for him. To please him. I want this to be her decision. "You want me to fuck that virgin asshole open?"

"Please." Her eyes are darkened with desire. She lifts off me.

My cock fucking weeps at the loss of that warm slick cunt. I sit up and capture her mouth with mine before she can move away. Thrusting my fingers into her cunt, I fuck her fast and hard. She trembles as she comes all over my hand.

"Stand, goody."

Hawk takes her hands and helps her stand, holding her against him as he explores her body. Damon gives me the lube, and I spread it on my cock while she watches. Her tongue darts out to wet her lips. I sit up on the edge of the bed.

"Straddle me facing out."

She bites her lip but does as I say. Hawk draws her forward to kiss him. I spread her ass cheeks and slide my lubed fingers into her puckered hole. She moans as I begin to fuck her ass, pressing on the sides to open her up to take me.

"Such a pretty little asshole." Damon sits beside me, watching my fingers work her. "Think how good it's going to feel to have us all fuck you, little devil. All three of our cocks plunging in at the same time."

She clenches around my fingers. Fuck. I never thought about fucking a girl with other guys. I've seen porn with multiple partners, but actually fucking seemed like a two-person thing. I never considered how just having them watch or watching them with her would be such a fucking turn on.

I pull my fingers out and bring her hips down, pressing my cock against her sweet little hole. When I push just the tip inside, she makes a little surprised noise.

Damon reaches between her legs to work her clit. Hawk slides his fingers over her breasts. She begins to rock in my lap. I ease her down a little more, pushing past the tight ring of muscles as she relaxes to let me in.

"You're doing so good, goody." I spread her ass cheeks to watch her take my cock inside her. I work her slowly, pulling her hips down a little before sliding her up and then bringing her down a little more. "Fuck, I want to fuck you so fucking bad."

"Yes, Cam. Oh, fuck," she leans her forehead against Hawk's chest. "Fuck me. Please."

I pull her down onto my lap, thrusting my cock deep into her ass. She cries out softly. I spread kisses all over her shoulder as she breathes.

"Good?" I ask, trying to hold back from fucking her or coming way too soon before I'm able to work my way up to fucking her ass. That would be fucking embarrassing.

She tips her face my way and I take her mouth. Her legs are spread around my hips. My cock deep inside her. I pull my mouth away from hers.

"Tell me what the others are doing to you, goody." I press my forehead to hers.

She breathes out. "Hawk is kneeling between our legs. His hands are spreading my pussy open. Ah, Cam, he's sucking on my clit."

"How does it feel?" Our chests rise and fall together. Her ass tightens around the base of my cock, squeezing.

"Oh, fuck. So full with you and empty without you in my pussy."

I chuckle. "We'll get there, but I'm not even fucking your ass yet."

"His fingers."

"I can feel them," I say as he thrusts his fingers in her pussy, brushing my cock through the thin layer of tissue separating us.

Moaning, she comes from Hawk sucking her clit.

"You're such a good girl, taking us inside this hot, little body." I slide my thumbs over her ass cheeks.

Her smile is sloppy, like she's drunk. "Fuck me, Cam."

Hawk grabs her hair and tips her head back. "Suck my cock while he fucks your ass, baby girl."

"Yes." She wets her lips.

He lowers her head, and I hold her hips while she parts her lips and Hawk thrusts into her pretty mouth. Damon stands and helps hold her waist, so I can get some leverage as I move to stand.

Spreading her ass cheeks, I watch my cock work in and out of her asshole. Sinking in deep before sliding back out. I don't think I've ever seen anything so erotic. Feeling her asshole like a ring tight around my cock.

Hawk groans as he comes down her throat.

Damon watches her ass take my cock with greedy eyes. He'll want to go next. Fuck, she's not a fucking ride we all take for spins, but it feels like that. Damon wanted her to fuck him, and she gives him what he wants. Because she wants it too.

She tightens around me as she comes, crying out, and I can't hold back. I release deep inside her with a roar.

"Oh, fuck," she pants.

I gather her against me and roll her to lay on the bed before pulling out.

"Get the plug," Damon tells Hawk as he lifts her hips, staring at her recently devirginized asshole before thrusting into her cunt.

She moans and buries her face in the covers. Her hands clutch at the sheets. I wait to go clean up as Hawk walks over with the lubed toy.

Damon parts her ass cheeks as Hawk begins to work the toy into her ass. I could seriously watch this all night.

She groans and squirms against the bedding. We're a lot, but this girl takes everything we throw at her.

"Don't worry, little devil. Next time it will be Cam in your ass while I fuck your pussy and Hawk fucks your mouth."

EvanAnn

Heat spreads through me as Hawk seats the plug in my ass. Damon pulls his cock out slowly, along every raw nerve. I'm ready to explode. He thrusts in deep, jarring the plug and making my brain melt. It was only a matter of time before I let one of them fuck my ass.

I'm done denying myself what I really want. I'm not delusional and think just because the sex is good, this thing we have will keep going.

How long can this really last? I want to experience it all with them, before they grow bored and move on. Maybe Damon will get his revenge on Chase and decide he no longer needs a little fuck toy.

Hawk smacks my ass, and I cry out at the suddenness and tighten around Damon's cock and the plug. Hawk rubs my stinging ass cheek as Damon begins to fuck me harder. Moaning, I tuck my head down and cling to the bedspread as he rocks my hips with his.

I shatter into pieces as my pussy milks his cock. I don't breathe for a moment, but it doesn't slow him down as he fucks into me over and over again. He groans as his warm cum floods me.

When he pulls out, Hawk thrusts in deep, stretching me even more.

I moan at how good it feels.

"That's it, baby girl. Take my cock like a good girl. I can't wait to fuck this pretty little ass into oblivion." He tugs on the plug, and my breath catches. "We'll keep fucking you all night long, taking turns fucking your holes. You'd like that, wouldn't you? Until you're dripping with our cum."

I can't think anymore. All I can do is feel as he pushes me over the edge. But there isn't relief in my release. I float, suspended in my orgasm, as he continues to fuck me until he comes deep inside me with a groan.

When he pulls out, Cam thrusts in deep, making me gasp.

"Is her ass better than her pussy?" Damon asks.

"Fuck, man, it's all good." Cam reaches between my legs and pinches my clit.

I spiral into another orgasm that devours me whole. They're definitely making up for the years I didn't have sex. And they aren't treating me like some delicate flower. No, they take me rough, and I love every fucking minute of it.

Every thrust is deep and hits me in spots that make me squirm with need. Cam fucks me hard, dragging me into another release before he comes inside me. My legs shake when he pulls out, and I wait for the next, staying in the same position, knowing they're staring at my used pussy and ass. Loving that they want me this way, full of them.

I pant in anticipation of the next cock, the next orgasm. Cum leaks out of my pussy, but I want more. I don't know if I can come again, but I definitely wouldn't mind trying.

Damon lifts me into his arms and carries me into the bathroom. When he sets me in front of the counter, my legs almost give out. I catch myself on the counter.

"I need you to relax, little devil." His hand sweeps down my spine and over my ass.

"You ask for a lot." I meet his gaze in the mirror and he smirks.

"You like it." He tugs on the plug, but doesn't pull it out.

"Maybe." I can't help my smile. He's not wrong. I do like it.

He twists the plug, and my insides try to spark, but it's a dull heat. I'm so tapped out. He removes the plug and cleans it in the sink as Cam closes in on my back and kisses my shoulder.

"You okay, goody?"

I meet his gaze in the mirror. His dark eyes hold mine. It was perfect. I've always been curious about sex, but worried about exploring it. Something about these guys makes me feel like it's safe to explore without being judged. Isn't that part of why they want me? So they won't be judged as they explore their sexuality?

"Yeah. Not sure I can walk."

"I'll hold you in the shower." He pulls me back against him and my skin buzzes where it touches his.

"Give me a sec." I grab my hair clip and quickly put my hair up so it won't get wet. "Ready."

He lifts me and carries me into the shower where Hawk waits for us. Hawk kisses my forehead.

"You did well, baby girl."

My insides shine. I've always been the smartest and most talented, but never have I been complimented on anything else. Definitely not something as physical as sex.

The shower is quick. I use the bathroom after Damon drags his shirt over my head. I'm not offered panties, and I don't ask for them. Anything they want to give me I'll take.

Chapter 16

Damon

I lie in the middle of my bed, waiting for Evan to come out of the bathroom.

"Is Chase going to be more of an issue?" Hawk leans against the headboard on one side of me, while Cam lies on the other side of the bed with his arms tucked under his head.

I told them about dinner with Chase's family and how we were basically told to play nice.

"He knows I'm all over his girl and have access." I smile. He doesn't realize how ruined his little good girl is yet.

"What if he tells people at school?" Evan asks.

I lift my head to find Evan standing at the foot of the bed. "Come here, little devil."

She crawls across the bed to my side. When she settles into her spot, I draw her in tight against me. This is where she belongs. In my arms. In my bed. Satisfied so many fucking times. Dripping with our cum. Ours.

"Are you worried?" I ask. "It doesn't have to change anything."

She laughs. "Are you sure you go to the same school I go to?"

"Your friend might have something to say about it," I admit. Mia's going to be a problem. I don't know how yet, but she'll become a problem for all of us.

"Mia doesn't know, and I kept it from her." She pushes up so she can meet my eyes. "I'm smart and talented, but that doesn't make me popular. It doesn't put me on the map of our school. Being here, with you, will. Girls will suddenly want to be my friends and maybe guys will actually notice I exist."

Cam scoffs. "Hate to tell you, goody, but they already know. And if they didn't before, that little outfit you wore last weekend put you on the map. You might be oblivious to the way the guys at our school watch you, but I'm not."

She looks so confused. I reach up and tuck her hair behind her ear. Her gaze drops to mine. Cam's right. She's gorgeous in a non-plastic way that's attracting more attention. It makes me want to claim her so they'll all back off, because she's mine.

"We don't have to say anything." I want to protect her because she's right. The girls will try to be her friend to get closer to me. "We don't have to change anything at school."

She draws in a breath and rests her head on my chest. "We're going to blow up his party? How do we do that?"

I rub my hand down her back. Maybe we shouldn't push with her and just stick to our other plans. What if Chase figures out Evan is part of my plan? What if he hurts her? For the first time, I hesitate to use Evan for my revenge. Maybe it was the way Chase put on an act for Evan and his parents. Making it seem like he's in love with her, and the adults fell for that shit.

Evan didn't.

I don't trust him with her. I never have. He needs to keep his hands off her. But she's right. This won't end well when everything comes out. If I want to hurt him, he has to know about us. If I tell him she's mine, it will put a target on her back. The girls will be jealous, catty bitches. The guys will want to see what the big deal is.

I'm not about to let her go through that. Not if sex is all that's between us. I don't know if I believe that anymore. There may have never been a way to have Evan without something changing.

"The normal ways a party spreads." Cam touches her hip. "Word of mouth. Eventually everyone hears about parties."

"Won't he be able to shut it down if he hears about it?" Evan yawns and her hand spreads over my ribs. Her touch is easy, comfortable. Most girls leave after sex. Most of the time I do the leaving. I thought Evan in my bed would make *her* want more.

My heart thumps a little harder as I realize it might have backfired.

"Not the way parties work, Annie." Hawk glances toward her, but she's tucked on my chest and I can feel her breathing evening out.

She works as hard on her play as I do on hockey. I respect that about her, which is unusual because I can count the women I respect on one finger. My mother had my respect and no other.

But Evan is earning my reluctant respect. She's doing what she can and adjusting to the things thrown in her path. Like me. I came at her like a fucking hurricane, but she just wrapped herself around me and slipped easily into being what I look forward to in my day. Those times I can see what she's doing or when I finally get the chance to be with her make my fucking day.

Holding her while she sleeps...

"She asleep?" Cam asks after she doesn't talk for a few minutes.

"Yeah," Hawk says and runs his hand through his hair. "What are we going to do? Chase has some power at school. Not as much as we do, but more than Annie."

"He wants her." Cam touches her hair. "Did you find out why?"

"His parents seem to think he's spending all his time with Evan." I picked up on that. But she has to be more than just his fucking alibi. "They seem really happy that he's with her. Like if you told your dad you got into Yale."

"Fuck." Cam shakes his head.

"Yeah, how will we get Annie untangled from him? Without fucking over her play?" Hawk turns on his side to look at her.

"First thing, the party. Let's take away his freedom." I glare up at the ceiling. Getting revenge and protecting Evan might not be something I can accomplish at the same time. Her breath skates across my chest. Right now, I'm not sure I'd choose revenge.

I wake up with Evan sprawled over me, my hand draped possessively over her hip. When I turn, her face is next to mine on the pillow, soft in sleep. Has anyone ever protected her?

It chased through my mind all night.

Has she ever had anyone she could turn to? When Chase abandoned her, she called Hawk. She didn't call me because I'd been an ass with Olivia. But she didn't call her mother or anyone else either.

How checked out of Evan's life is her mom? The counselor my dad sent me to after Mom died talked a little about how people reacted to grief differently.

Evan is the most capable, put-together person I know. My dad holds on to me tighter, but did her mom just give up? Because Evan is so capable of taking care of herself?

Fuck.

Cam kisses her hair as he and Hawk get ready to leave. "I'll start spreading the party rumor."

I nod, and Hawk kisses Evan's temple.

"You've got her?" Hawk's green eyes meet mine.

"Yeah." I tighten my arm around her. They can't be with her like I can.

I may not understand it, but right now, Evan is mine. I don't usually keep girls, but there's something about her that draws me.

The lock clicks as Hawk relocks it on his way out. I breathe in her woodsy scent. Fuck, maybe she was a mistake I couldn't resist. She was always meant to be in my path, whether by Chase or her mother. Always meant to be mine.

Her phone buzzes on the nightstand.

Thinking it's an alarm, I reach for it. I unlock it with the passcode she never told me. She was nice enough to unlock it right in front of the camera once.

UNKNOWN:

You can block my number but I'll always find you

You're mine, Evan

I know where you live

I watch you get in your car

I can get to you

Don't think I can't

And next time I'll finish what I started

Who the fuck is this? And what the fuck do they want with Evan? I take a screenshot and send it to my phone before checking the number. It's local. I delete the picture from her phone and put it back on the nightstand.

"Evan," I say softly. I need to watch her reaction to the messages. To get a clear view of what's happening.

She makes this soft little noise and burrows into my neck.

I chuckle. "Little devil, I need you to wake up."

"Too early." She wraps her arm around my waist and throws her leg over mine.

"Your phone's been blowing up." Unable to resist, I slide my hand under her shirt and over her bare hip, squeezing her ass cheek. I can't wait to fuck this ass.

"Really?" She lifts her head and blinks at me with those stormy eyes.

I gesture to where it sits on the nightstand. Her gaze jerks to it before she blinks at me again. Her gaze drops to my lips. Hunger, desire, heat. Fuck, we've created an insatiable monster.

"If you check it, maybe I'll have time to fuck you before we need to get ready for school." I arch an eyebrow.

She wets her lips and rolls to the side to grab her phone. When she unlocks the screen, her brow furrows, and as she reads, she becomes paler.

"What is it?" I ask like I have no idea what she's reading. I don't need her to change her passcode.

"I..." She puts her hand over her mouth and drags in a breath. Her stormy eyes meet mine. "I don't know who it's from."

"What is it?" *Come on, little devil. Tell me. Trust me.*

She draws in a breath. "I think someone is fucking with me."

"You mean besides us?"

She puts her phone on her chest and turns to meet my gaze. "It could be someone from my past or just someone trying to mess with me. Maybe they noticed you paying attention to me. Maybe it's Chase. I don't know. But honestly, it kind of scares me."

It's written on her face. "May I?"

She looks at it again before passing me the phone. She turns on her side to watch me read it. "It's not really a threat, right?"

I clench the phone. Anger burns through me upon reading it again. "You don't have any clue who this is?"

She blows out a breath and drops her gaze from mine. She knows. Somewhere deep inside her, she knows. But will she tell me? When she lifts her gaze, she's torn.

"It could be someone, but I don't know how he would have gotten my number. Or how he would know where I live. And I'm probably overreacting." Evan drops her gaze. That tracks with the girl I've gotten to know. Evan is logical. But fear isn't always logical.

"I don't believe you could overreact, Evan."

She lifts her gaze to mine. "It could be any of those possibilities..."

"Or? Tell me, Evan. I can look into it, at least."

She takes a deep breath. "When I was sixteen, the apartments we lived in, there was a boy who I knew from elementary school living there. He flirted with me and gave me candy and made me feel special."

From what I know about Evan, she's attention-starved. I'm sure it wasn't easy back then. If her mother was with her boyfriend, leaving Evan alone to take care of herself, someone paying attention to her would have drawn her. Like Chase did. Like we did.

"He caught me alone and kissed me. I froze. I didn't want him to kiss me." She holds my gaze like she's begging me to believe her. "If Mom hadn't come looking for me, I'm not sure what he would have done. I don't know that I would have fought whatever he had planned or if I could have." A tear slips down her cheek. "But I got away so..."

Something falls into place. I reach out and brush the tear away. "Your first kiss?"

She nods. "I'm being stupid."

But why wouldn't she tell us the name during truth or dare? Is it someone we know? I try to think of anyone at Deimos or Anteros who would live in an apartment complex. One of the scholarship kids?

She sits up and holds out her hand for the phone. I look at the texts.

"Someone wants you to be afraid." The more I think about these messages, the more I'm convinced whoever sent them wants her to be frightened. To be watching over her shoulder. Maybe they get off on that. The anticipation, her fear.

"It's not like I don't have a bunch of things happening right now. It might not even be him." She searches my eyes.

I put the phone in her hand. "Who is it, Evan?"

She lifts her gaze to mine. "Jackson Riordan."

Chapter 17

Damon

As soon as I get to school, I track down Cam and Hawk and pull them into an empty classroom. The whole ride to school my brain spun around what Evan revealed. I also followed her to school and watched her walk inside, keeping an eye out for anyone watching her.

"We have a fucking problem." I send both of them the screenshot.

They both look at their phones.

"What the fuck are we looking at?" Hawk looks pissed.

"This was Evan's phone?" Cam asks.

"The texts came in this morning." I run a hand through my hair. Part of me is grateful she gave me her story. But every piece of her she gives me ties me tighter to her. Makes me more reluctant to let her go.

"Did she show this to you?" Hawk raises an eyebrow.

"I saw them first. When she saw them, I asked to see them."

"Did she let you?" Cam is already doing a search on the number. He has access to all the numbers at Deimos and Anteros. If it's someone who's ever walked on this campus with us, he'll have it.

"Yeah, and she told me about her first kiss and the asshole who took it." There aren't many people I hate, but Riordan always rubbed me the wrong way. Too eager to please the adults around us. He thought he was hot shit on the ice as a kid. And he's good, but I'm better.

"Who?" Hawk asks.

"Jackson Riordan." I wait while they absorb that. Neither of them likes the asshole.

"She thinks these are from him?" Hawk looks like he's trying to figure it out.

"She said it could be anyone, but yeah, there was real fear in her eyes when she talked about him." I hate Chase Chadwick and think he's an overprivileged dick who needs to be brought down a few notches, but Jackson is different. He's not from privilege. He's talented and eager to escape his circumstances in life. It makes him more aggressive in a lot of ways. Willing to do anything to climb out of his situation. But it also makes him take what he wants.

"He was looking at her when he asked about the blond at the game." Hawk glances at Cam. "I knew he wasn't interested in Mia. Maybe it's intuition, but I can believe these are from him."

"He approached Mia and Evan at the football game." Cam runs his hand through his hair. "Fuck. What are we dealing with here?"

"He wants what's ours." I won't let her go. I can't.

"He doesn't know that. But if he's been watching her, he might have an idea. Fuck." Hawk leans back against the wall and puts his hands in his pockets. "Saying she's ours would put targets on her here, but it might protect her from him."

"Or our claiming her in public might make him more eager to claim her." Cam shakes his head. "He always wanted what Damon had."

"We don't know what lengths he's willing to go to get her." I want to punch something, but I don't. We can fix this.

"He might not try anything. Will Evan let us publicly claim her?" Cam sits in the chair and looks up at us. "She's not like most girls. She doesn't want to be popular."

"Claiming her won't make her popular. It will bring out the worst in people who want to get close to us, but it won't change Evan." I glance at my screen that shows where her phone is in the building. "We need to make him aware she's ours."

"We need to talk to Mia," Cam says.

"Why?" I don't want to encourage that bitch anymore. She thinks we're a sure a thing. That Evan would never stoop to fuck us.

Fucking Mia.

"Riordan talked to her at the game." Cam rubs his hands together. "If he was looking for an in with Evan, he might have used Mia. I don't know anyone else who would give him her number."

"I'll talk to Mia." Hawk steps forward. "I have class with her first period."

"We need a way to track Evan besides her phone." I glance at her moving dot on my screen. "Phones are too easy to lose or turn off."

"You want to chip her like a real pet?" Cam chuckles, but when I look like I'm considering it, he groans. "Fuck, man. You can't fucking chip the girl. But there might be another way. I'll find something."

"Until we have a way to track her, she doesn't leave our sights except during school." Some part of me still twists with worry, but I'm ignoring it. He can't get to her on school property, not when she's surrounded by other students.

"I'll look into him." Hawk checks the time on his phone. "Don't do anything stupid."

"Has she made contact?" I ask needing to make sure our other plan is in place.

"Hook, line, and sinker." Hawk shakes his head. "Ate it up like candy. She'll keep him on the hook until we're ready."

"I've got a few traps ready to spring next week too." Cam smirks. "But Chase is easy to manipulate. Jackson won't be."

We all nod. Fuck. I almost forgot.

"One thing Chase's dad brought up." I straighten. "He blamed Abby for drugs in Chase's room. Cam?"

"On it. As far as I know, he's not a user, but I'll see what I can find out. This number isn't a known student number, but I'll have to look later to see if it's a spoofed number."

"We can't discount Olivia may have found out about Evan." I glance toward the door. "I'll find out if she has a burner or an app that allows anonymous texts. Whoever it is, they won't touch her. Not without going through us."

Hawk

Jackson fucking Riordan. I walk into first. Mia sat near me the first day. Chase lingers next to her desk with a smirk on his face. I take my seat, and Chase wanders to one in the back of the class.

"Hey, Hawk." Mia leans on the desk toward me. She eyes me like she wants to fuck me. Fuck this girl. "Are we working on our history project this week?"

"We can talk with the others in third." I give her a smile because I need information. If she reads into it, that's not my problem. "I thought I saw you at the football game with Jackson Riordan. How do you know him?"

She smiles coyly. "I didn't. He seemed to know Evan and needed a place to sit for the game. After Evan disappeared, he got a call, but he said he'd show at the party."

"Did he show up?" I don't remember seeing him at the party, but I was distracted.

"No, he's as hard to track down as you guys." She flashes me a smile. "But I did get his number. He put it in my phone."

"Can I see that number?" I give her a quick smile.

She opens her phone and hands it to me. I glance at the number, memorizing it to write it down when class starts.

"He put his number in?" I hand her back the phone.

She nods and flips her hair back over her shoulder. "It was loud, and he didn't want to have to scream it."

Or he just wanted access to Mia's phone.

"Did he say anything to EvanAnn?" I'm careful not to call her Annie to Mia. I need her to believe what she sees.

"No, he was really focused on me." Mia leans in and says quietly, "But he's not the one I'm interested in."

Fortunately, the bell rings and class begins.

Cam

Evan is already in class when I sit next to her.

"How do you feel?" I ask with a cocky smile.

Her cheeks flush with heat, and she looks at her books. "I'm good."

I'm glad Damon pushed her last night. Fucking that tight little asshole was perfection.

She smiles shyly. Those blue-gray eyes meet mine. "We should set up a schedule for tutoring."

"Yeah." I run my fingers over my lips. "My guess is you have more on your schedule than I do. But if you can come over and meet my parents so they believe you're real and actually smart, then we'll be able to meet outside of my house the next time."

"How about tonight after rehearsal?" She gets her phone out and opens the calendar. "About seven?"

"Got it. I'll text you my address." I pick a piece of lint off her shoulder.

She looks at my hand and then meets my gaze. If I asked her to meet me in that classroom during the break, would she? Is she safe here at school? Those messages had an undertone of menace I can't ignore. If it's Jackson, he goes to another school, but it's possible it could be anyone.

Maybe someone who knew about Jackson's obsession with her.

"I'll see you tonight," she says.

The teacher walks in before I can say anything more. It's probably for the best. I shouldn't ask her to meet me somewhere that might not be safe. Besides, I wouldn't want to just fuck her hard against the door again. I'd want to explore every inch of her body. As the teacher begins class, I relax. I'll have her to myself tonight.

During class, I pull out the paper I ordered. It's red and while the teacher drones on, I carefully fold it like I learned in the video. The little drawing disappearing into the center of the flower. By the end of class I finish and set it in front of Evan before she can pack up to leave.

Her mouth opens as she lifts the paper flower. "This is beautiful, Cam. When did you learn to do this?"

"The other night." I lean close to her. "I wanted to bring you flowers but knew they'd wilt before you got home. This kind of flower won't wilt."

She looks about ten seconds from lunging in to hug or kiss me, which is not part of the plan. I turn to collect my things.

"Thank you," she says softly. Her gaze is on the flower twirling in between her fingers.

I brush my fingers over hers as I get ready to leave. "You deserve someone who brings you flowers, goody."

EvanAnn

I haven't done anything with the texts I received this morning, but they've lingered on my mind. Maybe I shouldn't have shown Damon. How stupid was it to tell him about Jackson? The boy stole a kiss.

Damon is no better. He stole a kiss from me too. The only difference is I craved his kiss more than my next breath. And I kissed him back. I sit down in the first seat in calculus. I haven't moved since that first class.

Cam's flower rests on top of my books until I can put it in my locker. Warmth fills me. It's something so simple, but he made it just for me.

Damon sweeps in and sits down in the chair next to me. There's been some shuffling, but we're the top two of the class. He takes his phone out and lounges in his chair, ignoring me. My phone buzzes and I glance at the screen.

It's a Snapchat message. Anticipation floods me. I open it knowing it's probably from Damon.

SEX GOD:

Sorry I didn't fuck you this morning

I glance around to see if anyone might have walked behind my chair and saw that. I glare at Damon, but he pretends he doesn't notice. Another ding.

SEX GOD:

I'll make it up to you tonight

Make sure you're full of cum before you go to sleep in my bed

I roll my eyes.

ME:

Promises

New phone who dis?

He chuckles and I can't help grinning. My heart warms at making him laugh. Mrs. Conrad comes in.

"Close your books. Pop quiz."

When we finish calculus and make our way to history, Damon closes in on my back, making me aware of his presence. Normally, he ignores me during the school day. Yes, the naughty texts are normal, but not this sudden attention.

I don't resist the urge to slow down so he looms over me.

We walk into history, and I take my seat. When he drops into the chair kitty-corner from me, his blue eyes are fixed on mine. I arch an eyebrow as if to ask *what?*

"We have a history project due," he says and leans toward me.

My breath catches. The temptation to flirt with him presses on me, but I shove it away. "So you want to discuss our project?"

"Not really, but if it's the only way I can have your attention..." He shrugs.

"You want my attention?" I look at him through my lashes.

He smirks. "Always."

My heart pounds so hard.

As more students are filing in, Hawk and Mia join us.

"Hey, I barely saw you this morning," Mia says.

"I was running late." I breathe out and turn to face her. "I need to tell you something."

"Sure, what's up?" Mia glances at the guys before giving me her attention.

This feels like a mistake, but I can't let Chase be the one to tell her. I don't trust him. I'm not sure I trust Mia fully, but if I want to be her friend, I need to give her a little trust. Trusting Chase was a mistake, but trusting the guys isn't. So it's a gamble, but I'm willing to take it.

"My mom moved us in with the guy she was dating a few weeks ago."

"Yeah? Is that hard?" Mia seems concerned.

I drag in a breath and hold it before bursting out. "My mom is dating Damon's dad. The house you were at... I live there now. Sorry I didn't tell you, but I really wasn't expecting it. And it doesn't really change anything. I'm still the same girl you met in the office."

How much of what I say is trying to convince myself I haven't changed? Because some part of me wants to cling to who I was and is scared of who I'm becoming. The Devil's trio's attention will fade. And if I'm not who I was, how will I deal with all this when it's over?

Mia's gaze narrows on me for a moment before it clears, and she smiles. "That has to be intense. Do you want to get coffee after rehearsal tonight to talk about it?"

"I'm tutoring someone tonight." I don't really want to tell her how much access I have to the Devil's trio. It's bad enough she knows I'm living with Damon.

"We're going to the game on Friday, right?" She's still smiling, but I can't tell if she's just acting. Fucking actors.

"Yeah, of course." I breathe out when she turns to the guys.

"We still need to work on our history project." She leans her elbows on the desk and looks between Hawk and Damon. "When?"

"This weekend. My place. After the scrimmage." Damon doesn't hesitate.

"Good." Mia smiles at me before turning her attention to the teacher.

Chapter 18

EvanAnn

After another long lecture and note-taking, Mia and I walk to the cafeteria with Damon and Hawk following us. I'm still not sure how Mia actually feels about me living with Damon, but I'm not going to push it. I still have to face Chase about dinner last night.

When I glance at Hawk, he smirks like he knows I'm hoping he'll bail me out again, but with a wink, he follows Damon across the cafeteria. I get my salad and head to the table where Mia meets me from the pizza bar.

"You aren't upset I didn't tell you, are you?" I ask as we sit down.

"Fuck, no. I get it. You moved in with Damon, and I told you I wanted to fuck the guy." She laughs. "I would have been wary in your position too. I figure he's pretty standoffish at the house, huh?"

"Yeah." Not sure how to explain anything that I've done with Damon since I moved in. She'd probably be happy I sucked his cock. But I'm still worried she might be mad I have them and basically told them they could never have her.

"What does Chase think about you living with that deliciousness?" She winks as she tears into her pizza.

"He just found out last night. So I don't really know how he feels yet," I admit. I don't know if he wants it widely known or if he's going to keep it to himself. It's one of the reasons I finally admitted it to Mia.

"Are you really going to get back together with him?" She looks at me warily. "I know we're new friends, but once a cheater, always a cheater. I get it if you want to stay with him. He's hot and seems sweet sometimes, but I'd also understand if you want to buy a bunch of feminine products and stick them all over his car in retribution."

I laugh, imagining his face if he came out and found his car plastered in pads and tampons. Mia smirks.

"I can help make that happen." She nudges me with her elbow. "After all, I'm your best friend."

"What are you making happen?" Chase stands behind us with his lunch.

"Nothing good." She winks at him but turns to me. "We'll talk later."

I smile at her. It's not a bad idea. Chase loves his fucking truck.

He takes a seat next to me and smiles. "How's your day been, babe?"

"I really don't like that pet name."

His hand freezes halfway to his mouth, holding his pizza. He clears his throat and looks at me. "Noted. How's your day been?"

I glance toward the courtyard and then look down at my meal. This is where I belong, but part of me wants to be where they are. Discussing Shakespeare with Hawk. Flirting with Cam. Damon, just being Damon.

"My day's been okay." I pick at my lunch.

"Did EvanAnn tell you about the party this weekend?" Chase asks Mia.

"No, what party?" She doesn't ask him, but me.

I swallow and turn to her. "Chase's parents are out of town and he's having a small get-together at his house. Just some football players and their girls if they have them. You and me, if you want to go."

"Wouldn't miss it." She winks at me before glancing at Chase. "Why small?"

"My parents would go nuts if I had a party like Fletcher's." Chase glances toward the outside. "I had one a couple years ago that got out of hand. They haven't forgotten. I'm surprised they decided to leave me for the weekend. But I couldn't miss rehearsal, and they want to leave early."

"Where's the party on Friday then?" Mia looks at Chase.

I look at him warily. He hasn't mentioned Damon at all. Maybe he would have been cool about it. But something tells me he wouldn't have.

I definitely wouldn't have told Chase about Jackson though. But Damon asked, and I don't know why, but he feels like a safe space.

Which is stupid. So is the way he makes me feel when he holds me at night or texts me outrageous things during the day or makes sure I eat or leaves me notes in the car. My heart thumps hard in my chest.

I put my hand over it, ignoring the conversation about where the party has moved to since Fletcher's is off-limits for a while. Yes, I'm having sex with Damon, Cam, and Hawk, but that doesn't mean anything.

It's just physical. They don't want more from me, and I'm not expecting more from them. Except amazing orgasms.

It's hard to separate my feelings entirely though. But it can't be more than physical.

"Everything okay?" Chase asks me quietly.

When I glance over, Mia is gone.

"She went to the bathroom." He leans his elbows on the table and studies me. "You checked out for a little there. Is everything good at home? I know your mom isn't around much, and this must have been a huge shift for you."

"Why are you being nice to me?" I whisper-shout and narrow my eyes at him. "You showed me who you were when you left me in those woods. I can't decide if this is just an act, or that's who you really are. Do you even know?"

He takes a breath and scrubs his hand over his face. "I shouldn't have even been driving that night. I had a few too many to drink and was high on the win. Everything was great between us. I know I'm the one who fucked up, but I didn't think you knew about the other girls. I fucked up and let the stress get to me and did things I wouldn't normally have done."

"Everyone knew you were a fuckboy. Even me. And just because you thought I didn't know doesn't make it right. You could have talked to me. Or broken up with me if I wasn't what you needed." I don't feel like I need to be considerate of his feelings. He showed me who he really was, drunk or not.

"Yeah, well, I tried to be better for you." He flashes me a chagrined smile. "I do think we could have a good future. And I want to have sex with you. Those other girls didn't mean anything."

I want to laugh because is that how those girls felt? Is it possible to hold back part of yourself when you're that vulnerable with another person? Yes, sex is fun, but there are moments that mess with my head. Desperate moments.

"I'm just glad you're willing to give me a second chance to prove to you I can be the guy you need." Chase reaches out and puts his hand next to mine. "You make me a better guy. I messed up, but I want to be better. I'll talk more."

I meet his blue eyes. I should put my hand on his to show I'm invested in this relationship, but I don't want to touch him.

Not now and not in the future. I don't want to be here with him. I want to be with them, and that spells trouble. Because what happens when they drag me into their world and abandon me there?

I can't run with that crowd. They'd eat me alive.

"I need to go to the bathroom." I push to stand and grab my tray.

Chase gives me a smile like he knows he's lost me. "Okay. I'll see you in class."

I'm not paying attention as I walk toward the restroom. Too much in my head. I don't even really need to go. I just didn't want to be near Chase anymore. He has all these excuses, but he's never been truly sorry. He just says the words to make things better.

Something drops on the tile floor and startles me out of my thoughts. I turn and don't see anything. It was nothing. I'm just paranoid. Being unaware is how I got into that mess with Jackson. I didn't sense the danger until it was too late.

The bathroom is empty. I figure I might as well use it quickly before heading to the theater. That's where I always feel safe.

Before I flush the toilet, the door opens to the bathroom. When I flush and exit, Olivia is there, leaning against the sink with her arms crossed. She's beautiful and rich and popular. Her eyes narrow at me.

"Hey, EvanAnn."

"Hi." I go to the far sink and wash my hands while trying to figure out why she's here.

"You're not dating Chase Chadwick anymore, right?" She glances at her fingernails like it doesn't matter to her. But she's not an actress. At least not a convincing one.

"We're on a break." I shrug. There's no reason she'd need to know that. My life should be insignificant to her.

"He's pretty hot." Olivia's smile is smug, like she's got something she doesn't want to tell me. "Your friend has been making waves too. Fucking the hockey team?"

I shrug. Again, this is none of her business and she shouldn't even be talking to me.

"What I don't understand is why Damon would be interested in you at all." Olivia looks me up and down like she finds me so fucking lacking.

"What makes you think he is?" There's no way she knows what happens in his bedroom at night. We've been extra careful at school. Just that one time for history class when I rode on his motorcycle. But normally, he ignores me.

Her smile is mean as she drops her arms and walks my way. "Something tells me you won't be run off like the others. See, they didn't want to see their social status drop, but you don't have that. So maybe what you really need is a glow-up. How much?"

Olivia levels her blue eyes on me.

"I'm sorry, but I'm not following here." I straighten. "You think Damon Storm is into me? Like, likes me?"

She rolls her eyes. "Maybe he just wants to fuck you, but it's getting in my way."

"How is it getting in your way?" I cock my head like I'm trying to figure her out. Because I am. I know she wants him, but he doesn't want her.

"I have one more year to get him. I mean, if I thought you might give it up quickly and he'd be done with you, I'd let it go. But you seem like too much of a challenge, and maybe that's what he wants." She narrows her eyes at me thoughtfully.

"If he wants a challenge, why don't you challenge him? Make him work for it." I shrug.

She chuckles dryly. "You obviously don't know Damon. He doesn't want a girl who tries too hard, but if you don't try at all, he'll ignore you. He's the most frustrating man."

"So why bother?" I ask.

She scoffs. "He's the best. And I get the best. If I can't get it by being the most beautiful, then I'll buy it. But I always get what I want. And I want Damon. So what's your price?"

"My price?"

"To give up trying to get him. He wouldn't be interested if you weren't giving him some kind of encouragement." Olivia looks at me like I'm not as smart as she is. "You may get great grades in school, but you have no social intelligence. If he gets no encouragement or outright rejection, he'll give up. He doesn't have time to seduce someone."

I think of those nights he works out and returns to our room hot and smelling like sin. He grabs me up and takes me into the shower with him. I've been fucked in that shower often. I'm hoping he'll fuck me tonight. He doesn't seduce me because he doesn't have to.

There's something between us that I never expected. He makes me want him.

I know he feels it, the draw, the magnetic pulse that's irresistible. I shake myself out of it and focus on the queen bee thinking I'm encroaching on her territory.

"So what? You want to pay me to stay away from Damon, but what happens if he keeps coming after me?" I raise an eyebrow. How stupid does she think I am?

"Tell him no. Duh?" Olivia pulls her phone out. "So how much?"

"You really think I can be bought?" I'm curious.

"Everyone has a price, EvanAnn. Besides, I've heard you're a cheap whore, so I'm sure the number won't even make my allowance flinch." That evil smile again.

"No." I turn to walk out of the bathroom.

"What do you mean, no?" she huffs out.

I turn back and smile at her. "That's what you tell someone when you don't want what they're offering. I know you might be unfamiliar with it, but my answer is no."

"So you won't stay away from Damon?" Olivia crosses her arms with a glare.

"You make a lot of assumptions about me and about Damon, but I don't think you really know what he wants, or you'd know he doesn't want someone to control him." I step toward her. "And if you knew me, you'd know I'm loyal to whoever I give myself to."

"I heard Chase had an open relationship with you." She smirks.

"That's what he thought, but it wasn't something we discussed." I laugh. "Is that the best you have? My fuckboy ex?"

"I fucked him this summer, gave him some quality road head."

My heart skips. She was the one in Chase's car, or was that another time? What if Damon wants to blackmail her instead to get revenge? My chest aches. I couldn't sit by and watch that happen. It would crush something in me I'm trying desperately to ignore.

"Maybe I should just tell Damon you're a stuck up virgin who won't give it up."

"Go ahead. I won't take your money to ignore Damon Storm."

She steps toward me menacingly. If someone more comfortable fighting with money than her fists could be considered menacing. "I can make school hell for you."

"And how would that be different from the past three years?" My anger that was on simmer burns through me. "Do you think it's easy to go here when you aren't rich? Do you think this has been easy for me? That I've been happy being alone? What are you going to take from me? My ex? My best friend, who I've known for a few weeks?"

"Damon is mine," she bites out.

"If he is, then I'm sure he won't even try anything with me because he'd be with you, so we wouldn't even be having this conversation." I take a step back and hold in the fact that he's mine. Maybe he won't be for long if he finds out Olivia was the girl in the car that night. My stomach churns.

"Maybe I'm wrong. I don't know why I ever thought he might want someone like you." She looks me up and down like I'm the trash beneath her feet. "He wouldn't even let you come near him. Even your name is stupid. EvanAnn? It's like your parents wanted to brand you as a loser. You're low class and have no future."

Fuck this bitch. Yes, she'll always have money, but that doesn't make her better than me.

"That's where you're wrong." I straighten. "I have a future. Whatever it takes, I'll rise, because that's what I'm meant to do."

She smiles. "Not if your play doesn't do well."

I shake my head. "One play will not make or break my career. Yes, it might set me back if I did something wrong, but that's not what's going to happen. And if you think you can threaten me—"

The door opens, and I turn to see who came in. I swallow as Damon meets my eyes. My body softens with his nearby. My chest aches. Will he want revenge against Olivia? Isn't that the whole reason he went after me to begin with?

"Did you miss me, lover?" Olivia smiles and knocks my shoulder as she walks over to Damon. She puts her hands on his chest. "We were just negotiating a deal."

I turn away. I can't watch her paw him. He needs to act the part to make her give up on her quest to pay me off. But that doesn't mean it won't hurt.

"Are you okay?"

"What?" Olivia practically shrieks. "She doesn't want you. She wants her skeezy boyfriend."

His hands fall on my shoulders, and I suck in a breath. I don't dare turn around, because I'm sure everything is written all over my face. Olivia will know. What is he doing?

"What are you doing, Damon?" Olivia is practically melting down. "She's nothing. She's worse than nothing. She's an ant."

I turn to glare at Olivia. Money isn't everything.

Damon gazes down at me with those sharp blue eyes, but I don't dare look at him. I try not to give anything away.

"Evan?" He tips my chin up, and I swallow. "Are you okay?"

"I'm fine." What is he doing? I search his eyes. This isn't the plan. I look at him like he's lost a screw.

His fingers glide along my jaw, sending a shiver through me. He smiles before he turns his head to Olivia.

"Are you still here?" He arches an eyebrow and gives her a look that would make some girls cry. "Next time you try to buy Evan, you might want to find out who owns her first."

Olivia huffs. "I suppose you do?"

"She's mine. And she's not for sale. You fuck with her, and I'll do something I never do." Damon's fingers glide down the side of my neck.

Something inside me is bursting. This is going to change everything.

"Why would you want her when you can have me?" Olivia narrows her gaze at me like I'm something she needs to destroy.

Damon moves between us and tucks me behind him, protecting me. It makes my heart ache because it won't last.

"Fuck around and find out."

She pouts. "What would you do?"

"I'll destroy you. I'll take away everything from you if I even think you have Evan in your sights." He steps toward her. "And don't think of having another guy go after her. I'm not playing. I don't want you. I belong to Evan."

My heart is in my ears. What is he doing? Maybe this is because of the texts? Did he find out Olivia sent them?

The door opens and closes. Olivia left. Fuck. I should have stopped her.

Chapter 19

Damon

Fuck. It was a bad idea but when I noticed Evan went into the bathroom and hadn't returned, panic shot through me. Her phone location hadn't moved on my tracking app. The guys and I talked about claiming Evan to make Jackson back off, but it would have been a controlled burn and not a scorched earth approach like I just did.

Honestly, for what we want, it doesn't make sense to claim her until we know why Chase wants her so badly. I wasn't supposed to do what I just did.

When I turn, Evan's face is pale and she's trembling.

This girl has me in a vise grip.

Her wide eyes lift to mine, a kaleidoscope of silver and blue. "What?" she asks dazedly.

I take her arms and pull her into my chest. "You were in here too long. I got worried."

"You're tracking me?" That's the first thing she wants to know? I almost laugh.

I shrug. "Are you surprised?"

After all, I've been filming her for weeks. She rests her ear against my heart.

"What did you just do, Damon?" she asks softly. Her hands grip my sides like she never wants to let go.

I drag in her scent and release my breath. "Blew up the world for you?"

She chuckles. "I don't think this is the end of the world."

"Maybe not for you." I cup her head against my chest. "I've never had a girlfriend before."

She pulls away and looks up at me with confusion. "Girlfriend?"

I smirk and run my hand through my hair. "What else would you be?"

Her smile softens and then falls. Her eyes widen. "What about Chase? Damon, this could fuck that up. You need to go after Olivia and tell her it was a joke."

"What? No." I grab her elbow and pull her toward the door.

She resists. "You didn't think this through. Our parents—"

"Can fuck off." I spin on her. "Did they consult either of us on whether we wanted to live together, or did they make the decision and hope that our feelings would remain that of reluctant siblings?"

Her mouth opens and shuts, and then she glares into my eyes.

"Olivia said she fucked Chase this summer," she bites out. She drops her gaze. "That she gave him road head."

My heart stops. The blond in the car? Could that have been Olivia? It doesn't matter now.

"I don't care."

Her eyes flip up to mine in shock.

I narrow my eyes on her. "Did you think I'd go after her if you told me that, little devil?"

From the look on her face, she did. "It doesn't matter," she says.

"Yes, it does." I back her into the wall. She looks up at me with those panicked eyes, but I'm done. "You fucking matter, little devil. I'm done watching you take everything everyone throws at you. I'm done pretending. At least here at school. We can do whatever we need to at home to make our parents comfortable so they don't try to move you to the other side of the house."

"Damon—"

"You're mine. You're ours. I need whoever is coming after you to know that. Chase, Olivia, Mia... anyone who wants to get between us. They need to know you're protected."

"This won't work." She puts her hand over my heart.

"I'll make it work."

EvanAnn

I'm numb. What the fuck did he do? We don't have classes together in the afternoon. So unless Olivia spreads it around, no one knows what happened in that bathroom.

And I doubt Olivia will tell anyone. It wouldn't feed into her story.

I'm just going to pretend Damon didn't make my heart leap in my chest like he might feel something more for me too. I sit in my acting class wondering if I shouldn't have told him about Jackson.

Maybe it's just misplaced protectiveness. We're together in our own little bubble, but he's poking holes in that bubble. I may belong to them, and they belong to me, but no one else knows.

Maybe he's just tired of Olivia coming at him and he wants to use me as a shield. That makes more sense than I mean something more to Damon. Before class, Mia chats at me like nothing's changed.

But my lips still feel stung by his kiss. I didn't let him drag me into the hallway from the bathroom. He kissed me and left. I waited until after the bell rang to slip into the hallway and find my way to my class.

The topic today in our lecture series isn't one that interests me, but I can always rewatch it later if I need to study.

What I really need to do is figure out how this is going to work.

It's in Olivia's interest to keep it quiet. That only leaves Damon. Has he told Hawk and Cam what he's done? Does his claim include them? I rub my pounding temple. I need to focus on school, not on what's going on in my social life.

Laughter bubbles up inside me because I have a social life. A sex life. I'm fucking three guys. I may not have a status at this school, but I do have a reputation as a good girl. Damon will taint that reputation, but wasn't that his goal all along?

Take me from Chase. Make it hurt.

I'm on board with hurting Chase. He didn't deserve my loyalty or any piece of me. He fucking used me.

But I never really thought through what it would be like when it came out. Maybe Damon would throw it in Chase's face, and then Chase would go away. But that's not realistic. Damon wants to destroy Chase and just me being with them wouldn't be enough. Chase's pride would be bruised, but he could just let me go quietly. Start fucking around again.

But if Chase doesn't want me to break up with him, then what would he do if someone took me from him? Especially if it's Damon doing the taking.

Everyone is bound to find out what I've done. It's just a matter of time. My chest tightens.

"Are you okay?" Mia's words echo Damon's and I almost laugh again.

"I don't know," I admit. And then there's Mia. Would she be hurt by me dating Damon? She can't seriously just carte blanche claim all the guys in school and leave me with the only asshole. She did tell me I should suck his cock.

"If you need to talk it through, I'm here for you." She touches my arm and I look into her blue eyes.

"Thanks, Mia. I'm good. Honest." I give her the smile I use during auditions.

She takes it. "Okay, I'm going to go get fucked in the closet. Liam wants to prove that he's enough for me. I've decided to let him try."

I shake my head and gather my things before heading for the black box.

"Hey, boss." Keira catches up to me in the hallway. She frowns. "What's eating you?"

I stop and take a deep breath. "Nothing."

Keira looks up and down the hallway. "Yeah, you're not in the right headspace." She grabs my arm and pulls me into an empty classroom. When she shuts the door, she cocks her head and narrows her eyes. "Okay, pretend I'm the best friend you've never had and spill."

I smile and shake my head. "I'll figure it out."

"Not while we're orchestrating the finest performance of Shakespeare this school has ever seen." Keira crosses her arms. "Now out with it. I'll go first. There's this guy I've been seeing outside of school and he's being really pushy for sex. I keep telling him no, but then he kisses me and ugh. That boy can kiss. But it's a relationship that's going nowhere, so I should just tell him to fuck off."

She inhales and smiles, shaking her hands. "That feels good. Your turn."

My mouth opens and closes.

"Come on, Evan. I know something is going on with Chase and Hawk and Damon. It's not like I'm the person anyone comes to to hear the latest hot gossip. Your secret is safe with me."

When I open my mouth next, I can't stop myself. It all spills out. I tell her about my mom and Adam Storm. Finding out Chase was cheating on me. Damon blackmailing me. The nights in his bed. The revenge against Chase (though I leave out that he hit Damon over the summer). Olivia and the bathroom with Damon. Him saying I'm his girlfriend, but that might mean that Hawk and Cam are my boyfriends too.

My hands are on my stomach as it all pours out. While I pace, Keira stands against the wall watching me.

"I don't know what to do." It's the truth. I don't.

"Okay, that's a lot to take in." Keira smiles. "Damn, girl. I thought maybe Hawk. And that time with the salad, I was curious about Damon. But Cam too? I'm fucking impressed."

My laugh sounds tortured. "I feel like I'm going to vomit."

"Yeah. So here's what we're going to do. You're going to take some deep cleansing breaths. You said no one but Damon and Olivia know so far, right?"

"And you," I whisper.

"Steel vault, boss." She smiles before getting serious again. "We tuck this away for rehearsal. You have the whole cast waiting for you."

"Waiting for us," I point out.

"Yup. But we need to focus on one thing at a time. If this really does come out, we'll do what we can to mitigate the damage. Chase isn't going to give up his dream role to fuck you over. No matter how vindictive an asshole he is. It sounds like Damon is offering you his protection. It takes away Olivia's power, but she's going to try to come back around."

"How do you know?"

"A girl in Deimos last year tried to get with Damon, and she was actually on his radar." Keira winces. "Olivia slandered her until the girl crawled away with her tail tucked between her legs."

"How's that helpful?"

Keira smiles. "Damon didn't claim that girl. Yes, Olivia made her life hell, but only because she thought Damon was claimable. So if he wants to claim you, then claim him."

"But what about getting back at Chase?" I ask.

"That can't be the only thing driving you with this relationship, right?" Keira sits next to me. "Damon wants you. Hell, three guys want you. Your ex was an asshole who fucked you over. Him seeing you with those three will drive him crazy. It's the best revenge a girl can have."

I smile, but will it be enough revenge for Damon? Will he want to go after Olivia since she was part of his accident? I can't watch that. Stand by and let him do whatever he wants as revenge? I don't know what I would do, but I couldn't be present for him trying to get one over on Olivia by seducing her.

I won't know until I have a chance to talk to him tonight. After rehearsal and after Cam's tutoring session. Until then, I need to do what I always do. Compartmentalize and go on with the show.

"Are you ready now?" Keira asks softly.

"Yeah, let's go."

Chapter 20

Hawk

I got to the black box early in the hopes of finding Annie alone or close to alone. Enough that I can at least flirt with her before the rest of the cast shows up. But she's not in here, so I take a seat in the audience and pull out my phone.

I have a few contacts at Riordan's school. I reached out to see what I can find out about the guy since we haven't been around him in years. If he's the one coming after Annie, we need to get ahead of him. There's no way I'm letting her get trapped with him or Chase alone again.

With Riordan, what I don't get is why now? Why is he suddenly interested in her again after two years? That day at the rink. He looked at her with interest, but it wasn't obsession. At least I don't think it was. I need to talk to Annie about it.

Chase walks into the room and looks at the table where Annie usually sits. He's disappointed she isn't here too. Maybe he does want her more than just as an alibi for all his wrong doing. Or maybe he's just an asshole who doesn't want his toy taken away.

He looks me over. I smile because Annie's mine. If I thought she'd let me, I'd drag her to a closet and fuck her until she screams, so everyone knows. But that's not the plan. No, Annie needs to find out why he wants her so much, and we're going to show him exactly how he made her feel.

Chase nods at me. Apparently, eye contact and a smile was an invitation to come over and talk. He crosses the stage and sits down near me.

"You're here early." He glances at me like he wants to take the temperature of my involvement with Annie maybe. Either that or he wants to talk about Damon having access to his girl.

I'm all over his girl. If I could have found her, I would have given her a stress break because she looked at me for help at lunch and I couldn't do a damn thing to help her. Not without hurting her. We don't know if our interest in Annie is why Riordan wants her. If it will make him back off or want her more.

Fuck, this is complicated. Since Chase didn't ask an actual question, I give him the non-answer.

"You and Damon are friends, right?"

I lean back in my chair and close my eyes. "Yeah."

Where the fuck is he going with this line of questioning?

"I'm trying everything I can to get back with EvanAnn. Could you let him know to back off? She's not the kind of girl he's used to." Chase's voice is low and private.

I straighten and meet his eyes. "And what kind of girl is Annie?"

He swallows and glances toward the door. "Inexperienced. I was with her for months and didn't get any. So if he's hoping she'll fuck him—"

I laugh and he cuts off. He doesn't know how quickly we got her into our bed.

But he tries again, "EvanAnn is cute. She's not as hot as most of the girls in our school, and she's not fast."

If he only knew.

"So you want me to tell Damon to, what?" I arch an eyebrow.

"She's in his house. Just ignore her like he does at school. Give me a chance to figure out my shit with her." Chase runs a hand through his hair and glances at the doors. "He'll just hurt her."

I scoff. "You're fucking around on her."

He looks at the ground. "I'm done with that. I was stupid. But she's willing to forgive me."

"Are you done fucking around on her?"

His gaze jerks to mine.

Smirking, I lean forward and give him a look. "You want to make sure Annie doesn't have any options but you? Why?"

"She's smart and talented." He tugs at his tie. He's fucking lying. "I like her. Okay? I messed up, but I'm sure she'll give me a second chance."

"You want me to go to Damon and tell him to ignore the hot little piece in his house?" I rub my chin like I'm thinking it over. Instead, I'm thinking about how she looks spread open and needing my cock buried inside her.

"She's not a hot little—yeah." Chase rubs the back of his neck. "I think I still have a chance."

The doors open, and Annie and Keira walk in. Annie has a rule about not flirting or fucking around during rehearsal, but fuck, I want to go kiss her right now to make this asshole realize Damon isn't the only competition he has.

Annie glances my way, and her cheeks flush pink. She seems on edge. I wish I could pull her into a closet and see what's wrong. If it's just stress, I could make her come to ease some of that tension. She glances away.

"I'm offering her a future." Chase clears his throat. "Can Damon say the same? We all know he fucks girls and that's it. That's not what EvanAnn needs."

"What do you know about what Annie needs?" I'm curious what he thinks she needs.

"Connections. She thinks she'll get them in college, but she needs people like my parents who are already connected and want to push her to the next level. My dad is already setting her up with a director who mentors students. She needs someone who believes in her and her process and will do anything to support her."

"And that's you?" I arch an eyebrow.

He smirks. "I have the money to grease the wheels, but also the connections she needs. I can make her dreams come true. All Damon is going to do is break her heart."

"And what do you get?" I'm curious if he'll finally come out with why he needs Annie.

Chase's eyes narrow on me. "EvanAnn is enough."

EvanAnn

The school is dark as Mark and Mia walk out with me. We just finished our rehearsal. They have amazing chemistry on the stage. They embody Desdemona and Othello. All the other bullshit doesn't matter. This is what's important.

And I'm floating a little because of how great rehearsal went.

"Evan."

Damon. My heart stops.

I turn and see him striding toward us. Fuck. I pushed that whole bathroom incident to the side while I worked, but I really don't want to explain why Damon is suddenly possessive of me to Mia or Mark.

"You guys go on. Damon will make sure I get to my car." I smile. "Again, great job tonight."

Mark nods. "See you tomorrow."

Mia hangs back for a moment. "Are you good?"

"Sure. We'll talk later." I glance toward where Damon strides toward me.

Yes, I'm still keeping secrets from my new best friend. I don't know how I'm going to unravel all this, but it's not like Damon asked me to be his girlfriend. He blackmailed me into a physical relationship and then decided to announce it to the girl who wants him while she was trying to pay me off. The girl who may be the reason I was a target in the first place. But he didn't actually ask, and I doubt being my boyfriend is what he really wants.

Seriously. How is this my life?

Besides, we can fix this. It's not like everyone knows he called me his girlfriend and that a big part of me really liked that the guy I'm fucking wants to claim me in public and not keep me a secret, but...

But there's something else we have to deal with. And yes, I may have a potential creep trying to scare me, but that doesn't mean Damon has to make a big deal out of what we're doing. Or that I need to like the idea of him holding my hand or bringing me to school. We're not dating.

We're fucking. That's a huge distinction I think needs to be discussed.

"Don't go anywhere alone." Those are the first words he says to me when he finally reaches me.

I glance across the parking lot as Mia and Mark stop to talk next to her car. Mia glances back toward us and waves. I lift my hand to acknowledge I saw her.

Damon closes in on me, and I inhale his earthy scent. "You have someone potentially stalking you. You need one of us with you at all times."

"Don't be ridiculous." I turn and head toward the car. "I was walking out with other people."

He falls into step next to me. "I'm not being ridiculous, little devil. I'm being realistic. Jackson Riordan and I played on the same team when we were kids. He's obsessive about things."

"Sounds familiar." I arch my eyebrow.

"This is serious. He thinks he fucking owns you, Evan."

"And as my current owner, does that piss you off?"

When I unlock the car doors, he closes in on me, pressing me against the side of the car.

"I'm trying to protect you."

I meet his sharp blue eyes as his head drops toward mine. Biting my lip, I turn my head to the side and look toward where Mia and Mark were. I don't see them.

Damon grabs my chin and turns me back to him as his lips crash down on mine. His hand sinks into my hair to hold me there. I give up and clutch the t-shirt he must have put on after practice.

Parting my lips for his tongue, I sink into the kiss, needing to feel him. I don't know what any of this means. It doesn't need to mean anything, but him offering it to me might be enough. It's not like we can tell our parents we're dating.

They'd definitely move me to another bedroom. And Damon wouldn't have that.

He lifts his head. "Let me take care of you."

I search his eyes in the parking lot lights. "We can find a way to do that without pretending to date."

"No one's pretending, little devil." He leans down and kisses me softly.

My heart skips a beat. "Can we talk when I get home? I need to go over to Cam's to tutor him. He's expecting me."

"I'll follow you there. Text me when you're getting ready to leave."

"That's not necessary—"

He tugs on my hair. "Let me take care of you."

He kisses me like he can make me do it by fucking my mouth with his. Honestly, I'm okay with it.

Chapter 21

Cam

I'm sitting on the porch waiting for Evan when she pulls in, another red paper flower ready for her. A motorcycle follows her, and he flashes his lights at me as I hold up my hand. Damon's a possessive fucker.

He heads off as Evan gets out of her car, and I walk over to her. She takes the flower with a soft smile and pulls me down to kiss me quickly. Smirking, I take her backpack and put it over my shoulder before leading her into my house. Her eyes go everywhere, but linger on the pictures of my family at various ages on the wall. She slips her shoes off at the door and follows me in.

"My parents just want to meet you, and then we can go work in the family room." I told them about Evan, and they're wary. Especially Dad. He thinks I'm just asking a girl over to screw around with. He's not exactly wrong. I do want to screw around with Evan, but I know we won't get away with it until I actually show improvement in my grades.

"I'll help where I can, but I also need to use this time to work on my homework too." Her blue-gray eyes capture mine, and she gives me this serious look.

"We can do that." I open the door to the living room where my parents are watching a movie. They pause it and turn to us. "Mom. Dad. This is EvanAnn. The soon to be valedictorian of Deimos and Anteros. EvanAnn, these are my parents, Alex and Lisa."

Mom stands and runs her hand over her slacks. "It's a pleasure to meet you, EvanAnn. Cam says you're super busy, so we're glad you can find time to help out Cam with his classes."

She holds her hand out to Evan, and Evan shakes it. "It's a pleasure, Mrs. Warwick."

"Lisa, please, dear." Mom glances at Dad as he stands behind her. "You can call him Alex."

Evan holds her hand out and he shakes it. "It's a pleasure, sir."

Dad looks her over until Mom elbows him with an overbright smile.

"It's good to meet you." Dad puts his hands on Mom's shoulders. "I hope you can do something to make sure he gets the grades he needs to get into Yale."

"I'll do my best to help him get his grades up." She glances back at me.

Yeah, that's enough of that. "Okay, we'll be in the family room."

"If you need any snacks—"

"We're good, Mom." I smirk as I lead Evan down the hallway. I gesture to the opening. "We can work here."

I set her backpack on the table in the corner. This room will be the best for my parents since there are no doors to close. It sucks for me though.

"Okay, first thing we need to do is figure out where you are and make a plan to get you caught up or improve your grades." She sets the flower in front of her with a smile before she pulls out her laptop and opens it. "WiFi?"

I give her the information. "You really are a nerd, aren't you, goody?"

Her smile makes my chest tight. "Probably. But I've been the one driving my education. I love my mom, but she's not focused on me or getting good grades."

"I wish my dad were a little more lax, but maybe a happy medium?"

As she begins to plan what I need to work on, I fill in the details when she asks for them. She takes control. I never imagined listening to her boss me around would be so hot.

When we have a plan, she sets me to work on homework for one of my classes she's not in while she begins on her calculus homework. It's probably been a half hour when I hear footsteps.

"How are you two doing?" Dad stands in the doorway. His gaze takes in everything. I'm sitting next to Evan instead of across from her, but we both have our texts and laptops out and are busy working.

"Good. Evan's a good instructor."

She blushes but smiles at my dad. "He's not really behind. We put together a schedule, so he can stay on top of his assignments and a study schedule, so he won't be doing it all the night before."

My dad nods. "Who are your parents?"

Too many of my friends are from families he knows. But Evan isn't like the other Deimos kids.

Evan clears her throat. "Heather Ward. My father passed years ago. Cancer."

"Oh, sorry for your loss." Dad straightens. I can see him trying to figure out the last name and if it's someone he knows. Or a friend of a friend.

Evan smiles. "It was a long time ago. I miss him, but he's always with me."

Dad nods. "You're in Deimos?"

"Anteros. I'm in the directing program." A good thing about our school is that they train us to deal with situations like this. She has no problem rolling with the questions. "I've always excelled in school as well."

"Well, if you can help Cam, we'd be grateful." Dad steps away with a nod and leaves us alone.

"He probably counts it as a win that I'm not out partying tonight." I roll my eyes as I focus on my screen.

Evan's fingers stop on the keyboard. "Do you really party on weeknights?"

Is she concerned about my drinking? I couldn't be there when she needed me because I was too drunk.

"I'm done drinking."

She arches an eyebrow skeptically.

I smirk. "Maybe one, but that's it."

"Why did you go out on weeknights anyway?"

I shrug and meet her eyes. "Sometimes it's better than being at home."

"I spent a lot of time alone at our house, but I kept myself busy with school." She glances at the computer. "I never got into the party scene. Honestly, I don't like alcohol all that much."

"I'll find a drink you can love." I slide my hand over hers on the table.

She startles, but smiles and turns her hand over so we're holding hands. It's weird, because I don't think we've done this and it seems strangely intimate given what we did last night and other nights.

"Damon told us about your texts." I pull her hand down onto my thigh below the table, still holding it.

She glances my way. "I'm sure it's nothing."

"He said they scared you." I want her to know I'm taking this seriously.

She shrugs. "It's someone trying to make me afraid. They succeeded. I'm sure it doesn't mean anything."

She swallows and I realize she's trying to convince herself. I've never had anyone like Evan in my life. There's this instinct to protect her no other girl has made me feel. I squeeze her hand to reassure her.

"Well, I'm taking it seriously, and so are Damon and Hawk."

Her eyes look at me like she's trying to figure me out. I'm a simple guy though. I love fiercely and protect what's mine. It's why I'm protective of Hawk and Damon. They're my friends, and they feel the same about me.

"When we decided to come after you together, it felt like fate or some bullshit." I draw in a breath. "We didn't know we'd be getting you, goody. You're more than a conquest to us. You have to know that by now."

She blows out a breath and glances toward the doorway. She leans in and says quietly, "If this is because I gave you my virginity, it really doesn't matter to me. It's a construct."

"It's not about that. It's about you." I don't know if I'm explaining this well. "What's happening between us is more than physical."

She looks down at our hands. "Cam—"

"None of us knows what we're doing here, but we like spending time with you. It's not all about the sex."

When she gives me a look like she doesn't believe that, I laugh.

"It's mostly about the sex, but we want to take care of you too. So don't hold this shit back. Tell us when you're afraid. Your instincts probably aren't off. If something frightens you, tell us. If you get a weird feeling. Whatever. You need me? Call. I'll be there and sober."

She searches my eyes, but I'm being sincere here. We're a lot. But she takes everything we throw at her. There aren't many girls who would be cool with the way we treat Evan. Most girls would cry if Damon took videos of them in their private time. Not Evan.

"Fuck, Evan. You're going to make me say it, aren't you?" I give her a small smile and raise my eyebrow.

"What?"

"You complete us." When she doesn't reply, I lean in and whisper like she forgot her line, "This is where you say you had me at hello."

I chuckle.

She shakes her head, but her lips curve into a smile. "You didn't even say hello."

"Hmm, that doesn't matter. You give us something more than sex. You can read into that what you want." I squeeze her hand and reach out to tuck a strand of hair behind her ear. "Just consider this might be something more than a blackmail and revenge pact."

She blinks at me, but she gives me a small nod. I'll take it because I'm not letting this girl go, and I need to convince the others this is what's best for all of us. That she's what's best for us.

She blows out a breath. "There is something."

"Whatever it is I'll help if I can."

"I need to talk to you and Hawk." She sighs. "It's about Damon."

I pull out my phone and text Hawk. "He can be here in ten."

We study for a little until Hawk walks in. He runs his hand through his hair as he checks out us working.

"I'm guessing this isn't a bootie call?" Hawk smirks at Evan.

Fuck, he's going to get me in trouble. He needs to knock that shit off in case my dad comes by.

I shake my head. "You know my parents are still up, right?"

Hawk shrugs and sits on the edge of the couch. "Come here, Annie."

She stands and walks over to him. He pulls her down onto his lap and hugs her. I follow her over and sit down next to them.

"What's going on?" Hawk asks.

Evan blows out a breath. "Today during lunch, Olivia confronted me in the bathroom."

"I told him not to encourage her." Hawk growls softly as he rubs her back. "What did she do?"

She laughs bitterly. "She wanted to pay me off. Give me money to have me discourage Damon from coming after me."

"How much did you get?" Hawk asks.

"I didn't take it," Evan says offended.

I shake my head. "Money is what Olivia is used to. She figures everyone has a price. She's fucking desperate for him. That's the part that doesn't make sense. It's not like she couldn't get another guy to fuck her."

"She said she gets the best and he's the best." Evan shrugs. "She said she cheated with Chase over the summer, even gave him road head."

"Fuck." I stand and put my fingers against my lips. "Did you tell Damon?"

Will this change his strategy at all? I'm not on board with leaving Evan.

Nodding, she blows out a breath. "That's the thing. She was trying to pay me off, which I'm not down for, but then Damon comes into the girls' bathroom."

My gaze collides with Hawk's and his widen.

"He's apparently tracking me and said my phone hadn't moved, so he wanted to make sure I was okay." She takes a breath and looks at both of us. "Not really surprised given there are cameras all over our rooms. But he told Olivia I was his and that he was mine. When she left, he said he wanted to protect me. He called me his girlfriend."

She meets my eyes. "Did he tell you guys?"

I shake my head and sink down onto the couch next to her and Hawk. Fuck. What would that even mean? We talked a little about how to protect her from Jackson, but we decided it might be best not to poke the bear.

Jackson's always been jealous of what Damon has.

"I don't think it's gone further than Olivia because she wouldn't spread it. It would just make her look bad." She glances at Hawk. "How do I tell Damon this is a bad idea?"

Hawk looks at me, but I shake my head. Damon's off script.

Hawk sits back and pulls Evan to rest against his chest. "I don't know that you can convince him, but it would be better to get through the weekend before we claim you. If that's even advisable. I'm not convinced that our having you isn't half of why Riordan is after you again. If he's really watching you, he has to know about all of us."

"Olivia might tell Chase." I rub Evan's thigh. "If she wants to get back at you, that probably would be her move to call you out. Especially if she thinks you want to get back together with him. But she might not, hoping you'll get back with Chase and she'll have another go at Damon."

"Why did Damon do that though?" Evan closes her eyes. "Everything has been going according to plan. Mostly."

"I already told you, goody." I wait for her eyes to meet mine. "You complete us. Maybe he's tired of being your side piece."

Her mouth opens for a second before she snaps it shut.

"My side piece?" Indignation colors her words.

I smirk. "I mean, you did have a boyfriend."

She narrows her eyes, but I boop her nose.

"Just talk to him, Annie." Hawk rests his hand on her back. "He's worried about you. Maybe he overreacted, but when he sees a threat to someone he cares about, he takes care of it."

"He wants me to let him take care of me." Evan looks thoughtful.

"I know this didn't start out with best intentions." Hawk shrugs when I scoff. "But this isn't something we want to end. Maybe Damon is pulling the trigger a little sooner than any of us expected. But I'm okay being yours and letting you claim me at school."

Evan's eyes widen. "That's not part of the deal. I mean, Chase finding out is definitely part of the plan, but—"

"Just because we didn't start that way—" I clear my throat, "doesn't mean we can't grow into something new, Evan."

"But our parents—"

"Don't need to know the details." I lean back.

"They might make me move if they know about Damon. Or if they think I'm single." She nibbles on her lip. Yeah, she doesn't want to move away from him.

"Then claim one of us is your boyfriend." I smirk. "They might freak out if they knew you were dating all three of us. I'll definitely take the role."

"Get in line," Hawk says.

Evan smiles and shakes her head like she doesn't believe us.

"Probably best to go with the golden boy who can do no wrong with the parents. You're ours and we're yours. That's all that matters." I glance toward the doorway before pressing my forehead against hers. "I do agree with Damon on one thing."

Her blue-gray eyes meet mine.

"Let us protect you."

Chapter 22

EvanAnn

"Our parents are out." Damon opens the car door for me. He rode over to Cam's, and he and Hawk followed me home like Damon said he would. Hawk split off from us to go home. Apparently his parents are in town. I look at the house and grab my bag. It's late.

My head is still spinning from talking with Hawk and Cam. Could what we have be more?

Damon leads me into our house. We take the back stairs to our rooms. When we walk into my room, I set my backpack next to my desk as he locks the door.

I can't look at him to say what I need to say. Not after he claimed me in front of Olivia. It feels like I'm trying to let him down, but that isn't the case.

I've been worried about this ending, but I never thought it would keep going. That they would want to make us something more official. How would that even work? I'm going to have three boyfriends?

I was thrilled to just have one a few weeks ago. The problem isn't being with them.

The problem is school. If I thought living with Damon would be bad at school, having the Devil's trio as boyfriends will be ten times worse.

But will it? There's a part of me that wants to believe this could be something more and that it could be as easy as it was to fall into bed with them.

Right now, we need time to discuss this. We need time for Damon to get his revenge on Chase. And that means I can't be theirs yet. Not in school. Not anywhere but here.

"You can't claim me at school, Damon. I've thought this over and it's not going to go well. Not with Chase and Olivia still in power. It just won't work."

"Why not?" He closes in behind me and runs his hands up my sides, drawing me back into him. This man. His touch. Everything.

I melt, because how can I not? "Olivia won't say anything. She wouldn't want to admit that I have you. You can tell her you were just messing around."

"I wasn't." He pushes my hair off my nape and presses his lips against the sensitive skin. My breath catches. Already I want to turn into him and let him take me to bed. That's where we make sense. That's where we belong together.

"Don't you want your revenge?" I turn to him and he grabs the back of my neck, but I'm not trying to get away. I search his eyes. "Don't you want Chase to pay for everything he's done? I thought that was the whole point of this."

I gesture to my room. He runs his thumb along my jawline.

"Chase has lost you. He just doesn't know it yet." His blue eyes search mine. "You're ours, and it's time he knows he can't have what's mine."

"But—"

He cuts me off with a kiss. I sink into it but try to hold back a little. When I don't part my lips, he presses small kisses along my jawline. I tip my chin up to give him more access.

I groan because he's making it hard to think. "Damon."

"Evan." He lifts his head. "I know what I'm doing."

I put my hand over his heart. It beats so hard against my palm. Searching his blue eyes, I want to give in to him so badly. To be his. To go out at lunch and sit with him, Hawk, and Cam. To not have to pretend to be happy with my life the way it was.

"What are you doing, Damon?" I ask softly. "Why now? Is this because of Jacks—"

"I'm protecting you." He traces his thumb over my lower lip as he tracks the movement.

"Why?"

"Because no one else does." His eyes turn hard and focus on mine.

My breath catches and my heart thumps hard.

"Not even the people who should protect you." He undoes my tie and drops it on the ground. "I watch you, Evan. I know your life."

He's wrong.

"You don't—"

"I've watched you be alone a whole week. If we hadn't shown up, it would have been only you. No mom. No boyfriend. No friends. Fuck, Evan. You belong to us, and I'll do whatever it takes to protect you. You don't have anyone else. Let me take care of you."

I can't speak. What can I say to that? But he doesn't understand my life at all.

"You caught a glimpse of my life. That's not my whole life. My mom works."

"She was here every night. How do you think I got in to place the cameras? Why do you defend her?"

"Because we lost my dad, and it tore her apart." I pull away from him, but he follows me, backing me against the wall and unbuttoning my shirt. "Stop, Damon." I don't grab for his hands though. But I do search his eyes. "You should know what it's like. To watch your parent get sicker until you know it's going to end. That there's nothing left for you to do but prepare yourself. She didn't just lose my dad. She lost her life partner. The man she planned to spend the rest of her life with. How was I supposed to demand she pay attention to me when she needed to take care of my dying father?" Tears stream down my face.

Those last months were so hard. I went to school, but I didn't live. Every piece of me was grieving and waiting for the end. I lost weight. I barely slept. I'd go into their room at night to make sure he was still breathing.

Holding my breath as I waited for my dad's chest to rise.

I brush the tears away, but they don't stop. Damon's brow furrows, but he doesn't stop unbuttoning my shirt.

"I took care of me so she didn't need to. After he died, we had to deal with the bills and her having to work after she hadn't been able to. So yes, she got used to me being on my own, and so did I. I'm okay taking care of myself so she doesn't have to."

He pushes my shirt off my arms as I brush the tears away again.

His voice is low when he asks, "What about Chase? Where was he that first week of school? Where was he when we pushed into your house?"

"He was busy. He had football—"

"And fucking around on you." He undoes my bra.

"He's a bad example, but you know that." I take a breath as he bares my breasts.

"He should have been there with you." Damon reaches beneath my skirt and pulls my panties down. "If you were mine, I would have been there with you. Even though you weren't mine yet, I was there."

I suck in a breath as his gaze meets mine, holding me pinned in place.

"I spent every night watching your every move." He grabs the back of his t-shirt and strips it off, dropping it in the pile of clothes. His jeans come off next as I press my hands against the wall to keep from reaching for him. "I noticed you. I watched you. We worked together. Ate together. Got off together. Slept together."

My breath catches as he stands naked before me. I only have on my skirt, but I don't move to take it off. I can't breathe. He was there with me. He's been here with me every night. I haven't been alone and neither has he. We've had each other.

My heart pounds as I search his eyes.

He stands before me, breathing for both of us.

"I don't know when it happened, Evan, but you became part of my life. The part I look forward to." He brushes his thumb down the track of my tear. "I'm not about to let you go. Someone else isn't going to take you from me. I can't protect you unless you let me, little devil."

I step forward into his arms, surrendering. I'm so fucking tired. So done having to carry everything. When he lifts me, I wrap my legs around his waist. He brings me into his room. Our room.

He lays me down on the bed, following me down and capturing my lips. My insides are always on fire when I'm near him. When he reaches between us and notches his cock at my entrance, he lifts his head. Our eyes lock as he eases inside me. Connecting us on a primal level.

"You're mine. Every fucking inch of you. Stop denying me." He fills me so fucking full of him. My lips part on a gasp.

I thread my fingers through his hair and drag his mouth down to mine. It's insane. In here, we work, but out there in the real world no one will accept this. Yes, if we were just fucking around, people would nod, because that might make sense.

The Devil's trio fucks girls, but they don't have girlfriends.

Every piece of me already belongs to him, Hawk, and Cam. I want to claim them. And let them claim me. I want them to be able to push other girls away. Because they're mine.

"I'm yours," I whisper against his lips before I kiss him. We surge together, our hips moving together and apart as we fuck, but we never release each other. Our tongues parry as our hearts beat to the same tempo.

"Come for me, little devil." He reaches between us to circle my clit.

I'm so fucking close it's enough to push me over the edge. I cry out as I come, tightening my fingers in his hair.

My release drags his out of him. He groans as he hovers over me, filling me with his warmth. For a second, we continue to breathe each other in. Our hearts pounding. My hands in his hair.

When he pulls out, he kisses down my neck, down my chest as I breathe raggedly. When he reaches my stomach, he kisses it and stops, resting his head on me, the rest of him sprawled between my legs. His hair tickles my skin.

Combing my fingers through the strands, I don't know what to think. We didn't really come to any sort of agreement about anything. All I know is I don't want to fight what's happening between us. And it sounds like they don't either.

It's fucking terrifying and elating at the same time. I tried to keep them at a distance, but my walls were never that strong.

My fingers toy with his hair as my heartbeat slows. We still need to wait to come out at school. At least until we're finished with his revenge. And honestly, mine since Chase led me to believe we had something special and used me.

I release my pent-up breath. Tomorrow is soon enough to tell Damon.

My fingers trace his temple. For a moment, I wonder if he's fallen asleep, but then he speaks.

"My mom didn't find out until it was too late."

I don't stop touching him. His fingers skim over my hip bone in small circles. I hold my breath, waiting for his next words.

"It wasn't quick. They offered her radiation and chemo, but she refused treatment. She didn't want to spend the last year of her life in the hospital." He turns and kisses my stomach. Unzipping my skirt, he slips it down my legs, dropping it off the edge of the bed.

He returns to his position, head on my stomach, sliding his fingers in patterns on my bare skin. Gentle, calming touches. Something I wouldn't have believed Damon Storm to be capable of last school year.

I comb through his soft hair, feeling it tickle my bare skin. Holding my breath, waiting for him to continue.

"Dad let her make that decision. He let her choose to die. I hated him. I didn't understand it was her decision to make, and he probably struggled with it. All I knew was they gave up before even trying. I sat next to her bed every day for a few hours, telling her about my day. Washing her hair. Feeding her when it got too hard for her to feed herself."

The tears start again. I couldn't hold them back if I tried. This time for Damon and what he went through. But I continue to stroke his hair, to comfort him. Quietly crying while I listen to his pain.

"I couldn't understand why they didn't try. Anything had to be better than this. She grew weaker, thinner until she couldn't even get out of bed." A tear slides across my stomach and my heart breaks for him. For us. For the unfairness of it all. "He let her die. I know that's not the truth. It was what she wanted, and he was respecting her wishes. But I hated him for it."

When he lifts over me, he cups my head in his hands and presses his forehead to mine.

"I will do anything to protect you, but don't ask me to sit back and let you walk around in danger." He kisses me. "I can't do that. I can protect you by claiming you, by letting everyone know you're mine. Chase won't protect you. But I will. I'm not going to lose you, Evan."

I breathe Damon in. This pain I understand. The helplessness. The waiting. The anguish when it's over so quickly but goes on for so long.

"Okay," I whisper.

I can't fight him on this. Not this. I could tell him the texts don't scare me, but he knows it isn't true. He wants to protect me, and I just want to be theirs. I don't need a fancy title or a public display. I just need him, Cam, and Hawk.

The public part of whatever we choose makes me scared, but I'm not scared to let them in. Not anymore. We have things to sort through. But tonight in his bed, I'll give him what he wants because it's not in me to hurt him.

"Yeah?" he asks. His nose brushes mine. He smiles and it lights up his eyes.

My heart beats a little harder. "Yeah, I'm yours."

Chapter 23

Damon

I want Evan to ride my bike to school. I want to put my arm around her shoulders and make sure she gets to her classes. Instead, I follow behind her as she drives my car, watch her park, and walk into the building. Alone.

She's right. While we showered, she told me all her reasons for not wanting me to claim her right now. And she's right. We don't know why Chase wants her. I haven't taken everything away from him yet. We're so close.

But my revenge means nothing if I lose her because of it.

This was never supposed to happen. This feeling welling up inside me. It wouldn't have happened if it had been anyone else. Anyone except Evan.

I text her when I get to first period. She's with Cam this morning. She sends me her location on her phone. I smile a little. Like I don't know where she is.

Olivia breezes in and sits at the desk next to mine. "I'm assuming you're through with whatever yesterday was about. Maybe it was a test to see if I'd spread the rumor around."

She arches her eyebrow and taps her pen on her notebook.

I don't say anything. I know Evan wants me to tell Olivia it was a joke. That I didn't mean it. But fuck this girl. Olivia wants something from me she's never going to get. It's time she knows it's not happening.

The real question is, was Olivia the girl in the car with Chase? Because she's just as guilty as Chase if that's the case. And with the way she came after Evan, she needs to be taken down.

"I mean, she's cute I guess, but no one would ever believe you wanted more than a fuck from her." She sighs and looks at the front of the classroom like she's put out. "I appreciate you playing hard to get, but it's getting ridiculous, Damon. What if I were as big a tease as you are? You'd call me out on it."

I lean back in my chair and narrow my eyes at her.

"After all, this is our thing. Some girl chooses you, and I make sure she backs off. It's been fun." She turns and smiles at me. "I'll give you one thing. This one doesn't appear to be able to be bought. Which is new. She doesn't have any social standing I can take away. She's basically nothing, which is why I know this is just another one of your games."

Olivia smiles like she's figured me out. "Maybe it's just too early in the school year and you don't want to satisfy my curiosity quite yet."

I blow out a breath. I never should have let this bitch in. If I were still trying to fuck Evan over, Olivia was my best bet. But that plan's long gone. Evan isn't going anywhere. The only reason I continued to let Olivia believe she had a shot with me was to protect Evan.

"Maybe you should take the hint, Olivia," I say it louder than necessary and turn to look at her. "Maybe I'd want anyone more than you."

Some of the guys make burn noises in the background as her eyes narrow on mine. When some girls giggle, Olivia shoots them a look that makes them stop.

There's hell to pay in her eyes, but I'm done giving in to this bitch.

The teacher comes in. "All right, let's focus, people."

Olivia straightens. She glares at me before she remembers herself and smiles softly. This isn't going to end well.

When class ends, Olivia is out the door before I can say anything more to her. I blow out a breath. That might have done more harm than good. When I walk into second and Evan looks up at me with those eyes, my chest feels tight. It's not just Jackson I want to protect her from. It's everything and everyone.

Chase, Olivia, even her own mother.

We need to make sure Olivia hears me loud and clear that we're never going to happen. Not sex. Not a relationship. Nothing.

Without getting Evan hurt.

Hawk

Damon isn't happy, but Annie wants to stay the course. I want Chase to pay for what he did to Annie and Damon, so I'm all in on the revenge plan to take everything from him. The party on Saturday will take away Chase's freedom. Our other plan will cost him his dignity. We just need to find the right moment to pull the trigger. He's lost the girl he wants, but I want it to hurt when he finds out.

Cam did his job and everyone knows about the party. All we have to do is show up and make sure Chase's parents find out.

I'm waiting outside Annie's third period class when the bell rings. When she walks out, I wrap my arm around her shoulders, leading her to the doors instead of toward the cafeteria.

"Hawk, what are we doing?" She doesn't struggle. I love how she's never really shoved me off her, even when I shouldn't have been doing this. There was only one time she pushed me away. Back when she wasn't mine.

"We need to go somewhere we can talk."

She pauses next to the trash can and throws away three highlighters. I open the door and lead her to our motorcycles.

"Talk?" she asks suspiciously with a small smile.

I want to pull her in and kiss her because I love that she's as down as we are to fuck. But that's not the objective today.

Her eyes light up when she sees Damon and Cam ready to ride. Damon holds out her helmet. She goes to him, and he helps her put it on, but she turns to look at me.

"Go on, little devil, ride with Hawk." Damon pushes her hip, so she comes over to me.

I climb on and she easily slides on behind me. Her arms wrap around me, and she rests her head against my back. Her trust warms me. We start our bikes and take off.

Not the burger joint. Damon has plans, so he wanted somewhere private, where we can talk and not be overheard.

We drive to a park that's empty. It doesn't have playground equipment, just green space, so there are never a bunch of kids and moms here. When we stop to get off, Annie laughs.

"A picnic?" She hands me the helmet, and I put it on my bike before taking her hand. Damon has a pack and brings it over to a picnic table.

He takes out the food his chef made. She kisses his cheek, and he smiles.

"I swear your cook is trying to fatten me up." She takes the eggplant parmigiana.

"We'll help you burn it off." Cam sets a red paper flower in front of Evan before he straddles the bench next to her and eats a sandwich. He takes in every inch of her like she's next on his menu.

She smiles at him and touches his jaw. Her fingers touch the petals on the flower. Something inside me settles and acknowledges this is the way it should always be. At school, on weekends, every fucking night. Just us and our girl. Fuck everyone else.

Damon clears his throat, and everyone shifts our attention to him.

"We need to discuss what's happening." Damon sits across from Annie. "Evan is ours and I'm done pretending anything else."

Annie opens her mouth, maybe to protest, but snaps it shut at the look in Damon's eyes.

"Chase wants you to back off." I lean my elbows on the table. "He talked to me before rehearsal yesterday and basically asked me to tell you to fuck off and let him have Annie. Confident he meant me too."

"Good. He's nervous. We just need to keep poking until he explodes." Damon straightens. "He's going to be on lockdown after his parents find out about the rager at his house. We need to figure out why Evan is so important to him. It can't be just about fixing his reputation and having an alibi when he's out partying."

Annie watches Damon like there's something more there now. There's a softness between them. There's always been passion, but this is different. We're different with her. Fuck.

"We need to make sure everyone posts on social media at the party. That should do the trick if he manages to keep it under the radar by cleaning it up or some bullshit." Cam takes a bite of his sandwich. "We need to be careful about getting other students in trouble, especially after the bust at Fletcher's."

Cam is big on the party foul. The fact he took that video of Chase weeks ago is a testament to how much he wants to take Chase down. Or prove to Annie how big a sleazeball her boyfriend was.

"I'm not worried about the party. What we really need to talk about is Jackson Riordan." Damon locks eyes with Annie. She squirms beneath his gaze.

"What bugs me is why now?" Cam asks. "After all this time, if he's the one who sent the text, why is he coming after you now?"

Annie clears her throat. "It was summer when we lived at those apartments. We were only there for a few weeks. I didn't wear my uniform around him and didn't tell him I went to Anteros because I wanted to be a normal girl for once."

I rub her thigh under the picnic table, and she leans against me.

"When he kissed me, I stopped leaving the apartment. Mom was having some issues too, so she was eager to move. We never really talked about it. She found our house. Mom needed to change phone plans, so we both got new phone numbers. And I never let Jackson know."

"So you didn't see Jackson again?" Cam asks.

"I kind of ghosted him after the kiss. So, not until that night at the football game." She swallows. Her hand slides beneath mine and she laces our fingers together. "He called me *pretty girl* and asked to sit with me and Mia. Of course, Mia didn't know our history."

"And still doesn't know your history," I add. "I asked her about him. She gave him her phone to put in his number. Knowing she was your friend, he could have gotten your number then."

"That makes sense. I got my first unknown message the next day." She straightens.

Damon clears his throat. "At the football game, when I grabbed you and pulled you under the bleachers..."

"I thought you were Jackson at first." She ducks her head. "It wasn't rational. It's been two years since he kissed me. But my instincts say he's still after me."

"If we let everyone know you're ours, then maybe he'll back off." Damon looks determined.

"Or it might make him more desperate to have her." I push my food away and squeeze Annie's hand. "We knew Jackson from hockey when we were younger. He wanted to be friends with us, but there was something off about him. He tried too hard and felt fake, like a user. From what I've heard from his new school, he hasn't changed much. Maybe he's learned to blend in, but there's something not quite right about him. He never really apologized when he hurt someone, whether it was intentional or unintentional. Maybe he's a sociopath, but he's good at hockey, so he gets a pass even though he's unnecessarily aggressive and impulsive. The guys I know say he keeps to himself at school."

Annie shivers and Cam puts his arm around her shoulder.

"If he's really stalking her, he has to know about us." Cam clears his throat. "He has to know you're *with* us already."

Damon's mouth tightens, but Cam is right. Jackson either

watches Annie or he was bluffing about it. Something tells me he isn't the kind of guy to bluff.

"As soon as Chase is taken care of, we're claiming you." Damon's gaze meets Annie's. "Maybe this weekend we can get two birds with one stone. How can we bring down Olivia? Whether she's the girl in the car or not, she's threatening Evan."

"That's going to be difficult." Cam rubs his jaw. "She's been queen bee for a long time."

Cam glances at Annie and blows out a breath.

"There is something." Cam looks at Annie. "You're not going to like this."

"I haven't liked a lot of things. But I'm willing to do whatever we need to." Annie looks at each of us. "This is just another play, another performance. Let's do what we have to."

Cam nods. "We need something that will push her over the edge and catch her saying something on video that we can hold over her head."

Damon smirks. "If she caught me with Evan, that would push her over the edge. She had a mini-tantrum in the bathroom."

Evan bites her lip like she doesn't mind that idea. I glance around the park. It's abandoned. Would she let me fuck her here? Pull those panties to the side and slip inside her? Fuck her hard against a tree? Does the anticipation of getting caught turn her on?

"We'd need to set up cameras in his bedroom. She can meet me there and find us together. I want to show Chase the video when I finally let him know I have you. Just to rub it in his face that I fucked you in his bedroom." Damon rubs his chin. "Setting up the cameras won't be as easy as Evan's place was though."

"There's a party tonight." Cam leans forward. "All we need to do is get close enough to grab Chase's keys."

"I can get close enough." I run a hand through my hair. When Annie's blue-gray eyes lock with mine, I smirk. "He thinks we're acting buds."

"Maybe." Annie takes a drink and looks at each of us as she says,

"But I would be able to keep him close and distract him from figuring out they're gone."

"No." Damon narrows his gaze on her like she offered to take Chase up to a room.

Annie rolls her eyes. "It's acting, Damon. I don't need to do anything but pretend to be interested in him for a few hours while you guys go to his house and plant the cameras."

"Have you been in his room?" Cam asks, thinking.

"He let me use it to change into my bathing suit one time." Annie arches her eyebrow at Cam, waiting for what else he's going to say.

"I'm going to need to see that bikini, Annie." I wait for her because I know that will bring her attention back to me.

Her gaze flicks to mine. Her eyes darken. So many things we haven't done.

"There's a pool at Damon's house. Care to go for a midnight swim?"

"Later." She smiles and returns her attention to the others. "I can probably draw a rough map of the house if that's what you're looking for."

"Or you could come with." Damon smirks. "I'll set up the cameras while you poke around his room to see what you can find. And we can double-check the setup by recording me fucking you."

She releases a little breath. "What if Chase is already compromised? What if Olivia told him about you saying I'm yours in the bathroom? I didn't deny it."

We all pause. Olivia can be a vindictive bitch, but she also wants Damon. She wouldn't want people to think she's in competition with Annie and losing. It's possible she'd tell Chase to get Annie in trouble or make Chase double down on getting her back.

"Don't find yourself alone with him, goody." Cam runs a hand through his hair. "We need to make sure Evan is never out of our sights at either party. If he knows he's already lost you, he might do something rash."

Annie shivers. Having to pick her up in the middle of nowhere was bad enough. Chase could do a lot of damage to our girl if he thought he could get away with it. Yeah, I don't want Chase anywhere near her.

"This is a bad idea. We don't know if Chase knows that I claimed her. I'm not telling Olivia it was a joke, because fuck that bitch." Damon stands and takes his trash over to the waste bin. "I'm not risking Evan for my revenge."

"You aren't." Annie stands and walks over to him. "He's not going to get his hands on me ever again."

Damon slides his hand into her hair and lowers his forehead to hers. He closes his eyes and breathes.

It feels strangely intimate, like something I shouldn't be seeing, but also something that was inevitable. How could we have Annie in our lives without her pushing her way into our hearts?

Impossible.

"I'll get you the keys and keep Chase occupied." I ball up the paper from my sandwich.

"Or," Annie says as she walks over to me and sits on my lap, "You challenge Chase to beer pong. I get the keys while he's distracted, and you keep him occupied with the game while we're gone."

"Have I mentioned how brilliant you are?" I lean in and kiss her. "I'm going to fuck you so hard tonight."

Her blue eyes are bright when I pull away. "Why wait until tonight?"

"We need to get back to school." I kiss her again. "Can't have you late to your next class."

She sighs and stands.

"We need to figure out timing and find a way to turn off the alarm system." Damon pulls her against him. He drags his thumb over her lips. "Later tonight, little devil, you're taking all of us."

Chapter 24

EvanAnn

"Hey, I missed you at lunch." Chase sits next to me in acting class. He smiles and puts his hand on top of mine. "What did you do?"

I swallow down the urge to say the Devil's trio, because I'm so sick of pretending with him. Not that we fucked, but it was so nice to just be with them and not have to worry about everything else. But Chase and I? We're in this weird space where he thinks there's hope.

I'm curious if he knows what Damon said to Olivia. Maybe he'll think it's a joke or a way for Damon to push his buttons more. I can always lead him to that conclusion if he brings it up.

"I had lunch off campus." Stick as close to the truth as possible.

"Yeah?" He lounges back in his chair and runs a hand through his dark hair. He looks around the classroom and then returns his focus to me. "I would have gone with you."

"It was last minute. I didn't want to eat a salad today." I shrug.

He nods like that makes sense. I don't think I've ever seen him eat a salad. "Are you coming to my game tonight?"

"Of course. I wouldn't miss it." I give him a soft smile, like I'm into him.

He puffs up and leans into me. "I miss touching you, EvanAnn."

I want to push him away and tell him to go fuck himself because he's never touching me again. But I know how to act.

"Yeah?" I smile shyly at him, because I need him to believe I'm still trying to get back with him. If he suspects something is going on with any of the Devil's trio, will this work? I may need to up my game. Only for a little while longer.

"I think about you in that skirt from last Saturday a lot." His blue eyes meet mine. "Are you going to wear something like that this weekend?"

"Maybe." If I did, I'd be wearing it for my guys and not him, but he doesn't know that.

Mia plops down on my other side. "Olivia was an even bigger bitch at lunch today. She must be PMSing."

Chase glances at Mia before he turns to look at his phone.

"Yeah?" I ask, wondering if she's going to mention the guys weren't out there. Did Chase notice they were gone too?

"I swear I was about to douse her in holy water." Mia shakes her head. "She kept going on about Damon even though he wasn't even there."

I laugh. "She cornered me in the bathroom yesterday."

Mia leans in. "Really?"

I lower my voice. "Apparently she thinks Damon wants me or something and tried to pay me off to reject him."

"What a rich bitch thing to do." Mia glances toward Chase, who is still enraptured with his phone. "What'd you say?"

"I said she had nothing to worry about and refused her money." I shrug like it isn't a big deal and glance at Chase.

Mia laughs. "Where does she find the nerve? That girl wouldn't make it a day at my old school."

Chase drapes his arm around my shoulders and squeezes me. I give him a tight smile. At least he's not trying to kiss me.

Mia nudges my arm. "We on for Saturday?"

Chase goes back to his phone with a little humph.

"Going to the scrimmage?" I toy with my pen to not seem too interested.

"I was so lonely last time." She smiles. "You can come and cheer on your new roommate. That will piss Olivia off too."

Chase glares at Mia for a moment.

I clear my throat. "Yeah, I'll go with you. But I'm going to be with you, not because of the team."

Chase squeezes my hand like that's the right answer. Whatever he needs to think. I can't wait to be done with this charade.

Mia drives me to the football game. I don't know if the guys are coming, but they probably will show up. Anything could go wrong tonight. I need to get Chase's keys. The problem is I haven't figured out how yet.

Maybe I can offer to hold his things so he can really get into the beer pong game.

"So you haven't told me how it's been going living with Damon?" Mia sucks on a lollipop and looks unconcerned other people are around us and might overhear. We're in the student section toward the bottom so that Chase can see me when he glances our way. I need to convince him I'm really into making this work and resist the urge to flip him off.

What I don't need is a rumor going around about me and Damon. Fortunately the game isn't as packed, so we have some space around us.

"Uh, it's weird." I don't know what to say about it because I'm supposed to look like I'm trying to get back together with Chase. "I'm an only child, so I'm not used to having someone else around. Also, no one else at school knows besides you and Chase. I'd like to keep it that way."

"Understood." Her blue eyes sparkle as she meets mine. "What's the situation? Do you run into him? I was watching this one foreign show where she moves in with her stepbrother who is hot but older and there's this moment in the kitchen when... oof." She fans herself. "Honestly, I almost wish my parents were separated so I could get some hot stepbrother action."

My cheeks burn because she's not far off. Except Damon's dad is so rich, neither of us spends any time in the kitchen. "Our parents aren't married. But I guess I've seen him around the house."

I can't tell if Mia is trying to figure out how close Damon and I are or to figure out how to make something happen for her with Damon. I'm surprised she hasn't mentioned a sleepover yet. She could use my bed. I don't.

The cheerleaders are on the field holding a banner for the players to run through. I've seen things like this on TV and in movies, but I hadn't experienced it until this year. I just inhale and memorize this moment.

The excitement of the crowd. The cheers of the cheerleaders. The guys on the field. It's intense and I'm getting caught up in it as the game begins. Mia tells me a little about how the game works.

"You couldn't go to Sherman High without going to the football games. The stadium was always packed." Her cheeks are flushed with excitement as she watches the players. "They were amazing to watch. It was like they were so in sync with each other. Fuck, if I could have convinced Eli and Luke to join Jack, Caden, and me, I would have done all four of them at the same time."

Heat seeps into me, because the Devil's trio is planning to take me together tonight.

I bite my lip. "So how does it work with two guys at once?"

Mia arches an eyebrow at me with a smirk. "Curious, Evan?"

"It just seems a little impossible." I shrug. Though I've seen it in action, and Mia seemed to enjoy it. My guys have fucked me with a plug in my ass, and I enjoyed that. My cheeks flush with heat.

"Oh, it's so not." Mia glances around and leans in so her lips are close to my ear. "It burns a little because of the stretch, but once they're both in and moving, it's fucking spiritual. Overwhelming in a good way. If you know what I mean."

She pulls away and smirks.

"I seriously would do it all the time if I could. That and an Eiffel Tower. One in my mouth and one in my pussy, fuck it's so hard to focus as they fuck in and out of you." Mia licks her lollipop and puts it back in her mouth. Her eyes are a little unfocused as if she's thinking about it.

My heart pounds because I'll know after tonight. But I'll have all three of them, not just two. I cross my legs. I wore jeans to the game, and Damon tugged his sweatshirt over my head before he backed me into a wall and kissed me like he didn't want to let me go.

I'm trying not to read into what's happening with us. It's possible I'm misreading everything. It's not like I'm the best at understanding guys. They may just like that I'm willing to do anything with them. There hasn't really been any talk about feelings.

Yes, Damon wants to protect me and will call me his girlfriend to do that, but he didn't say he was falling in love with me. Last night though, things shifted between me and Damon.

It felt more real than any connection I've had in a long time. I don't feel alone in that house.

"Hey there, Annie."

My gaze jerks up and collides with Hawk's green eyes. "Uh, hi."

Cam and Damon stand behind him. Cam grins and winks at me.

"Mind if we sit with you guys?" Hawk gestures to the open seats.

"Oh, sure." Mia squeezes in closer to me to give them room. Honestly, I'm a little surprised she doesn't shove me away so that they can surround her.

Cam chuckles as he sits on the other side of Mia while Hawk takes the seat next to me and Damon sits behind me. I keep my breathing steady and don't close my eyes when Damon's fingers brush against the nape of my neck.

My hair is up in a ponytail. That might have been a mistake

because I have to suppress the shivers Damon's touch sends through me.

I don't think for a second that was an accident.

The heat of Hawk's thigh against mine sets my insides on fire. Was this part of the plan? Because I'm not prepared. I take a minute and breathe out and in, ready to improvise my way through this scene.

It would help if I knew what the purpose of the scene was.

I keep my gaze out on the field. Chase isn't playing right now. He stands on the sidelines and when he glances back, like he's been doing, his smile fades and he does a doubletake.

His arms drop and he almost takes a step toward us. He frowns and narrows his gaze. I act like this is completely normal, and it's not unusual for the guys to be sitting around me. I raise my hand to wave to him.

He lifts his hand to me, but the furrow remains on his brow. Damon brushes his fingertips down my nape, and an involuntary shiver rushes through me before I can stop it. Chase frowns, but his coach draws his attention back to the game.

Cam is talking to Mia, so I lean back against Damon's legs and turn my face slightly to him to say, "You're evil."

"You know it, little devil." He tugs my ponytail and I straighten.

We're probably drawing attention from the students around us, but I feel better knowing they're here with me. I don't think Jackson will show up at another football game. Last time could have been because we were playing his school. I don't know though.

Maybe I should have paid closer attention to him and where he went for high school. So I could keep track of things like that.

"Any new texts?" Hawk asks. He reaches over and tucks a strand of hair behind my ear.

I shake my head. "I blocked the number. Not that it will keep him from using another number."

My chest tightens. I don't know for sure it's Jackson, but I feel like it is. I don't know when he'll show up again. Maybe he won't.

Maybe he just wanted to scare me because I ghosted him. What if it's just a joke to him? And it's tearing me up inside for nothing?

I can't think about it. There's too much that needs to happen tonight at the party. I don't need to worry about him because I have the guys. They're going to protect me. Take care of me. Damon's shin rests against my back.

Mia turns to smile at me around her lollipop and give me a wink. She nudges me and jerks her chin toward the steps. I turn to look and see Olivia coming our way.

She comes down the aisle and stops directly in front of us. Her two friends stop behind her, effectively blocking the game.

"You're in the way," Damon says, leaning back against the bleachers behind him.

"Ha. Ha. Very funny, Damon." She glances at me. "I suppose you're as good a whore as any for him to use."

Mia stands and gets between me and Olivia. "My brother and I talk, Olivia." She looks Olivia up and down with disdain. "He said you were a decent fuck. A little too eager to get him into bed. Chase told him the only way to shut you up was to fuck your throat."

My breath catches. How long has she known about Chase and Olivia? Since that party when I found out about his cheating? But I continued to date him. She's supposed to be my friend. Why wouldn't she say anything?

"Whatever." Olivia gets up in Mia's face. "You don't belong here. You should go back to whatever public school rejected you."

Mia laughs and her face turns serious. "You don't know half of the shit that went down at my old school." Hands on her hips, she looks Olivia up and down like she's taking her measure. "Our queen bee doesn't offer people money to stop looking at her man. No, she gets real inventive. You wouldn't last a day there. She'd smack you down in an instant. If she didn't, someone else would put you in your place."

"Why am I not surprised? Violence is, of course, the answer. How common of you." Olivia looks at Mia like she's beneath her, but she doesn't back down. "You don't scare me, Mia. I've known girls like you all my life. The ones who can only get guys by putting out." She pouts. "How's that going for you here?"

"Just fine actually. Thanks for asking." Mia straightens and smiles politely. "Fuck off. No one wants you here."

Olivia glares at Mia before looking at Damon.

"Damon," she says it like he should stand up for her.

Damon leans forward and wraps his arms around my shoulders, resting his chin on my head. "Take a hint."

She stomps her foot and walks away. Her lackeys follow after her.

Mia sits back down as Damon straightens. He watches her warily, but she doesn't say anything to him. She does turn to me.

"When I told Tanner about Chase cheating on you last weekend, he told me what Chase told him about Olivia. I didn't want to say anything since you seemed to want to get back with the fucker." Mia shrugs. "I'm also not great at having female friends. And I didn't want to ruin our friendship."

I open my mouth, but I don't know what to say.

She sighs and looks up at Damon. "Nice move, by the way. Very possessive *grrr* energy. I approve."

"Mia..." What do I say?

"Evan, I thought I was hot shit at my last school." She blows out a breath. "My brother pulled a dickhead move with one of the top dog's sister. I didn't know the whole story until later. But he fucked up and deserved the shit they rained down on him. I thought he was just dating her because she was a freshman."

Her eyes glaze over as she stares at the football field.

"I didn't know how far he had taken it, or I would have beat his ass myself." She shakes her head and looks at me. "He's my brother. So I have to stand by him. I know none of this sounds good or like someone you'd want to be friends with. I also understand why you held things back from me."

She glances at Damon, Hawk, and Cam before returning her gaze to me.

"Honestly, I think they really like you. Trust me, I tested them to see if they could be led astray. I didn't even have to flirt five minutes with Chase to know he'd be all up on me if I let him." She shakes her head. "But I want you to know, I wouldn't take it there."

"I've never really had a friend since elementary school." I shrug. "I'm not sure how this whole thing works, but if you want to still be friends, I'm okay with it."

Damon lightly tugs my hair and I tip my face toward him. His eyes narrow slightly, and I can tell he's still not a Mia fan. I get it. Is she telling me all this to cover up any wrongdoings? Or is she being honest?

Only time will tell.

Chapter 25

Damon

Chase glances at us multiple times during the game. He didn't see me wrap around Evan since Olivia and her bitch brigade were standing between us and him. But I know Olivia wasn't the only one to see that time. She can keep thinking this is a game until I prove to her it isn't.

I don't care what she thinks as long as she leaves Evan alone.

Our team loses tonight. The football team isn't that great. Everyone files out of the stadium, and I keep a hand on Evan. It's too easy to get separated in a crowd like this. Cam ordered something that will help us track Evan, but it's not here yet.

I lean down to say in Evan's ear, "Ride with me to the party."

She glances up at me, and her eyes are filled with longing. "I shouldn't."

"Why not?"

"You're pushing it, Damon." She slows down so our bodies are a breath away from each other.

"I like pushing it, little devil." I wrap my hand around her hip.

She pulls away and smiles up at me. *Later,* she mouths before she hurries to catch up with Mia. When she grabs Mia's arm, she glances back at me.

Hawk steps up beside me and puts his hand on my shoulder. Cam is on my other side.

"We can follow them." He jerks his head toward our bikes.

I know I need to chill, but it feels like she's slipping through my fingers. That Jackson already has his sights on her and it's only a matter of time before I lose her too.

"Come on." Cam leads the way to the motorcycles.

We can maneuver better than Mia's car, and we're able to stay right behind them the whole way to Becca Anderson's house. She's Anteros, but she's having a party and she's rich, so it's going to be the place to be seen.

We pull up when Mia parks. She turns to look at us with a predatory smile. I'm not sure I believe any of the bullshit she fed Evan at the game. Maybe she really is trying to be a good friend and testing. But I know when a girl wants me, and Mia wants me. She may only want to fuck me, but she's willing to wait for her chance.

Mia's the kind of girl who would ask to spend the night with Evan and then crawl into my bed. I don't mess with girls like that.

We follow behind Mia and Evan as they walk up to the house. I keep an eye out for Jackson, but if he doesn't want me to see him, I won't. He's not like Chase. Chase can be a threat if we don't pay attention, but Jackson will be the threat we don't see coming.

Mia pulls Evan onto the dance floor and gets her to dance with her. Evan's eyes sparkle. I could drive a wedge between them so easily, but I know Evan wants a friend. Until Mia proves she's a disloyal bitch, I'll put up with her.

We move a little farther into the party, but I stop where I can still see Evan as Cam and Hawk go to scout the rest of the party. We need to figure out the quickest way out without being seen once we get the keys.

I wasn't joking when I said I want to fuck Evan in Chase's room.

His parents are already gone. We might run into issues with the security system, but Cam knows a guy who swears he can turn it off for us. The guy just wanted us to talk to a hockey player that's harassing him.

Easy enough.

A few girls stand near me, like they want to start a conversation, but I ignore them. There's only one girl I want. I keep my eyes on her, even when Olivia stops in front of me.

"I know what you're doing," she yells to be heard over the music.

I arch an eyebrow but don't look away from Evan. Olivia could have been the bitch in the car with Chase. I wish she'd bit his dick off and saved us all the trouble.

"You're trying to make me jealous," she says.

Hawk touches my back and moves into the room to take over watching Evan. I glance down at Olivia.

"And why would I do that?" I keep my tone even.

She smiles. "You want to make sure I'm into you. It's what I'd do."

She's lying. She doesn't think I'm doing that. Fucking fishing expedition, but I told her the truth already. Evan's mine and I'm hers.

"So did you lie about sucking Chase's cock?" I ask.

Her face twitches. "It was months ago. He was dating the little prude. We both hadn't had any for a while." She shrugs. "So yeah, I sucked his cock then rode it when we parked. I'm not ashamed of having sex."

"So you're back to Evan being a prude?" I cock my head at her as I stare into her blue eyes. It's possible she was the blond I saw with Chase. It was dark on the road that night.

"Why else would her boyfriend be cheating on her?" She can't meet my gaze though.

I lift my gaze to watch Evan again. If I look back over everything, she's always been honest with us. Never played a game. Sure, she didn't say she was a virgin and didn't know what the fuck she was doing, but we really didn't give her a chance to either.

Evan was the whore in the car with Chase. The interloper moving into my house with her mother. Friends with a girl who offered guys a blow job on day one at a new school. I didn't know then that they were all using her.

To me, she was someone I could use to punish the people who wronged me. Now, she's mine. Ours, because without Cam and Hawk, I might have broken Evan before I got to know her.

"See? This is why I think you're messing with me. She's nothing. She wouldn't even suck her boyfriend's dick. What kind of girl does that?" Olivia glances toward where I'm looking and rolls her eyes with a huff. "I get it. You want me to be so fucking jealous I start a girl fight or something. Is that what you want Damon?" She pauses and her tone changes. "Or maybe it isn't a girl *fight* you want."

I glance down at her. She's watching Evan with an evil little smirk.

"Maybe you want a threesome with the little prude? Maybe we can liquor her up and take her in one of the rooms upstairs." She moves closer to me and puts her hand on my arm. "I can hold her down while you do what you want to her. I don't mind making her cry. If you want, I can go down on her while you fuck me. I'm willing to be what you want."

Fuck this girl. Anger boils through me. I'm not a fucking rapist.

"Don't go anywhere near Evan," I bite out. "I'm not going to rape her."

"It's not like she wouldn't want it." Olivia tsks. "If you don't want her to cry, I have pills we can give her. Tanner was nice enough to give me a stash for sucking his cock. He gave one to me that night. It's a good trip. Made me want it so bad. The things I let him do to me... We could all take one. The two of us can worship your body all night long."

Every word out of her mouth makes me want to fuck up her life even more. Our plan is to make her blow up and get it on video. I need her to go full nuclear when it happens because even if I can prove she has illegal drugs, her parents would buy her out of any trouble she might find herself in with law enforcement.

But if I get her on video saying this kind of shit. Something no one could ignore or sweep under the rug. Push her to make sure she can't show her face at school again. Especially if everyone knows, the school would be forced to expel her.

That she thinks I'd be okay raping someone just solidifies our plan to take her down.

We need her angry enough tomorrow to really lay into me.

"While I appreciate the offer, I'm not into rape of any kind."

Olivia's mouth opens, and she turns to look at Evan. "It's not like she wouldn't want it. But sure, if that's not your thing, I get it. I want to give you what you want. You're a hard guy to figure out. You wouldn't even let me suck your dick."

She pouts up at me like that's going to make me want her anywhere close to me.

Chase walks in with some football players. Mia and Evan have started for the kitchen.

I need to shake Olivia permanently or at least until tomorrow night. Because tomorrow night I'll find a way to neutralize her for good.

"You want me?" I meet her eyes, and she smiles, but looks skeptical.

If she were smarter, she wouldn't trust me. But she's so fucking lust-blinded, she'll do anything I want.

"Find me a willing girl for tomorrow and we'll do exactly what you want. The three of us." I straighten from the wall. "I have shit to do tonight though."

"Any girl I want?" Her eyes light up.

"Yeah, you pick the girl and tomorrow at Chase's party we'll party in his room."

Olivia narrows her gaze. "You aren't tricking me, right?"

"I guess we'll find out tomorrow."

EvanAnn

We're in the kitchen when Chase finds me and Mia. Mia's flirting with Wayne, who came up to talk to me, but she drew him into a conversation with her. If I were single, I might have mixed feelings about it, but right now, I'm just grateful she did before Damon decided to claim me again.

"What are we doing tonight?" Chase asks and glances in the backyard where there's a beer pong table set up.

"It's a nice night. Let's go outside." I turn and head out, knowing he'll follow me. Mia's fingers brush mine. I smile at her and she gives me a wink before talking more to Wayne.

Chase puts his fingers on my waist, but I don't pull away. This time I'm using him. I'm no longer a pawn in his game. We go outside and, as I suspected, there's a bunch of Anteros kids out here. And some of my cast is at the beer pong table already.

I head in that direction figuring he'd want to talk to our classmates too. The beer pong is the ultimate goal, anyway.

"Hey," I say to Jason, who's watching the game.

He smiles and holds his fist out to Chase. Chase bumps it while Jason says, "Glad to see you guys. You planning on playing?"

He nods to the table and the cups. Perfect. I couldn't have scripted it better myself.

"I was planning on hanging with EvanAnn tonight." Chase's fingers ghost over the small of my back like he's worried I'll pull away if he actually touches me.

"I've heard you're the best at it." Jason smiles at both of us. It's almost like Jason knows the role I need him to play.

"Yeah," Hawk says. "Chase is the best?"

We both turn as Hawk joins us.

"I think it's time that Iago and Cassio get a chance to take each other on in a fair fight." Hawk smirks. "Winner gets the girl."

"I'm not winnable, Hawk." I roll my eyes and step closer to Chase, letting him think he has a claim on me. That I need him to protect me.

"Aren't you, Annie?" His smile is so knowing my insides tumble over themselves.

I turn and put my hand on Chase's chest. I smile up at him. "You should play, Chase. It's a good team-building exercise. And maybe I'll give the winner a kiss. And we all know who the winner will be."

I don't shift my gaze from Chase's, and he grins. I've watched him play, and if he's playing to win, he'll be focused.

"Fine. You're on."

Someone has reset the table for the next game. Hawk takes one end, and Chase takes the other. Hawk reaches in his pocket and holds out his keys to me.

"Here, Annie, hold my keys. Don't want anything to disrupt my game."

I take them from him and turn to Chase. He takes his keys out of his pocket and hands them to me. I nearly grin at how easy that turned out to be. But we have plans.

I open my purse and put both sets of keys inside. The guys move into position and people gather around to watch. Mostly Anteros kids but a few hockey players stand on Hawk's side.

"Best three out of five." Hawk bounces the ball, and it lands in the cup. A small cheer fills the air.

Chase fishes out the ball and downs the beer. "Fine."

I watch as they slowly go through both sets of cups. There isn't much beer in each cup. Hawk winks at me as he bounces the ball and it lands in Chase's last cup.

While they're resetting the game, I go to Chase. "I need to go to the bathroom. I'll be back."

He nods and glares at Hawk. "Don't worry. I'll win for you, babe."

I let the *babe* slide since he's had alcohol. When I touch his arm, he puts his hand on mine.

"I'm definitely winning that kiss."

I give him a smile before moving through the crowd. The party isn't as out of control as Fletcher's was, but there are still a lot of people. So much could go wrong with this plan, but everything in me is alert and aware. When I enter the house, Cam meets me and guides me through a quieter section of the house and out a side door. My helmet sits on a chair next to the door. He grabs it and puts it on me.

My heart is racing. Damon's already on the bike with it running.

"I'll text if something happens and you need to get back." His brown eyes search mine before he lowers my face shield.

I climb on the back of Damon's bike and wrap around him. He goes faster than he usually does when I'm on the back of his bike. I cling to him as he leans into turns and shoots down empty roads. It's like that first time with Hawk all over again.

Everything inside me braces for impact, even though Damon would never do anything to hurt me.

When we stop at Chase's house, I climb off and remove my helmet. Damon sets it with his on the bike and looks at his phone. My hands feel clammy as I glance around to make sure no one is out and sees us. Damon holds out his other hand, and I take Chase's keys out of my purse. I almost fumble them as I put them in his hand.

He catches them and my hand. Our gazes lock and I take a deep breath to help with my nerves. His phone beeps and he releases me.

"Okay, we're clear." He pockets his phone and takes my hand, leading me to the house.

My heart beats so fast. We could get caught. Any number of things could go wrong, but this is what we need to do for Damon to get his revenge. I hate what Chase did to him and what Chase tried to do to me.

Damon unlocks the door, and I take the lead, hurrying up the stairs and taking a few turns before we get to Chase's bedroom. When we step in, it's just like I remember it. Very masculine with his stuff everywhere. But tidy, probably because of the maids.

Damon moves to the corners. "See what you can find while I set these up."

I nod and go to Chase's nightstand. The drawer is filled with condoms and lube and other things I'd rather not think about along with a few magazines. Reluctantly, I take the magazines and flip through them to make sure he didn't leave a note or something in them.

As Damon positions the camera, he checks the angle on his phone. It's weird being back in here. Over the summer, I figured eventually this might be where I lost my virginity.

Chase's cologne fills the space. Would he have made it soft and gentle? Would I have liked that? Or would I have been so nervous it just would have been painful anyway?

I shake my head and walk over to Chase's desk. Damon catches my hip and tips my chin up so our eyes lock. "Did you expect to have sex in this room with Chase?"

I shrug and heat floods my cheeks. Now I know I was a fool. "He was my boyfriend."

Damon rubs his thumb over my bottom lip. "It's a shame."

Smirking, he moves to put up another camera. I take a breath to slow my pulse and sit at the desk to go through his stuff. Chase doesn't seem like the type to write down his evil plan though.

"What am I looking for again?" I glance at Damon.

He smiles as he checks the camera. "Something we can use against Chase. We know about the party. We know he wants you for some reason other than sex."

I narrow my eyes at him.

"We need anything we can use against him socially to drag him down." Damon finally looks at my disgruntled frown. He smirks. "Bitter because Chase didn't want to fuck you?"

"Honestly?" I blow out a breath. "No. I would have fucked him, but it's not like..."

Damon grins and steps away from the wall. "Not like us?"

Heat floods me.

"We've got time if you want to put on a show." Damon sets the camera and stalks toward me. He sucks the air away with every inch.

"What do you think?" He pulls me to stand, catches the back of my neck, and tips my chin up. "Want to make a porn, little devil?"

Chapter 26

EvanAnn

My mouth opens and closes. "We don't have time to fuck around. We'll be missed at the party if we don't head back soon. Besides, I thought tomorrow was the big show."

He lowers his head. "Consider this dress rehearsal."

"Damon—"

He kisses me, cutting off my weak protest. Every time he touches me, he drives me crazy with need. And now is no exception. I thread my fingers into his hair and push up on my toes.

He lifts me onto the desk, pushing papers onto the floor without releasing my mouth.

When I part my legs, he slides his hands over my ass, drawing me in close to him so I can feel how hard he is for me. My pussy throbs with need.

"You want to get your own revenge?" He kisses down my neck and nips at my shoulder.

I drag in a breath as I try to find some control.

"I didn't exactly dress for it." Why did I wear jeans? I run my hands over his hips.

"Get on your knees, little devil."

I lift my gaze to his blue eyes and slide off the desk as he backs up. I lower to my knees in front of him. My insides buzz with anticipation of what he gives me and the anxiety of getting caught. I undo his belt and jeans, pushing them down, while his fingers caress my face.

When I draw out his cock, I lift my gaze to his before leaning forward to take him in.

"Fuck, I love your mouth." He groans as I work his cock with my tongue and lips. I've had time to figure out exactly what each of them likes.

"He's fucking stupid to not take what you offer so beautifully." Damon grabs my ponytail and wraps it around his fist. I get so wet I'm sure my panties are ruined. I never offered Chase any of me. Not like I have with the Devil's trio.

He tugs on my hair, and I relax, placing my hands on his thighs and looking up at him. I know what he wants. Everything inside me wants him to take me. I want whatever he wants to do to me. No matter how filthy.

He holds my head as he thrusts his cock into my mouth, pushing in deep until I gag a little. He works his way up to fucking my throat, while I lick and suck when I can.

"Such a good little cum slut. You're going to swallow every last drop, aren't you, little devil?"

I hum my affirmation around his cock, and he groans as he comes in my mouth. When he releases my hair, I suck and lick to get every drop, keeping my gaze locked on his. He jerks me up and backs me against the wall, taking my mouth with his.

This kiss is all lips, tongues, and teeth. I taste him as he undoes my jeans and slides his hand down the front of my panties. He lifts his mouth and rests his forehead against mine as he slides his fingers over my pussy before pressing two inside me. I gasp at the stretch of him inside me.

"He never gets to see this. Never gets to watch you fall apart under his touch. It's mine."

I open my eyes to his blue eyes searching me.

"You're mine, little devil."

"I'm yours." I stroke my hands beneath his shirt, up his back.

"Fuck." He fucks me with his fingers, hiding me from the cameras and watching every expression of pleasure crossing my face. "Come for me, Evan."

I grab his arm as the tension winds tight and explodes. My moan fills the quiet room.

"So fucking sexy." He kisses me and pulls his hand out of my pants. He sucks his fingers to get the taste of me in his mouth, before he kisses me again. I can taste both of us. My heart races, and my breathing is uneven as he pulls away.

After we straighten our clothes, I notice the papers on the floor and pick them up. As I sort through them, Damon picks up some pens that must have dropped at the same time. It's all rehearsal notes and pages. Until the last page.

I stare at the list of colleges. Chase said he didn't want to go to college after high school. But there's something about this list that makes my stomach churn.

"What is it?" Damon looks over my shoulder at the list.

"These are the colleges I've applied to." Why would he have this? "I never told him where I applied to school."

"Maybe he paid attention and made a list." Damon slides his hands around my waist and rests his chin on my head.

I shake my head and point to the last one. "I added this one a week ago. No one else knows I applied here."

Damon takes the piece of paper and takes a quick picture with his phone. "We need to leave."

I nod, but the list bothers me. Why would he have that and how is it accurate? I don't have time to think about it now. We have to get back.

Damon takes my hand to lead me out. When we get to his bike, he claims my mouth.

"We're going to fuck you properly tonight." He promises as he puts my helmet on and fixes the strap. He offers me a mint, and I pop it in my mouth.

With his helmet in place, he straddles the bike. Closing my face shield, I climb on back and wrap around him, loving that his scent covers me. That when I'm standing next to Chase he could smell what we did if he ever bothered to notice. As we fly down the night streets, I enjoy the rush of what we got away with. So far.

We pull up to the side of the house where the party is in full swing. Damon takes off my helmet, and Cam comes out the side door.

Damon revs his engine as Cam and I slip inside. After the door shuts, Cam presses me back against the wall and kisses me. I grab his shirt and hold on. Fuck, I wish I could have them all every night. But tonight, I'll get my wish.

"Did you have fun, goody?" He kisses my cheek and backs away.

"I'll have more fun later."

He smirks and takes my hand. "Yeah, you will."

When we approach the party, he releases my hand. We slip inside, going separate ways. I head out to the beer pong table where Cam and Hawk are still going at it. More people surround the game, egging them on. It takes me a few minutes to reach Chase's side.

"Hey, babe." He smiles, more than a little tipsy. "One more game and I'll win."

Hawk smirks at us. "Probably not."

How much have they had to drink?

"I'm not feeling that well, Chase. I'm going to have Mia take me home." I reach into my purse and hand Hawk his keys before turning to hand Chase his.

He grabs my wrist. "Then I want my prize."

"You didn't win yet, Chase. I'll give you your prize tomorrow." I tug on my wrist and glare at him. "Let me go."

He winds me in. "Just a peck, babe. For luck."

He's definitely stronger than me. I try digging my heels in. No part of me wants him to kiss me, especially not in front of Hawk.

Suddenly, Hawk is between us, in Chase's face.

"She said no, asshole. Let her go."

Chase releases me and straightens. "I'm the asshole?"

"Yeah."

"At least I'm the one offering to be EvanAnn's boyfriend and not just toying with her." Chase runs a hand through his hair and glares at Hawk. "He's just messing with you, babe. He doesn't really want you any more than he wants any of these girls. Oh, sure he'll fuck you, but he doesn't do relationships."

I put my hand on Hawk's back because I know he's getting angry. He's held back going after Chase this long. It's just a little longer and we'll get revenge on him.

His back muscles flex beneath my touch. "It's not much of a relationship if you're off fucking other girls behind her back, is it?"

The crowd makes noises, some surprised, most not, but I'm focused on Hawk. Cam moves through the crowd and steps between Chase and Hawk.

"You two need to chill out. Everyone go find someone else to fuck." Cam pushes Hawk back, and I stumble back to not get trampled.

An arm wraps around my waist, and I jerk.

"Little devil." Damon says it so softly I barely hear him, but he draws me back against him into a darkened corner. "Time to leave."

I nod and turn to leave with him. I'm sure Cam and Hawk will meet us.

Damon

We pull into the garage. The house has some lights on, but that's not unusual for this time of night. She follows me. We're still trying to stay under our parents' radars, and my dad's car was in the garage.

"Out late again?" My dad's voice. I freeze, and Evan stumbles behind me into his view. "EvanAnn?"

He looks between us like he's figuring shit out. Fuck.

"I called Damon to pick me up." Evan steps forward. "My designated driver decided to drink too much."

My dad's face clears. If I'd said that, would he have believed me? I keep my face blank even as the anger churns to the surface.

Evan turns to me. "Thank you for the ride. Good night."

She walks away from us, heading to the stairs.

"Sorry, I thought you were out partying late again." Dad runs his hand through his hair. That's the first time he's said he's sorry in a long time. "Is everything okay with her?"

The muscles in my jaw twitch. Now he's worried about Evan? It's been weeks since she moved in. They didn't think anything of putting her right under my thumb. I want to yell at him and her mother, but if I start, I'll spill everything.

And he'll take her away from me. I'm never letting that happen. I draw in a steadying breath.

"She's fine. She's smart and driven and doesn't want to fuck up her future by getting into a moving vehicle with someone who's been drinking." I straighten. "I'm heading to bed. It's late."

Dad nods. "We should have a conversation tomorrow."

"Scrimmage and then I'm busy with schoolwork."

"Sunday dinner, then." Dad steps forward. "You have to eat."

"Fine." I turn and walk away.

I go to my room just in case he follows me, but he doesn't. I lock the door and pass through the bathroom to find Evan sitting cross-legged on her bed, plucking at the comforter.

"Quick thinking." I sit on the edge of the bed next to her.

She smiles. "Improv. It comes in handy every now and then."

We both stare at the door like someone's going to knock it down and split us up. Does she worry about that? That if we come out, our parents will try to force us apart?

They can try, but nothing will keep me from Evan. Especially not Jackson Riordan.

When I grabbed her, she jerked at the party.

"How bad was it when I grabbed you?" I watch her face. She's good at lying, but she's got tells. Her eyes try to slip from mine before she makes them focus when she wants to lie to me.

She sighs. "It only took me a moment to realize it was you." She lifts her gaze to mine. "Honestly, I didn't have any issues until I got those texts. Seeing him was messed up, but it was easy enough to put that down to chance."

Except it wasn't. I put my hand on her leg, and she puts her hand over mine. But I don't say anything, hoping she'll give me more. More of herself.

"I figured it was years ago and he'd moved on. I definitely didn't encourage him." She breathes out. "He grabbed me and kissed me before I could even register what was happening. But I felt trapped and frozen, unable to get myself out of that situation. I thought I'd gotten past it." She shakes her head.

I turn my hand over and tug her hand toward me. Without hesitation, she crawls to my lap, straddling me. I release her ponytail from the holder, and her blond hair falls around her shoulders. Soft and beautiful, just like Evan. I comb my fingers through it.

She leans into my touch like she always does. It settles the burning inside me. When Chase grabbed her, I didn't think. I would have beat him worse than last weekend. But Hawk got in his face. Cam broke them up, pushing Evan back toward me. So I took her.

The others know. I met Cam's eyes before I ushered her out. There were too many people trying to see the potential fight for all of us to disappear at once. The others will be along.

"Should we go somewhere else?" She runs her thumbs along my jaw, her hands around my neck. She glances at her door. "Our parents are here."

"They aren't going to interrupt us, little devil." I turn her chin back my way. "But if you want, I can ask Hawk if his parents are home. We can go there."

Her cheeks flush as she meets my eyes. "I don't want to worry about them coming to talk to us or have to be quiet."

I smirk. "We wouldn't want that."

Chapter 27

Hawk

The ride home doesn't cool me off. Fucking Chase Chadwick. If Cam hadn't stepped in the way, I would have kicked his ass for daring to touch Annie and not respecting her when she said to let go. It wasn't at school, so I wouldn't have gotten in trouble, but with the play, it could have fucked things up.

Knowing Annie is in my bedroom waiting for me helps with the anger. Because in the end I get to win the girl. She's mine, not Chase's, and we're the only ones she's going to kiss.

Cam pulls in behind me, and we head into the house. The hallways are dark on the way up to my room. I open my bedroom door.

When I stop in the doorway, Cam comes up beside me. Annie and Damon are topless, kissing. Obviously warming up. She straddles him on the edge of my bed. They're so into it, they didn't even hear us come in. Fuck.

Her hands tangle in his hair as she arches her neck for him to kiss down it. His hands cup her ass, holding her tight against him. She lets out this little whimper that always drives me fucking wild.

My cock grows harder. I need her now. To fuck her cunt open for us. To flood her with my cum. To claim her as mine.

I take off my shirt and strip out of my pants and boxers on the way to my bed. I pull Annie's head back by her hair and catch her surprised gasp in my mouth. When her tongue slides against mine, something inside me settles. This is my prize. Fuck that asshole for thinking she could ever be his.

I lift her from Damon, setting her on her feet. His chuckle is dark. Her breast is wet against my chest from Damon sucking on it. As I strip her jeans and wet panties off, she grabs my cock, stroking it. Her face is flushed with desire. Her lips swollen.

Fuck, I need her. When I lift her, she wraps her legs around my waist. Holding her in the middle of my bedroom, I slide my cock against her clit before notching it at her entrance. Pressing my forehead to hers, I wait until her eyes open and meet mine. She whimpers, and I thrust deep inside. So fucking tight.

When she gasps against my mouth, I smile.

"Hawk," she whispers.

I back her to the wall, bracing her body against it with mine, and grab her hands to hold next to her head. "Do you think I'm toying with you, baby girl?"

Chase's words cut to the quick. Fuck that asshole for assuming what this means to me. What she means to me. We might have started there, but we've gone so far beyond toying with each other.

She shakes her head as she squirms against me to get motion, rocking her hips, but I have her pressed tight against the wall. She tightens her cunt around me.

"Use your words." My voice is firm, demanding.

She whimpers. "No, I don't think you're toying with me."

"Tell me you're mine." I drag my cock out until just the tip is inside her.

"I'm yours." Those stormy blue eyes meet mine and don't stray to my friends. Right now, she's all mine. She wets her lips. "Make me come. Please, Hawk. I need it. I want your cum so deep inside me."

Fucking perfection. I capture her lips and thrust into her hard.

"Again," she whispers against my mouth. "Please."

I pull out and thrust in deep over and over again. It's not romantic. It's a fucking claiming. She matches me, trying to take me deeper. Our kiss is almost brutal as we fuck. Finally, she cries out in my mouth. Her pussy milks my cock with her release as she trembles against me.

"Please, please, please," she whispers, pressing kisses against my lips and jaw with every word. Begging me so prettily, it makes my balls ache.

I thrust a few more times, feeling my release swell before I come inside her. Her hands clutch at mine as we stare at each other. Our breathing is chaotic. Our bodies still joined. Hers pulses around mine in aftershocks.

"He touched you, baby girl." I search her eyes.

"He wouldn't let go." She rests her head back against the wall. "Thank you for protecting me."

"For you. Always." I lift her and walk over to the bed where Cam and Damon wait, naked. I pull out and lower her feet to the floor. "Now show them how grateful you are."

EvanAnn

I reach up and grab the back of Hawk's neck to pull him down to kiss me. The way he fucked me was almost desperate, and I loved every minute of it. His hands rest on my hips as we kiss, but then he pulls away.

When I turn to the others and move toward Cam, he shakes his head and grabs a bottle of lube. My insides churn. I climb onto Damon's lap and kiss him. He claims my mouth as I sink onto his cock. My lips part. Fuck, this is what I need. I need more. I want more.

To be connected to them so thoroughly. I rock my hips against his, and he slides his hands over my ass. Tonight is about taking them all. They may have set out to claim me, but fuck if

I'm not going to claim them back. Here, in this room, with all of them.

I need them all inside me. He lies back and pulls me down with him. My pussy pulses around his cock as Cam slides his slick fingers between my ass cheeks. I shiver against Damon and turn to meet Cam's eyes. He spreads lube around my asshole before pushing two fingers inside.

I moan, still sensitive from the rough fuck against the wall with Hawk.

"You ready for us, little devil?" Damon pushes his hand through my hair, brushing it behind my ear. My hips rock with every thrust of Cam's fingers, shifting on Damon's cock too. I'm on fire and ready to burn with them.

"I've waited my whole life for you." I lean down and take his mouth with mine as Cam works his fingers in and out of my ass. It feels like I've been holding my breath for years and now I can finally breathe. They let me breathe.

Damon kisses me like he needs me just as much. I rest against his chest as Cam works me until I want more, need more. I'm on the edge when he draws his fingers out. A whimper escapes me at the loss, then Cam spreads my ass cheeks apart.

"I've got you. If you need me to stop, you tell me, goody. Just say anything and I'll stop." Cam is right behind me and the blunt tip of his cock presses on my asshole.

I hold my breath. So ready for this, but afraid at the same time.

"Breathe, baby girl." Hawk slides his thumb across my lip. "Breathe and relax."

I take his thumb into my mouth and suck while meeting his green eyes. Cam eases his cock into my ass slowly. It burns, but I can feel his cock pushing in next to Damon's with only a thin wall separating them. It's different than someone fucking me with the plug in my ass.

"Fuck, you're so fucking tight, goody." Cam pulls my ass cheeks apart as he sinks in deeper.

I moan at the burn of him pushing past the ring of muscles.

Damon breathes out, blowing my hair. His hands flex on my sides. "I can feel you making her even tighter around my cock. Fuck."

Hawk pulls his thumb out of my mouth and presses his cock against my lips. "Let us all in, baby girl."

I part my lips and take him inside, sucking to make taking Cam easier. Cam thrusts in the final inch. I groan at how full I feel. We all pause for a second as we take in that we're all connected.

Warmth blossoms in my stomach and spreads through me. While I adjust to feeling Cam and Damon inside me, Hawk fucks my mouth. Not rough, just slow and easy. I suck and lick, feeling my body pulse around the cocks buried within.

"Such a good little slut." Hawk presses in deeper, and I relax my throat to let him in. He thrusts a few more times before coming with a groan. I swallow around his cock with my eyes locked on his.

Hawk backs away as the others adjust. Damon presses to sit up and then he's lifting me. I wrap my legs around his waist and my hands around his neck. He stands with Cam, and they both slide in deeper.

I press my lips against Damon's chest and suck on his skin. He'll be covered with my marks tomorrow. Pleasure bursts through me thinking about them. Hidden below his jersey, but I'll know they're there. That I've left my mark on him. That he's mine.

They start moving slowly at first. Cam pulls out and sinks back in. Damon curses and pulls out before he thrusts back inside. I'm so full I can't think of anything else as I cling to Damon. When I bite his chest, he hisses.

"Pull out while I thrust." Cam pulls out.

When he thrusts back inside, Damon pulls out. I suck in a breath at the way that makes my body sing and moan on the next thrust. Fuck.

"You're amazing, goody. Taking our cocks."

They fall into a rhythm as I hold onto Damon. Cam slips his hand between Damon and me to slide a finger over my clit. I can't stop the overwhelming orgasm that surges through me, taking my breath, as I pulse around them.

Cam groans, and warmth floods me. I can't move as they press me between them. All I can do is feel.

"Fuck," Damon whispers. "I can feel that."

"Me too." I tug his head down to mine, capturing his mouth, and he thrusts a few times before he's coming inside me too.

"Fuck, that's…" Cam says.

"Exactly." Damon kisses me.

After pressing kisses to the nape of my neck and my shoulders, Cam pulls out and heads to the bathroom. Damon holds me in the middle of the room. His cock is still hard inside me.

Hawk steps up behind me. "Look at how pretty your ass looks wrecked."

I turn my head and catch his green eyes. "Take me. I want to feel you inside me."

His eyes darken. "You sure you want me to wreck this ass more, baby girl?"

His fingers slide over my asshole, and I clench at the burst of pleasure that spirals through me. I want more, to feel them fill me over and over again.

Biting my lip, I rest my head against Damon's chest. I ache at how empty I feel. "Yes, do it. Please, I want to feel you inside me."

He rubs his cock with lube. My breath catches as his tip presses against my hole and eases in steadily.

My mouth opens as he stretches me open. A whine works its way out of my throat.

Damon kisses my shoulder. "Such a good little cum slut."

"Your cum slut." I tangle my fingers in his hair. So happy to be theirs, to be able to please them.

He gives me a cocky smile. "I'm going to fuck you all night."

Hawk thrusts in deep, and both Damon and I groan.

"You good, baby girl?" Hawk kisses my shoulder blade.

"Mm-hmm." It's intense, the burn, the stretch, the feeling of them both inside me.

"After this, we're going to keep fucking you." Damon pulls out to thrust back in. "We'll take turns so we get some sleep for the scrimmage tomorrow."

"You can sleep if you want, baby girl. I'll still fuck this ass or your pussy." Hawk's words light me on fire as he begins to fuck my ass in rhythm with Damon. My breathing is ragged.

"Feel free to use us if we fall asleep, little devil." Damon tips my chin up. "I like waking up to you fucking me."

Hawk thrusts a little harder into my ass and I moan. Fuck, it feels so good, so full. I wrap my arm around Hawk's neck and lean back into him, turning so he can kiss the side of my mouth. Cam returns from the bathroom and sits on the edge of the bed. He fists his cock and watches the guys fuck me.

"You take cock so well, goody." His dark eyes flick up to mine for a second, like he doesn't want to miss anything.

My chest swells with heat as I fall over the edge. Everything tightens and stars erupt behind my closed eyes. I cry out to release some of the tension building inside me. It doesn't feel like I'll ever come down.

And I don't want to. I want to stay in this moment forever.

Chapter 28

Hawk

I lean on the counter waiting for Annie to come out of the water closet. She's barely slept. None of us have. The temptation of her body is too much.

There's still enough time to get a few hours before we have to be up for the scrimmage. I'm tempted to sleep with my cock buried inside her.

Annie steps out of the water closet wearing my Devils t-shirt, and walks over to the sink to wash her hands. Her eyes stay on mine, even though I'm not wearing a stitch of clothes.

"Where are your parents?" She turns and dries her hands. "Why aren't they here?"

I blow out a breath and pull her over in front of me, my hands on the hem of the shirt and the softness of her thighs. Her eyes search mine.

"They travel."

"For work?" She puts her hands on my chest, and I draw her hips against mine.

"And other things?" I cock my head to the side. "You worried about me, baby girl?"

"It's just unusual."

I blow out a breath. "They're kind of separated. So when one of them is here, the other is usually gone. I guess they got used to always being away to avoid each other."

"What about you?" She slides her hand up to my neck and rubs her thumb against a hickey she left there.

I smirk. "Haven't you heard? I'm the golden boy who can do no wrong?" The words taste bitter in my mouth. "I'm the one my friends' fathers wish my friends were more like. That mothers point out to their daughters as someone who's going somewhere in his life. What do I need parents for?"

She wraps her arms around my neck and hugs me.

I shake my head and pull her in close to me, smelling her hair. "What's this for?"

"You're more than that." She rests her face against my chest. "I need you, Hawk. I need you to make me beg you. To fuck me so hard I'm going to be sore tomorrow. To sleep with me and wake me up with your head between my thighs."

I chuckle. "You've got two other guys who can do that for you."

She lets out a little huff and looks up at me. "It's more than sex. Right? I like holding your hand and riding on the back of your motorcycle. I love talking Shakespeare with you and watching you perform. I like when you put your arm around my shoulders and claim me as yours. There's more here."

The uncertainty in her voice has me taking notice. "Your mom hasn't been around much either. Has she?"

Her lips press together, and I know she's going to defend her mother. It's what Annie does. It's why she tries to defend me.

"You don't have to lie to me," I say softly as I cup her jaw and look into her eyes. "I know it hurts. That you do everything to make her life easier, so she won't need to worry about you. But sometimes you wished she'd slow down and notice. Not just praise you for your accomplishments but see you."

"Hawk?" Her voice trembles as she looks up at me. The lights in here are dim and make her eyes almost appear silver.

"Yeah, Annie."

"Do you think they'll notice you?" The question is simple and it pierces my heart. I know what she's going through because I do it too.

"They do. It's just not often." I lift her onto the counter and step between her legs. She puts her hands on my jaw, and I lower my forehead to touch hers. "It's difficult when you make their lives easy. I'm sure they haven't forgotten about us. And they'll be there for the big things."

"I'll be here for the small things." She lifts her mouth and touches her lips to mine. "And the big things and the ordinary things. I want to be with you for all the things."

Something clicks into place inside me. "I want that too, baby girl."

EvanAnn

Thankfully, the rink is cold as I lower myself onto the seat a little gingerly. Everything aches. They took me every way they could last night. I woke in a tangle of limbs with Damon fucking my ass.

I came so hard I screamed. My voice is a little hoarse this morning even after drinking tea.

"You sure you feel better? You seem a little off still." Mia sits next to me in the hockey rink. "Maybe you shouldn't drink at parties if you keep getting sick."

I haven't been drinking at parties. I've been sneaking away to fuck the Devil's trio. My pussy clenches, and I almost groan at the ache. Yeah, we might need to take a little break.

"Just a little exhaustion from all the work." I try to keep the heat from my cheeks.

"You work so hard. We have our history project to do this afternoon. Tell me if you want me to leave you with either or both. Fuck, you want those guys, I'll negotiate terms for you." Mia seems a little too eager. But I don't need anyone to negotiate for them, they're mine.

"I'm good. Besides, we have the party with Chase tonight." Also I don't think I can take another cock right now. But if Cam, Hawk, or Damon asked, I'd try. My insides spark as the guys skate out onto the ice. I could always use my mouth and so could they.

"I know. It's such a difficult school. It's a wonder anyone has time for anything but a quickie between assignments." Mia watches the guys.

"Have you started decorating your room?" I ask, trying to steer the conversation to something besides my guys or the players she wants to fuck. It seems like that's all we talk about. As I think about it, it kind of is.

"A little." Mia glances toward me. "Honestly, I'm not very good at decorating. You just moved too, right?"

"Yeah. I haven't done much. The house kind of runs on its own. I didn't even have to unpack. It's so different from what I'm used to. I think they even unpacked the box that didn't get unpacked the last two moves."

Damon flies by and shoots a puck into the net. My attention gets captured watching him, Hawk, and Cam warm up. They glide around each other as they skate. So in sync. My insides warm. They definitely figured out how to be in sync last night. I cross my legs, not sure if the ache is pain or want.

"They really are gorgeous." Mia sighs. "Are you sure you want to give Chase a second chance? Because I'm sure any of them would be better for you than him. Even if it's only for a night."

Last night was like sinking into pleasure. Every moment they took me from one orgasm to the next. It was intense, but there were moments where things slowed down. Where it was just me and Hawk and him taking me slowly on the bed, sinking into me over and over. Or Cam and I in the bathroom. He took his time cleaning me up before I begged him to fuck me again. Our eyes locked. Breathing the same breath.

The guys skate back to their bench as they prepare to start the game.

"Hey, Mia, right?"

My blood freezes. My breath catches as my chest tightens.

"Oh, hey, Jackson." Mia is all smiles. "Are you here to scope out the competition?"

"Of course." His voice is all charm.

I don't turn around, but everything inside me wants to run. My finger scratches at my jeans. I can move. I can leave. But then he might get me alone. That can't happen.

"You can sit next to me." Mia grins. At least he didn't sit beside me.

He steps over the back of the seats and sits down, leaning forward to see me around Mia. "Hey, Evan."

"How do you know each other?" Mia asks.

"Elementary school." Jackson smiles. "She was the pretty blond with pigtails, and I was the kid too nervous to tell her I thought she was pretty."

I take a breath and turn to meet his dark eyes. Was it all fake? The laughter? The sweetness? He acted like he really liked me, but was it all obsession?

He smiles like we're old friends. "Honestly, I had the biggest crush on her, but she never noticed me."

I narrow my eyes on him. He's not mentioning that summer. Maybe it didn't mean anything to him. Maybe I was just an available girl.

"She's currently trying to make amends with her cheating boyfriend. You should convince her she shouldn't give him another chance." Mia wiggles her eyebrows.

"I'm okay, really." I don't want his attention. Let him focus on Mia.

Mia gives me an odd look but then turns to smile at Jackson. "She's shy, but I've told her that once a cheater, always a cheater."

"You're full of all sorts of good advice." Jackson chuckles, but his gaze strays to me, and there's an intensity that's unsettling. Am I just imagining it? I don't think so.

Something bangs against the boards in front of us. I jerk my gaze and meet Hawk's green eyes before he spins away from the guy he shoved against the boards.

When I swallow, something settles inside me. They're here. They'll protect me. I just have to stay here and not leave the game. He can't get me here.

But after the game, the guys will go down to the locker room together, leaving me with just Mia as backup. She doesn't know Jackson might be dangerous to me, but we're in public.

"I didn't realize Evan went to your school until my team played yours in a scrimmage."

Mia looks like she's buying his sugarcoated words. But she doesn't know him or about the texts he's sent me. Should I confront him? Ask him why he sent them?

Would I sound like a crazy person if it's not him? Because as much as the guys and I believe it's him, is that because he's the only suspect? There are people who don't like me, like Brandt. He might fuck with my mind to get me off my game for the showcase. Olivia definitely doesn't like me, but she's already offered to buy me off, so I don't think she's moved to scare tactics yet.

It might just be a coincidence Jackson realized I still exist. Maybe he just wants to apologize for frightening me. Maybe he really hasn't thought of me at all since that summer.

"Are you still acting?" Jackson asks.

I'm not being hunted. This is standard catching up talk. "I direct now."

"She's the best at it." Mia smiles. "I'm one of her actors. She's putting on Shakespeare and she's brilliant."

"She was always the smartest girl in school." He smiles like he's remembering.

I try to remember if I ever knew him in school. But I barely remembered him when he started talking to me at the apartment building. He was a cute boy who seemed interested in me. The first boy who ever approached me and seemed to like me.

He didn't look at me like I was an ant or a have-not. He saw me.

Fuck, I fell into the same trap with Chase. Am I doing the same thing with the Devil's trio?

They paid attention to me, and I just let them in. Okay, that's not entirely true.

They came at me hard, but I didn't exactly cave to them. Not at first, but they made it so hard to ignore them.

"Sorry, she checks out sometimes." Mia's words bring me back to the present.

"Sure, it's not a problem." Jackson meets my eyes. "There are few people who actually know Evan."

Yes, and they're all on the ice right now and not able to claim me in front of him. But I belong to them in ways I've never belonged to anyone else. Chase knows about my needing silence, but only because I told him.

Damon takes care of me in a way I haven't been in years. He makes sure all my needs are met. I lift my gaze and see him on the ice. My heart thumps hard.

Cam knows what it means to be lonely. He balances the other two out.

Hawk is passionate, and when I needed him, he was there. No questions asked.

I feel like they all get part of me and want all of me.

But they haven't said they love me. They want me and want to keep me for now, but will they ever be able to love me? Is that possible? Because I'm losing my heart to each of them.

For a while, Mia and Jackson trade stats back and forth. He thinks she's really impressive with the knowledge she's gained, and she preens. At least, he says that. He could be trying to charm her. As Mia flirts with him without trying to push him on me again, I start to relax.

I focus on the guys skating around their competition like the opposite team is standing still. I try to figure out more about the game and ignore Mia and Jackson.

But my mind keeps spinning. I should be engaging with him while I'm safe.

Is there a way to find out if he's my creepy texter? The fact he's shown up at a football game and now the hockey game definitely points in his direction. So maybe that's the way to out him.

"Don't you have a scrimmage today?" I ask, interrupting whatever they were talking about.

Mia looks at me curiously.

Jackson smirks and runs his hand through his dark hair. "Nah, it's a bye week for us. There's an odd number of teams in the league."

Okay, that's a good reason. He said he was checking out the competition. "Didn't you guys already play Deimos?"

"You should know, pretty girl, you were here."

My heart stops for a second. He was here and I didn't know it. How vulnerable was I? I was with Chase the whole time, but did I go to the bathroom alone? Fuck, I'm here. I was safe. I push aside the fear trying to drag me under. "Then why are you here?"

"We play the Coyotes next week. Coach encourages us to go to games when we can." That's the opposing team. Jackson's smile is a little tighter. "Besides, I wanted to see if Mia was here again. I haven't heard from her since the football game last week."

Mia smiles. "Like I said, her boyfriend's being a dick. She's had a rough week."

"It's not a problem. They're good questions. She's looking out for her friend." His eyes sparkle with mischief when he catches mine. "Evan has always kept me on my toes. I thought I lost her."

Those words. Fuck, is he toying with me? Making me sound like the crazy one? Maybe he just wants to punish me for disappearing on him after he kissed me.

The buzzer sounds, and I look out as the teams leave the ice. Damon hangs back, skating slow circles around the rink. My heart buzzes when he meets my gaze. *Let me take care of you.*

"That's weird." Jackson nods toward the ice. "Usually the coach would call in everyone so they can clean the ice."

"Damon's going to go pro." Mia sighs as she watches him skate. "There aren't many who do. But he's definitely going to draw attention when he goes to college. He's the real deal."

"He's okay." Jackson scoffs. "If you like a wealthy kid making it. He had all the best equipment and daddy to pay for extra training."

"You're the underdog story then?" Mia asks, curling her hair around her finger.

"I got into a great program because I earned it, not because daddy paid for my spot." There's bitterness in Jackson's tone.

I swallow. What will he do when he knows Damon's claimed me? What will he do to Damon? I'd like to believe nothing. But then I'm there in that moment with Jackson kissing me while I couldn't do anything. There's something dangerous about Jackson.

And if he's really watching me like his texts said, then he probably knows about the guys already.

"Hey, Evan." Cam drops into the seat next to me. He nods to Mia and Jackson.

I glance at the ice, and Damon has disappeared. Cam runs a hand through his wet hair.

"Checking out your competition?" Cam asks Jackson. "The Coyotes were okay, but they're too weak to play against us."

Jackson laughs. "I doubt we'll have any issues then."

Cam puts his arm on the armrest between us and presses it against me. He's so warm. I didn't realize how cold I'd gotten. I want to lean into him but don't want to antagonize Jackson.

I've seen flickers of the predator. They're brief and I'm not sure he meant for me to see them.

"Did you like the game, goody?" Cam asks. "Did you see the goal I made?"

I smile softly. "Yeah."

He puffs up his chest, and I want to laugh. His brown eyes sparkle and his arm brushes against my side.

He helps thaw the ice inside me.

"You going to play in college, Cam?" Jackson draws our attention.

"Maybe. It's not my long-term goal, but it might be interesting." Cam glances over his shoulder. I follow his gaze to see Hawk heading our way. The tightness in my chest vanishes. One-on-one Jackson might have a chance, but not two on one.

"We're working on homework with Hawk and Damon this afternoon," Mia explains to Jackson like he asked. "Cam is just a bonus."

"Did you hear that, goody? I'm a bonus?" Cam sounds amused. "Evan is tutoring me. Maybe I should come along and get ahead on my studying with the schedule she's set out for me." He meets Jackson's gaze. "She's a hard taskmaster, but I like it."

Hawk sits behind me. "Annie."

My cheeks heat remembering him fucking me against the wall yesterday like he couldn't wait to get inside me. My body warms, but I'm careful not to look at him.

"What's up, Jackson? Didn't have anything better to do on a Saturday morning than to come and talk to my girl?" Hawk leans back in the chair like he doesn't have a care in the world.

"Your girl?" Jackson looks at Mia.

"News to me." Mia looks at me.

"He's teasing." I don't need Mia telling Chase I'm with Hawk before we can get through tonight.

"You don't have girls at your school, Jackson?" Cam asks.

"Not like Mia here," Jackson says, but his eyes are on me.

A cold chill runs along my spine.

"You should come to the party tonight." Mia straightens. "It's a small get-together. It'd be nice to have a date with me. Evan is going to be with her ex all night."

Jackson's face flashes with anger before it's gone again. It's so quick, I might have imagined it.

"Yeah, maybe. I still have your number." He smiles and begins to rise. "Just don't block me." He winks at her, but his gaze goes to mine.

She laughs. "Trust me I won't."

Jackson nods to the guys. He focuses those intense dark eyes on me. "I'll be seeing you, pretty girl."

He heads down the aisle as Damon comes my way from the opposite direction.

"Did he say anything?" Cam asks.

Mia looks confused.

"Just some things that sounded like the texts, but nothing concrete."

Hawk turns to Mia. "We'll see you at Damon's house. We have Annie."

I stand and Damon closes in on me. He pulls me into his arms and glares at Mia. I don't care. I'm safe here. I breathe him in and let him hold me.

"I'll see you at the house then." Mia leaves.

"Come on, little devil. You ride with me."

Chapter 29

EvanAnn

We walk in together and head to the basement. Cam waits upstairs for Mia to get here. Damon holds my hand and doesn't let go. It's a risk, but the likelihood of our parents actually being here is low.

Besides, I need him. I need them all.

When we get to the rec room, he sits down on the couch and pulls me onto his lap. Hawk sits next us and puts his hand on my knee.

"What did he say?" Hawk asks.

I shake my head. "I don't know. I froze a few times. Mia invited him to the party tonight."

That's what stuck with me. Him coming tonight. That, and he really hates Damon. Did Jackson see him take me into his arms? Why didn't I wait to make sure he was gone? But the relief was so intense to have all them with me.

"I asked why he was at the game, but he had a good excuse." I shrug and tell them the other things he said that sounded like the texts.

Damon runs his hand over my arm. "You don't leave our sight tonight."

I swallow and lean my head against Damon's shoulder. I don't pull away when I hear Cam and Mia on the stairs. Just a few more minutes and I'll be warm enough to be without him. To pretend I don't need them.

"Oh," Mia says as she comes down. "Is everything all right?"

I breathe in Damon's earthy scent. I don't want to act like I'm not theirs. Like the guys are just Damon's friends and I happen to live here. No more pretending. Damon squeezes me against him, like he's not going to let me move even if I want to.

"Sit down, Mia." Hawk gestures to the chair across from the couch. Cam comes to my other side and sits. He rests his hand on my back, and I can fucking breathe. How did I breathe before them?

Mia sits and looks at the four of us. "So this is more than fucking I guess?"

"I don't know if you're playing a game here." Damon tightens his hand on my hip. "But don't fuck our girl over or we'll make your year hell."

"Fair." Mia lifts her eyebrow and leans back in the chair. "You don't know me, but I've been around guys scarier than you and they did make my year hell. I'm not looking for that kind of treatment here. I'm getting my diploma and getting as far away from this area as possible. I was serious when I said Evan is exactly the kind of friend I need this year. She's smart and driven. I didn't know she was going to end up in a reverse harem situation."

"Reverse harem?" I ask.

Mia winks. "I'll give you some books. Very educational."

Hawk sits forward. "If we trust you and you stab us in the back, you'll find out those guys weren't shit compared to what we'll do to you."

Mia takes in a breath. "I take it we're all on the Chase is a dick train?"

She looks over all of us, but we don't say anything. She nods.

"Are you going to let me in on the plan? Because normally I'd just be looking for someone to fuck at the party, but if you need my help, I doubt I'm going to find much to entertain me at Chase's house."

Cam glances at Damon, and Damon gives him a nod. We're willing to trust Mia for this. It might bite us in the ass. But there are so many moving parts that could break, having someone else in the know might not be a bad thing.

"This summer Damon was struck in a hit and run."

I cup Damon's scar on his jaw, and he turns and presses his lips to my palm. His blue eyes meet mine and hold. I could lose myself in him.

Cam continues, "Chase was getting head from some blond at the time and didn't see us. But there's no way he didn't know he hit someone and see the bike go down."

"Fuck." Mia glances at us, but I don't look away from Damon.

Hawk sighs. "We thought Evan was the girl. What better way to get back at a guy than take his girl. Especially when everyone knew she was a good girl."

My gaze flicks to Hawk. What? They came at me accusing me of being a whore.

"Ruin the good girl." Damon's voice brings me back to him. I search his blue eyes trying to see the truth. "Show everyone how wrong they were about her."

My breath catches. I didn't give in until I knew Chase was cheating, but what if I had before that? When did the plan change? Because Damon still blackmailed me, but I was good with whatever they wanted. I gave in so easily, proving to them I was the whore they wanted me to be.

"So you set about seducing Evan thinking she'd be the key to getting back at Chase?" Mia taps her fingers against each other. "It's not a bad plan, but why stay with him? I'm sorry, but even I figured out the guy wasn't exactly boyfriend material. He hit on me pretty quickly after I got here. But in the interest of full disclosure, I met Chase when I interviewed at Anteros. It was brief, but he definitely was interested. I didn't have time to fuck around, but promised him if I got in that we could."

Mia cocks her head, waiting for my reaction. Her expression remains flat.

"Did you fuck him?" I ask. My stomach churns, wondering if she's already betrayed me and would I recognize if she lies to me about it?

"Fuck, no." Mia sits up straight. "I may be a bitch and quite proudly a slut, but I'm not about to break girl code. You don't fuck your friend's boyfriend. I mean, I did years ago, but I'm trying to be better."

It doesn't really matter to me if she fucked Chase, but if she has, I won't be her friend. I'll be friendly like other students. That arm's length friendship we all seem to have in the theater department, because you never know who you'll work with in the future.

"Chase fucks everything that moves, and you want us to believe you didn't tap that?" Cam raises an eyebrow. "You would have fucked any of us if we gave you the chance."

Mia laughs and puts her hand on her chest. "Slut. You see this body. Who wouldn't want to show it off and do what it does best?" She winks, but turns back to me. "Believe me or not. I didn't cheat with your boyfriend. Did he offer? Yes."

Damon's hand tightens on me. But I don't have any emotions when it comes to Chase's cheating, besides anger in him using me. No, the only time I felt the bite of jealousy is with the Devil's trio.

Her face is serious when she continues. "I didn't want to hurt you. I've had friends blame me for their guys hitting on me. I'm a flirt and can't stop it if I try. I'm not looking to stir trouble here. Standing up to Olivia is just fun, but fucking your boyfriend...?" She sighs. "I just want to be your friend and fuck as many guys with six-pack abs as I can before I head off to Hollywood. My motives are really fucking simple. I didn't want to lose you as a friend because you decided to stay with your scuzzy boyfriend. And didn't want to lose you for telling you he was scuzzy."

"I didn't trust you because I've had friends who betrayed me before. Taking the guy I said I had a crush on." I inhale. "Having to smile while they kissed the guy they knew I wanted." I exhale. "Maybe that's why I didn't want to tell you about the Devil's trio. Or that I was moving here. I didn't want you to use me to get to them."

Mia laughs sharply. "I'm not going to say I wouldn't take advantage when you had a boyfriend and they were single, but all I want is for you to be happy. If that meant you trying to get back with Chase, I would accept it, if that's what you wanted, but encourage you to leave him. I'm still trying to find my footing at this school."

"Jackson might be stalking me," I blurt out.

"Evan," Damon growls like I've overstepped.

I turn and meet his eyes. "She needs to know so she doesn't accidentally let him back into my life."

"The guy gives me the creeps, but sometimes that can be hot in sex." Mia shrugs. "He doesn't ask me about you, but he knows we're new friends. I thought he was obsessing about me." She gives me a wry smile. "Oh, well, there's a lot more guys in hockey that I haven't gotten to yet."

"An unknown number started sending some texts after we saw him at the football game. The texts might be from someone else, but there were a few things he said today that made me think he wants me to know it's him." I shiver, and Cam rubs my back.

Damon shifts me to lay back against him, draping his arms around my waist. Hawk rests his hand on my knee. Their touch helps center me.

"Okay, so inviting him tonight was a bad move." Mia gets her phone out. "I can just text him."

"Has he been texting you?" Hawk asks. He holds out his hand, and she unlocks her phone and hands it to him.

"Not really. I was surprised he showed up today." Mia leans back in the chair and crosses her legs. "He was super interested at the football game. And then asked if he could give me his number. I sent him a quick message at the party to ask if he was coming, and he never responded. Then he showed up today, and I meant to ask to make sure his number was correct in my phone."

"Could be one of his burner numbers." Hawk glances my way. "What are the numbers he used to reach you?"

I unlock my phone and hand it to him. He compares the two unknown numbers with the one on Mia's phone. He shakes his head.

"Not a match." He hands our phones back.

"So that may or may not be his number." Mia shakes her head. "What a dick."

"Tonight's party isn't going to be a quaint little get together like Chase is planning." Cam rubs my knee. "He's going to get a few hundred more people at his house. We need people posting to social media during the party. Spread the word as much as you can."

Mia nods. "No problem. What else do you guys have planned?"

Cam looks at Damon. A look passes between the two of them.

"Chase will get in trouble because he's not supposed to throw a party. We have some plans to help put Olivia in her place." Cam squeezes my leg.

"Can't stand that bitch." Mia nods like this is exactly what they should be doing.

"Annie shouldn't be left alone with Chase." Hawk takes my hand. "We don't trust him. With us circling, he's getting more desperate to hold onto her. But if Jackson shows, we need to know right away. Some of what he texted is threatening. He's not to get his hands on her."

"If he shows up again, I'll give him the cold shoulder." Mia leans forward and meets my eyes. "I'm sorry I talked you up to him. I just wanted you to realize there are other options than Chase. You seemed so determined to stay with him, and I couldn't understand why. Though I get it now." Her eyes drop to Damon's hands wrapped around me. She smirks. "I know you aren't like me. It's one of the things that attracted me to you. I figured if I went with someone better than me for a friend, someone who took the time to fix a stranger's tie, maybe some of that might rub off on me. Or I would, at least, have a drama-free senior year."

"That ship has sailed." I shake my head. "Sorry, normally I'm completely drama-free. Except when we're on stage."

Mia laughs. "So, are we working on our history assignment? Because I need a good grade in this class."

"Yes," I say as Damon helps me stand. "I need to go grab my books."

I start toward the stairs and then hesitate. She's trying and I want to try too. Maybe I can let Mia in a little more.

"Do you want to see my room?" I ask Mia.

She smiles like I offered her a Golden Globe. "Sure."

Chapter 30

Cam

We wait until we're sure the girls are upstairs. Damon takes out his phone and pulls up the feed to Evan's room. Evan laughs at something Mia says and shows her the room and her closet. Mia goes nuts over the clothes, and they start talking about what Evan should wear tonight.

"Is this smart?" I ask what we're all thinking. Girls like Mia don't really change.

"Evan wants a friend." Damon's eyes soften. It's odd to see on Damon, but I don't think it's a bad thing. He needs someone soft in his life. Someone like Evan.

"Her assistant director, Keira, seems like a better option than Mia." Hawk runs his hand through his hair. "I guess we just see if she decides to *test* us again."

None of us believes she was testing us. She wants to fuck us. She doesn't care who we belong to.

"Do you think she slept with Chase? She's blond. She could have been the girl in the car." Will Damon want to get revenge on the girl? It made sense with Evan because she was dating Chase, and her gold-digging mother was moving in with Damon's dad.

He hasn't really mentioned the mother in a while. Hurting Evan isn't the plan anymore.

And while her mother might be a gold-digger, pushing her out now would hurt Evan.

"She might have." Damon drags his fingers across his lips as he watches the two of them in Evan's room.

"We're not hurting Evan." Standing, I glare at Damon. "I don't give a shit if she was the girl in the car or Olivia was. I'm not giving up Evan for your revenge."

Damon lifts confused eyes to me. "Why would we give up Evan?"

Hawk grunts. "You wanted Annie because she was the girl in the car. It's not unreasonable to think you might want to fuck over the girl who was actually in the car since we know it was never Annie."

"Don't be stupid." Damon looks down at the screen. "Evan is ours. If we get our revenge, it won't be by giving her up."

Hawk meets my eyes. We haven't talked about Evan's mother. Now isn't the time to bring it up though. Not when Evan might accidentally overhear us. I don't know how Evan feels about her mom, but she might not like that part of our seduction plan was to get her and her mother kicked out.

"Olivia talked about drugging Evan so I could fucking rape her." Damon raises hard eyes to us. "Olivia doesn't get close to Evan or her drinks. Evan needs a drink, we provide it. It sounds like Olivia has some sort of rape drug she got from Mia's brother."

"Does that make us trust Mia less?" Hawk asks. "It's possible she doesn't know about the drugs or that she uses them too. Do we trust her with Evan?"

I glance at the camera where Evan sits on her bed with a smile as she chats with Mia. It's hard to imagine anyone being malicious to Evan, but then again, we didn't have the best intentions at the beginning. But we don't spread our shit, so the only ones who know about the plan to get rid of Evan's mother are us.

"Fuck." I run my hand through my hair. "Can we just claim our girl and be done with it?"

"Soon." Damon lifts his gaze to me and then Hawk. "Tonight, Chase doesn't get a chance to draw her off on her own. Evan is ours."

"Good." I glance toward the stairs. "What about the other plan?"

Hawk nods. "She's keeping him on the hook. When we're ready to pull the trigger, all we have to do is say when and where."

"We need to make sure Evan is safe when it happens." Damon glances down at his phone again.

I stand. "I've gotta run home and grab my books. I'll study while you guys work on your project."

Hawk nods. I head out. The ride home is quiet, and when I get there, I worry this is a mistake. That Dad will try to make me stay home. I'm supposed to be on lockdown, but my parents aren't really helicopter parents who know everything I'm doing.

As I pass the living room, Dad says, "Cam?"

I blow out a breath and stop. I hoped he was out.

"How was the scrimmage?" He gets up from the couch and puts his book down.

"Good." I lean against the doorjamb. "I'm heading over to Damon's to study."

My dad chuckles. "You expect me to believe that?"

"Actually, yes." I straighten. "EvanAnn's mother is Damon's dad's girlfriend. Evan will be there to make sure I stay on task."

Dad's gaze narrows on me, suspiciously. "She's a cute girl."

"Most girls who go to our school are cute or downright gorgeous. Just par for the course." I shake my head. "I really want to get my work done."

"If your grades improve, I'll thank the girl myself." Dad clicks his tongue.

"Don't worry, they will." I turn and walk up to my room. It's not like my grades are in the tank, but the partying did make it hard to compete with my classmates. I grab my schoolbag and head back downstairs.

"Your mother and I are going out tonight." Dad calls after me when I pass the doorway.

I backtrack. "Okay."

They don't usually tell me where they're going or when they'll be home. But I've also never been on lockdown before.

"You'll be here tonight?" He tries to make it a statement, but it comes out as a question.

"Where else would I go?" I smirk, but fuck that shit. "Oh, wait, I'm eighteen, and it's a weekend, so I think I'll go hang out with my friends."

"Cam." His tone is a warning.

"Look, we have this year left to hang out. It's my senior year, and sure, we'll keep in touch after graduation, but I doubt we'll even be in the same state next year, so cut me some slack. I'm studying on a fucking Saturday. My friends will only give me sodas because they don't want me to get in an accident because I drank too much."

Dad's eyes widened during my speech. "Fine. But only if your homework is done."

"On it."

EvanAnn

We work on our history project while Cam does some of his homework. Before Cam heads out, he puts a red paper flower next to me. I put it with the others on my desk.

Mia helped me pick out an outfit for tonight. It's not as revealing as the outfit Damon picked out last weekend, but it's still showing a lot more skin than I normally do.

I didn't tell her the whole plan, and neither did the guys, but she knows to distract Jackson if he actually shows up. I hope he doesn't. It will just complicate things. My nerves are frayed by the time she leaves, and she'll be back after dinner to do my makeup.

I don't know what to think about Mia. The things she said and knew and didn't tell me. Testing the guys? My boyfriend? I knew she wasn't really my speed of person, but I do believe in second chances. She hasn't hurt me.

Yet.

I don't plan on giving her enough trust to actually hurt me.

"Evan," Damon says from the bathroom doorway. He has on jeans and a black t-shirt that hugs his body.

My insides flip as I meet his blue eyes. I can't imagine not being here. Not sleeping in Damon's bed. Not fucking the Devil's trio. It's hard to remember what my life was before they stormed into it.

"Dinner?"

"Yeah." I stand and run my hands over my jeans and straighten his sweatshirt on me.

He closes the distance between us. Will I ever not get a rush when he touches me? Will I get used to having all three of them? Will they grow tired of me?

He takes my hand and leads me through the bathroom to his room. He grabs the sweatshirt and pulls it off over my head, leaving me in only my bra. His finger trails over the lacy edge, making me bite my lip.

"No time." He goes to his drawers and pulls out a t-shirt.

His obsession with dressing me in his clothes is odd. I don't think I even wore one of Chase's sweatshirts while we were dating. I can't say I don't love it though as he helps me put it on.

"I am capable of dressing myself." I give him a small smile.

"Far less fun." He smirks and lifts my chin. He searches my eyes. "How's your pussy?"

I arch an eyebrow. "A little worse for wear. How's your dick?"

He chuckles. "Hard, aching. I want my cum inside you at that party. I want to smell me when I get close to you."

My panties grow damp just thinking about it. I press my thighs together at the ache.

"We're meeting the guys out to eat." Damon takes my hand and leads me down the back stairs and out to the garage. Riding with him on his bike is almost second nature now.

We ride to an Indian restaurant. When we stop, he asks, "This is good, right?"

"Yeah, this is good." It's perfect, but I'd make anything work for what appears to be a date.

When we enter the restaurant, Cam and Hawk already have a booth for us near the back. Of course they're sitting across from each other, making me choose who to sit beside.

I slide in next to Cam, and he throws his arm around my shoulders and kisses me. My cheeks flush with heat as I pull back and look around.

"No one we know is here, little devil." Damon reaches across the table with his palm up, and I put my hand in his.

"This feels really weird. Like I shouldn't be here with you guys." I glance around the small restaurant, but there are only some random people. We're still not out as anything. Not even friends. Though they do interact with me at school and parties occasionally.

"How else are we going to treat our girlfriend?" Hawk winks. Happiness floods my insides, but I don't know how this can work long-term.

"Is that seriously what we're going with?" I tuck my hair behind my ear and meet each of their eyes. "I'm your girlfriend and you all are my boyfriends?"

"We're basically already that, right?" Damon leans back in the booth and looks at me with hooded eyes. "We spend all our free time together. Eat together. Fuck together."

"Blackmail me with videos to get me to sleep with you. Force me to stay with my ex to punish him." I arch an eyebrow. It hasn't all been fun and games.

Damon smirks, Hawk laughs, and Cam squeezes my shoulders.

"You liked it, little devil." Damon's blue eyes lock on mine.

He's not wrong. I enjoy every moment of being theirs. So I give up my little defiance. Besides, they all know I'll give them what they want in the end. I always do and I'm okay with that.

We chat about classes a little while we wait for the food to arrive.

"There's got to be more to you than your classes, Annie." Hawk pauses while the server puts our meals in front of us. "What kind of movies do you like?"

"Oh," I pause with a bite of turmeric rice on my fork. I set it down. "I love all kinds of movies. My dad had this long list of movies he wanted me to see. I used to watch them with him."

I haven't thought about that list in a while. I couldn't make myself look at the incomplete list after he passed. All the things we didn't get to, because we ran out of time. And then everything seemed to move so fast.

"What kind of movies?" Cam asks.

"Movies from the 80s and 90s mostly, but some classics as well. He wanted to encourage my acting, since I was being typecast as the serious kid even at ten. He was determined for me to watch them all." I straighten and meet Damon's eyes. "Most of the time he'd fall asleep during them, but I still stayed and watched the whole thing. He'd wake up at the end, and we'd talk about them for a little while before he got tired again."

My heart still aches when I talk about him. Damon doesn't look away, and I know he understands. That he sat beside his mother's bedside the same way I sat beside my dad's. How would our lives be different if they hadn't died? Would he have ever looked at me twice? Would I have ever dated Chase? I shake it off. What ifs don't matter now.

"We didn't get to his favorite genre though." I smile, remembering the list and the section labeled for when I'm older. "Mostly horror movies or movies that weren't appropriate for a ten-year-old."

There's a box that list was in. I saw it when I was in my closet with Mia. It was obviously memorabilia, so whoever unpacked my room didn't unpack that. Pictures of my family when it was whole. A necklace Dad gave me when I was little with a broken chain. Cards he gave me, birthday and encouragement. Letters from when I was at camp.

I rub at the ache growing in my chest. It's been so long since I let myself think about him. I was too busy taking care of myself and Mom.

"We could watch them." Cam leans forward. "I mean, I like movies and I'm always on board for horror or R-rated movies."

My mouth opens and closes. Ready to tell them no, that's not necessary.

Hawk and Damon nod, and warmth bursts in my chest.

"I'd like that." Even my cheeks are warm. I can't believe I'm blushing at this.

"I don't like to know about a movie before I watch it." Hawk draws my attention. "Trailers too often spoil shit or make the movie seem like it's something it's not."

"I've done that. Though there were a few movies I wished I'd watched the trailer for first." I smile and eat as we discuss movies and TV shows. And for a moment, I forget we're in public and really shouldn't be. That tonight we're going to take down the queen bee or at least put her in her place. And gather more evidence on my ex.

After Damon pays for our dinner, he takes my hand to lead me outside to his bike. It hits me that there's a lot that can go wrong tonight. But dinner was perfect, and this was the best date I've ever been on.

Chapter 31

EvanAnn

Mia and I pull up to the party. Cam told everyone to show up after ten, but Chase's party starts at eight. Cam said people would start showing up around nine because they were bored.

We're getting there a little late. Eight-thirty. I don't want to be without the guys for too long. I'd prefer to walk in as the party really gets started, but it will be nice to see Chase's panic too. Yes, the drama major wants drama.

Jackson hasn't reached out to Mia, so we don't think he's going to show. Thank god for that.

If I were directing this, it would be an elaborate trap. I would have Mia be a double agent and working with Chase to steal me away and make me his Stepford wife before the guys arrive. But that's not real life. I don't trust Chase. I kind of trust Mia. But the guys will get here soon. And in the meantime, I can protect myself.

I get out of the car in a skirt a little longer than the one Damon had me wear last weekend. My top shows my midriff and is tight around my breasts. Damon fucked me in the shower and sucked on my shoulder until it almost hurt, marking me as his.

My shoulder twinges as I walk up the drive with Mia. A smile plays on my lips because I'm theirs, and they want more.

When she takes my hand, I glance over at Mia with surprise.

"I've got you." Her blue eyes seem sincere. "You need out of this one, let me know and we're gone. Promise."

I smile. Fuck, I want to trust her to be a good friend the way I wanted Chase to be a loyal boyfriend. Maybe I'm just delusional.

I trust the Devil's trio now. But there was that moment when Damon brought me to the hamburger place where I thought that might have been his grand plan. Humiliate me in front of everyone.

Ruin the good girl.

I didn't know about their original plan. My heart pounds when I consider those words. That was their plan, but the hamburger place was obviously too soon.

What if part of the price to take down Chase was to hurt me? Not physically, but they could do a lot of damage emotionally. I tried to keep my walls up. Keep things strictly physical.

But they kept battering my walls until I was vulnerable to them. They're inside and I'm beginning to depend on them for more than just orgasms. My emotions are all tangled up in them.

Chase can't hurt me. Mia can't hurt me. But the Devil's trio? They could destroy me.

I don't think they will, but a small bit of fear remains. At one point I thought Chase was a loyal boyfriend. Maybe my judgment isn't the greatest.

We walk in the door, and there are voices out by the pool. I drag in a breath. Maybe I should listen to everything that's warning me this is a trap. And maybe not the one I helped to set.

My guys, I trust. Maybe it's stupid to trust them, but I do.

But I wouldn't put it past Chase to have something planned for tonight. But I'm committed, so I walk confidently next to Mia out to the pool. There are a few girls and football players playing in the pool and some on the deck drinking. An arm wraps around my waist and pulls me into a hard body.

My heart stops, but Chase says, "You came. Awesome."

I try to relax in his hold. Act like his girlfriend or at least the girl willing to give him a second chance. I'd rather shove him into the pool, but this won't be for much longer.

"Hey, she's my date tonight." Mia pushes Chase's shoulder. "Get off her."

He releases me and laughs. "Sure. Everyone knows you like dick, Mia."

She shrugs and puts her arm around my waist and pulls me in close. "It's a friend date, and you didn't invite anyone I'd want to fuck, so I'm hanging out with Evan."

Chase shakes his head. "Whatever. EvanAnn can decide what she wants to do."

"You said I could bring Mia." I give him a wide-eyed look and lean into Mia. "I'm not abandoning her."

Chase runs a hand through his hair but forces a smile. "Great. The more the merrier." He gestures toward the pool deck.

Mia keeps her arm around me, and we take a seat on the loveseat, making it so Chase has to sit on an armchair or the couch alone. He chuckles as he takes the armchair.

"I wanted to apologize about last night." He leans forward and takes my hand. His blue eyes seem sincere. "I drank too much, and I was an ass. Hawk was right to get in my face. I was wrong to say what I said. I wish I didn't have to keep asking you to forgive me."

He gives me this look he probably gave his parents when he did something bad. I wonder if they ever bought it. Even his words feel practiced.

I smile. "It's okay. We all need to blow off steam after this week." I glance around at everyone giving us space. "It's nice this is so low-key. I'm kind of partied out."

"Yeah, I don't get to do this too often. My parents don't like to go out of town without me." Chase leans back and nods toward the pool. "We could get in if you want. I'm sure my mom's suits would fit you two."

"I'm good." I resist the urge to glance at my phone to see how much longer I have to sit here and try to "reconnect" with my ex. Especially when I can feel Damon's cum leaking in my panties.

"Yeah, I don't want to ruin my makeup and hair." Mia smiles.

"You going to another party later?"

"Nope, I'm staying here. I just like to look my best for my friend." Mia leans her head on my shoulder.

"How about I get you two drinks?" Chase rises.

Don't drink anything anyone else gives you. Damon told me about what Olivia wanted to do. Yeah, that's Olivia, but with Chase and her, who knows? And his parents did find drugs in his room. Better safe than sorry. I hold up my full water bottle.

"I'm good."

"You could have a drink, Evan. You're safe and among friends." Chase smiles. "It'll help loosen you up."

Yeah, that's what I'm afraid he's trying to do.

"No, thank you." I say firmly and meet his blue eyes.

He holds his hands up with a small smile. "Got it. Mia?"

"Sure." She leans back on the loveseat. "Bring me something pink."

"Pink." He shakes his head as he walks away.

"Do you think he's pissed off?" I ask.

"I hope so. He's such a fuckboy." Mia shakes her head. "Don't get me wrong, fuckboys are usually good lays, but they aren't loyal for shit."

"Have you ever had a boyfriend?"

Mia glances at me. "When I was fifteen, a senior noticed me, and I thought I was the hottest shit ever. I'd done a little before then, but I hadn't had sex yet. He coaxed me into it.

"He was kinky." She gets this unfocused look. "He liked watching his friends take turns with me. The whole senior football team fucked me that year. I loved every minute of it. Even let him fuck my ass, so I could take more guys at a time. He enjoyed watching." She refocuses and looks over at Chase at the bar. "I was really popular with the guys because they could fuck me however they wanted." She shrugs. "I like sex. A lot."

I slide my hand in hers and thread our fingers together, leaning my head against hers. "You're worth more than just your body, Mia."

She laughs a little bitterly. "Yeah, I'm an actor. My body will always be an issue. My casualness with sex will only help me in my career. I won't get hung up on guys who just want to use me."

"Mia." I feel it like an ache in my soul. I can picture her as a girl who craved new things and sex and how that guy exploited that fact. And taught her guys only wanted her for one thing. Of course, she's gorgeous so she could have heard that her whole life.

She turns her face toward me and smiles a little too brightly. "I use guys and they use me. Fuck guys, Evan. They aren't worth my time except to get me off."

"You're the only one I know who can list the stats of any player in a league." I straighten and look at her. "And I love how I'm able to really breakdown a character with you when we're working on the play. You're more than just your body. You're smart and you're nice to me. And I don't want to have sex with you."

Mia laughs. "Damn, I thought I'd get to experiment." Her eyes soften on me. "This is why you're an amazing friend, Evan. You see this old tart and find a way to make me sound like apple pie." She squeezes my hand. "Thank you. You're an amazing director so it's fun to discuss character with you."

I return her smile.

Chase walks over and hands Mia a glass. He offers me one. "You sure?"

"I said no." I arch an eyebrow like he's being an asshole, because he is.

He settles in the armchair and takes a drink. "I didn't know if you changed your mind."

"Why isn't there music?" Mia asks and takes a large drink from her cup. "Is this a party or what?"

"I have to keep the noise down, but I can turn on the surround sound. It just can't be loud enough to disturb the neighbors." He unlocks his phone and sets the cup on the table while he taps something on the screen.

Music comes out of the speakers, and a small cheer comes from the pool.

"I wanted to make you more comfortable here than at those larger parties." Chase leans in. "I know they aren't really your scene, and you go to them for me. Besides, we could always chat about Shakespeare since we don't have to yell over the music."

I give him a soft smile because that does sound more my speed. Even if I don't want him and don't think he's really after me for the right reasons, I can see how I might have fallen for him if he hadn't been a huge cheater.

We talk a little about the play. Mostly Chase argues with Mia over whether Desdemona actually slept with Cassio or not. He swears she actually did.

The wave begins slowly. A few girls arrive, and they seem to be with the football players. Chase notices but doesn't do anything about it, figuring girls aren't generally a problem.

Suddenly, a tidal wave of students arrive, like they all came together. Chase stands.

"Fuck. Just a minute." He walks off, and Mia takes my hand.

"Don't lose me," Mia says as the backyard fills with students. Liam arrives with Fletcher, and they immediately zero in on Mia.

Liam smirks as they approach us.

"Hey, kitten, mind if we join you?" He sits on the couch with Fletcher. He nods at me. "EvanAnn."

Mia's cheeks flush a little pink as both Liam and Fletcher flirt with her. My cheeks heat remembering seeing them fucking for the first time. I take a drink of my water and try to focus elsewhere. Part of me wants to give them time to talk, but I also know Damon will punish me if I don't stick to Mia until one of the Devil's trio is with me.

The party around us begins to fill in, and the music gets louder.

Chase is lost in the crowd. My gaze stalls on green eyes. Hawk smirks as he saunters toward us. He has on dark jeans and a green shirt that makes his eyes pop.

He looks like the embodiment of the privileged Cassio, and he's mine. My insides buzz.

"Hey, Liam, Fletcher. Mia." His gaze stops on me. "Annie."

My name is soft on his lips. He takes Chase's armchair. Mia's hand tightens on mine.

This is it. The pieces are falling into place and our play is about to begin. The problem is, most of the actors don't realize they're on stage. But we'll guide them through their parts.

The number of people in the backyard grows exponentially while we talk.

"Hey!" Keira stops next to our chairs. "I think the whole cast is here tonight."

"We could do an impromptu performance." Mia grins.

"Except Brandt's here too." Keira frowns. "He'd insist on his production getting equal time."

"We can't have that." Hawk winks my way and warmth bubbles through me.

Keira's attention is pulled away from us. She gives us a smile. "We'll catch up later, right? No beer pong tonight."

Hawk chuckles. "No beer pong."

Keira wanders off, and we settle in, waiting for the next explosion.

Chase comes over. His hair stands on end like he's run his hand through it. "Fucking Brody probably opened his big mouth. I never should have invited that asshole, but he said he could bring some party favors."

Party favors? Like drugs? Fuck, I'm glad I didn't take that drink.

Chase lifts his gaze as he realizes Mia and I aren't alone. His gaze bounces from Liam to Fletcher to settle on Hawk. His jaw tightens.

"Are you seriously flirting with my girl again?" he asks Hawk.

Hawk chuckles and rubs his jaw. "Is she your girl? Last I heard she broke up with you."

Chase straightens. "We're on a break. Right, babe?"

"Not your babe." I meet Chase's eyes. "And I did break up with you. We're trying to work through it, but we're definitely not back together right now."

Chase's gaze narrows on me. This is the guy who left me out in the woods, but this time I'm not alone. Mia's got my hand and Hawk is right here. Motion catches my attention, and my gaze collides with sharp blue eyes focused on me.

Damon.

Chase seems to remember what the fuck he's doing. "Sorry, you're right. I need to do better."

He sets his drink off to the side and glances at the party ramping up behind him. "I don't know what to do. I can't have this many people over. And it's not like I can kick everyone out."

"That sucks, dude." Fletcher smiles. "Did you lock your bedroom? Otherwise, you never know who will fuck on your bed."

"Fuck." Chase turns to head for the house. "I'll be back."

"Might want to lock your parents' room too," Fletcher calls after him, then turns to us. "Poor bastard. Not sure why he thought he could keep this a secret."

Hawk smiles at me, and I return it. I'm not sure where Damon went, but he's somewhere nearby. I'm sure Cam is helping someone bring in kegs. After all, this is going to be the party of the year. We'll make sure of it.

Chapter 32

Damon

Hawk has Evan, leaving me free to do what I need to do. I'm sure Fletcher reminded Chase about locking bedrooms. If not, Hawk will. The good news is Chase doesn't have a keyed lock on his door. He'll set the lock and use an interior door key to get into it later.

Most people will try a knob and move on if it's locked, figuring it's occupied.

I'm planning for the girls to come to his door at the right time because Olivia is supposed to be bringing me someone willing and drugged. Fuck this girl. Like I need to mess around with chicks high on drugs. I've got Evan to take care of my every need.

Olivia's desperation is worrisome. Is there no boundary she won't push? Is she really that bored? Or is it something more? I don't know her home life or what might be going on outside of school. But I don't give a shit because she's decided to focus on me and threatened to drug Evan. She also helped Chase ruin my life. The problem is her father is rich enough to get her out of anything, including a drug charge.

The only reason I can find why she wants me is because she can't have me. Nothing else makes sense. She's not asking me to date her.

She wants to fuck me. Maybe it's a numbers game. A collect-them-all type of thing.

Or maybe she thinks once I've had her, I won't want to give her up. Fuck that noise.

About ten minutes ago, Olivia showed up at the party. She's looking for me, but I'm avoiding her. My job is to make sure Jackson isn't here and get our game pieces lined up. Cam is playing party captain. Hawk's goal is to keep an eye on Evan.

We have plans to ensure we come out on top. It just depends on the moves of the other people. The main plan is for me and Evan to put on a performance for Olivia and catch the storm on video to use as blackmail or to broadcast at school. Olivia's choice.

I'm not showing anyone an inch of Evan though. The plan is to use the video later for Chase. We talked it through in the shower as I fucked her against the tile wall—slowly, since she's sore from last night. Her skirt tonight will hide whether we're actually fucking. It just has to look like we're fucking to get Olivia to explode.

"Why don't we just fuck?" Evan's voice was breathless. Pretty sure my little devil likes to put on a performance. But not this time.

"Because that's for us, little devil. Only us."

Every inch of her is ours, and I'm not sharing it with anyone else.

As much as I want to fulfill her every fantasy, I may be too possessive to show anyone else that part of us.

We need to keep track of the players and make sure the girls head to Chase's room at the right time for optimum results. Cam will keep Chase distracted so he won't come investigate or notice Evan isn't where he left her.

Olivia has her friend Megan with her. They both have on short skirts and barely-there tops. Their pinkies hooked together as they walk through the party.

Megan might be collateral damage. It can't be helped. Olivia's overstepped one too many times. It's time she learns the hard way she's never going to have me.

EvanAnn

This isn't like last weekend's party at Olivia's where the room was dark. Hawk and I are out in the open. Mia continues to flirt with Liam and Fletcher. It won't be long before they end up in one of the bedrooms upstairs.

Hawk leans forward to talk with me. It's casual looking, but his knuckles brush my bare knees, sending sparks through my system. We talk about *Romeo and Juliet*.

It's nothing like the blatant flirting happening next to us, but I love that Hawk wants to talk Shakespeare with me. And not just surface stuff like Chase does.

My phone buzzes.

SEX GOD:

Now

I glance up at Hawk and nod.

"Should we move inside?" Hawk rises.

Liam and Fletcher stand with him like they're in on the plan, but the only ones who know are the four of us, and Mia knows some. Mia squeezes my hand as we follow the guys inside.

The outside was quiet compared to in here. Music plays, drowning out other noises. The lights are down low, and people are making out on every available surface. There's a group sitting in a circle on the living room floor spinning a bottle.

Two girls crawl to each other and kiss while the others cheer. I never really explored parties with Chase. He stayed outside by the beer pong table. It was a safe space I never wandered from. I never participated, and he never pushed me to do anything more.

Honestly, the fact he didn't really want me did me a favor. He didn't push me.

Now I belong to the guys I was always meant to belong to.

Our play is in motion. I haven't seen Chase since he wandered off to try to keep his house intact. For all I know, he's upstairs having sex right now.

I really don't want to walk in on that.

I've already caught enough live shows to last me our high school career. Cam is supposed to distract Chase from looking for me. Tonight I'll be the one giving a performance. Anticipation and performance anxiety wind through me. Hawk slips back and nods to Mia, who moves up to walk between Liam and Fletcher.

Their arms go around her. I kind of hope they're serious about her. She deserves someone to love too. Or at least someone who wants to take care of her.

Hawk slides his hand onto the small of my back where my skin shows. His hand is warm, and I can't wait to be able to turn into him and kiss him like he's mine. I glance up at him through my lashes. He leans down to talk in my ear.

"You're gorgeous tonight, baby girl." His lips brush my ear and send a shiver through me.

I turn and lead him down a hallway. Either no one has found it or no one is inclined to use it. Being alone tempts me to make something happen with Hawk, but we're on a time crunch. We make our way up some back steps and turn some corners until we're almost at Chase's bedroom.

Before we turn the corner, someone knocks on a door. Hawk presses me into the wall as we wait to see what's happening.

"I don't feel well," a girl mumbles.

"Shh, you're fine," Olivia snaps. "I promised to bring you somewhere you could lie down."

Olivia. They're early. Fuck. My eyes meet Hawk's and he presses his forehead against mine. All we can do is work with what we've got.

The door opens.

"What the fuck?" Damon's voice. He was probably expecting me to be on the other side of the door. Not Olivia and whoever is with her.

"Well don't just stand there. Help me. The ant is heavier than she looks," Olivia says. "I got you a little theater nerd. Just like you wanted."

What? I meet Hawk's eyes. Who did Olivia get?

"I said willing." Damon's voice is tense.

Olivia shrugs. "She will be."

"Fuck." Damon's word is soft, but there's a slight groan of pain from the other girl.

Hawk nods at me and we round the corner, stepping into the open door to see Olivia leading Keira to the edge of the bed.

I press my hand to my mouth as I rush in. "What did you do?"

"Why are you here?" Olivia says at the same time and releases Keira.

I help Keira sit, tipping her chin up. Her eyes are seriously dilated.

"Damon, why is she here?" Olivia is so fucking confident in her ability to have Damon. I wish I could knock her down, but she'll always be rich, and she'll always have power.

Damon closes in on Olivia. "You were with Megan. Why are you with this girl now?"

Olivia shrugs like this is all beneath her and glares at Damon.

"Megan doesn't like how the drugs make her feel." Olivia scoffs. "Besides, she's a greedy bitch and would have wanted all your attention."

"What did you give Keira?" I ask, checking her pulse. It's steady but fast. I lift my gaze to Hawk's. "We need to get her to the hospital."

Hawk nods and begins typing on his phone.

Olivia laughs. "Oh my god, she'll be fine. It's just a little party upper."

Damon narrows his eyes on Olivia. "Did she know she was taking a drug?"

"Why are you angry? I did what you wanted." Olivia glares at Damon. "You wanted a little theater nerd, so I brought you one."

"I also said willing. This doesn't look willing. Did you slip her the drug?" Damon glances at us. I sit next to Keira on the bed. She sways like we're on a boat.

Olivia glances at Keira. "It's her fault. She drank what I gave her without asking questions. Honestly, she should know better."

"I don't feel well." Keira clutches her stomach.

I go into Chase's bathroom and wet a washcloth with cool water before coming back in. Olivia has her arms crossed like we're interrupting her fun time with nonsense. I sit beside Keira and put the cool cloth on the back of her neck.

"That feels nice." Keira's smile is loose, and her words slurred.

Hawk squats in front of her and meets my gaze. "Cam's finding someone who can give us a lift. She can't ride in this state."

I nod, but I'm nervous for Keira. She's been nice to me. Honestly, she's been more of a friend than Mia. Rage wells inside me. Where does Olivia get off with targeting us? Is it because we can't fight back?

"Why are they here, Damon?" Olivia demands. "You told me it would be just us."

"You told me you'd bring someone willing. Not that you would drug some random girl at the party so you could rape her." Damon's voice is colder than I've heard it in a long time.

"Girls can't rape girls." Olivia looks away.

"Did she consent, Olivia?" Damon stalks closer. "Did she say yes, I want to fuck you and whoever else you get to party with us? Did she ask to be fucking drugged?"

"This was all a fucking trap anyway, so what do you care?" Olivia looks like she's ready to storm out.

"You put drugs in someone's drink." Damon's voice is low. "You don't know what else she might have in her system that would fuck with it. Instead of getting her medical attention when she said she wasn't feeling well, you brought her here to rape her. Fuck you, Olivia."

"What about your whore?" Olivia gestures to me with her chin. "That's the real reason I'm here, right? You're going to tell me to fuck off again. Like you don't want to fuck me."

"I don't want to fuck you!" Damon says. "Get it into your fucking head already. I've never wanted to fuck you."

Cam shows up in the doorway. "Truck's outside."

His gaze roams over all of us.

"Will you carry her?" I ask softly.

Cam nods and scoops Keira up into his arms. She groans and clutches her stomach. "We'll grab a bucket on the way out."

When I stand and turn to follow them, Damon pulls me into a hug. I rest my head against his chest and breathe out, taking comfort in his warmth.

"Go on. I'll take care of this." Damon presses a kiss to the top of my head.

I draw away and look up into his eyes.

"Yes, run away." Olivia smirks. "Don't worry, I'll keep your man warm."

Something settles inside me, like the center of a storm. She's never going to give up on Damon. Fuck this bitch.

I straighten and turn to Olivia. "What the fuck is it going to take to make you see he'll never be yours because he's mine?"

"For now." She scoffs and rolls her eyes. "I've been waiting years for him."

"Why can't you get this into your head?" I run a hand through my hair while Hawk stands next to Damon and Cam holds Keira next to the door. They're all watching me.

Fuck it. I step closer to Olivia. Her heels make her taller than me, but I don't give a shit.

She looks down her nose at me and crosses her arms over her chest. "You're just something he wants to play with right this minute. I'm fucking endgame."

"You don't know the first thing about him." I narrow my eyes. Why does she want him so much?

"He's popular, plays hockey, and fucks you like you mean nothing to him. What more do I need to know?" Olivia arches an eyebrow, but she doesn't get it.

He's a fucking trophy to her. She's never looked into his eyes when he's buried deep inside her and felt that raw connection. She's never felt him curl around her in his sleep, holding her tight so neither of them have nightmares. He's never brought her a plate of food because he's worried she hasn't eaten enough.

And she never will know that side of him, because it's mine.

"When I say he's mine, I mean he's mine and I'm his. We care for each other. We aren't just fucking around to get off." I turn to look at him. Damon sits on the edge of the bed and watches me. My heart beats a little harder. "You're right. He is those things, but he's also so much more. I'd get it if you wanted more than sex from him, but that's not why you keep coming after him. Is it?"

She presses her lips together and glares at me.

"He's your fucking prize in the box of cereal. The participation award you deserve for going to this high school. You don't give a shit about Damon."

I can't keep doing this. She needs to stop, and Damon isn't going to be able to do it. It's up to me.

"You want something you can use against me?" Laughing bitterly, I look around at the guys before glaring back into her eyes. "I love him. I love Damon and Hawk and Cam and whatever the fuck we're doing. It's not typical. It's not all sexy times and getting off. It's real and emotional and everything I've ever needed. We take care of each other. And that means finally dealing with you."

"Watch how you speak to me. You can't get any lower, ant."

"Watch how you speak to her," Damon steps up behind me. His warmth is a wall surrounding me, but not touching, just supporting. "I've told you who she is to me and still you persist. I love Evan. I'm not giving her up. Not for you or any of your machinations."

"You can't be serious." Olivia stomps her foot.

"Why do you want him?" I lean back against him, giving into the need. "What's the fucking point? He doesn't want you."

"But he should. He should want me more than any other girl in this school. I'm everything. Beautiful, rich, popular. He belongs to me." She eyes me up and down with disdain. "Not you. You mean nothing to anyone at this fucking school. Yes, they love trotting out the poor, little, talented kids, but you won't make it in the real world. Do you know how much Chase and I laughed at the fact you honestly thought he really wanted you?"

Her laugh is bitter. It stops abruptly as I smack her across her face.

Chapter 33

Hawk

Olivia straightens like she's going to say something else to Annie, but Annie hits her again. Annie's face is twisted with hate. Fuck, this was worth it. Watching Annie claim us is fucking perfection. Olivia snarls as she straightens.

Before Olivia can gain her bearings, Damon steps between the two of them, facing Annie, and backs her up a few steps. He tips her flushed face up.

"That's enough, little devil. Go with Cam and take care of your friend." Damon glances over his shoulder at Olivia. "I'll make sure this goes away. For good."

Annie looks like she wants to protest, like maybe she just wants to fight Olivia and be done with it. But we wouldn't let Olivia touch Annie.

"It's okay. Let me do this for you." Damon lowers his forehead to Annie's and closes his eyes. She releases her breath and closes her eyes, resting her hands on his waist. They stay like that for several heartbeats until she draws in a breath.

When he opens his eyes, she whispers, "I love you."

His smile is softer than I've ever seen it. "I love you."

Annie steps back, and as tempted as I am to go with her and Cam, I'm needed here. No one trusts Olivia, and I'm not sure she won't provoke Damon. As much as I hate her, Olivia can't have a way to bring Damon down.

"I'll stay here with Damon." I take Annie's hand and want to say so much, but my throat closes up. She said she loves me, but now isn't the time for me to figure out how she makes me feel. I clear the lump from my throat and say, "Keep me posted, Annie."

She nods and turns with those worried eyes to Cam. He jerks his head, and she follows him without a glance back. Tears are drying on Olivia's face as Damon turns to her. Her face is red on the cheek Annie struck.

He nods at me. I close the door so there won't be any more interruptions.

What Olivia has said so far might not be enough for the police to get her on drugging a minor, but we're close. Olivia's parents will pay off Keira, and Olivia will likely get a slap on her wrist. Maybe even do a stint at a rehab center. Rich kids rarely go to jail, and Olivia's father is a well-connected, powerful lawyer.

"Keira's sixteen," I offer.

Olivia's angry eyes lift to mine. "So?"

Damon walks to the desk and sits in the chair facing Olivia. "You can do time for drugging a minor with the intent to sexually assault her."

"Bullshit." Olivia straightens and wipes at her cheeks. "There's no proof it was me. She was at a party drinking. It could have been anyone."

"Except you admitted it to us." I lean against the wall.

"Yeah, but it's not like anyone would believe you guys over me. It would be your word against mine. Even if I did put a drug in a drink, there's no proof I was the one who gave her the drink. Besides, this is all posturing on your part." Olivia looks at Damon like he's contracted a deadly disease. "Maybe your reputation has been oversold."

"How's that?" Damon cocks his head to the side.

"You want me to believe that you..." She gestures to him, waving her hand up and down. "Are in love with an ant? I mean, I believe her when she says it. Fuck, she dated Chase, who is a known manwhore, for months. She's pretty desperate, and you're hot. But you loving her? I don't believe it. I assume this is some sort of revenge plot? Because that's the only thing that makes sense."

She's a little too close to the truth. We may have started out with revenge on our minds, but that seems so long ago. Annie's become more to all of us. If she weren't on board with bringing Chase down, we'd have ended this farce of her trying to get back together with him.

"You just can't let go of the fact I chose Evan over you." Damon smirks and shakes his head like she's so far beneath him.

Olivia narrows her eyes at him. "Everything I've done has been for you. I even stooped low enough to find an ant to entice you with. Another little director nerd. Used my scarce supply of pills on her so you'd both have a good time. How was I supposed to know she couldn't handle it?"

"You drugged her. What did you expect to happen?" I ask.

Olivia turns to me. "I've taken it before. I was fine. Maybe her destitute body couldn't handle designer drugs? That's not on me."

"Except she didn't know you were giving her a drink with drugs in it." I relax my hands on my legs when I really want to throttle this girl. Drugging Keira is bad enough, but she wanted to pull that shit with Annie. Not on my watch. Not ever.

"Whatever." She folds her arms across her chest and turns to Damon. "You've got nothing but your word. My father would crush you in court, so that's not going to help you. Maybe I'll go find a real man to fuck me since you only seem to want to slum it. I hope she's worth it."

Damon's smile tells her everything. "She is."

Olivia's eyes narrow and she heads to the door. Before she can touch the doorknob, Damon clears his throat. I smile because this is when he shuts the trap.

She stops and huffs, "What else can you possibly have to say?"

"Did I forget to mention this whole thing has been recorded?" Damon leans back with his legs spread and his hands threaded together over his stomach. "Video and audio."

Olivia glances around.

"Don't worry. I'm not poor. I can afford the high-quality stuff. You'll never find them."

She glares with a glint in her eyes. "You're bluffing."

I hold out my phone with the video playback from when she came into the room. "Definitely not bluffing."

Olivia goes still as she watches herself help Keira into the room. She pales and the martyred look drops from her face.

"I'm betting the police will be real interested to find out what happened in this room when a sixteen-year-old turns up at the hospital with alcohol and a date rape drug in her system." Damon glances my way. "How long is the federal jail time for drugging a minor with the intent to sexually assault them? Up to twenty years?"

"Sounds right." I'm not confident in my answer, but it seems legit. "State and federal would both want a piece of you, plus they'd want to know your supplier. Drug dealers get pretty twitchy when someone like you might turn on them. Especially for a reduced sentence."

Olivia staggers like I hit her. "What? But Tanner—"

"Is probably a dealer." Damon stands but doesn't approach her. "I mean, why else would he willingly give a chick like you drugs? The first time is always free. He probably wanted you to spread it around so he'd make bank selling party favors."

Real fear plays across her face. "What will it take?"

"What will what take?" I stand and lean against the wall like I have all day. "You drugged my girl's friend. Once the cops get involved, there's not much we can do."

Damon smirks. "Except be law-abiding citizens and turn the video in."

"You must need something, or you wouldn't be here talking to me. You would already be showing the police that video." Olivia glares at both of us. "What do you want from me?"

"Leave Damon alone."

"Oh, that ship has already sailed." She shakes her head. "I've already worked too fucking hard for low results."

"I need to hear you say it." Damon straightens off the wall and takes a step toward her. "You won't come near me or Evan again."

"Fine, I won't come near you or EvanAnn again." She crosses her arms over her chest. "Anything else?"

"You're going to make sure Keira gets a generous scholarship to the college of her choice." I make sure to meet her eyes. "A full ride, tuition and living expenses."

"And how am I supposed to pull that off?" She throws her hands up.

"Tell daddy the truth. I'm sure he'll pay whatever it takes to keep Keira and us quiet." I know we all come from privilege, but Keira is a scholarship kid just like Annie. And tonight could have fucked up Keira's future. So I'm going to make sure she gets what she needs for the future.

"Fine." Olivia turns like she's going to leave.

"Not so fast." Damon's words make her pause and flinch a little. "I still have one more thing I need from you."

She drags in an impatient breath. "What?"

"Did Chase hit something while you were giving him road head?" Damon leans against the wall like this isn't that important. Like this isn't the whole purpose of everything we've done this year. This bitch and Chase Chadwick ruined Damon's future. But it also gave us Annie.

"He swerved and it sounded like he might have hit an animal. I'm just that good," she snaps with attitude. "Not that you'll ever find out now."

"Don't worry." I give her a mean smile and glance at Damon. "You aren't missing anything."

We fucked a while ago. A party hookup I barely remember. She glares at me.

"You said you laughed with him about dating Evan. Why is Chase so desperate to keep dating her?" Damon asks. It's what we've all been wondering. She's not giving him sex. Yes, he uses her for an alibi, but when she broke up with him, why not find another girl? Why keep trying to get Annie back?

Olivia smirks. Her eyes dart to the healed scar on Damon's face as if she's beginning to put things together based on our questions. She laughs, but it's abrupt and bitter.

"I was right, wasn't I?" Olivia gets this look like she thinks it's precious. "You want revenge on Chase Chadwick, so you stole his girl. I tried to warn you she was a prude."

"Tick tock, Olivia," I say with my hand on my phone. "I can just send this to the police, and they can take care of you. Or you can tell us what we want to know."

She glares. "That's the question everyone asks, why the little nerd?"

I'm tempted to send the file and fuck this bitch over. Honestly, we might send it anyway. I don't trust her.

"If you don't have the answer..." Damon shrugs. "It's not like you know everything."

"Oh, I know some of it." She's smug now.

"Fuck it. Let's just send it to the police and let them sort it out." I press a few things on my phone.

"No!" Olivia's façade drops. "But I don't know all of it. His dad wanted him to date someone like EvanAnn. Someone smart and going places. A good influence. Chase figured he'd use her this year. Daddy wasn't going to introduce his whore son with a drug problem to his friends who could make him a star." She chuckles. "Chase isn't that bright, but he knows how to use people to get what he wants. He gave EvanAnn what she wanted. A boyfriend. And in return, she polished his reputation with his father. She may be a scholarship kid, but there's a reason she's at Anteros and why they'll splash her name over any future recruitment efforts."

She gives a cold smile. "And Chase wants to attach his career to her rising star. In his father's eyes, EvanAnn can do no wrong. And with Chase dating her, Chase gets a shiny new respectability with his father. And the connections his father wanted to withhold."

Chapter 34

Cam

I hand Evan a soda and take the seat next to her in the waiting room. Her focus remains on the doors they took Keira through ten minutes ago. We told the nurse what we knew. Now we just wait.

"She'll be okay." It seems like the right thing to say, but I don't know if it's true. Had it been anyone else in that room waiting for Olivia, would they have even questioned it? Would they have raped Keira?

This isn't something that can be swept under the rug. We won't let it. Someone like Olivia won't ever stop if she doesn't get punished at some point.

But right now, I need to take care of our girl. "How's the hand?"

Evan blinks and turns to me. "Hand?"

I smirk and reach for her hand. "You smacked the shit out of Olivia Carmichael."

"Oh." Evan glances down at it. "I guess I did."

I take it and check it over before threading my fingers through hers and holding it on my lap. "I'm sorry about your friend."

She blows out a breath. "I thought I was used to this school." Her blue-gray eyes lift to mine. "I thought I knew everything they could do to us, but this..."

She gestures toward the hospital doors and shakes her head.

"Won't go unpunished," I say with conviction.

Evan meets my gaze. "There's not much you can do to her. She's untouchable. Fucking rich bitch."

That makes me smile.

She cocks an eyebrow at me. "What?"

"You amaze me." I bring her hand to my lips and press a kiss to her knuckles. "The shit you put up with. From us, from Olivia, from Chase." I shake my head. "Most girls would have given up at some point, but not you."

"I'm not giving up on my dream just because of a few roadblocks." She scoffs.

"Someday this will all be a memory of a really sucky night." I bump her gently with my shoulder.

"Tell me Olivia's going to pay for this." She looks up at me with so much hope.

I brush my thumb along her jaw. "We have a plan, but we need to work fast. First thing that needs to happen is we need to clean up the recording. No one needs to know about us. At least not yet. Especially not your mom or Damon's dad."

She nods and processes what I'm saying. "Then what?"

I smirk. "Then we send a copy to the authorities, Olivia's father, the DA, and post it online tagging our school."

Her mouth opens and closes. "Will that be enough?"

"Depends on what they find in there." I gesture to the doors. "Usually drugs can be hard to find after the fact, but Olivia just gave this one to Keira. It should show up on her workup. That plus Olivia basically walking Keira into the room." I shrug. "It will definitely get everyone's attention, but there's no guarantee she'll do time for it. But she'll be tried in the court of public opinion. And probably be asked to leave Deimos Academy."

Evan gives me a look. "Asked to leave? Not expelled?"

"Unfortunately, that's the world we live in." I rub my thumb on the back of her hand. "Our parents will do anything to make us who they want us to be. My dad wants me to go to Yale. He's going to be disappointed to find out I can't get in, but maybe he'll figure out that's not really what I want or need."

She rests her head against my arm and squeezes my hand.

"Olivia's dad will do what's necessary to keep his daughter from doing jail time. But he'll also make her life unpleasant enough that she wishes she was in jail instead. And that's what will punish her. Will it make Keira's life better? Probably not. But I bet she walks away with something more than trauma from being drugged."

"You mean Olivia's father will pay her off." Evan sounds sad, like the world isn't living up to her expectations. I wish I could change it for her. Make the world exactly how it should be. Everyone gets exactly what they deserve.

"Why do you think we didn't go after Chase directly?" I turn and press my lips against her hair. "Because he would have gotten away with it. Yes, there would have been a little punishment, but not nearly as much as Damon was owed."

She sighs. "If I did any of this shit, I'd be in prison."

"Nah, goody." I tip her chin up so I can search her eyes. "First, you wouldn't pull any of this shit because you're way too smart for any of us. Second, if you did, you'd be smart enough not to get caught. And third, we wouldn't let anyone take you away from us."

She gives me a soft smile, and my heart beats a little faster. "I meant what I said."

Those words. Fuck. I could spend a lifetime and not be good enough for this girl, but that doesn't mean I'll let her go.

"Good, because no take backs." I wink and brush my lips against hers.

She releases a sigh and turns to look at the doors. "Do you think they'll let us back there?"

"When she's ready."

EvanAnn

It was almost thirty minutes after they took Keira in that they let me know she wanted to see me. Cam gave me a kiss and said he'd be out here waiting. While we waited, he told me about some of his family vacations as a kid.

Places I only dreamed of going, they went to on a whim.

I follow the nurse back, and she opens the door for me. When I close in on the bed, Keira looks as pale as the sheets behind her. I round the bed and take her hand. It's so cold. I rub it between my own.

She opens her eyes and smiles groggily when she sees me. "Hey."

"Hey." Tears press on my eyes, but I blink them back. She was in that room because of me. Because Olivia thought Damon wanted someone just like me.

"Could you...?" She waves her other hand toward the cup with a straw in it.

I reach for it and hold it in front of her, guiding the straw to her lips. She drinks a little and then pushes it away.

"What happened?" Her eyes search mine for the answers.

I sit on the edge of the bed and tell her about the spiked drink. How Olivia brought her into the room, and how I was right there. I even tell her about me slapping Olivia.

Keira laughs, but her throat is still sore from her stomach being pumped. "I wish I could have seen that."

"I think we have it on video." Smiling, I squeeze her hand. "Where are your parents?"

I glance over my shoulder toward the door. Someone should have been notified she's here.

"Mom's at work. Dad's usually asleep around now." Keira looks down at her lap. "I wasn't supposed to go out tonight, but..."

"I get it." It's hard to feel like you're not part of the school. To be on the outside looking in. I thought not going to the parties wasn't a big deal, but so much of our social lives happens there. "Did they call?"

She nods. "Dad should be here soon. Mom can't leave work."

"I'll stay with you until they get here if you want."

Her eyes brighten as they meet mine. "That would be nice, but if you need to go—"

"I don't. This is where I need to be right now." My chest feels warm. "Cam's out in the waiting room, but he'll stay as long as I need him to."

She smiles. "Those boys must be gone on you."

"I like them too," I admit.

We talk about classes and some movies while we wait. Nurses come in and check her vitals every now and then.

"Will you get in trouble?" I ask. "For going to the party?"

Keira shrugs and looks away. "Not so much trouble. But Dad needs his sleep. He works first shift and Mom works third. They want to be home for my younger sister in the evenings. She's twelve."

"Is she trying to get into Anteros too?"

Keira shakes her head. "No, she would do excellent on the Deimos side, but she doesn't really have a thing like us. She's just really smart. Wants to be a scientist when she grows up."

Before I can say anything, there's a knock on the door. A large man comes in and glances at me before his green eyes settle on Keira's.

"You took years off my life." His voice is low and soothing. He's upset, but not at her, at the situation. "What the hell happened?"

"Someone gave me something in a drink at a party." Keira blows out a breath. "This is EvanAnn. EvanAnn, this is my father, Bruce Fox."

He looks at me like somehow this is my fault. I don't think an adult has ever looked at me like that.

"Dad! She's my friend. She realized what happened and got me to the hospital." Keira draws her father's attention. "If she hadn't been there—"

She cuts herself off, and her eyes water.

"I'm sorry." Bruce gets to Keira's bedside and reaches for her shoulder like he wants to comfort her but forgot how.

"It's okay. It's just been a long night, and I'd like to go home." Keira breathes out a shaky breath.

He draws his hand away and fists it at his side. "I'll go find the doctor." He glances at me. "Will you stay with her?"

I nod and sit in the chair beside the bed. It takes another half hour before they release her.

"Do you need a ride home?" Bruce asks me as we walk beside Keira in a wheelchair.

I shake my head. "My boyfriend is waiting for me."

He nods. "Thank you for being there for my daughter."

"Anytime." I ignore the twist in my gut that says this is partially my fault.

"I'll text when I get home." Keira takes my hand and squeezes it before she's wheeled off, leaving me alone.

I turn to the doors to the waiting room. It's late now, and I pull out my phone as I head that way. The guys checked in on me a couple of times to make sure everything was okay, but otherwise, they just let me be.

I appreciated that, but I'm also not sure how Cam and I are going to get home. The guy who dropped us off left to return to the party. When I push through the doors, Damon, Hawk, and Cam rise to their feet.

A rush of warmth goes through me at finding them all here. Cam steps forward and draws me into his arms.

"How are you doing, goody?" He rubs my back as I sink into him.

"So tired."

"Come on. We went and got Damon's car." Hawk nods toward the exit.

Cam wraps his arm around my shoulders, and we follow Damon and Hawk to the car. Cam gets into the back seat with me, and I rest against his shoulder, suddenly drained of all my energy.

An alt rock station plays softly as we drive into our neighborhood. Instead of going to our house, Damon heads to Hawk's. I breathe out a sigh of relief.

I don't know if my mom would have been home or not, but I'm not ready to talk to any more parents. And crawling into bed with the Devil's trio sounds like heaven right now after everything we went through tonight.

Chapter 35

Hawk

We left the party quickly after our discussion with Olivia. It didn't sit well with either of us, letting her walk out of that room thinking she lost Damon, but she wouldn't face consequences for her actions.

She can think that tonight. Because we have work to do and need her to stay quiet.

I like Keira. She's a good person and a better fit as a friend for Annie than Mia. If we didn't have the video, Olivia would have walked. But with the video in the right hands, she'll face punishment. Maybe not as much as she deserves, but more than a slap on the wrist.

Cam, Damon, and I talked in the waiting room about what needed to be done. And what was left of our plan. We just need to loop Annie into it.

We also discussed timing for the other plan for Chase, but we need to find a way to make sure Annie is safe while we execute it.

We climb out of the car and head into the house. I stop to grab a few bottles of water to bring up with us. Damon heads to my computer and pulls up his cloud account.

"What do you need to edit the video?" Damon glances at Annie.

We don't want to hand Olivia proof of her "assault." It can be her word against ours. But we'll win, because we always win.

"Drop it in my file and I'll work on it when I get to my editing software." Annie sits on the edge of the bed and releases a breath. She's tired and worn out. Tonight was a lot.

Damon nods and copies it. I hand Annie a bottle of water, and she gives me one of those soft smiles. There are so many things I want to tell her. I'm all in on this girl.

Before we can get into anything, Damon hits play on the recording. Cam sits beside Annie, and I lean against the wall as we all watch the playback.

"You promised her you wouldn't send this to the police?" At the end, Annie sets her drink down and stands. "Without this, she's definitely going to get away with it."

"She's not getting away with anything." Damon leans back in my desk chair. "We had to let her walk tonight. There wouldn't have been a way to get her out of the party without her making a huge scene. We'll send the video tomorrow, and they'll have the evidence to prosecute her."

"Keira didn't remember much. She talked to the police officer at the hospital, but her test results should be enough to prove she was drugged." Annie runs a hand through her hair. "But they need the recording to prove Keira didn't take the drugs herself."

I step up to Annie and put my hands on her shoulders. She meets my gaze.

"Olivia isn't going to get away with this." I pull Annie into me for a hug. "She doesn't get to get away with this. I don't think she'll receive prison time, but she definitely won't be at Deimos for long. They have a reputation to uphold."

She rests her ear against my heart and wraps her arms around my waist. "I never thought something like that could happen to someone I know."

I want to hold her like this forever. Keep her from anything or anyone who wants to hurt her.

"It shouldn't have happened," Cam says. "We may have parties, but we would have heard if someone was slipping drugs into drinks."

"Olivia said she got them from Tanner." Damon leans back and rubs the back of his neck. "Maybe no one's had access to them before he came into town. And most people may be using them recreationally without saying anything. Not trying to assault other students."

Annie takes in a deep breath and releases it. "We need to talk."

She releases me and steps away. I let her. Her blue-gray eyes lock on each of us.

"I need to know what the plan was and what it is now. You told Mia the plan was to ruin me." She wraps her arms around herself but lifts her chin. "Obviously, you know how I feel about you, but that doesn't mean you don't intend to hurt me."

Cam and I turn to Damon. This is his revenge. He scrubs his hand over his face and looks down at the floor between his feet.

"I meant what I said." He lifts his gaze to Annie's. "I want to take care of you. I love you. But before that I was willing to hurt you to get what I needed."

Damon

Evan's eyes search mine. I could let Hawk or Cam tell her how this started. Let them smooth out the rough spots, but it all starts with me. And if she's going to be angry with anyone, it will be me. I could lose her. My chest aches, but I have to tell her.

"Okay." She blows out a breath and moves toward me.

I can't do this if I'm touching her. Because even though I don't want to hurt her now, this still might burn. I glance at Hawk, and he guides her to the bed beside Cam and then sits on her other side. He takes her hand and she takes Cam's. They all face me.

"I didn't know you. Chase hit me. You were his girlfriend. It made sense you were the girl in the car."

That night is burned into my memory. Glancing over and seeing her sucking his dick. The moment the car swerved into me, too quickly for me to react, to get out of the way. Falling. I take in a shuddering breath, jerking myself out of the memory before the pain.

I rub my leg, even though the pain is mostly gone.

"I was so fucking angry at Chase for stealing my dreams." I shake my head and lift my gaze to meet hers, because I'm not going to hide from her now. "Juniors was my mom's and my dream. It was one step away from the NHL. It's what we worked so hard for. But it also meant spending a year in someone else's house and going to school up there while playing hockey. Dad wouldn't see reason and wouldn't let me go, even though I had recovered for the most part."

Evan swallows. She knows what it's like to have a huge dream. One that seems unattainable, but she'd do anything to get it.

"I was stuck here this year. No more Juniors. No more NHL. And then my dad tells me he's moving in his girlfriend and her daughter." My smile is not nice as I remember them offering her to me like a present. "Imagine my surprise when the daughter was the girl who helped cause my accident."

Evan doesn't react. She's got a great poker face, but she knows most of this. Nothing I'm telling her is new, but Evan also loves her mother. And I have to tell her the whole story if I want her to trust me going forward.

My hands tighten into fists, and I drop my gaze. "My dad's brought other women around. Gold-diggers. Women who could never compare to my mother. He didn't deserve to find happiness with someone less than her. Not after what he did to her."

Evan shifts, and I jerk my gaze up to hers. She knows my thoughts on my mother's death. The guilt and anger. But her desire and need to comfort me is laid bare on her face. The others hold her back. She doesn't know I don't deserve it. I don't deserve her.

"We were at a party, and I was still calculating how best to get revenge. I knew I had to get rid of the gold-digger, but she was bringing you into my territory. Giving you to me. I didn't know who you were. You were an ant. Smart, driven. Dating Chase Chadwick. I saw you at the party and you didn't fit in. Your hair up in a messy bun and a sweatshirt and jeans, hanging next to the beer pong table while your boyfriend ignored you."

It feels like forever ago.

"It was before school started. Olivia wanted to talk to me, so I asked her about you. She waffled between calling you a prude and obviously giving it up to your boyfriend because everyone knew he got around. Like he wanted a good girl to clean up his rep."

I tap my foot and look away.

"The plan was to get you to fuck around with us on your boyfriend. Take you from him and prove to everyone you weren't the good girl everyone thought you were." I meet her stormy blue eyes. "It would have hurt Chase, you, and gotten your mom to leave. It was everything I wanted."

Her chest stops rising and falling like she caught her breath.

I laugh, but it's bitter now. "It was so easy to convince my dad to use the room for the daughter my parents never had. The one connected to mine. Changing the locks was simple, and since he rarely comes into my room, he never noticed."

I shake my head. "It shouldn't have been so fucking easy. To get to you. To make you mine. Not if you were the good girl everyone said you were. I never imagined I was forcing an innocent to play my warped little game."

I blow out a breath and meet her eyes, expecting to find disgust in them. But they're almost silver. Her face is carefully blank. I wish I could read her right now. My heart thumps hard in my chest. I don't know how, but if I've lost her, I'll get her back. I'll force her back into my bed and remind her how much she loves me.

She releases the others' hands and stands. Will she leave me now? Have I lost the only good thing in my life because I was a vindictive asshole? I deserve it.

She crosses the floor to stand in front of me. I straighten and brace myself for the slap I deserve. The anger she should let loose on me.

Instead, she straddles me and sinks onto my lap. Her hands cup my jaw and she searches my eyes. Her breath spills onto my lips, and I breathe her in like she's the air I need to live.

"Okay. Tell me what the plan is now."

I rest my hands on her skirt bunched up on her hips and release the fear. She's mine. Fuck, I don't deserve her, but I'll spend my whole life making it up to her, giving her everything she needs.

"To make Chase pay and to keep you safe."

"And how do we do that?"

"Olivia falls." I draw in her woodsy scent. "Chase gets punished for the party, and then he finds out he's lost you. We make sure Jackson can't get to you. You stay ours."

Her lips press into a thin line. "What about my mom?"

Evan has defended her mom. I want to look away, but she's holding my face and searching my eyes.

"I can't lose you," I say softly. My heart is torn. I want to keep Evan but send her mother packing. But that's not how this works. I can't protect my mom's spot in my father's heart. If he wants to give it to Heather, I can't stop him. Because I can't hurt Evan like that. I can't force her out. She's mine.

"Damon," she whispers and presses a kiss to my lips. "My mom is just looking for love and happiness after loss. The same thing your father is doing. They know each other's pain, and they respect the love for the person who isn't here anymore. I can see it when they talk. I'm used to not having my mother's full attention, but that doesn't make her a bad person. And I don't think she would have moved us in with your father just because he has money."

I breathe out. "It doesn't matter if she is. You're here, and that's all that matters. If it's not your mother, it would be someone else. Dad is ready to move on. Even if I'm not."

She slides her hands into my hair and rests her forehead against mine. "We'll never be ready to let go of our parents. Your dad and my mom are just doing the best they can with the hand they've been dealt. They aren't trying to replace or erase your mom or my dad. They're just trying to continue to live."

I nod, and she kisses me again. This time slow and tender until I want to sink into her so she'll never get me out.

When she breaks the kiss, she smiles softly. "Do you have a plan to take down Chase or are we just improvising at this point?"

I slide my hands down to her bare thighs and slip under her skirt. "I would have shown him the videos of us fucking if he'd already seen the way you come. But he hasn't and he never will. That's ours."

"Then we need to come up with a new plan." She's got that determined look on her face that's so hot.

And those eyes, when she lets me in... I could spend hours watching her eyes as she's fucked. By me, by the others, it doesn't matter.

"First we need to take down Olivia." Hawk stands and paces the room. "Remove the queen from the board. She's too fucking unpredictable."

"We've cornered Chase. He's out of moves." Cam leans forward, putting his elbows on his knees. "The party didn't get busted, but there's no way he'll be able to hide it from his parents."

"The party hasn't gotten busted... yet," Evan says. Her fingers tighten in my hair and my cock aches to be inside her. "We could call in a noise complaint."

"Fuck, the police breaking up two parties? The party scene will be dead after that." Cam runs his hand through his hair.

"You need to study, anyway." Evan glances at him over her shoulder.

"Besides," Hawk says with a smirk, "we already have a party."

His gaze takes in Evan. She's hot in this outfit. The shirt clings to her breasts and covers my marks on her shoulders. I want to tear it off her and mark every inch of her delectable little body.

"Fine, it won't shut down all the parties," Cam says with a cocky smile at Evan. "But everyone will be leery of big parties for a while.

Things will be kept small. And we can focus on what's important. Like Evan."

Hawk gets his phone out.

"How are you going to make sure the police don't trace it to you?" Evan asks.

Hawk smirks. "I know the neighbors. Or at least one of them. A freshman on the hockey team. He can have his mom call, and we'll give him some extra training on the ice."

"I'll text the hockey team to get the fuck out." Cam is already texting.

"Mia's with Liam and Fletcher." Evan's still focused on me. Her eyes are dark kaleidoscopes. Her hands in my hair. Our faces close together. Her bare skin under my fingertips. "Make sure she gets out too."

"On it."

"I don't want to hurt you, Evan." The words are soft, and I mean them.

Her eyes soften. "I would do anything to help you get your revenge. Anything you needed me to do. But I can't help you hurt my mother. She's already been through enough pain."

"I was still mad at him. Mad at my mom for making that decision not to fight. I didn't think he deserved to find someone else. He should have to live with that pain." I breathe her in. "I won't get in their way. Getting your mother out of my house is no longer a priority. You are my only priority. That means keeping you in my bed."

"And getting into the NHL." She brushes her thumb against the corner of my jaw.

"That's a given." I slide my hands beneath her panties and grip her ass cheeks.

Her eyes darken, and she arches an eyebrow.

"We also need to figure out how to neutralize Jackson," I say.

She shivers in my arms. "He hasn't really done much besides make his presence known."

"He threatened you, baby girl." Hawk tosses his phone on his desk and tips Evan's face up to look in her eyes. "He wouldn't threaten if he didn't intend to see it through."

"What do we do then?" Evan's throat is taut in front of me.

Irresistible. I lean in and suck on her soft skin.

"We keep you safe with us." Hawk lowers his head. "As long as we're fucking you, no one else can fuck with you."

He claims her mouth, and a low moan works out of her. I slide my fingers beneath her panties and over her wet pussy. When I press inside, she whimpers in pain.

"Are you sore, little devil?"

Hawk lifts his mouth from hers.

"A little," she admits.

"Police are on their way to the party." Cam stands and takes off his shirt. "I'm sure we can find some way to amuse ourselves without fucking that pretty pussy."

She bites her lip as her gaze lowers to meet mine.

"On your knees, little devil." I release her and she slides to the floor between my knees.

Her hands are on my belt. Hawk slides to the floor with her, kneeling behind her.

"I need that pussy, baby girl."

She moans and looks at him as she undoes my pants. "It's yours."

He kisses her and smirks up at me as he lies on the floor and puts his head between her legs under her skirt. She lets out a moan as he begins to work her with his tongue.

She frees my cock and lifts her gaze to mine before taking me into her mouth.

This isn't the hurried fuck in Chase's room. She takes her time, tasting me, sucking me, licking me. Her breath hitches when Hawk hits the good spots. I draw her hair out of her face so I can watch her.

Cam sits on the edge of the bed with his cock out, stroking it. His gaze doesn't stray from her. Every inch of this girl is ours. I slide my hand along her neck before squeezing slightly on the sides of it.

She gasps around my cock and jerks her hips against Hawk's face.

He grabs her to hold her still. Her release takes her as she sucks on the head of my cock and moans. I push her down onto my cock as I come, flooding her mouth, making her take every drop.

Her throat works against my hand to swallow me down.

"I love you," I whisper.

Her eyes open and meet mine. My future used to be hockey. It still is, but I can see my future in Evan's eyes now.

Chapter 36

EvanAnn

Damon lifts me off the floor and carries me to the bed as my pussy still pulses from my orgasm. He lays me down, and they surround me. Dragging my clothes off until I'm naked and spread out between them. Anticipation swells inside me. Cam takes Hawk's place between my legs, licking my pussy before sliding back to tongue my asshole.

I suck in a harsh breath at the sensitive nerves sparking with his attention.

When Hawk draws my head his way, I part my lips, and he slides his cock into my mouth. Damon touches me softly everywhere, on my breasts, stomach, neck, gliding his fingers over my skin in shivery little patterns. I focus on sucking on Hawk's cock, making him feel as good as he made me feel.

His green eyes lock with mine as he guides my head over him, thrusting into my mouth. My whole body trembles beneath their touch. I don't need an apology for the way they came after me. Maybe I would if I hadn't been as willing to work with them. To explore this connection and attraction.

The blackmail wouldn't have made me do something I didn't

want to do. It's not like it would have ruined my career. Maybe my relationship with Chase. But that was already gone. I never wanted Chase, but he was a social life. He made me feel seen and wanted.

But I wanted Damon, Hawk, and Cam. They truly see me, know me. And being here with them is worth whatever pain I might have had to endure to get here.

The fire they stoke in me consumes me. I arch as Cam rubs circles on my clit with his fingers while fucking my asshole with his tongue. Moaning, I come for him. Hawk thrusts deep into my throat and groans as he releases.

"Fuck," he whispers. "I'll never get enough of you, baby girl."

He leans down and kisses me, tasting himself on my tongue.

"I love you, Annie. I'll protect you no matter what."

Cupping his jaw, I search his eyes. "I love you."

He smirks and kisses me before trailing kisses down my neck and capturing my breast in his mouth. Cam pulls away and stands between my legs.

"Such a beautiful mess." His dark brown eyes settle on mine as he strokes his cock.

The others hold me down with their mouths and touch. I'm helpless against what they do to me.

"I could come all over your creamy skin."

Hawk and Damon each grab one of my legs, spreading them wide and holding me open for Cam.

"You want my cum on your pussy, goody?" Cam's gaze focuses on my pussy.

"Cam," I whimper, wanting it, needing it.

He steps closer and rubs the head of his cock through my slick folds. Damon bites my breast and sucks on the hurt. Hawk swirls his tongue around my nipple. I'm overwhelmed and needy. Cam's cock teases my entrance. He doesn't thrust in, but he pushes slightly inside before sliding his cockhead along my clit.

My release is sudden, and I cry out as I arch between them. Hot, sticky cum jets out over my pussy as Cam groans. He slides his fingers through the mess and eases it inside me. My pussy pulses around his finger as I try to come down.

"I could spend the rest of my life fucking you, goody, and not get enough."

The others move out of the way as Cam sweeps me up against him, our bare skin hot against each other.

I slide my hand into his thick brown hair and take his mouth with mine. He opens for me as he carries me into the bathroom. He walks into the shower and turns the water on before pressing me against the shower wall.

When he lifts his mouth, he searches my eyes. "I love you, Evan."

I smile and brush his hair back from his face. My heart is going to burst because of these guys. "I love you, Cam."

His smile is huge. The water is warm on my legs, and he steps back to lower me to stand.

"If I didn't want to sleep in the bed, I would have come all over you, goody." He runs his head under the shower.

I laugh. "You say the nicest things."

He smirks and draws me against his wet naked body. "You have me, goody. Body and soul."

"Movie quote?" I arch an eyebrow because it sounds familiar.

"Not this time." He stops and thinks. "Probably not."

We finish showering and head back out to the bedroom. Hawk passes Cam one of his Devils shirts, and Cam tugs it on over my head. I yawn.

"It's done." Damon offers me his phone.

I press play on the video, and it's Chase's house with cop cars pulling up.

Cam sighs and sits on the edge of the bed in his boxers. "It's going to be a while before anyone will be able to have a party."

"Think of all the homework you'll get done," I say.

He grabs the hem of my t-shirt and tugs me toward him. I stand between his legs and look down at him. My fingers tangle in his damp hair, and he rests his head below my breasts.

"My reputation as a party boy is going to suffer."

"That's not a bad thing. Maybe your hockey will improve along with your grades." Damon sits on the bed next to Cam and his blue eyes dance as they meet mine.

Hawk comes up behind me and rests his chin on my head. I breathe them in. I was so happy at the beginning of this year to have a boyfriend and a potential new friend. But now I have three boyfriends and two friends.

And an ex and a stalker, but who's counting them?

We stay in bed Sunday morning. Just talking. I don't remember the last time I didn't do anything. Cam wants me to find that list so we can start working on the movies my dad wanted me to watch.

"My dad wants to have dinner tonight." Damon plays with my fingers.

My head is on Hawk's stomach. His fingers stroke my hair. Cam has my feet in his lap. I turn to meet Damon's gaze. I should work on something, but I don't want to move from this spot. Ever.

"Want me to join you?"

He smirks. "Of course."

He sets my hand on his tight abs. I can't wait to explore each of their cut bodies slowly. Without any distractions from the others. My phone beeps, and I want to ignore it, but I know I can't. It's already late.

I roll over, grab my phone from the nightstand, and shut off the alarm.

"Keira won't be at practice today." I frown. "She's feeling better, but her dad and mom want her to stay home."

"Not a problem." Hawk rubs my back. "I'll be there if you need help getting people into line."

I roll toward him and kiss him because I can. His smile when I draw away is everything I need.

"I need to get home." I don't want to, but I need to.

Damon climbs off the bed and tosses my clothes from last night onto the bed next to me.

"Is this going to be the walk of shame?" I arch an eyebrow his way.

"If you want to walk, little devil, you can, but I have the car here." Damon smirks.

I shake my head and get dressed. Cam hasn't moved so I lean over and kiss him.

"We're studying tonight?" I lower my head slightly and narrow my eyes.

Cam chuckles. "What else am I supposed to do? There are no parties."

"Good." I kiss him again and meet Hawk's gaze. "See you in a few hours?"

"Wouldn't miss it." Hawk winks.

"Maybe you should ride with Hawk to rehearsal." Damon catches my hip and draws me into him. "That way we've got you from door to door."

"What would I say to Chase?" I haven't gotten any texts from Chase. But if he's in trouble, he might not be able to text me.

"Tell him the truth." Damon tips my chin up and gives me a cocky grin. "That you're fucking Hawk, Cam, and me, and it's the best sex of your life."

"Half of that statement is true, but can I really say it's the best if it's the only sex I've had?" I give him my best innocent look. "I should really gather more data points before making that determination."

He growls, and shivers race through me.

"You better go before Damon feels the need to provide proof." Hawk shakes his head.

I tap my finger on my lip like I'm trying to decide. "I do have to go..."

"Come on, little devil." Damon takes my hand, and I let him drag me out of Hawk's house.

We park in the garage and take the backstairs up to our rooms. Damon gives me a searing kiss before smacking my ass and heading down to workout. I take a shower and when I get out, I touch all the marks they left on my body last night.

There's one on my neck I'm going to need a lot of makeup to cover up. Part of me doesn't want to. Doesn't care who sees it. But even though we know a little of why Chase wants me, it doesn't explain the college list we found.

After I get dressed and settled at my desk, there's a knock. I set my planner down and open the door.

Mom stands there. Her fingers on her necklace as she stares down the hallway.

"Hi, Mom."

She turns, seeming almost startled to find me in the doorway. It's weird, but I leave the door open and head back to my desk.

"I have practice in an hour, but I'm planning on being home for dinner." I glance back, and she's stepped in and is looking around my room. I should really be pulling the covers down on the bed every night to make it look like I slept there.

But maybe the cleaners just think I'm a really tidy kid.

Her gaze jumps to the bathroom door, which is cracked slightly. She's acting weird. I stop and really look at her. She's dressed how she dresses now, her clothes a fancier version of what she's always worn. But she seems distracted.

I glance at the date in my planner. Did I forget one of the important dates? I've been a little caught up in my own drama lately.

Mom blows out a breath and turns her gaze on me. "Are you okay here, Evan?"

Okay, that furrows my brow. "Of course. The food is delicious. The bed's comfy. I have more clothes than I can ever imagine wearing. All my needs are being met."

My cheeks burn at that last one. But I wasn't talking about that. Not with my mom.

She slides her pendant on her necklace and looks at my bed. "Chase seems like a nice boy."

I sit in my office chair and watch her closely. She's looking for something from me, but what? Her motivation in this scene is a complete mystery. Normally, she checks on me, but never with this nervous energy.

"Is something wrong, Mom?" I'm in jeans and a sweatshirt. Something I've always worn on the weekend.

"No." Mom straightens. "I just—"

She cuts herself off and blows out her breath. Some of the tension leaves her body, and she sits on the end of my bed.

"I should check on you more." Her eyes dart up to mine before lowering to her hands. "But you're fine, right? School's good? The play is good? Your boyfriend is good?"

"I'm good, Mom. What's bringing this on?" There's this buzzing feeling inside me, like something's terribly wrong.

"I did this all wrong." She looks up at me. "I didn't mean to spring the move on you or leave you by yourself so much."

"It's okay." I go over and sit next to her on the bed. "I adjusted. It was a surprise, but I'm made of tough stuff."

She reaches over and takes my hand between hers. "Adam thought I should see a therapist. So I've been going, and we've been talking about things." Mom's eyes are watery when she lifts them to mine. "It was easier just to press on than to dwell, but I didn't take the time to worry about you."

The tears spill down her cheeks. I reach over to my nightstand and take a tissue out of the box to hand to her.

"You were only ten, but you were doing so well. Top grades. Applying to programs I never dreamed of. You never complained and didn't seem to need me. And I was so lost." She dabs at her tears. "Your dad and I were with each other since high school. I didn't know how to be alone. And the worst part is, I wasn't alone. I had you, but I couldn't be there for you."

"Mom." I squeeze her hand. "I'm fine. This move is good. I'm focused on school and the play."

I can't tell her that I have Damon, Hawk, and Cam. That even though things have been messed up, I've never felt more alive. Never felt more loved. Never felt more like I'm part of something amazing.

I pick up the box of tissues and hand it to my mom.

"It's like Adam shook me back to life." Mom blots at her tears and gives me a watery smile. "It was fast, and I know that, but I really love Adam. I've been sleepwalking through life, and he woke me up. He's worried about you and about Damon. You both went through trauma like we did, but it's different for you. I'm so sorry I wasn't more present. I'm going to do better."

My chest buzzes with that feeling again. Mom hasn't ever been truly present. What will that mean? Will she suddenly realize that maybe putting her eighteen-year-old daughter in a room connected to her boyfriend's eighteen-year-old son wasn't maybe the best idea?

Or is this temporary? Because she gets this way after a break-up. Maybe this is new because she isn't breaking up with Adam and just wants to feel closer to me. It will last a couple weeks, and then things will return to normal.

I just know I'm not ready to give up Damon.

Chapter 37

EvanAnn

I cling to Hawk, not because he's going too fast, but because I like the way his body feels against mine as we ride to the high school. He parks and waits for me to climb off before setting the bike on the kickstand.

He takes our helmets and puts them in his storage bags. When he reaches for my hand, I look around. We're the only ones here, but I don't want to out us. He smirks and puts his hand on my back to usher me into the school.

We make our way to the black box room, and Hawk moves to turn on the lights. My mind is already on practice mode, and I sit down at the table to pull out my notes for today. As I pull my script and highlighters out of my bag, Hawk sets down a new package of highlighters next to mine.

I glance up at his smirk and then down at the highlighters. These are the fancy kind they don't sell at the dollar store. The tips are see-through.

"What are these for?" I ask, not touching them.

"They're for you. I've watched you throw away twice as many as these during rehearsal. Figured you needed some new ones." He lifts the package. "These are supposed to be long lasting."

He hands me the package. *I'm about to make a fool of myself over highlighters.* Those words race through my head before I hug Hawk.

"Thank you."

He hugs me. When I sit back to look at the highlighters, he smiles and touches his knuckle to my cheek. "I love making you smile."

I blush and glance up at him. "I'm afraid it's pretty easy and not at all expensive to make me smile."

"That's one of the reasons I love you."

Hawk sits down next to me and leans back in the chair with his feet up on the desk. I pull out the highlighters almost reverently and open the purple one to draw a line. Fucking perfection. A thrill goes through me.

"This is obviously the best seat in the house."

When I glance over at him, he winks. I shake my head. "You should do some warm-ups."

"I'm the only one here, baby girl."

"Hawk," I chastise. My cheeks heat at the endearment that most definitely doesn't belong in rehearsal. I glance at the door. People will arrive at any moment.

"Sorry, Annie." He puts his feet down and stands to stretch. His shirt lifts, and my gaze snags on his abs. Fuck, he looks yummy.

He chuckles, and I look up to find him watching me. He leans forward and wipes at the corner of my lip. "Got some drool there."

I swipe at his hand but can't help my smile.

Mia walks in and looks at the two of us. "You know, if I didn't know, I'd know."

Hawk smirks. "I'm going to go get you a soda, Annie."

Mia walks over to me as he heads out into the hallway. "So did everything go as planned last night?"

She sits in the seat next to me.

"Not exactly," I hedge. "Did you get the message to get out before the police arrived?"

She grins. "Fortunately, we were finished with round one and recharging before round two. So we got out of there in time."

I would have felt like shit if Mia had gotten caught up by the police at Chase's party.

"How was your night?" Mia wiggles her eyebrows.

My gaze lifts as the doors open and Hawk comes back in, talking with Mark Green. My cheeks flush.

She smiles and pats my hand. "Don't worry. I won't tell."

Hawk comes over and puts the soda on my table before walking with Mia back to Mark. I focus on what I need to do today. Where we are in the play. What we still need to accomplish. I wish Keira was here. She keeps me on track.

We've texted this morning. She's feeling fine and understands her parents wanting to keep her home, but she's like me: the play comes first. Anger and guilt war within me, but Olivia will get what's coming to her.

I finished editing the tape of Olivia this morning and sent the final version to Cam. He has someone who can send it anonymously and make sure everything identifying is scrubbed off the file.

A few extras come in, and they glance at me before talking behind their hands. I ignore them as I put together the scene order for today. My mom's sudden need to be involved was unexpected, and I didn't get as much done this morning as I should have.

I probably shouldn't have lazed the morning away in bed with the Devil's trio, either, though. I shake my head and focus. The noise levels rise as more of the cast shows up. I glance at my phone and stand.

"Five minutes, people." I take in the crowd, figuring out who's here and who's not. There are some actors who are late every practice. I'll need to talk to Mr. Watson about those students.

Some of the actors watch me with interest, which is not normal, but maybe they're wondering where Keira is. Or maybe they wonder why the hell I'm still willing to be with Chase. Or maybe they saw me talking with Hawk last night and then us disappearing.

Whatever has them talking, I ignore it, but I notice Chase isn't here. Which is unusual. He's usually one of the first to arrive. Fuck, if his parents are out of town, it's possible he might still be at the police station if his party got busted.

"What's wrong?" Hawk asks.

I lift my gaze from my phone. "Chase isn't here yet. He's never cut it this close before."

"Maybe he's skipping because of last night."

I shake my head. "I have to report all absences to Mr. Watson, and they have to be excused or points will be docked from his final grade. He wouldn't risk it."

"Give me a minute." Hawk takes out his cell phone and walks into the hallway.

I text Chase.

ME:

Practice is about to start.

Are you okay?

I set my phone down. We'll have to go on without him. "Jason?"

He glances my way, and I gesture him over. "Can you play Iago until Chase gets here?"

Jason looks around like he's surprised Chase isn't here. "Of course."

I hand him the script in case he doesn't have his copy. Hawk comes back in and squats next to my chair. I lean down to listen to what he has to say.

"The party got busted. Chase didn't get taken in though. Apparently his dad is friends with whatever cop came. So most people didn't get taken in, but they were sent home. Chase claimed the party got out of control and more people showed up than should have."

"So why isn't he here then?" I ask.

"I don't know." Hawk straightens.

I glance at my phone and know I can't wait any longer to start. I nod and stand. "All right. We're doing a full run-through today. Scripts in hand, but please try not to use them. Act one, scene one. Places."

The actors get into their spots, and I lean against the table. The people who aren't in the scene file into the chairs behind me to watch.

There's always some whispering in the stands, especially as we go through the same scene twice. But I keep picking up words like *Devil's trio*, *Chase*, *Olivia*, and even *Keira*. I want to tell them to shut up and speak up at the same time.

I burn inside, wondering what they know. Letting Olivia leave unscathed wasn't the smartest thing to do. And slapping her was stupid on my part, especially since it gave her all the ammunition she needs to bury me.

Or did I trust my info with the wrong person? Mia smiles at me since she's not in the scene. She knows about me and the Devil's trio. Is she as cool about it as she's acting?

"Whore!" Chase's voice captures everyone's attention.

I stand. My skin crawls. I must have misheard him.

He's in the back making his way toward me. Jason tries to stop him, but Chase pushes through. His eyes are ablaze as he focuses on me.

"Whore!" he shouts, and some of the girls twitter with nervous laughter.

I straighten. "You're late for rehearsal."

His smile is nasty. "You played the little virgin for me, but you fucked your stepbrother and his friends."

The blood drains out of my face.

"What the fuck are you doing, Chase?" Hawk steps in front of him before he can close in on me.

Chase shoves him with both hands, making Hawk stagger. "You ruined her. She was mine."

My heart is in my throat, and I can't move. Frozen with fear. My heart beats loud in my ears, but I can't move.

Hawk rights himself and goes after Chase. Chase swings, but Hawk ducks under it.

"Whoa," Mark steps in. "Seriously, what the fuck!"

Mia moves to stand next to me and puts her hand on my arm.

Chase laughs. "She has everyone fooled, but she's a whore!"

He yells the word, shouting down the rafters. My knees go weak.

"You need to calm down," Mark says.

"Calm down! My whore of a girlfriend is fucking him and his friends." He gestures at Hawk, who glares at him. Hawk is keeping himself between me and Chase.

"I'm not your girlfriend," I say it calmly, but my insides are on fire.

This is my stage. My practice. I'm in charge, and something rushes through me, unlocking me.

"Leave." I straighten to my full height and meet Chase's angry eyes. "You need to leave this rehearsal right now."

He narrows his eyes and glares. Hatred. A chill rolls through me, but Mark and Jason escort Chase out of the room.

"Are you okay?" Mia asks softly.

"Take ten. That's enough drama for the day." I want to crumble into myself, but I can't.

Everyone moves to go to the bathrooms or just exit the room so they can talk about me and Chase and the Devil's trio. By the time they get back they'll have texted everyone. Oh god.

I sink into my chair, and Hawk is there.

"I've got you." His green eyes flash with anger.

"How did this get out?" I say it more to myself than anyone in particular. But I threw it in Olivia's face and then smacked her. Twice. Unless. My gaze lifts to Mia.

She recognizes what I'm thinking, and her face goes blank. "If I did it, I wouldn't pretend to still be your friend. I would have brought popcorn to watch you burn. But I didn't and I wouldn't. You trusted me with that, and I'm not about to blow up the only friendship I have at this school."

I didn't want it to be Mia, but I don't know her well enough to trust her. I rub my temple.

"It was probably Olivia," I say. "I did smack her."

Mia grins. "No shit? Fuck, how did that feel? Oof, smacking her must have felt so fucking good."

A ghost of a smile haunts my lips. It really did. "Yeah."

"What do you need, Annie?" Hawk pulls my attention.

"The show must go on." I try to gather the riot of feelings flowing through me. Embarrassment, fear, humiliation, but also relief. Fuck, I don't have to pretend anymore. Olivia set me fucking free and probably would hate to realize that.

"I don't have to pretend anymore." I meet Hawk's gaze, and he smiles. Leaning forward, I touch my lips to his. Just a graze, but his lips curve into a smile against mine.

He holds my head when I try to pull away. "Does that mean I can flirt with you during practice?"

"No." I search his eyes with a smile. "We're still professionals."

He leans in and kisses me briefly before straightening. I glance at Mia.

"I didn't want it to be you." I blow out a breath. "But—"

"But we're both a little broken from what we've been through." Mia touches my hand. "No hard feelings, and you're still my bestie. We'll get there. Trust is earned not given."

Hawk

ME:

He called her a whore

Screamed it at her during rehearsal

DAMON:

Fucking Olivia

CAM:

Do you need backup?

Sending videos now

ME:

He left

We need to move up our plan

This can't stand

DAMON:

Start today

Thursday night

CAM:

What if she gets hurt?

DAMON:

She won't

CAM:

He could target her

ME:

We'll protect her

CAM:

Should we let her know?

DAMON:

No

Better if this is all on us

Chapter 38

EvanAnn

The rest of practice goes off without a hitch, and the whispering stops. Apparently, no one was sure, but everyone had heard various rumors. But now it was confirmed. At least that I'm fucking the Devil's trio. Not the dating part.

I don't know how school will go on Monday, but practice continues because we're professionals. I did write an email to Mr. Watson, detailing my side of the story. Chase blew up in front of practice, so I have witnesses if I need them.

At the end of practice, I call Jason over to me.

"Are you okay being backup for Iago too?" I have to ask, otherwise, I'm going to need to find another understudy.

"Of course." Jason smiles and winks. "If you want, I could also understudy Desdemona. I look great in a wig."

"Hopefully that won't be necessary." I make some notes, but I honestly don't know what else to do. Chase can't get away with coming into practice and calling anyone he wants a whore. Especially not his director.

Granted, he did just find out I was fucking three other guys behind his back while he thought he had a chance to get back with me. But he was using me too, so fuck him.

If he can't control himself, I'll have to replace him. The bigger problem is Chase needs the play for class. Though that's not my problem if he can't be professional. He'd have to go work on Brandt's play as a stagehand. It would serve him right.

Hawk comes over and sits next to me at the table. "How do you feel?"

I take a deep breath. "Honestly? Good. I don't have to pretend to like Chase after he ditched me in the woods and fucked everything that moved."

"I was fooled. You're a very talented actress, Annie." He smirks.

"Thanks." I close my folio and stand. "Let's get out of here. I have dinner with my mom tonight, and I have no idea if I should tell her I've broken up with Chase."

"Why wouldn't you?"

I blow out a breath, remembering her attention earlier. I don't want to lose what I have. The way things are is perfect, and I don't want anything else to change.

"She's waking up and paying attention. If she thinks about it too closely, she might realize putting her daughter in an adjacent room to her hot future stepbrother probably isn't the smartest choice." I walk with him toward the parking lot. "And I like sleeping in my bed."

"You mean Damon's bed." He hands me my helmet with an arched eyebrow.

"I mean, *our* bed."

He leans in and kisses me. I don't hold back or check to see if anyone is in the parking lot. I didn't know how much not claiming them in public really bothered me until now. The freedom I feel to express myself is almost overwhelming.

He pulls me in tight against him. When he lifts his head, I open my eyes and drown in pools of emerald green. "No more hiding."

I blow out a breath and look around the parking lot. "It's not all going to be easy. The girls are going to hate me."

"Fuck the haters." He kisses me and then helps me put my helmet on. "We have better things to worry about than some butthurt girls."

I chuckle and turn on the Bluetooth as he gets on the motorcycle. When I climb on, I turn and see a car close to the edge of the parking lot. A little chill goes through me. It isn't hidden, but the windows are dark so I can't tell if anyone is in it.

Hawk and I were the last ones to leave practice.

"Hawk?" I say softly as he lifts off the kickstand.

"Yeah?"

"Do you know whose car that is?"

His head turns to look. "It's not familiar. Let's take a look."

I hold my breath as he starts the engine and drives across the asphalt toward the car. The headlights turn on, and the car starts right for us. Hawk curses and turns the bike out of the car's path.

As it speeds off into the night, my heart pounds. What the hell!

"Fuck. I could catch up." Hawk turns to head that direction, but he hesitates.

"No." I cling to him. They didn't even brake. They came right at us. "It's not worth it. I can't. I have to get home."

"I'll get you home, Annie."

The car is long gone as we pull out of the parking lot, going the opposite direction. The text messages said he was watching me. But I remember at the football game, Jackson said he rode a motorcycle. So was that him? Or was it someone else?

Damon

The dining room table is set for four. Two on each side. Interesting. Is this a united front thing? I sit down on the side Evan normally sits. This week is going to need pacing for all the shit we need to do. Chase won't know what hit him until it's too late.

My dad is the first one to walk in. He takes the seat across from me and sets down his drink. Something amber on the rocks.

I slouch in my chair and watch him. He's the one who wanted me here.

He leans his elbows on the table. "How's school?"

"Fine." I don't need to tell him I'm working harder because Coach says I need to get into a good school for hockey. My plan had always been Juniors and when I got in, I might have been less than attentive at school last year.

"Hockey?"

"Fine." Is he just going to list everything? This could have been a text conversation.

He arches an eyebrow at me as Heather comes into the room. She glances over her shoulder.

"Evan isn't here yet?" she asks the obvious.

I don't scoff. I also don't point out that she's probably getting home about now from play rehearsal. Something her mother should know. I get she's Evan's mother, but my dad is more attentive than Heather is.

Heather sits next to my dad, and he kisses her briefly. It's a greeting, but unexpected because my dad generally isn't into PDA of any kind.

"Hi, Damon." Heather turns to me. "How is everything?"

"Fine." Why change the party line?

"Sorry I'm late." Evan hurries into the room. Her eyes are bright, and her cheeks flushed.

I smirk. How long did Hawk keep her in the driveway kissing those pouty lips?

"Glad you could join us," my dad says as Evan sits in the chair next to me.

She purposely doesn't look my way. Part of me hoped she'd sit and give me a kiss, but she missed that portion of our dinner theater. I could imagine the explosion that would cause. I'm not ready for them to take Evan away from me. I won't ever be ready.

But fuck, I love fireworks.

"How was rehearsal?" Heather asks as the server begins to bring our meals out.

Evan's cheeks glow a little brighter. "Interesting. Apparently, Chase had a party last night and showed up late to rehearsal. He may have been a little drunk still. I had to send him home."

Heather frowns. "Your boyfriend, Chase?"

"Mm-hmm." Evan takes a drink of water. Apparently, Evan isn't ready to give me up either.

"Isn't this the weekend Tom and Jess were supposed to be out of town?" My dad glances at his phone, but Heather puts her hand over the screen. He smiles at her and puts it face down on the table.

"I think so." Heather's gaze flicks between me and Evan. We're not even close enough to touch.

"I guess Tom will have to deal with that when he gets back." My dad shakes his head. "At least you weren't there. Either of you."

"I'm not much for the party scene." Evan takes a bite of her pasta.

"Evan's a good girl." Heather smiles and clears her throat like that reminded her of something. She sets her fork down and looks at my dad with an expectant look.

He smiles and looks at us. "Heather and I have been talking."

I brace myself because if this is an engagement announcement, I might need to leave the table. Fuck, I might need to leave the country. I told Evan I wouldn't do anything to hurt her or her mother, but this would be way too soon. Even Evan has to realize that.

She glances my way, and her fingers twitch like she wants to reach for me.

"We know moving in together was sprung on you two fairly quickly."

Heather blushes and glances at Evan. Yeah, Evan didn't know until the week prior. At least I had a little more heads up.

"And that the two of you are both busy with school and your extracurriculars," Dad continues.

I almost laugh at extracurriculars. Her directing and my hockey are our futures. Not something we do just to get out of the house. I put my fork down and lean back in my chair. Part of me wants to reach across the table and take my dad's drink.

"But we feel we need to work on our family. So we want to make sure to schedule two dinners a week. Wednesdays and Sundays. If you can make others, great, but we figured those nights are the best for you two."

Heather squeezes my dad's arm before she looks at both of us. "We really want you to get to know each other and us."

I almost laugh, but that would blow things up. Evan and I know each other very well. Spending time with our parents won't solve anything. It won't wipe away the pain and anger I carry, or the years of neglect Evan dealt with.

"That sounds like a good idea." Evan sits back in her chair. "I don't have any issue with it."

"It's doable with my schedule." I noticed Evan hasn't said anything to her mother about her and Chase breaking up or that things are even rocky between them. I get it. We're sleeping together, and if our parents look too closely, they might figure it out.

That doesn't mean I like it though.

Heather releases a breath like this will solve everything. Fix the fact her daughter was so fucking lonely, monsters sought her out. Granted, I was one of those monsters, but now I have to deal with the other ones.

We continue to eat, and Heather asks Evan more about the play. Evan and Heather keep the conversation going while my dad sits back and watches me. Does he suspect anything? It's reasonable to assume I'd ignore the hot little piece he moved in just out of spite.

I don't give anything away though. Not even when I look at Evan while she's telling a story about rehearsal this past week.

"I'm so glad we're doing this." Heather sounds overly excited about the dinners. "We should schedule a movie night too."

"Just like a happy little family." I stand with a glare at my father.

What I want to say is, this is your girlfriend. Stop trying to push me to be family with her. It's not going to happen.

But Evan seems happy, so I don't let the vitriol I feel come out my mouth.

"My schedule is still seriously swamped with homework and the play." Evan glances at me. It's brief but loaded, and I hope Dad doesn't notice.

"Whatever time you kids can make." Dad stands and helps Heather up from her chair. "We just want to make sure everyone feels heard in this family."

My insides burn. *Family?* I bite my fucking tongue and leave the room before I explode.

I head up to my room. The door opens and closes behind me. I turn ready to tell my dad to fuck off, but Evan stands there. My heart still pounds, but I can't yell at her. Not the way I want to yell at him.

She locks the door and grabs my hand, drawing me toward the bathroom. I let her because, fuck, this girl has me in a fucking choke-hold. She leans in and starts the shower and then goes into her bedroom and locks her door before returning to me.

She stops in front of me and pulls off her sweatshirt, silently undressing while meeting my eyes. Her jeans join the sweatshirt in the hamper.

My marks litter her body. Every one of those marks is mine. She's mine.

She drops her bra next, and I reach out to touch the slight bruise from my bite on her breast. Her breath catches, and she lowers her panties so she's naked before me. I touch her side, her breast, her hip, almost reverently. Her skin is soft. The burning pit of anger lingers, but the heat of her body makes me want.

The steam from the shower fills the room as she reaches for my belt. I grab my t-shirt in the middle of my back and pull it off with one hand. Then I help her push my jeans and boxers to the floor before stalking her into the shower.

She backs against the wall and lifts her gaze to meet mine. Her hands rest on my stomach. "You can use me, Damon. That anger, I can take it."

"Can you, little devil?" I smirk down at her. So small. Something easily broken, but she's proven I can't break her. "Can you take my anger?"

She tips her chin up. "Olivia outed us at the party. Chase called me your whore."

Hawk told me. I step closer to her until our skin brushes. "Are you? My whore?"

Her silver eyes spark up at me. "Yes. I'm yours. Yours to use. Yours to love. Yours to fuck."

I put my hand around her neck, but she doesn't flinch. I squeeze lightly, and her eyes never stray from mine. Her trembles are desire for me, not fear.

"Let me hunt you tonight." I lower my mouth to hover over hers. I need to burn off this wild energy. "We'll ride out and meet Cam and Hawk. We can play our game."

Chapter 39

EvanAnn

"Tell me something," I say into the Bluetooth. It's just us as we pull out of the driveway. Away from our parents, away from the chaos that's becoming our lives.

"What do you want to know?" Damon's voice is still rough. He's on edge. But I get it. Our parents want to force us to be a family.

"Tell me about your other love." I squeeze around his middle. "Tell me about hockey."

He chuckles, but I can feel the tension ease a little from his body. "The ice beneath my skates. The way it glides so easily, giving me speed, helping me stop. My mom loved to skate. I think she wanted me to be a figure skater like she used to do in school."

The way Damon moves, I can believe it. There's a grace and elegance even when he's being brutal.

"From the minute they put a hockey stick in my hand, I was captivated." He chuckles. "I love skating, but give me a puck and a stick and it becomes so much more. She always came with me. Helped me practice. Cheered me on from the stands. It didn't matter if it was a real game or scrimmage. She was always there."

I clutch tighter to him. "My dad was like that. He took me to rehearsals and auditions and lessons. He made sure I had everything I needed to succeed. If he couldn't go, Mom would take me. They came to every play, every performance."

We fall silent for a few moments. Lost in the memories of the people who helped us get to where we are.

When we hit the town limits, two motorcycles join us. It's dark and the moon isn't quite as bright tonight. I packed a small bag for afterwards. Damon picked out my outfit and dressed me.

"Looking hot, goody." Cam's voice comes through the Bluetooth connection.

"We all riding to school tomorrow morning?" Hawk asks.

My heart pounds a little harder. This I can handle, but school tomorrow might be another thing entirely.

"We have no reason not to." Damon shifts against me. "Olivia thought we wouldn't want it out there. Let's show her how wrong she is."

The others laugh. I drag in a breath. Damon was angry earlier. He mocked that we were a happy little family, but when his father called us family, Damon grew cold. The reality is, these three feel more like my family than anything I've had before. And yes, my mother dating Damon's father made that possible.

They pull into the lot, and I climb off Damon's bike. My skirt is black, and while he tried to put me in a bright colored top, I refused. I have on a tight black crop top. My panties are white and lacy, fragile things really, but that's kind of the point.

I hand Damon the helmet as Cam's arms engulf me from behind. My ponytail bounces as he lifts me off the ground and swings me around. My laughter fills the air.

He sets me down and turns me. His lips capture mine in a kiss that makes my toes curl. When he pulls away, he holds me out a little from him and takes in every inch of me.

"Fuck. I need you to play naughty teacher with me sometime, goody." He cups my breast and my nipple hardens to a peak. "I'll even let you use a ruler on me."

I close in on him and look at him through my lashes. A little thrill goes through me at the possibilities. Do I want to play act with Cam? Absolutely. "You want me to punish you, Cam?"

His eyes light up and he grins. "Yeah."

"If you want to keep your panties, little devil, I suggest you run." Damon closes in on me. "Pussy or mouth. You catch her? You fuck her how you want to."

Hawk touches my cheek, and I turn to him. "You need this to stop, say red. Need to pause, say yellow."

"Like traffic lights." I breathe them in, putting one hand on Cam's chest and the other on Hawk's waist. Damon looms over my back. I love being surrounded by them.

"You can fight us if you want, baby girl. We're going to be rough with you." Hawk's words light me up inside.

Damon slides his hands beneath my skirt and pulls my hips back against his. "Are you wet for us?"

"Always," I whisper.

His chuckle is delightfully dark. "Count of twenty. Twenty, nineteen."

The numbers go down quickly as I take off. This time I have on sneakers, but I don't think it's going to help. I hurry through the trees and then force myself to slow my movements and hide, creeping from one location to the next and staying low.

My heart pounds in my ears, but I can still hear the numbers counting down to one. I freeze when *one* rings out, and the only sounds are crickets, a lone owl, and the frantic beat of my heart.

Last time we did this, I was worried what it would feel like. Now I know, and it's not going to hurt. It might, but not in the same way. I close my eyes and try to control my breathing, to slow my heart, and to listen for them.

The dried leaves should give them away, but I don't hear anything. I bite my lip and turn to look through the forest, searching for moving shadows. My eyes have adjusted to the dark, but I don't see anything moving.

Suddenly a shadow shifts in front of me. A hand covers my mouth before my scream can reach my throat. His other hand presses against my stomach, holding me against the tree. My eyes are wide, but I can't make out the figure in front of me.

I reach for his arm to pull his hand away from my mouth, but he presses in tighter against me. My hands touch his bare sides. There's nowhere to go.

"Shh." The noise is quiet and still doesn't tell me who has me. He slides his hand from my mouth down to my throat and then his mouth crashes down on mine.

Hawk. I melt into the kiss. I should be struggling and fighting to get away, but fuck, I love the way he kisses me. It's possessive and dark. He lowers his hand on my stomach and reaches below my skirt. His fingers wrap around the crotch of my panties, his knuckles brushing my pussy, before he rips them off me.

The tear is loud, and I gasp against his mouth. He slides his tongue against mine as his fingers thrust inside me. I bite back the moan that will give my location to the others. I tremble in his hold as he fucks me with his fingers, winding me tighter and tighter.

Hawk leans into me and squeezes the sides of my neck, just enough to restrict my breathing a little. His lips touch my ear. "Do you like us hunting you? Because your cunt is dripping all over my fingers. You need a thick cock in that pussy, don't you, baby girl?"

I whimper, feeling everything tighten. He takes his fingers out of me before I can come. His breath is harsh against my ear as the backs of his hand brushes my stomach while he undoes his pants. The drag of his zipper is louder than my breath and makes my pussy clench.

"Do you want my cum, baby girl? Do you need me to fill that needy little cunt?"

His words throw gasoline on the fire he's burning inside me.

"Fuck me, Hawk," I whisper, turning my lips to his ear. "Fill my greedy cunt with your cum. Make me yours."

"Fuck," he groans. He releases my neck and lifts my legs. I grab onto his shoulders as he thrusts his cock deep into my pussy.

I cry out at the stretch and the fullness. Oh, shit! His mouth covers mine, but it's too late. My pulse jumps. Branches break from off to the sides. The wolves are coming for me.

Hawk pulls out and slams back into me, pressing me into the tree at my back while holding my hips. I cling to him as he changes angle and hits a spot so deep that lights me up inside.

"Hawk," I whine into his mouth, so fucking close.

"Shh, baby girl." He thrusts in deep, holding his throbbing cock inside me, pinning me against the tree with his hips. He lifts his hand to his mouth and spits on his fingers. "I'll make you feel better."

He slides his fingers over my clit and rubs me hard and fast, using the spit as lube. I arch and tighten around his cock as he pushes me violently over the edge. I swallow my scream as I come hard, milking his cock.

"Good girl." He grabs my legs again and fucks into me hard and fast. This time is for him.

I hold on until he groans and his warmth floods me. My breathing is chaotic as he presses his lips to mine.

He chuckles as he pulls out and lowers my shaky legs to the ground. "Good luck, Annie. You might want to run."

A shadowy figure looms to my left, and I shriek before sprinting to the right. My legs feel like jelly, and I stumble a little, but I keep running. Arms catch me and lift me off my feet against a hard body. The adrenaline of being chased surges through me, and I struggle against him, wiggling and trying to drop, but he has a good hold on me.

He spanks my ass, and I let out a surprised *ouch*. He chuckles low enough that I can't tell if it's Cam or Damon. I don't know where he's taking me. I use my feet, trying to push off his legs. Everything in me wants to fight as much as I want him to fuck me.

He hoists me higher and turns me to toss me over his shoulder. I land with a humph, knocking the wind out of me. He holds my legs with one hand and touches my pussy with the other. When he finds my pussy wet, he grunts and thrusts his fingers inside.

I wish that didn't feel so good. Part of me wants to give in and let him have me, but that's not the game.

I slap his back, but it doesn't have the desired effect. He drags his fingers out of me and smacks my ass. I let out an indignant noise. When I slap him again, he smacks my ass again. It's not really painful, just startling. He thrusts his fingers back into my pussy and teases my clit with his thumb.

His shoulder makes taking a deep breath difficult and my struggling isn't changing anything, so I hang like a doll as he fucks me with his fingers, making the need for release crawl through me. I can feel my arousal and Hawk's cum sliding down my inner thigh. Hear how wet I am with every thrust of his fingers.

My captor stops and lowers me to my feet. My pussy aches for release. He takes off his shirt and lays it on the dirt in front of me.

"Knees." The word is low and harsh, meant to disguise his voice.

I bite my lip. If I run, he might tackle me. He's offering me somewhere somewhat nice to put my knees on. A branch cracks behind me, and a hand closes on my shoulder.

"He said knees, little devil." Damon shoves me onto my knees on the shirt, coming down with me to kneel behind me. His hand rubs my ass beneath my skirt. "I should take this pretty little asshole."

They haven't prepped me for it. It would be as painful as when I lost my virginity without lube. The remembered pain sparks fear inside me. He cups my pussy under my skirt and I flinch away from him. He wraps an arm around my waist and holds me against his hard, lean body.

Even if I wanted to get away, I couldn't. They'd be on me the second I moved.

Cam grabs my ponytail and brushes his cock against my lips, smearing precum on them. "Open, goody."

I press my lips together and jerk against Damon. They want the struggle as much as I want to be taken by them. But this is a game, an act. No matter what, they'll take care of me after, and I have the power to make them stop.

"If you're going to say a color, I suggest doing it now." Damon thrusts his fingers into my pussy and rubs my clit. I melt against him. "Otherwise, your mouth will be full."

"You can tap my leg three times if it's too much, goody." Cam jerks on my ponytail. "Do you understand? Say yes."

"Yes," I whisper, caught between the two of them and not hating the feeling at all.

Cam wraps my ponytail around his fist and pulls on my hair hard. I cry out, and as soon as my mouth is open, he thrusts his cock in deep. I gag slightly.

"Relax, little devil. We all know how much you like to suck cock." Damon's fingers continue to work my clit and thrust inside me, not quite fast enough. My hips roll trying to find the right rhythm, but he keeps changing it. "You were a little virgin and let us shove our cocks into that sweet mouth. Use you like the little cum slut you are."

I groan because he's right. I am their little cum slut, and I love being that for them.

Cam fucks my mouth, holding my head still as tears stream down my face. My body is on fire, aching for release. When Cam pulls out, I drag in a breath. He lowers to his knee in front of me and tugs my head down.

It sparks that need to get away again. But I'm also so fucking aroused I don't care how they take me as long as I get off. I grab onto his bent knee to stop my hands from landing in the dirt.

"Open, goody." He jerks my head down to his cock and bumps his cock against my lips.

Damon pulls his fingers out of me, leaving my pussy wet and aching. I try to jerk away from Cam, but his hold is too tight on my hair. Damon grabs my hips and slams his cock deep into me.

I cry out and Cam thrusts into my mouth. So fucking good. They fuck me together, thrusting in deep, making me gag, brushing my womb. I moan around Cam's cock as my release washes over me, fast and hard, pulsing around Damon's cock.

"What a good little slut, coming all over my cock." Damon digs his fingers into my hips as he holds me still for his brutal thrusts. "You're so wet I could fuck your ass with your cum."

I clench around him as he chuckles. He spits, and it lands on my asshole. He spreads it with his thumb before pressing his thumb inside. I whimper at the stretch. My insides are a tangle of desire and nerves and adrenaline.

I'd let him fuck my ass. I'm helpless to resist him at this point, but I'm sure it will hurt.

Damon will take care of me. He promised.

"Fuck, little devil. You must want me to fuck that ass. Such a good little cum slut." Damon presses his thumb in deeper and fucks me harder. "Too bad I want to fill this pretty little cunt. Your ass will have to wait its turn."

Cam keeps fucking my mouth as Damon fucks my pussy and fingers my asshole. I shiver and never quite come down from the high. They keep pushing me higher until it's almost too overwhelming. Damon quickens his strokes and groans as he fills my pussy. When he pulls out, he smacks my ass.

Cam pulls me off his cock. "I don't want to fill your throat tonight."

Hawk kneels in front of me to brace me as Cam goes behind me.

When Cam thrusts into my pussy, I release my breath. That feels so fucking good. My head hangs down and the thick feel of him inside makes me moan and push back against him.

"So warm, goody. So sloppy wet from all of us." He pulls out, and I feel his fingers slipping in the mess between my legs. "Need to make you come again."

His fingers rub my clit as he fucks me hard. I'm already so close, everything so sensitive. I make a noise like an animal as I shatter.

Cam groans as my pussy milks him for everything he has. Like I haven't gotten enough. His cock jerks as he paints my insides. I collapse against Hawk as Cam pulls out of me. My thighs are wet and sticky. I don't think my legs could carry me if I wanted them to.

"Better than last time?" Hawk asks as he lifts me into his arms.

I wrap my arms around his neck and sigh against his neck. "So much better."

Damon runs his hand along my bare hip. "I'm bringing lube next time."

I give him a sloppy smile and sigh. This is everything I ever wanted.

"Feeling better?" I ask.

He smirks. "If you want to do this every time my dad makes me angry, I won't say no, little devil."

Chapter 40

EvanAnn

My thighs press against the outside of Damon's as we ride to school. He offered to drive his car, but fuck it, if we're going to make an entrance, we might as well make an entrance. Cam and Hawk ride beside us.

I haven't ridden with Cam yet. I'm sure I will, but it's weird I haven't. Is it intentional? He seems to ride the same as the others, but he doesn't have a spare helmet on his bike.

It's something to focus on besides walking into school with everyone aware these guys are fucking me.

I'm confident Olivia probably said they were just fucking me. Not that I was their girlfriend or that we love each other. No, that would have looked bad for her. To her, I'm fucking the guy she wants.

So her making sure everyone thinks I'm just a slut would make her feel better. I'm just hoping the video that Cam posted of Olivia takes some of the heat off me.

My chest feels tight as we pull into the parking lot. I don't know what's going to happen at school, but I know this is going to change everything. I'm an actor, so I don't mind standing in the spotlight, but there's something satisfying about staying behind the camera. Being the one pulling the strings, controlling the action.

We stop, and I climb off the bike. Before I lift my hands, Hawk is in front of me, undoing the chin strap and taking the helmet off. Some girls make disbelieving sounds behind me. One coughs *whore*.

My hair is in a French braid this morning. So I don't have to worry about helmet hair. My scalp is still a little tender from Cam pulling my hair last night.

"Don't give them anything today, Annie." Hawk pulls my braid over my shoulder, letting the end slide out of his fingers.

Not giving the students what they want is my mantra today. I won't fall apart or cry or yell at them. Just hold my head high and walk past them as if they aren't even there.

Damon takes my hand and threads our fingers together. When I look up at him, he takes the back of my neck and kisses me like we're alone. I may be a good actor, but this is so much more. I sink into his kiss and press in closer.

Unfortunately, this kiss will feed the rumor that we're all just fucking.

He pulls away and brushes his thumb across my lower lip as our eyes meet.

"I've wanted to do that for a while." Damon's eyes glint with possession as he draws me toward the entrance. That possessive streak shouldn't make me feel warm, but him wanting to own me makes me come alive.

I've walked into this school for the past three years and never felt like I needed to make sure my skirt wasn't tucked into my underwear like today. Eyes follow us down the hall. Whispered words haunt our steps. I run my hand over my butt just in case, but I know the reason everyone is watching is because the Devil's trio surrounds me.

The rumor might have died if we'd kept everything the same, but we're owning it.

Cam walks beside me while Hawk follows us. Damon holds my

hand. A thousand stares follow us, but I keep my head high. I earned this. I earned them. And I'm keeping them.

Normally I'd go hide in Mr. Watson's room until the first bell rings, but today is about letting everyone know I'm not just their fuck toy. I am, but that's not all I am. And only my guys can call me that.

When we stop at my locker, I put my books away and pull out what I need for morning classes.

"Chase is only in the class I have with you and acting," I tell them. "Mia's in my first class and acting too."

"We don't want him to have a chance to come at you again." Cam glances around. "We'll get you between classes."

There's not a lot that can happen at school. They're overreacting, but Olivia might be here. And Chase did come at me pretty hard at rehearsal.

I blow out a breath. "Except you can't this afternoon. You have your classes on this side of the school while I have classes on the Anteros side. Even the time schedules are different. I have senior acting with Mia and Chase before my directing intensives."

I glance over my shoulder and see some girls whispering behind their hands across the hallway. Our gazes collide, and they roll their eyes before looking away. I shake my head. I'm not looking for acceptance. Just trying to avoid retribution.

"I'll let Mr. Watson know about Chase and the issues I'm having." I close my locker.

Damon doesn't look happy. If he could, he'd probably follow me to every class today instead of attending his, but that's not how this will work. I need to be my own person and stand on my own.

I put my hand over his heart and smile up at him because there are definite benefits to being out as whatever we are. Yes, it might make me a target. It already has, but it's worth it.

"We don't have to hide. At least not here." Home is another matter. That I'll have to deal with eventually, but not now. "I don't have to eat lunch with Chase."

A hint of a smile teases his lips. "You'll be with us."

I want to ask them to sit inside the cafeteria with me, but we have to make a statement. Part of that statement is being seen and showing everyone none of this bothers us. While hiding would be more comfortable, it's not an option.

They all walk me to my first class. Mia looks up at the door as I enter. Damon waits until I'm seated before he turns and walks away.

"Fuck, I thought he was possessive at the game, but damn, girl." Mia fans herself with her notes. "I think I'm getting secondary burns from the heat you two generate."

I chuckle and then sigh. "I don't know how I'm going to get through today."

Mia smiles. "What I learned by being an unrepentant slut is you don't let other people's opinions of you matter. Hold your head up and let them eat your dust. They're just jealous anyway."

"Jealous." I nod, but I don't believe it. It feels like I'm encroaching on someone else's territory. I have no desire to be popular like Olivia. But I'm going to have lunch outside with the Devil's trio and pretend I belong because I'm fucking the hottest guys in school. The guys want me there. That's all that matters.

"Jealous. Trust me." Mia winks as the teacher walks into the room.

My phone buzzes. I look down.

SEX GOD:

Look out the window

I glance toward the windows and see police cars parked outside. I'm not the only one who's noticed. Students stand and hurry over to the windows.

"What's going on?"

"Who do you think those are for?"

"Probably Olivia. She drugged an ant this weekend."

"Did you see the video?"

"What video?"

"Here's the link."

I don't stand and join the crowd, but I hear the whispers about Olivia and the video that got leaked from the party. I keep my face blank even though I want to smile.

SEX GOD:

Got you a present

He sent me a video from his class. When I press play, Olivia sits down and ignores him, but soon an officer knocks on the door. A man with a stoic face dressed in a suit stands beside the officer. I have the volume off, but I watch as Olivia stands with a huff and grabs her books. She walks out like she owns the place, and this is a mistake.

But it's not. The people at the window sound shocked, so the police must have brought her outside. Is their shock because she might actually get punished?

"That's enough." Ms. Adams claps her hands. "Back to your seats. You can gossip in the hallway between classes."

When class ends, Mia steps into the hallway with me. Cam gives her a nod before offering me his hand.

"See you in acting!" Mia waves as Cam leads me down the hallway.

He pulls me into Mr. Ridgeway's classroom and leads me to our seats. He sits sideways and grins. "Did you see the video?"

"Nothing less than what she deserves." I keep my voice down.

"You're not wrong." He trails his fingers down the side of my face. "I can't wait until lunch."

"Are we going out again?" I can't help the hopeful tone of my voice.

He chuckles. "No, goody. You're eating with the Devils."

He turns and when he turns back, he holds out a red paper flower for me. I smile, loving that this is his thing with me.

Hawk walks in and takes the seat behind me as I twirl the flower between my fingers. "We need to get some time alone, Annie."

I meet his green eyes with a smile because I want that. I love being with all of them, but I definitely would like to spend some alone time with both Cam and Hawk separately. Even though Damon and I spend the most time together, we don't actually talk that much.

"I don't have a lot of free time." I glance at my busy schedule in my phone.

Hawk smirks. "I don't need a lot of time."

A little shiver rolls through me. No, he doesn't. I'm hoping he's talking about the closet again. Damon walks in and, before he takes his seat, he tips my chin up and kisses me softly. For a second, the classroom noise fades.

When he pulls away, his smirk makes my already wet pussy clench. He takes his seat and the roar of whispers commences. My cheeks are hot.

Chase walks in. His eyes narrow on me before he takes his seat near the front. That first day of class, I'd worried about not sitting next to him. Now, I'm so fucking happy the guys took his spot and didn't let me change seats.

Today would be even more miserable with him beside me.

"Figures he wouldn't get suspended after rehearsal." Hawk shakes his head.

"His father makes large contributions to this school." Cam watches Chase. "If he'd actually hurt one of you, it would have been harder. But unlike Olivia, there's no video of the incident."

"They can just sweep it under the rug with all the other bullshit he gets away with," Damon says.

There might be consequences for him with the play from what he pulled on Sunday. I'm just glad I don't have to listen to him and whatever he wants to call me today.

Whatever Chase has to say to me, I won't like, but fuck him. He used me. He used the fact I was lonely against me. It must have been so easy for him to just give me a little attention, and I was willing to be his.

I hate it was that easy for him. That I wasn't suspicious at all when one of the hottest guys in the theater department suddenly wanted me. That he made me feel special and it was all a lie.

I was more suspicious of the Devil's trio's attention at the beginning of the year.

But they haven't lied to me. They wanted to use me to fuck over Chase, and I think we've accomplished that. I doubt he'll be partying or anything else this year. Not anytime soon.

I feel bad I haven't told my mom about breaking up with him. But the situation is complicated. If I'm dating Hawk, maybe putting me next to Damon would be a bad idea suddenly. Or did they put me there because they trusted I wouldn't be seduced by Damon? Or worse, what if they assumed Damon wouldn't want to seduce me?

I rub my neck. It doesn't matter. Damon's mine. I'm not changing bedrooms, and my mom doesn't need to know I'm sleeping with her boyfriend's son. And his friends.

As soon as the bell rings, Chase is out the door. I breathe a little easier, but that just means he might be waiting until he can get me alone. Away from Damon, Cam, or Hawk.

And he'll have that opportunity this afternoon.

Cam

As soon as Evan comes out of third period, I fall into step beside her.

"Hey, goody." I wrap my arm around her shoulders, and she bumps into me.

"Hey."

Her woodsy scent intoxicates me.

The guys would kill me if we're late, but I'd love to drag her into an abandoned room and spend lunch making her come over and over again.

Instead, I lead her to the cafeteria and stand in line with her at the salad station. I go ahead and get lunch from there, but after I eat this, I'll have to find something else to eat.

We head to the doors, and Evan looks longingly at the table she usually sits at.

"If you want, we can sit there, goody." I'm not as big on the whole we have to prove shit to everyone. If she wants to be comfortable, I'm all for it.

Evan shakes her head. "No, it's time to face the music."

"At least Olivia won't be there." I smirk, and Evan gives me a genuine smile. I could seriously live on this girl's smiles.

We enter the courtyard, and Mia waves from Abby's table.

"You can invite her to eat with us," I offer. Maybe having her friend with us will make it easier.

"Not today." Evan straightens. "Today is about showing everyone you guys are mine as much as I'm yours."

Grinning, I set my food next to hers on the table before pulling her into my arms. She tips her head back to meet my eyes. Our arms are draped loosely around each other.

"I like it when you claim us, goody." I wink.

She smiles. "Same."

I give her a kiss before turning her to the table and sitting next to her, straddling the bench so I'm facing her. She glances my way as she takes a bite, but something captures her attention over my shoulder.

She sets her fork down and frowns.

"You'll sit out here as their whore, but not as my girlfriend?" Chase fucking Chadwick. Still a fucking stupid name. I should have known he'd do something stupid.

Evan goes pale, but she doesn't cower. She arches an eyebrow like he's beneath her.

"Did you have something to say to my girlfriend?" I stand and turn to face Chase.

We're about the same height and build, but I'm quicker and not a wuss like him. He glares at me.

"Girlfriend?" he spits out. Chase laughs, sharp and bitter. "You don't honestly want us to believe you're not just toying with her. Using her because she's naive."

"Fuck you." Evan stands next to me, but I put my arm in front of her and try to push her back behind me. She moves around my arm. "You fucked anything that moved while we were together. Then, when I wouldn't put out, you left me in the middle of nowhere. Oh, you would have come back to save me after you fucked someone at the party. Such a gentleman."

Chase narrows his eyes, and I step between them. Evan shifts again. This girl is going to kill me. And where the fuck are Hawk and Damon? They should be done by now.

"It's not like you'd even touch my dick, EvanAnn." He sneers at her. "We were dating months. What did you expect me to do when all I got from you was a few kisses?"

"I don't know? Maybe wait like you said you would, or break up with me." Evan's livid. "But that wouldn't work with your plan for your dad, would it? You couldn't bring a different girl home every night because then daddy wouldn't tell his producer friends what a reliable guy you are. Instead, you said you were with me."

He takes a step toward her.

I lower my chin and get in his face. "Take another step toward her, and I'll fucking flatten you. I don't give a shit if I get suspended, but my guess is you don't want that right now. Daddy's probably on the warpath since your party blew up."

Chase's blue eyes search mine. The moment he realizes what we did hits him. There's a flash of anger, but then a mask falls over his face and he smiles like there's absolutely nothing wrong in the world. He steps back.

Fucking actors.

"I wouldn't get comfortable, EvanAnn." Chase glances toward her. "Everyone knows the Devil's trio don't keep girls for long. You'll be back." His blue eyes meet mine, and he smirks. "They always come back."

Chapter 41

EvanAnn

I was ready to have it out with Chase at lunch, practically vibrating with rage, but he disappeared into the school. He's wrong though. I'm not stupid enough to go back to him, ever. Fool me once...

My hands are still trembling as Cam and I settle back at the table, when Hawk and Damon come out. The other tables are still talking about the confrontation. Damon's mouth presses tight while Cam tells him what happened.

I take Damon's hand and lean into him so he won't go and do something stupid. Hitting Chase at a party is one thing. Hitting him at school would get him suspended. Suspension might mean no hockey. I'm not letting Chase Chadwick take anything else away from us. I'll protect Damon's future with all I have.

Damon settles, but Hawk looks too still, like he's planning something. Cam glances at Hawk, and Hawk subtly nods his head. What the fuck are they planning?

I can't be everywhere the guys are, but I need to try to make them think this through. Before we leave lunch, I clear my throat to get their attention.

"No one gets suspended because of that asshole." I meet each of their eyes. "We can take care of him outside of school."

Hawk smirks. "Yes, Annie."

He draws me into him and kisses me.

I shake my head at him as he winks. Cam kisses me next.

He lifts his head. His face is serious as he searches my eyes while cupping my face. "If I put you behind me, that doesn't mean find a way around, goody. I like you fierce, but if I needed to take down that fucker, I could have hurt you."

My heart swells as I grab his wrists. "I need to stand up for myself too."

"And you're hot when you do." He kisses me again. "We'll figure it out."

When he releases me, I turn to Damon, still sitting at the table. He grabs the hem of my skirt and pulls me toward him. I climb onto his lap to straddle him like I always do at home and put my hands in his hair. He tugs my hips into his and rests his head against my shoulder.

"If he tries anything..." His words are for me alone.

"I'll tell a teacher. That's why they're there." I lift his head and look into his blue eyes. "You can't always be there to protect me. I love you for it, but I can hold my own, especially with Chase."

"That's my little devil." He gives me a cocky grin.

I lean in and kiss him. It's so easy to lose myself in the hint of mint and taste of Damon.

Someone clears her throat. I pull back and look over my shoulder at Mia. She gives a little finger wave. Heat washes through me at how intimately Damon and I are locked together. At school. Not being able to touch him made it easy to avoid touching him through the school day. Now that I can, all I want to do is touch him.

"Figured you'd like some backup heading to acting?" Mia smiles, and her eyes sparkle.

Damon helps me stand. "Text me if anything happens."

I nod, but my cheeks are red. It's so hard to think when they touch me. The courtyard wasn't completely empty. Abby and her friends stand off to the side. When they notice me noticing them, they give me a look of disdain and head inside.

So, business as usual.

"I've got her from here." Mia winks at Damon, who rolls his eyes.

The guys follow us to the intersection of the schools and then head off to their afternoon classes while Mia and I head to the black box theater. We're a little early, so I touch her arm as I head over to Mr. Watson.

"Can I talk to you?" I gesture toward the sound booth.

He nods and leads the way.

"Did you get my email?" I ask when the door is shut. I can see Mia, but I know she can't hear us in here.

Mr. Watson rests his hip on the counter and crosses his arms. His back is to the glass. "It's your production, EvanAnn. What do you want to do?"

"I don't want Chase to fail because we broke up, and it wasn't an easy split." I sigh and watch the classroom fill with students I've been with for the past three years.

"The difference is that you didn't blow up at him while at practice." Mr. Watson sighs. "It doesn't matter what you did or what he did. What matters is how you behave during rehearsal time. That's sacred space. He wasted everyone's time and threatened another student."

Mr. Watson isn't wrong. I didn't so much as blink at rehearsal after Chase left me out in the middle of nowhere or after I found out about the cheating. Hell, I saw the cheating. Chase just heard about it from Olivia.

"We can bring Brandt into this discussion if it would make you more comfortable." Mr. Watson straightened. "If Chase needs to be off your production, then he would need a spot on Brandt's. There might be someone you could exchange for."

"If I were to recast, I would have Jason perform as Iago and whoever came in would need to understudy Cassio." But the real problem is Chase is Iago. "I do think Chase is the best actor for the part still."

Mr. Watson nods thoughtfully. "After class, we'll talk. You, me, and Chase. If we can't come to an agreement, then we can talk with Brandt to see if he has a solution."

"I think that will work." I'm still not sold, but at least we have a course of action now.

Chase sits in his chair like a sullen toddler. Legs kicked out. Arms crossed. A frown on his face. He looks ridiculous because he didn't get his way. He didn't get to keep me and fuck around too.

We sit across from each other, and Mr. Watson sits between us.

"What we need to know, Chase," Mr. Watson begins, "is if you're going to be able to keep this production professional and keep your personal life outside of rehearsals?"

Chase's eyes narrow before he releases his breath, but he keeps his lips pressed shut. Fine. I can be the bigger person.

"I'm willing to ignore Sunday's interruption," I say. "But that's the extent of it. You don't bring negative energy to my rehearsal, and you don't waste my actors' time."

He leans forward. His gaze flicks to me before he looks at Mr. Watson. "What are my options?"

My chest tightens. Jason will do fine as Iago, but Chase would give a brilliant performance. I wasn't blowing smoke up his ass about him being suited for Iago. And the more I find out about the real him, the more I see the character Iago is part of who he is.

Mr. Watson leans forward and clasps his hands between his knees. "You have a lead role in *Othello*. If you don't think this will work, we can discuss with Brandt what he can do for you on *the Crucible*. But it won't be a lead role and may not even be a walk on. You might have to work backstage."

"I could get something in the spring showcase though." Chase glances at me, like I'm the one who will be disappointed if he quits my show.

I arch an eyebrow. "It's early. Jason would be able to learn your part. If you want to go to Brandt's show, that's up to you. I won't stop you."

Chase chuckles and rubs the corner of his lip. "Why would I give up my part in the play?"

"I don't know, Chase." I lean back and cross my arms. "It would be a stupid move, but it's not like anything you've been doing has been smart."

His eyes flash, but he hides it quickly.

Mr. Watson clears his throat. "I'm not saying this will be easy, but if you need me to supervise for a while, I can come to rehearsals to make sure things remain civil."

"I'd appreciate that," I say.

Chase straightens. "Fine. I can be a professional."

Mr. Watson stands and glances at his watch. "You have time to get to your next class."

I grab my stuff and stand to leave. We'd moved to Mr. Watson's office so the students in the acting class afterwards wouldn't have to wait in the hallway.

As soon as I step out of the office, Chase touches my shoulder.

I flinch and spin to face him. He holds up his hands in surrender.

I straighten and glare at him. "Outside of the production or class, you don't have any reason to interact with me. You definitely don't have permission to touch me."

He smirks, and the confidence that always surrounds him makes itself known. "But you will need me. When those three decide you're no longer worth playing with."

I press my lips together, but don't give him anything, because he doesn't know anything about us. He still thinks they're toying with me. And there's nothing I'll need him for even if they do leave me. I've never needed him.

He drags his gaze over me like he has any right. "I've always been playing the long game with you, EvanAnn. Those other girls were to stave off a need. You?" He smiles like we're something more. "You're endgame. But I get it. I fucked up, and you need to teach me a lesson."

"That's not what this is."

"But it is revenge, right?" He steps forward, but I don't step back.

I'm not going to let him see me afraid of him.

"Damon's revenge. Your revenge." He smiles down at me. "Doesn't matter, does it? You've had yours. He's had his. What do you two have left? Fucking?"

My cheeks heat, but I don't say anything.

"And then he takes off to fulfill his hockey dream, and you... what? Follow him to a school that has a mediocre theater program?" Chase chuckles. "Or maybe you'll try to do some film festivals and make it from there?"

I glance at the door, hoping Mr. Watson comes out.

"That's not the way you achieve your dreams, EvanAnn." Chase shakes his head like I'm being silly. "You need someone like me and my family. Money. Connections. He might have you now, but it won't last. But don't worry. I'll take you back when you're ready."

Chapter 42

EvanAnn

When I get to rehearsal after school, there's a bag and a paper flower waiting for me on my table. Mia smiles when she sees it.

"Someone's got boyfriends," she teases and sits in the audience area, pulling out her laptop to do homework until everyone else gets here.

I set my backpack on the floor next to the table and peek in the bag. There's a salad and a pack of nuts. I pluck out the folded note.

Need to eat, little devil

—D

Smiling, I pick up the red flower Cam made me. Each flower is a little different. I'll add it to the collection of them on my desk at home. I put the sack on the floor and get out my notes and my new highlighters. This is what I thought being in a relationship meant. Being excited to be together. Thinking about each other when we're apart. Doing little things to make the other happy.

Keira didn't come to school today, but she messaged to let me know she'll be back tomorrow. Tonight I have a few scenes that have been tricky to go over. Including the scene with Chase, but since Hawk has practice, Jason will be playing Cassio.

Mr. Watson comes in and takes the seat beside me at the table. "If this doesn't work out with Chase, let me know. Brandt did say he could use Chase as an extra and give you one of his extras in return."

I look at the stage and consider. If I need someone to do backup for Cassio, I need someone who could step onto the stage prepared. I glance at Mr. Watson.

"Why don't we wait and see? I think we'll still have enough time if Chase doesn't behave." And right now, I need time to think about who I might use to replace Hawk if something happens and he can't be there.

Everyone comes in and I begin rehearsal. We run the problem scenes until everyone has their lines correct. I glance at my phone when Cam sneaks in to sit in the back and do his homework. Mr. Watson furrows his brow, but doesn't say anything.

After another five minutes, Damon and Hawk walk in and sit next to Cam. Mr. Watson raises an eyebrow, but they remain quiet and work on homework. I breathe out and finish rehearsal.

As I'm packing up, Chase walks over. Mr. Watson is still at the desk.

"I just wanted to thank you for giving me another chance." Chase seems sincere, but he's an actor. He's just had time to practice his lines. "I want to apologize to you and the whole cast tomorrow at afternoon rehearsal, if you'll let me."

"I appreciate your apology." I grab my trash from my salad and pick up my flower. "I can give you a minute, no more, at rehearsal tomorrow. You've already taken up too much of my time."

Chase's eyes flare, but he smiles. "Of course. Thank you, director."

He walks over to his bag and snatches it off the ground.

"Good work today. As always, I respect your professionalism." Mr. Watson heads out after Chase.

"Come on, Annie." Hawk touches my waist, and I turn to see the others waiting for me. "We need to hurry or we'll miss the show."

"The show?" I ask, but let them usher me outside.

Chase gets into his truck right when we step out. He turns on the engine and glitter fills the cab. My mouth opens in shock, but then I giggle.

Cam drapes his arm over my shoulders. "Not the most subtle of pranks, but it's a good start."

I glance at Damon, and he nods toward the bikes. As we head over, Chase's truck door flings open and he steps out, shaking glitter onto the ground.

"Best thing about glitter," Cam whispers. "It gets everywhere and takes forever to clean up. Unfortunately, Chase's car is still in the shop. Apparently, it got pushed behind some other cars."

I smile. "You guys are awesome."

"We know. Come on, let's get you home."

"Damn, man, did you go to the strip club?" Some guy laughs down the hallway behind me.

"Fuck off," Chase snarls.

I turn as I walk to the acting seminar with Mia to see Chase with glitter on his uniform. It's Tuesday and somehow a video of the glitter bombing has been passed around. Chase still has glitter everywhere. As a girl who loved dresses with glitter when I was little, I remember how I'd leave little piles of it everywhere I went.

"Couldn't have happened to a nicer guy." Mia laughs. "I've played that video at least three times this morning. Though I still say we could have plastered his truck with feminine products."

I shake my head, and we go into our acting studio. Chase sits as far away from me as possible and in the back of the auditorium. I'm grateful. He ignores the snickers and looks at his phone.

I block him out as class starts and don't even think about him as we head to our rehearsal. Hawk catches me before we go into the black box room, pushing me against the wall. Mia shakes her head and goes in without me. He puts his hands on either side of my head on the wall as he looms over me.

"It's not rehearsal out here." Hawk smiles down at me. "Out here you're my girlfriend, not my director."

I put my hand on his chest and push up on my toes to kiss him. I'm getting used to the touches and kisses during school. It makes me worried that when we're at home, I'm going to slip up and kiss Damon where our parents can see.

But here? Hawk smiles against my lips as I pull away.

"It's time for rehearsal." I slip out under his arm and open the door to go in.

He follows behind me and leans down to whisper in my ear. "I'm spending the night tonight, baby girl. Have to make sure Damon is treating you right."

A shiver rolls through me as he chuckles darkly and heads over to where Mark stands. Damon and Hawk together. I can't wait. Heat flows through me. I wish I had time to fit in a nap.

"So that's happening?" Keira asks with a smile.

I grin and hug her. "I'm so glad you're back. How are you?"

I look her over like I'll be able to see if anything's wrong.

"I'm good except for missing most of Saturday night." Keira shakes her head. "It's weird knowing I was there, but not remembering any of it."

I glance at the cast. "I might be able to help with that."

Keira cocks her head to the side.

I lean in close. "I have the full video from that night. If you want to come over tomorrow, we can watch it."

Mr. Watson comes in and stands at the door.

"I'd like that," Keira says as I stand, getting ready to start our rehearsal.

I look out at everyone. "I know we had an exciting weekend, but we're moving forward with the cast we have. For now." I glance at Chase. "Chase has something he wants to say."

Chase steps forward and little pinpoints of light sparkle on his clothes. I manage to keep a straight face, but Hawk grins and winks.

"I just wanted to apologize for my behavior on Sunday. It was unprofessional and uncalled for. I plan to show you that I can behave in a professional manner from here on out." Chase nods and heads back to stand with the cast.

Sophia lets out a snicker and covers her mouth. Crystal smiles and straightens. Hopefully that was about Chase and not about me and Hawk. Chase tenses but doesn't say anything.

———

Keira walks into my house with her eyes wide and taking everything in. It's become my usual now, but it wasn't long ago, I felt that same sense of awe as I walked in for the first time and found out Damon and I would be living together.

I never imagined that I would be where we are now in our relationship. I'm his girlfriend and he's my boyfriend. He still makes my heart pound, and between him and Hawk last night, I barely got any sleep. But he made sure I had coffee and fruit before we rode to school.

I take her up to my room and cue up the video on my laptop. When it's over, Keira releases a breath.

"It's weird to watch myself and know I was there, but I don't remember any of that or the hospital really." Keira rubs her temples like she can make herself remember.

"At least we have you on video so you can see what happened." I would hate to have a blank spot in my memory. To have to rely on others to fill it in. At least she was safe.

She looks around my huge room. "So, your mom and Damon's dad?"

I nod. "It's taken some adjusting, but the move's been good."

She smirks. The guys touch and kiss me a lot at school. If anyone doubted their intentions toward me, those people definitely know the Devil's trio is into me. But they also see the guys caring for me in little ways. Damon brings me food before hockey practice and rehearsal.

Cam works on his homework in the audience after practice to be near me. Hawk gives his all on the stage and watches over me, ready to step in if Chase makes a move toward me.

No one trusts Chase.

When I told Damon what Chase said about going back to him, Damon just laughed. "There's no way you'd go back to him. You don't need anyone to help you make it."

"Do you think it will last?" Keira asks. She glances toward the bathroom door.

"Honestly, I haven't thought a lot about the future." I look down at my hands. "I'm just getting through the next day, the next week, the next month, at this point."

"Probably for the best. Do you know where they're going for school?" Keira asks. "Or where you're going for school?"

I bite my lip. "Hawk's going to Columbia. Cam wants to go the Crowne Mawr. Damon wants a good hockey program, so a D1. And I'm going wherever I can get the most contacts in the industry and can afford."

"This glow up doesn't include a college fund?" Keira arches an eyebrow.

I shake my head. "My mom isn't married to Adam, and I wouldn't expect him to pay for my college even if they were."

"You'll get a scholarship pretty much anywhere you apply, anyway." Keira blows out a breath.

"Hopefully." I don't want to ask if Olivia has reached out about what Hawk told her to do. Since the guys released the video anyway, is giving Keira college money null and void now? "Do you want to see the entertainment room? It has a huge TV and surround sound."

Keira's eyes light up. "Yes, please."

Chapter 43

Cam

"How was dinner, goody?"

She looks up from her laptop. "What?"

We're in the family room, studying. I wish we were in my bedroom doing other things, but she insisted we needed to study during study time.

"Wednesdays are family dinner, yeah?" I lean back in my chair. If I read one more paragraph, my brain is going to explode.

She's got on jeans and a sweatshirt. Her hair is in one of those messy buns.

"Yeah." She bites her lip. "It actually wasn't bad. Damon even managed to behave."

"Is it weird?" I ask, tapping my pen on the notebook.

She narrows her eyes on me. "Is what weird?"

"I don't know, being in a relationship and hiding it from your parents." I shrug.

"Cam, what's going on?"

I've barely seen her this week, and we're freaking studying. But I can't say that, because that's what she wants to do.

She shuts the lid on her laptop, and her blue eyes meet mine. "Why don't I ride with you?"

"What?"

"You were the first one to offer me a ride on your motorcycle, but I've only ridden with Damon and Hawk." She sits back with her hands in her lap. "Is there a reason?"

"Besides, those two being obsessive bastards?" I smirk.

That gets a smile out of her. Fuck, I want to make her smile more.

"We can fix that." I stand. "Come on, goody. Let's go for a ride."

She glances at her work and then shrugs. Taking her hand, I pull her up, and we head outside. She grabs her helmet on the way. Damon dropped her off earlier.

I help her put it on and then put on my own. "You tell me if I need to slow down."

She nods, and I get on my bike. She straddles the bike behind me and tucks in nice and close. Her arms wrap around me. Why haven't we done this before?

Because those dicks are possessive assholes who don't like to share.

"You good?" I ask.

"Yes, Cam." Her voice is in my helmet, and I love it. "But this counts as studying time, so I'm going to quiz you for English lit."

"That tracks." I chuckle as I pull out of the driveway and head toward the highway. She quizzes me as I drive around town, and then we hit the open highway. She squeezes me tighter at the increase in speed.

After a little while, I pull off in a spot we like to come to that overlooks the city. I shut off my bike. She climbs off and removes her helmet. Her messy bun sits a little crooked. She reaches up and lets her blond hair fall around her shoulders.

"I like your hair down, goody." When I lean back on my bike, she turns and smiles.

"We should head back soon." She turns to look over the city below.

"I like you on my bike."

"I like being on your bike." She walks back over to me.

She leans in and kisses me. When she goes to pull back, I catch the back of her head and hold her there while I explore her mouth slowly. She whimpers, and I help her climb onto my lap to straddle me on the bike.

Her fingers weave into my hair. I could spend an eternity kissing her and not get enough.

"Fuck, goody. Why are you wearing jeans?" I kiss down her neck.

"They're better for riding." She tips her head back, and her silky hair brushes my hand, resting between her shoulder blades.

"But not great for access."

She laughs, and the sound fills the night air. I smile because I love to hear her laugh. Even better if I'm the cause of it.

She cups my jaw and looks into my eyes. "Why don't you tell your dad you don't want to go to Yale?"

I drag in a breath and pull her in tighter against me. "Part of me still doesn't want to disappoint him. He's always wanted me to go, to follow his footsteps."

"But it's not what you want?" She slides her hand down my chest. My cock twitches, already uncomfortably hard. Evan should only be allowed to wear skirts.

"I just don't think I'm Yale material." I rub my thumbs over her hips. "Deimos is a challenge, and I know Yale will be the same, if not more challenging. I want a break. College is going to be hard no matter where I end up. I'm not deluding myself and thinking Crowne Mawr will be easy. But it's close, and I'm not ready to leave here yet. I'm not ready to be without Hawk and Damon. You're going to go off and do amazing things and leave us."

She smiles sadly. "Isn't that what high school romance is for? To break our hearts?"

"It doesn't have to be."

"My parents were high school sweethearts." Evan leans back on the gas tank. Fuck, she's like temptation incarnate. I slide her sweatshirt up, baring her stomach, and she smirks. "They made it, so I'm not saying it can't happen. But we're all going different directions. It's not just two of us trying to make it work. It's four of us. So instead of worrying about the future..."

She sits up and takes off her sweatshirt before lying back on the tank, all pale skin and a pretty blue, lacy bra. "Maybe we just enjoy being young."

I run my hand up from her stomach to her neck. "Fuck, goody, you know how to change a topic."

"I'm just focusing on what we might be able to take care of now." She smiles and undoes the button to her jeans. "Prioritizing."

"I like the way you think." I reach for her zipper, and she reaches up to hold the handlebars. She's everything I want in a partner. Willing to try anything. "Fuck, goody."

"I've been promised multiple times I'd be fucked on a motorcycle." She lifts an eyebrow.

"Don't need to ask me twice." I tug her jeans down her hips and reveal the matching blue panties. "I never thought I'd say this, but Damon has really great taste in underwear."

She laughs. Fuck. This road is fairly abandoned. The guys and I have sat here practically all night and not seen another car, but I'm not about to get my girl completely naked, no matter how much I want to. But the jeans have to go.

I lift her leg and undo her shoe, dropping it on the ground. "One leg or two?"

She arches an eyebrow. "For what?"

"I can leave your jeans on one leg to do what I want to you, or I can take them off completely." I smirk. "Lady's choice."

She lifts her other foot to my shoulder. "Both, show me what you can do."

"Someone might catch us," I warn.

Her flush works its way down to the tops of her breasts. "Then we better put on a good show."

"Fuck, goody. I fucking love you." I take off her other shoe and then drop it. I tug off her jeans with her help, leaving her spread before me in her bra and panties.

When she starts to sit up, I put my hand on her stomach. "Grab the handlebars again."

Her eyes light up, and she does what I ask.

"Next time, I'm bringing something to tie you like that. This is like a fantasy brought to life." I slide my hand up to cup her breast.

She arches into my touch. Her pussy pressing against the front of my jeans. My other hand trails up her thigh as I watch her. Her breath catches and her thighs tighten around my waist.

"Cam," she sighs.

I stop at the edge of her panties, my thumb teasing the edge. "You need more?"

I slide my finger beneath the lace of her bra and circle her nipple.

"Yes. I need more. Fuck, Cam. I want you." Her hips rock.

I smile, loving the way the moonlight glows on her body. I slip my thumb beneath her panties and tease her bare pussy. She lets out a little whimper.

Leaning over her, I push her bra to the side and suck her nipple into my mouth at the same time I thrust my thumb into her. All wet and warm. She lets out a soft moan.

"Please," she whispers.

"You want someone to find us, goody? You'll have to be louder than that." I suck her nipple and fuck her pussy with my thumb. She's so wet. My cock aches.

Her cry is the loudest thing in the night.

When I bite her nipple, she arches into me. I straighten and look down at her. Her eyes are hooded. Her nipple exposed and her panties drawn to the side so I can see how wet she's making my thumb.

I push her bra off her other nipple before leaning in and taking it into my mouth. She moans louder than before. Her hips rock with my thrusts.

When I feel her tighten around my thumb, I pull out.

"Cam," she whimpers as I straighten.

"Don't worry, goody. I've got you." I undo my belt and fastenings to pull out my cock. Lifting her legs to press against my shoulders, I make sure I have both feet on the ground to steady us. "Tell me what you want."

She looks at me through those lashes. Her blond hair a halo spread across the black of my tank. Her hands gripping the handlebar. She looks ravished, and I did that to her.

"Fuck me. Hard." She pushes against me.

I line up my cock with her entrance and thrust in deep. She cries out, scaring some birds into flight. "Like that?"

"Harder."

"Louder, goody."

"Fuck me harder, Cam," she yells with a laugh.

"That's my girl." I lean, pushing her legs up as I fuck her tight pussy.

"Oh fuck, that feels good." She grins up at me as she yells the words. "Harder. Faster."

We fuck on my bike. Her tits bounce with my every thrust. Her eyes dare me to give her everything. I fuck her harder and faster until she's trembling beneath me. I want to give her everything. Every piece of me. Our moans fill the night air.

Noisy with no care if someone finds us, we fuck.

Her cunt squeezes me as she cries out her release. I groan, knowing I'm not going to last long now. I reach for the handlebar next to her hand and slide my other hand down her panties to tease her clit, extending her release.

"Fuck, Cam," she yells and arches as her pussy gushes another release all around me.

"Fuck, goody." I thrust deep a couple more times before coming inside her with a groan.

I collapse on her and let her lower her legs. The night is silent around us until she giggles.

I kiss her lips before asking, "New kink unlocked?"

"Definitely." She combs her fingers through my hair, and I lean into the touch.

I lift and look her over, thoroughly debauched on my bike. "We can take a ride anytime you want."

Chapter 44

Damon

"It's a calculated risk, but my dad and Heather are in tonight. We pick up Evan at seven and take her home. She'll be safe there." I grab my shoes out of my locker. "We get Nina to text him to meet her at eight."

"What if he recognizes us?" Cam rubs his hand over his hair. "If he gets hurt..."

I look at Cam, and he nods. Yeah, I don't care if the fucker gets hurt.

"He needs to know how it feels." Hawk tosses his towel on the bench. "He needs to fucking learn from his mistakes. Not be rewarded."

We finish getting ready. Cam heads into the back of rehearsal while Hawk and I check the parking lot. The car Evan and Hawk saw that tried to run them over hasn't been back, but we don't want to risk it.

Maybe the texts were just to make Evan scared because we haven't heard from the fucker since. I've checked her phone. Mia hasn't heard from Jackson either.

Hawk and I head out to make sure everything is ready for tonight.

Cam has our girl, and Evan has a project she's been working on all week. She even told me in the shower this morning that she needed to focus when she got home tonight. It's the perfect night.

By seven, we're back at the high school waiting for Cam and Evan. The cast walks out. Chase still has glitter on his uniform. I'm tempted to pour more into his truck. It's satisfying but not enough.

This might not be enough. It will get him back for what he did to Evan though. That's the goal.

Evan comes out. Cam's got his arm around her shoulders, and she leans into him. I suppose something like that should make me jealous, but I'm not. Evan is just as much mine as she is his or Hawk's. Her smile grows when she sees us.

But when she gets to us, she turns serious. "I need to work tonight."

"That's the plan, little devil." I smirk, knowing she'll think I'm implying sex.

"You need to make yourself scarce." She shakes her head before putting on her helmet. "You're a nuisance and a distraction."

She's referring to earlier in the day when I trapped her in a closet and fucked her so hard I had to cover her mouth to muffle her screams so no one would think someone was being murdered.

"Don't worry. We'll keep him occupied." Hawk closes the distance between them. "But it will cost you, baby girl."

She narrows her eyes like she's going to tell him off too.

"After you're finished with your assignment. Of course." He kisses her hand, and she blows out a breath. "You want a full bed tonight, don't you?"

She puts her visor down and turns on the Bluetooth. "Yes, but later."

Perfect.

It's dark. It's one of those nights the moon plays hide and seek in the clouds. Our bikes are hidden, and Nina drove her car out to meet us. We recorded her voice and told her to wait with our bikes. Once he's in, she can head out.

We have on black clothes and masks with voice modulators. Nina's been working on him for a week, telling him her deepest, darkest desires. He's taken the bait.

We find our places. Hawk goes to the right, and Cam goes to the left. I have my phone ready to press play.

It's five to eight when Chase's truck pulls into the parking lot. The same one he left Evan at two weeks ago. He parks next to Nina's car.

When he climbs out, he runs his hand through his hair and looks into the car.

"Nina?"

I hit play. "Come and find me."

"Fuck." The word is soft and carries on the wind. He takes a breath and moves into the woods. He has his phone light on as he walks slowly.

"Maybe this wasn't a good idea. We should just fuck in my truck." Chase shifts to the left. "It'd be more comfortable."

"I want you to chase me." She ended that take with a little giggle.

He moves farther into the woods, until he passes where Hawk and Cam are. They step out like shadows and move to follow him.

The car engine roars to life, and Chase looks behind him.

"What the fuck?" He swings his phone toward the road and catches the two figures in black, their masks lighting up in the flashlight beam. "What the fuck?"

He turns and runs deeper into the woods. The others follow after him while I track him, waiting for the right moment. I step out and he skids to a halt.

"I have money. You can take my truck." Chase holds his hands up in the air. The smell of urine fills the air.

"You wanted her enough to come into the woods." Hawk's modulated voice breaks the growing silence.

"Yeah, man. She's hot." Chase turns to look at the other two, his hands still raised. "I swear my dad will pay you a lot of money if you just leave now. No one has to get hurt."

"That's not what you promised her." Cam's voice is low with reverb. "You wanted to fuck her."

"She texted me," he almost screeches. I always knew he was a coward.

"Not Nina." I let that wash over him.

"This is about EvanAnn?" Chase straightens. "Damon?"

A fourth person steps out from behind a tree and then a fifth.

Chase's eyes widen. "I don't know what you want from me, but I'm willing to pay."

"You will pay, Chase. On your knees."

He starts to cry as he falls to his knees. "I didn't mean it. I wouldn't have hurt her."

"You wanted to hurt her. You left her out here for hours." Hawk's modulated voice is loud over Chase's sniveling.

"I would have come back. I did. She was gone when I got back." Chase's head swivels to watch all of us surrounding him.

I snatch his phone out of his hand and open the timer app. I set the time to the exact amount of time Evan sat out here alone.

"When this timer goes off, you can come and get it at your truck. If you come out before, we'll teach you another lesson in obedience."

I set the timer and we walk away. All five of us toward the truck. He doesn't move, but we hear him sucking in gulps of air. Good.

We get to the truck and I set the timer on the hood. We wait ten minutes to make sure he doesn't try to come out. Cam pulls a hunting knife out and jams it into the sidewall of the back tire.

"Insurance." He pulls it out and the tire releases its air.

We walk to our bikes and Liam's car. I pull off my mask.

"Thanks for your help." I grab Liam's forearm, and he grabs mine.

"Anytime." Liam knocks Fletcher in the arm. "We've got a girl to see."

They head out. We wait a few more minutes, watching the camera I have set up on him. There's one on the truck too. It's more than he gave Evan. It's more than he deserves.

The alarm goes off. Chase looks around him before getting to his feet. An owl screeches in the night, and Chase takes off running toward the sound of the timer. He falls but he scrambles to his feet and races to his truck.

He jerks his keys out and snatches his phone before getting in. When he tries to pull out, he realizes his tire is flat.

We take off. He's got his phone and his truck. That's more than Evan had when he left her.

Chapter 45

EvanAnn

Chase shows up on Friday wearing a knee brace in an obvious foul mood. He doesn't even look at me during class. The guys were in a great mood when they came home to me last night. They weren't quick and took me through so many layers of pleasure, but we were still asleep at a decent enough hour.

The day goes smoothly and without rehearsal after school, we plan to go to dinner and a movie as soon as they finish their practice. I've had enough of football games.

When we're at dinner, Mia texts me that Chase is stuck on the sidelines due to his injury.

"Chase is out of football this week. Something about his knee." I look up from my phone in time to see Damon smile. It's a curious smile, because it's smug like he caused this.

Cam coughs and takes a drink of his soda.

"You want to see the new *Conjuring* movie?" Hawk looks at me like he wants to get into a heavy discussion about the horror genre.

I don't know what they're keeping from me, but I let Hawk lead me into a discussion about modern horror and films because I don't want to spoil our date night.

It's been an awesome week, but there's this countdown happening in my mind. We haven't really talked about the future. Cam, Hawk, Damon, and I. We're living in the present, but our present has a deadline. The end of school means the end of us unless we make plans. Plans that will change our futures if we want to stay together.

And while we have time, admission deadlines are fast approaching.

Adam and Mom still don't know about us. Or that I've officially broken up with Chase. I don't know why I'm hesitant to tell them about Chase. It's not like Mom cares who I date. She would understand if we broke up.

I could always claim Hawk as my boyfriend. It feels wrong to not acknowledge the other guys in my life. To pretend I'm not in love with Cam and Damon. It might make my mom more comfortable leaving things the way they are.

So I don't say anything to her about it. Eventually, I'll have to, but I just want to enjoy this time with them.

Today is Chase's dad's birthday party. The guys had a bye week for hockey, so no scrimmage this weekend. The party is this afternoon. We took our time getting out of bed and getting ready for today.

Cam and Hawk left early so Adam wouldn't know they spent the night. Again. It's almost like they take turns creeping in to sleep with Damon and me. I wish we didn't need to sneak around at all. But I don't think Mom would be cool with me sleeping with any of my boyfriends let alone all three of them.

While Damon got ready, I put on a simple dress that goes down to my knees. Makeup covers the little love bites littered across my collarbone, but I know they're there. The marks the Devil's trio leave on me. Claiming me as theirs. Now, Damon sits on my bed in nice dress slacks and a black collared shirt, propped up on his hands as he watches me put jewelry on.

Even after everything we've done, awareness of his cocky grin spins my insides like a carnival ride, leaving me dizzy and aching for him in the same breath. Will I ever get enough of him?

"Did you find the movie list?" he asks.

"It's in the box in my closet." I gesture with my elbow. We're all planning on watching a movie from the list tonight over at Hawk's so we have some privacy. He also has a movie theater room I haven't seen yet. I can't wait.

Damon stands and stretches, showing off his lean muscles before going into my closet. He brings out the box and sets it on the bed. I put on my other earring and go over as he opens the box.

When he picks up the list, he offers it to me. Smiling, I read over the movies. I haven't really looked it over in the past eight years. Some of the more recent ones I've seen, like *Get Out* and *The Quiet Place*.

"There's a few I can cross off." The list is still long, with movies spanning almost four decades of cinema.

"What's this?" He holds up a small jewelry box and opens it. I glance over at him and give the jewelry a wistful smile.

"It's a necklace my dad gave me for my tenth birthday." I watch the chain slip through Damon's fingers. "It broke a few years ago, and I didn't want to risk losing it."

I don't add that I couldn't afford to get it fixed and didn't have the time to do it myself.

It's a small gold heart pendant on a delicate chain. Damon returns it to the case and sets it in the box. There are a few other things in there. Cocking an eyebrow, he holds up a stuffed bear that has seen better days. Dad gave it to me when I was five, and I slept with it every night until he passed away.

I shrug. "I was ten."

He finishes shifting through the box and then closes it to put away. I check the mirror again. I'm going with Mom, Adam, and

Damon to Tom's birthday. Unfortunately, now would be the best time to tell our parents Chase and I broke up, but I still haven't.

I don't want to fuck things up by telling them. This week has been really nice. Even dinner on Wednesday with Mom, Adam, and Damon was pleasant. I'm definitely not ready to tell them I'm technically dating Hawk, Cam, and Damon. So I've done nothing, and that might bite me in the ass today.

I walk downstairs with Damon to join our parents.

"You look so pretty, Evan." Mom touches my blond curls.

"Thanks." I lower my eyes and step away from Damon.

"Are we ready to go?" Adam opens the door.

Damon and I follow our parents out to the car and get into the backseat, sitting far from each other. The drive doesn't take long and Adam has music on, so we're not expected to converse.

When we walk up to the house, I fall into step beside my mother so I don't accidentally take Damon's hand. One of these times I'm going to forget and lean into him for a kiss. It's so easy at school.

The attention on us there hasn't really waned, but I'm loving having three boyfriends and getting to claim them as mine. In a school that caters to art students, the teachers don't really raise an eyebrow at unusual pairings or groups like ours. As long as we don't become disruptive, we can do whatever we want.

We stick to their table at lunch with a few guys from the hockey team. Mia joined us with Fletcher and Liam on Friday. It was nice, but I can't get over the girls watching us, whispering to each other. It's not like any of them were dating my guys before me.

Adam hands the keys to the car to the valet. The party is around the pool in the back, so we walk through the house. We follow Adam to Tom and Jessica. I itch to step closer and grab Damon's hand as my stomach churns. This could be the end of the lies.

What did Chase tell them about our breakup? Did he tell them I cheated on him? Will they hate me? What if they ask me to leave? Damon wouldn't hesitate to take me out of here.

They don't look like they hate me as they smile at us. Is it fake?

"We're so glad you could make it!" Jessica kisses Adam's cheeks, then my mom's, then mine, but when she reaches for Damon, he steps away. Not missing a beat, she laughs and touches his arm. "So good to see you."

"It feels like it's been forever since we've seen you, EvanAnn." Tom shakes his head. "I'm sorry we had to ground Chase this past week, but that party should have never happened last weekend. He should have known having a few friends over would get out of control."

I smile and nod. Maybe Chase hasn't told his parents either? Why wouldn't he though? Oh, right, I'm his little trophy. Fucker. As long as he's dating me, he gets free rein.

"Chase," Tom says, looking over my shoulder. I tense.

Chase touches my waist, and I flinch. "I've been waiting for you, EvanAnn."

Damon's lips flatten, but he can't do anything about this. Not if we don't want to blow up everything. And everything's been going so well.

"Hey." I turn and give Chase my plastic smile. "Can we talk for a sec? You don't mind, do you, Mom?"

"Of course not." Mom smiles.

"Don't stay away too long." Tom nods toward a group of people standing off to the side of the pool. "I haven't forgotten. I need to introduce you to my friends."

Smiling, I nod at Tom, trying not to let my gaze stray to the director he promised to introduce me to when I was dating his son.

"Show me the bathroom," Damon says to Chase. Chase nods.

I let Chase lead me toward the house. Damon isn't far behind. I still don't want to be anywhere alone with Chase.

We walk inside and down a hallway away from the party. I shift from Chase's touch, closer to Damon, but not touching him in case someone comes after us. We can still hear the low murmur of voices and soft music from the party.

"What are you playing at, Chadwick?" Damon's words are a harsh whisper. He balls his hands into fists.

Chase laughs and leans against the wall. He doesn't have the brace on his knee, but I noticed a slight limp when he walked. "I figured you wouldn't be in a hurry to tell your parents about the two of you banging. And while EvanAnn has three boyfriends at school, I doubt your mom would approve. It was a calculated risk. You didn't tell your mom I left you out in the woods either. So I guessed you don't want your parents to know we've broken up because they might look a little too closely at what's going on in their house."

I release my breath. He's not wrong, but he has his reasons too. "It's not like you're going to tell your parents you've broken up with me and lose your free pass."

Chase shrugs with a cocky smile. "What I propose is you act like my girlfriend at this party so you can meet your favorite director and the people who can help you get into that long list of colleges you've applied to. A few of the faculty are here from your top choices."

"What do you get out of this?" Damon demands.

"The pleasure of her company." Chase smirks and looks me up and down like he's asking to fuck me and not just pretend to be my boyfriend for an hour.

When Damon jerks forward, I put a hand on his chest to keep him from decking the asshole. Stepping between them, I wait for Damon to give me his attention. He shifts his gaze to me reluctantly. He doesn't want me to do this, but it's in public. Chase can't do much to me at his father's birthday party.

"It makes sense," I say softly. Logically, Damon has to know that.

"Yeah, lover boy. It makes sense." Fuck, Chase is begging for Damon to kick his ass. Or maybe I'll kick his ass.

"Shut the fuck up, Chase." I keep my voice low. "Or I'll go out there and tell your parents exactly how you treated me as your girlfriend."

He doesn't make a noise, so I don't turn to look at him, keeping my focus on Damon.

"Fine." Damon backs off. He touches my jaw and grinds his teeth. His sharp blue eyes lock on Chase. "Touch her and I'll end you."

"It's a part." Chase chuckles softly and shakes his head. "What happens when EvanAnn gets a part in a play or movie, and she has to kiss some other guy onstage? Are you going to go mental on him? Or is it just me? Am I an actual threat?"

Damon chews on that. "No, you're just an asshole."

I don't know if we'll ever be in that situation of me playing a part, but Chase is kind of right, even if he's also absolutely wrong. This is about trust. That I'm not easily swayed away from Damon. Because nothing would make me go back to Chase after the shit he's pulled. Even if I didn't have the Devil's trio, I do have some self-respect.

"You trust me, right?" I cup Damon's jaw to get him to look at me. When his gaze meets mine, I search his blue eyes. "Damon, you trust me."

He takes in a breath. "Yes, little devil. I trust you."

I release the breath I was holding. "Good."

When I turn to Chase, I glare up at him. "If you touch me and I don't like it, I will knee you in your balls so hard you'll be tasting them at Thanksgiving with your turkey. And I'll tell your parents about your cheating and the woods."

"Understood." Chase glances at Damon and winks. "Does that make her hotter for you too?"

"Stop taunting Damon." I shake my head. "He's not the one who will destroy you. I will."

"Yes, ma'am." Chase gives me a cocky smile.

This is going to be a disaster. But it's just a part.

Chapter 46

Damon

Fucking Chase Chadwick. We walk out of the house, and he flashes me a grin before putting his hand on Evan's back and leading her to his father. If we hadn't made him cry like a little bitch in the woods, I'd be even more angry. But I have the video ready to upload the second he tries something I don't like.

I'm tempted to go to the bar and get something hard to drink, but Dad wouldn't be cool with that.

Instead, I get a Diet Coke and sit beside the pool. Dad and Heather walk around talking with people. She keeps her hand on his arm and they seem happy. It doesn't cut me quite as much as it used to, but it still doesn't feel good.

Tom takes Evan and Chase over to a woman in her late forties. Evan seems excited to meet her. She practically glows as she talks.

"Did your parents drag you to this too?" A brunette steps between me and my view of Evan across the pool.

I lift my gaze to her face, but the sun is behind her.

She drops into the chair next to me and holds out her hand. "I don't think we've met."

Around my age, she's definitely plastic from her designer dress and heels to her manicure. Like she belongs at this party. Across the pool, Evan wears a dress that she must have bought before moving in. It's nice, but not as nice as the dresses surrounding her. She looks beautiful in it nonetheless.

I shake the girl's hand, noting the expensive rings and perfume. The perfect makeup. This is a wealthy girl. "Damon Storm."

She nods and leans back in her chair. "Elizabeth. My parents forced me to come. Said I should mingle like my brother."

She does air quotes around *mingle* and scoffs. "What I really need is a drink, but since that can't happen, I figured I'd come and talk to the hot guy staring off into the distance."

I could tell her I was looking at my girlfriend. There's nothing about this girl I want, but maybe she can keep me occupied so I don't kick Chase's ass for commandeering my girl with logic. I want Evan to get the future she wants. She talked about the director a little last night and seemed so excited about the prospect of meeting her. I can't take that from her. Not if this is her opportunity.

Even if it means letting Chase touch what's mine. I'll just fantasize about breaking every bone in his fingers.

"I honestly hope we won't be here long." Elizabeth glances over with a smile. "But you know how it is when your parents are in the biz."

"The biz?" I don't know why I ask. There's nothing about this girl that interests me. I glance over, and Evan is still chatting with that older woman. This is what Chase said he could give Evan. Connections to make her dreams come true, but at what cost? Shackling herself to someone like Chase for the rest of her life?

He wouldn't know how to give her what she needs.

"My parents are producers. I am definitely not in the family business." Elizabeth laughs like that would be ridiculous. "It's not for me. But my brother loves it. He even goes to a special high school to teach him to be an arrogant prick."

I look at this girl again. "What school?"

"Anteros Conservatory." She waves her hand. "I could have

attended. They have another school, but your grades have to be practically perfect to get in. Besides, I love my boarding school. Not having to live under Mom and Dad's thumbs. Priceless."

My gaze flows over the crowd again, looking for whatever rich ant is her brother. I'm not familiar with all the students in either school. That wasn't my focus.

"Hey, big brother." Elizabeth says.

I turn and see Brandt Stanwell standing there. He smiles at me and offers me a hand like we're old buds.

"Damon Storm, the myth, the legend. What are you doing at this tea party?" Brandt takes the chair on my other side.

"Probably dying of boredom like me." Elizabeth smiles like we have an inside joke.

"My dad is business partners with Tom." I lean back. I don't know Brandt very well. I've heard the name, and occasionally Evan will say something about him. But he goes to our school, so he has to know Evan and I are together.

"I'm surprised to see EvanAnn with Chase." Brandt nods toward them. "Especially after the breakup."

"They're still friends." I act like it's not a big deal.

Brandt smirks as he watches me. "It's never easy when your girl is friends with her ex. Is it?"

I don't comment.

Elizabeth laughs. "Can you ever really be friends with your ex?"

Brandt shrugs. "EvanAnn's a nice girl. I'm sure you have nothing to worry about. She's usually too focused on school to worry about guys. Frankly, I was shocked when she agreed to date Chase. I figured he wouldn't have a shot with her. I told him if he could get EvanAnn, he needed to keep a girl like that."

"A girl like what?" I keep my tone neutral. And study the guy sitting beside me. Why is he telling me this? Why is he talking to me at all?

"Ambitious. Going places." He smiles and nods toward her.

"She's not the hottest girl at school, but with the right leg up, she could definitely make it big in this business."

"You and this business," Elizabeth scoffs. "I swear that's all you care about. Besides that one girl. Oh, what was her name?" She snaps her fingers toward Brandt, which has her hand in front of my face. "Olivia. That was it. She was fun."

"How was she fun?" I ask. Is she talking about Olivia Carmichael? It's possible there are other Olivias at our school. Or outside of school.

Elizabeth laughs and glances at Brandt with a smirk.

"She was a bit obsessive." Elizabeth leans over to me like she's telling me a secret while she looks at her brother. "She came around a few times, but she kept going on about this hockey player. She'd pretty much given up on having him. But Brandt said she deserved him, and the guy was just playing hard to get. That she should focus all her attention on the guy. Convinced this girl he would be the trophy she needed for the future. What did you call it, B? Oh, arm candy. Every girl needs a nice piece of arm candy."

Elizabeth shakes her head and laughs like it's their own personal joke. "You never did tell me, B, did she ever get her arm candy?"

"No," Brandt says with a smirk. "But she got a new pair of bracelets. Not the quality she's used to though."

"Hmm." Elizabeth settles back into her chair.

For a second, they're both silent. What's their game? Is he the reason Olivia came after me so hard this year? It doesn't make sense though. Who is this asshole?

"I was surprised to hear about you and EvanAnn." Brandt kicks his feet up and glances over at me almost casually. "She's not your normal *speed* of girl. But you weren't supposed to be here this year at all. What happened to that hockey program you were going into?"

"Dad wanted me to stay here." I don't mention the accident. How much does this guy know? I need to ask Cam about him when I get back. He always knows everyone's deal, no matter which school they attend.

"Got into an accident this summer, right?" Brandt nods like he doesn't need me to confirm it. His gaze strays to Chase and Evan across the pool. They're still talking to that woman. "Odd how Chase had to repair his car. Big, ugly scrape and dent. They never caught the guy who ran you off the road, did they?"

I cock my head at him. "No. Probably never will. Dark road. Late at night. No witnesses."

Brandt rubs his jaw. "You didn't see anything? Don't guys like you use cams on your motorcycles?"

I smile slightly. "We don't wear them most nights. And I don't remember much of that night."

We definitely don't wear them when we're riding like our namesake.

"Odd." Brandt turns to look at EvanAnn and nods his head toward them. "That's Sandra Cox EvanAnn is talking to."

I glance over like I wasn't already aware of this. Evan seems in her fucking element, talking to a director who can mentor her. She practically shines.

"She's very pro-woman in the industry. Loves giving internships to rising stars. The connections that could unlock for EvanAnn would be amazing."

"Why aren't you over there chatting her up then?" I ask, curious. I'm not stupid. He sought me out for a reason. Like his sister said, there are a lot of professionals here he could be rubbing elbows with, so why me? And did he use his sister to have an in to talk to me?

It feels like he's trying to find what wound is raw so he can pick at it.

"Why aren't you over with your girlfriend?" Brandt replies, instead of answering. His eyes narrow on me even as he smiles.

I don't say anything. Brandt is Evan's competition for the fall showcase. From everything I've heard, he's not as talented as her, but he's better connected.

Looking like the cat that caught the canary, he leans towards me with his elbows on his knees. "I've been watching this play out, and I think I've got it figured."

"Have you?" I cock an eyebrow.

Elizabeth chuckles. "He's the smart one in the family."

"You get into an accident and can't go to the hockey thing because of the injury or just because daddy doesn't want his only son going off. Maybe it's a mortality thing. The problem is, someone ran you off the road. That someone happened to have a girlfriend. Granted, he was fucking anything that moved behind her back, so maybe he wasn't the best boyfriend."

I set my drink down but keep my face blank.

"But then you and your friends pay attention to his girl. And shit starts to get interesting. They breakup, and you three are dating her, fucking her, whatever you want to call it. It's epic. Like a play brought to life, upsetting the norms. But what I don't get is what's the endgame."

"The endgame?" I ask.

He smirks. "You took his girl. You blew up his party. But what do you need a girl for? You could have any number of girls. Better girls even. Including my sister."

When I glance at Elizabeth, she gives me a knowing smile and a little wave.

"So what are you doing with a girlfriend? And why is her ex parading your girl around? Confusing." Brandt shakes his head like he doesn't understand. Then his gaze locks with mine. "It got me thinking maybe you don't actually want the girl, but are stuck now. But then I see your dad with a familiar blond. See, EvanAnn's mom shows up to productions. She's always sweet to everyone, but kind of off, like she doesn't pay that close attention to what EvanAnn is doing. So my guess is your parents don't realize you two are fucking around. Maybe it's that forbidden aspect that keeps you with her. Or maybe them finding out would end badly for both of you."

Chapter 47

Damon

Brandt's a good guesser, but he's off. I shrug. "Does it matter?"

He straightens and looks me over. "Probably not. After all, Hawk's going to Columbia in a year. You'll find your way back onto someone's list for college hockey. Maybe somewhere in New England or Michigan. And Cam? Cam's your wildcard, but he's definitely focused on Crowne Mawr."

Interesting pivot, but I let him continue.

"And EvanAnn?" He smirks and gestures to her shaking the director's hand. "She'll go places with or without the showcase. She's got a long list of colleges she's considering."

My eyes narrow at that comment, but he doesn't notice. He's watching Evan.

"She could go anywhere, but probably not the places you're going." Brandt shrugs and relaxes back in his chair. "You guys are a ticking bomb just waiting to go off. Maybe that was the plan all along. Throw her off her game. Maybe your parents will split you up. Or maybe you'll make it through the school year, but after this year..." He makes an exploding motion with his hands. He shakes his head and puts on his sunglasses. "It'll be a fun ride, but all rides end."

Evan and Chase move away from the director. Evan chats at Chase and he watches her with a smile. My heart burns seeing her give him attention.

"You know there are other options to keep your bed warm for the rest of the year," Elizabeth says. She touches my knee.

I glare at her, but she smiles at me like she isn't doing anything wrong. This is all a game to both of them.

I stand and glance at Brandt. "Whatever game you're playing, you need to stop before it gets you in trouble."

Brandt chuckles. "I'm not like Olivia. My emotions don't drive me. But something tells me they drive you. I'm going to sit back and watch the sparks fly when you go reclaim your ant."

He takes a sip from his glass as humor dances in his eyes.

Manipulative asshole.

I glance toward Evan and Chase as they walk over to a man and woman. Chase introduces Evan, and she turns on again. Ready with the right answers. Are these the drama professors at the college she wants into? This would be the equivalent to the coaches I need to get in front of.

Chase keeps his hand on her back. When he notices me watching, he smirks and leans down to kiss her hair. She doesn't pause in talking with the people, but she shifts away from him.

I should go claim her. Fuck our parents. But I also know Evan doesn't want that, so I walk the other way. Maybe there's a bar inside where I can add some rum to my Diet Coke.

"There you are." Tom's voice stops me as I reach for the glass door.

When I turn, I freeze at who stands next to Tom.

"Roger, this is the young man I've been telling you about. Adam's son." Tom's smile is huge.

I offer him my hand. "Damon Storm, sir. Huge fan."

Roger Farrell laughs and takes my hand. "Hopefully of my coaching as well as my hockey career."

"Both, sir." I straighten as we shake. He's been coaching at Yale for the past five years. Before that, his team won the Stanley Cup with his help. "I'd hoped to meet you when I was in the USHL."

Roger gives me that pitying smile people give you when they know your sob story. "Tom told me about your accident. It sucks to have to sit out a year and miss an opportunity like that."

I nod, but keep my gaze from drifting to Evan. Without the accident, I never would have gotten a chance to know her. She just would have been the daughter of Heather, the bitch who moved in with my dad while I was gone.

"I've been watching your stats for years," Roger says and gestures for me to join him in some chairs.

"I'll leave you two to it." Tom waves before heading off toward Evan and Chase.

We sit and he talks about the program at Yale a little. I ask questions when I need to. Yale would have been a stretch for me with my grades last year, but this year I'm focusing. It's not Boston, but it's definitely a step up from a new D1 program.

"I'd love for you to come visit for the weekend in a couple weeks." Roger meets my gaze. "You're the kind of player we've been looking for. Good grades, excellent school, and a coach who trains his players as if they're already in the NHL."

"We have the best coach." I agree. "And I'd love to visit."

"Your parents and sister can come with you too."

Sister. "She's not my sister. My dad and Heather aren't married."

Roger doesn't even skip a beat. "That's fine. Your dad is a good man. It'll be nice to see him on campus again. He got his law degree from Yale, I'm told."

I nod. Is that what this is? Legacy? Does it matter to me how I get in?

Not at this point. I'm just happy to have the opportunity again. Even if I apply to the Ivy Leagues, there wouldn't be a guarantee I could get on the team. Most teams already have their new players chosen for next year.

"We're always happy to have legacies. Even if your dad didn't play hockey."

I smile and we chat for a few more minutes before shaking hands and going our separate ways. I didn't keep an eye on Evan while talking to Roger, and now I look for her. Chase is standing with Elizabeth. Flirting.

But I don't see Evan. I circle the pool and find Evan sitting with Sandra Cox. What if Brandt is right? If I go off to Yale, Hawk's going to Columbia, and Cam goes to Crowne Mawr, where does that leave Evan and us?

Where would she even go for the internship? LA? And her colleges are all over the place. I've looked over the list Chase had. There's a couple in the northeast, but how do we all see each other?

Would she have time to travel if she gets an internship and college? And I'd have hockey, Cam's joining a fraternity, and Hawk will dig into school. None of us will see each other except maybe at breaks if I don't have a game and Evan doesn't have a performance.

I drag a hand through my hair. Maybe we do have an expiration date. A fist closes around my heart. I'd lose my best friends and my girl. Sure, we might keep in touch, but will that be enough? Maybe we need to start looking at what kind of future we might have together.

Is it too soon to be looking at that? Will that freak Evan out?

Her gaze lifts and she looks around. Her eyes find me and she smiles so fucking big my heart hurts. The future is months away. We have time to come up with a plan.

EvanAnn

"We're taking submissions over the next month." Sandra Cox tells me. Me! "I'd love to see your application."

"This means everything to me." I'm not about to be shy about this opportunity.

"When Tom told me about you and what you've done at Anteros, I knew you'd be a perfect fit for the program." Sandra smiles and touches my arm. "It's a year-long internship, but you'll be working with me the entire time. My interns usually have their choice of colleges or work when they finish. And we'll keep in touch."

The amount of industry contacts I could make in a year makes my head spin. I turn and look for Damon. He was talking to a man earlier, but now he sits alone, and his focus is on me. I can't help but smile.

"Here's my contact information."

I get out my phone so she can AirDrop the info to me.

"I'm really looking forward to reviewing your application." She points to the information on my phone. "You can access the application here."

I nod. "I'm so glad I got to meet you. You really are who I want to be someday."

Sandra stands with me, and she kisses my cheeks. "You'll go far, EvanAnn."

She leaves me, and for a second, I just breathe in the fresh air. Fuck. Sandra Cox is excited about my application. I want to run to Damon and jump into his arms.

"How did it go?" Chase comes up beside me. His hand hovers near my arm, but I glare at it. He doesn't touch me, thankfully.

I give him my practiced smile. "It went well. Thank you."

"You should give your boyfriend a hug." He arches an eyebrow.

"I will give my boyfriend a hug as soon as we're alone." I move away from him a little, and he drops his hand.

"You could be a little more grateful, EvanAnn." Chase closes the distance between us and leans down so no one else can hear. "I got you one-on-one time with your future, and you didn't even have to suck my cock."

I narrow my eyes at him. He's right on the edge of the swimming pool no one is using. The blue water ripples from the gentle breeze. I give him a fake grin and move like I'm going to give him a hug. He opens his arms, and I shove him enough that he loses balance. I'm careful to scramble away so he doesn't drag me in with him.

He lets out a yelp as he crashes into the pool. I cover my mouth to hide my smile but keep my eyes wide.

"Oh my god, babe," I say. "Are you okay?"

Chase runs his hands through his wet, dark hair and lifts his gaze to mine. He's careful to hide his anger, knowing he's the center of attention. "Must have slipped."

He swims to the ladder and climbs out. Mom stops beside me.

"Are you okay?" she asks.

I almost giggle but hide it. "I'm fine."

I turn to look for Damon, and his blue eyes dance with amusement. Chase makes his way inside as his mom offers him a towel. He snatches it from her. Damon walks over to us.

"Seems like a fitting end to the party." Damon nods to his dad as Adam joins us. "I'm ready to go when you are."

I wish we'd come separately from our parents. That we could take off on his bike and ride up into the hills.

Tom approaches us, shaking his head. "I don't know what to do with that boy. You'd think he'd be more graceful from all the acting classes we bought him."

I shrug. "I might have thrown him off balance."

Swallowing my laugh, I glance at Damon. He doesn't give anything away, but I really can't wait until we're alone so we can laugh about it. Cam and Hawk will be pleased too.

"You should stay for dinner, EvanAnn," Tom announces. "It'll just be us and Chase. Seems like you two haven't gotten a lot of time together lately."

"I already have plans to hang out with friends. Chase said he'd be busy tonight." It's just a line in the part I'm playing as Chase's long-suffering girlfriend.

"That's too bad." Tom glances toward the house. "I have to say goodbye to people. Hopefully, we can get together again soon. I'd love to hear about who you talked to and what opportunities might have come your way."

"It's a little busy right now with family, the play, and school. Thank you so much for introducing me to Sandra Cox. She's amazing."

Tom smiles. "I knew she'd love you."

"Who wouldn't?" Damon says softly. He's close enough to my back I can feel the heat coming off him. But far enough away to be appropriate.

"I always knew my little girl would go far." Mom touches my hair and smiles with a little sadness. Like she's remembering Dad and his love of movies. I could use a hug, and it looks like she needs one too.

I step into her and wrap my arms around her waist, resting my chin on her shoulder. "I love you, Mom."

She hugs me back and rests her head against mine. "I love you, too."

Chapter 48

Hawk

"And then Sandra told me she couldn't wait for my submission." Annie sits on the edge of her seat at my kitchen table. Her plate of pasta has grown cold, but she was so excited when she and Damon arrived. "I still can't believe it happened."

She holds her hand out, and it shakes. "I can't stop trembling."

Damon takes her hand and kisses the back of it before lowering it to his lap. "Eat your dinner, little devil."

She smiles at him before finally eating the bite of food on her fork.

"She also pushed Chase into the pool." Damon smirks.

"He slipped." She grins and takes another bite. "Who were you talking to?"

Damon glances at her. "Roger Farrell."

"No way." Cam leans back in his chair. "I swear my dad would faint if Roger Farrell spoke to me."

"Who's Roger Farrell?" Annie asks, glancing at all of us.

"The head coach for the Yale hockey team," I say. I meet Damon's gaze. "What did he say?"

"He wants me to come up in a couple weekends. Unofficial visit." Damon glances at Annie.

She squeezes his hand. "That's amazing, Damon. It's a good team?"

"One of the best." Damon's smile has an edge to it, like he's not happy. Annie hasn't noticed, but Cam glances at me, and I give him a small nod that I've seen it too. We'll let it go for now.

He told us about Chase. The coward hadn't told his parents about their breakup, so Annie played along to get introduced to the right people. But she probably would have met them without playing along. Chase threatened to tell her mom though.

Cam should have punctured two tires.

I don't want to rain on Annie's parade, but this needs to be fixed. "You need to tell your mom about Chase, Annie."

She looks up at me with wary eyes and sighs. "I know."

"If you're worried about being single, just say you're dating me or Cam. Or me and Cam." I smirk. "It's not a lie. If you don't, Chase will keep finding ways to use you."

"I know." She sets down her fork and stares at her cold pasta. "But what if she makes me change rooms?"

"Then you can still come to my room at night, little devil." Damon puts their hands on the table.

She bites her lip like she can't decide.

"We can figure that out after the movie." Cam nudges her plate. "Eat, goody. It's not like the special effects are going to make you hurl."

The first movie from the list Annie picked is *Poltergeist*. She wanted to make it a haunting-type weekend.

Annie picks up her fork and spears a few vegetables. "I do want to tell my mom what's happening in my life." She glances up at each of us. "I just don't like leaving any of you out. I love you, and I'm not ashamed of that. But I don't know what my mom would do if she found out about Damon and me."

"She won't take you away from me." Damon's voice is determined.

"You don't know that." Annie shivers. "The only place that always has availability on short notice is that apartment complex Jackson lived at. I don't know if he's still there, but I don't want to go back there. I don't want to be afraid."

"You won't have to." Damon blows out a breath. "She doesn't get to control your life."

Annie laughs bitterly. "Yes, she does. That's how I ended up in the bedroom next to yours."

"Just say you're my girlfriend." I sit in the chair next to her.

Her stormy eyes meet mine.

"We have a good story." I glance at her fork meaningfully, and she takes the bite. "You're the director. I'm the actor you didn't see coming. We fell in love on stage. Easy."

"Probably better than you blackmailed her into sucking your dick." Cam grins and runs his hand through his hair.

Annie sticks her tongue out at him, and his smile grows.

"Personally, I think we could have found something sexier on that list of movies." Cam winks.

"I don't think *Nightmare on Elm Street* will be particularly steamy." Damon's tone is flat as he arches an eyebrow at Cam.

Annie continues to eat as we argue over whether *Friday the Thirteenth* is sexier than *Nightmare*. She laughs a few times at our reasoning. When she finishes eating, I take her hand and lead her through my house.

We haven't really explored it much since we tend to stick to the bedroom. Her gaze bounces around at the artwork, molding, wallpaper, and statues. It's a little over the top, like my parents.

She pauses in front of a painting of a naked woman. It's one of the more tasteful pieces. She glances at me like she's trying to decide how to ask me something.

"Go on, baby girl. Ask your question."

She looks from me to the painting, and back again. "Did you grow up with all this... art?"

Cam chuckles. "It's the best thing about Hawk's house."

"It's tastefully done," I insist. "But to answer your question, yes. My parents are collectors. My house has always had a few more naked people than most."

She nods. "Is that what you like?"

"Are you asking if I want a house full of nudes in the future, baby girl?" I guide her toward the movie theater.

"I don't know if that's the sort of thing you like or expect." She shrugs as I open the double doors, and she steps into the theater. When the dim lights come on, she gapes at the size of the screen. The rows of leather recliners. The smell of fresh popcorn.

"Holy shit! I'm never leaving this room." She pulls away and walks all the way to the front before turning back with a wicked smile. "You guys have watched porn in here, haven't you?"

"We could watch you fucking us in here if you want," Damon pulls her against him. "You could fuck me while we watch."

Annie swallows. "We're supposed to watch *Poltergeist*."

She wants to watch us fucking her though. I smirk.

"We can do both." I pick up the remote and cue up the movie. "Do you want to be satisfied before or after watching the movie?"

Annie raises an eyebrow and looks at all of us. "Both?"

Damon chuckles. He tosses me his phone as Cam goes to lock the doors, just in case. My parents have been MIA, but they show up from time to time. Usually at inconvenient times, like when I have my girl naked in my movie theater, needing my cock.

"These are completely unedited." Damon lifts her shirt off before grabbing the waistband of the little skirt she wore for us and pulling her into him. "Very amateur until you edit them."

"I told you before, I'm not editing your blackmail videos."

Damon tsks as I pull up the file on his phone and cast it to the big screen.

"I don't need to blackmail you to be mine, Evan." Damon drags his finger along the lacy edge of her bra as she sucks in a breath. "You'll give it to me even if I erase all the videos."

Her lips part as Cam closes in on her back. He reaches under her skirt and drags her panties down her legs.

"You'll do anything to have one of our thick cocks buried in your cunt. Won't you, goody?" Cam kisses her shoulder, and she releases a little whimper that makes my hard cock throb.

I move down the center aisle and take a seat in a recliner toward the middle. There's a collection of videos on Damon's phone. His private server we have access to. I click on the night Cam took Annie's ass for the first time.

The sound of ragged breathing fills the room as Damon leads Annie to the chair beside mine. Cam sits on my other side.

"I want you to watch while you fuck my cock." Damon sits down.

Annie stands in front of him with just her skirt and bra on. She's the sexiest thing I've ever seen. Her eyes dart up to the video playing. Her fingers touch her lips, and she presses her thighs together.

"Are you dripping, baby girl?" I undo my pants and release my cock.

Her eyes catch on the movement of my hand stroking my dick. She wets her lips.

"So wet." Her voice is low, and she clutches the hem of her skirt.

"Lean against the back of the chair and show us." I gesture to the chair in front of me.

She faces the big screen and spreads her feet to either side of mine before leaning her arms and chest against the back of the chair, presenting her ass to me.

"Lift your skirt for me, baby girl." I stroke my cock at the glimpse of her wet pussy shining before me.

She drags the hem of her skirt up to rest on her waist, exposing her pussy and ass to me.

"Fuck." Cam squeezes his cock in the chair next to me.

She whimpers and her pussy clenches in front of me, aching for a cock to fill it. I glance up at the screen she's watching. In the video, the light is on in the bedroom at this point, and she's lowering that sweet ass down on Cam's cock, inch by inch. My cock weeps at the sight.

I lean forward and press my lips against her pussy.

"Hawk." She pushes back against me.

"So needy." I grab her hips and swipe my tongue up her slit. She moans almost as loud as she does on screen. "Do you like watching yourself get fucked?"

"Make me come, please. I want it. I need it." Her hips try to rock in my hands.

"Oh, baby girl, I'm going to make you come so hard and then you're going to fuck all of us with that sweet, tight pussy until you're dripping with our cum. Then you're going to sit on our cocks while we watch your movie. Moving between us after we come again."

She shivers, and I catch her wetness on my tongue, swallowing the sweet taste of her.

"Do you want that?" I ask and slide my tongue along her slit before pausing at her entrance.

"Yes. Fuck, yes, Hawk."

I grin against her pussy and then fulfill my promise.

Chapter 49

Cam

Evan is passed out on my dick and it's the best thing ever. Though she's missing the movie. I've got the recliner tipped back. She's draped against me, her back to my front. Her face is turned and pressed against my shirt. My cock buried in her cunt. She's practically naked, but we're still clothed.

"We're going to have to rewatch this one," I say.

My chest moves under her with every word, but she's conked out. The movie is at the part where they're waiting for something to happen, monitoring the house.

"When you're done, I need that pussy." Damon smirks at me across Hawk. "I don't mind if she's asleep."

I chuckle, and she shifts on my cock. Fuck, she's dripping wet. Granted some of that is from us filling her up, but most of it is all her.

"What's up with Yale?" Hawk turns to Damon.

"Yeah, why isn't that the most exciting thing from today?" I ask. "It's a step toward the NHL."

Damon scrubs his hand over his face before looking at Evan. "We haven't exactly talked about what happens next with us."

I slide my arms around Evan's middle. "You mean like the future and shit?"

I haven't really thought about college all that much. Obviously I'm going, but with Dad pushing for Yale, I haven't figured out how to tell him I'm applying early admissions to Crowne Mawr.

"That list of colleges Evan applied to is long, but it's selective." Damon shakes his head. "What if we don't end up in the same state or even the same part of the country?"

Hawk runs a hand through his hair. "This seems like a conversation Annie should be part of."

"Probably, but I'm not waking her up," I say. "She needs her sleep."

Especially if she's going to keep up with us three and all the other things she does.

"We have this year, but after graduation and summer, we'll probably be going separate directions." Damon's eyes are soft as he looks at Evan. He's possessive of her. That he shares her with us is amazing, but I wouldn't want it any other way. "I'd say we could see each other on weekends, but how reasonable is that? I'm going to be busy with hockey. Evan has her theater program. Hawk has academics. And Cam will have his fraternity."

I drag in a breath as I get what he's throwing down. Long distance won't work for us. Not if we can't even visit each other. "We won't have time to travel to each other."

I'd come to terms with losing my best friends when we went off to college, but I can't imagine losing Evan too. Starting over is a little scary, but doable. Except I don't want to lose this. Evan has brought us closer together.

"What if we tried to go to the same college or at least the same city, maybe state?" Hawk glances at each of us. "That could be a possibility, right?"

"You're going to give up Columbia?" I scoff. That's a huge ask. "You've been wanting to go there all your life."

"Their team is D2, but it's New York City. Surely we can all find a college in or near that." Hawk glances at Damon. "Boston isn't that far from New York City."

"Yeah, but Boston isn't exactly knocking on my door." Damon zips up his pants. "At this point, I need to go with whatever hockey program will take me. That might be Yale." Damon glances my way.

"Well, my dad would be thrilled." I blow out a breath. "I don't know if I'm Yale material though."

"You're smart enough if you stop dicking around." Hawk fastens his pants. Apparently party time is over.

But I still have Evan on my dick. And while this isn't a sexy conversation, her muscles clutch me every so often, keeping me hard.

"It's not about being smart enough." I lean my head back. "It's about how much I want to work through college. Deimos sucks, man. And it's a guarantee that any of the Ivies will be just as intense. I know Crowne Mawr will be difficult, but..."

I scrub my face. The future sucks. I just want time to keep being a punk before having to get on with my life.

"You could manage with us helping." Damon leans his elbows on his knees.

"Fuck." I straighten and Evan's hips roll against mine even though she's still asleep. "Give me a minute here."

I slide my fingers between her legs and work her clit gently. She moans softly and rolls her head. When I grab her breast with my other hand and squeeze her nipple, a breath rushes out of her. Her hips rock against mine. The others are watching, but right now she's all mine.

I rub her clit in little circles until her pussy clamps down on my cock as she comes. She arches against me as her cunt milks me. It's enough to push me over the edge and finish inside her.

Her breathing is ragged as she shifts on my chest. "Did I fall asleep?"

"Yeah, goody. Time to go to Hawk." I lift her, and Hawk helps her sit on his lap.

She blinks a few times and glances at the screen. Hawk pauses the film at the point in the movie where the ghost lights dance down the stairs.

"I guess we'll have to watch this one again?" she asks as she snuggles against Hawk and yawns.

"Yeah." Damon brushes her hair behind her ear. She gives him a sleepy smile. "We were talking about what happens after high school."

"That's a heavy conversation." She stretches and glances over her shoulder at me.

Damon continues, "If we want this thing to last long term..."

She straightens. "Oh."

"Do you not want that, Annie?" Hawk brushes his hand over her back. "If this isn't something you think can work for you, let us know. We'll still fuck you this year, but we'll stay the course with our plans."

She bites her lip and looks at each of us with wide eyes. She's definitely awake now.

I take my shirt off and pull it on over her head. "Easier to focus with you covered, goody."

She bites her lip and looks down at her hands. "Is it realistic for us to go to college together?"

Her gaze goes to all of us before settling on Damon. "We're both on career paths that may not even end up in the same country. A lot of filming is done in Canada or around the U.S. You need to be flexible to go with whatever team picks you, but it's possible to be traded, right?"

Damon nods.

She looks at Hawk. "Your dream is Columbia University. Are you really willing to give that up for me? What happens in a year when we break up because we're growing apart?"

No one says anything. Her blue eyes lift to mine. There's determination in hers.

"You may not have a career picked out, but you do have a plan. It's not a bad plan either. So who has to give up or compromise on their dream to keep a relationship we've had for a couple weeks?"

"What if it's not a compromise?"

EvanAnn

Damon's words make my heart leap. This whole conversation is more than I expected from them. But I also have to be real here. Even if they don't want to. There's no guarantee we'll make it through the school year. Let alone go to college together.

I blow out a breath and turn to search Damon's eyes. "Do you really believe that? That the four of us can find somewhere that has D1 hockey for you, feeds into a stellar law school for Hawk, has a film directing program for me, and provides a good school/life balance for Cam?"

If my heart wasn't breaking, I'd laugh. It feels impossible. One of us will have to compromise. Even if I got into Yale, I might not be able to afford to live there even with a scholarship.

"We can try." Hawk tips my face his way. "It may not be one perfect school, but schools close enough together where we can see each other more than once a year have to exist."

"I don't think this will work long-distance." I'm throwing that in because it won't. "It's not like I can make myself available for you to fuck as frequently as we've been. I have ambitions and dreams. I don't want to compromise on school or my career for the guys I fell in love with in high school."

Standing, I turn toward the screen so I can think straight. "I'm fucking this up. I love you." My gaze catches on the lights on the screen. I wish what was happening with us was a movie and I knew it would all work out. But that's not real life. "Do I want to figure out a way to make this work? Of course. I don't want to lose you now or at the end of the school year when we go our separate ways. But I'm not going to compromise my future to be with you. I've worked too hard to get to where I am."

I turn and look at them. My face is dry, even as tears choke me. "And you shouldn't have to compromise your future to be with me."

"So we do nothing?" Damon rises and towers over me. "We don't even try?"

My breath catches, and I put my hand over his heart. The hurt in his voice is obvious, but this is different than his mother. "Damon, I want to be with you as long as we can. I just don't know how we find a future where we're all happy with our choice. Where someone doesn't have regrets. Do you honestly think we'll still be together next year at this time?"

He sinks his hand into my hair. "I have never wanted anyone the way I want you. This need I have to be near you. I will stalk you wherever you go. Watch you sleep. Make sure no one touches what's mine."

"Damon..." I don't know how to explain to him this won't work. That I'm trying to save us the heartache. But part of me wants to be theirs forever. To try to make this work. Even though in the end, it might go up in flames.

It's ridiculous. When Chase talked about the future, I blew it off because he didn't matter. He was always going to be a footnote in my story. But these three? My heart aches at the thought of being separated from them for even a week, let alone months.

"Tell me you won't ache for me when you're alone on set." Damon brushes his lips against my forehead. "That you won't dream of Hawk or need Cam. That we're better off following our dreams if they take us away from each other."

I lift my gaze to his. I've never been good at telling Damon no. And my heart doesn't want to.

"It won't work," I whisper, but he smiles because he can hear how weak my protest is.

"Then it doesn't work, little devil." Damon brushes his lips against mine, too brief of a touch. "That doesn't mean we plan for the end."

Hawk brushes my thigh with the backs of his fingers. I meet his steady gaze.

"We plan for both, baby girl. We figure out how what we want fits together. Take the time to research how we can do this. How we can stay together."

I turn to look at Cam. He drags his hand over his face.

"I can apply to Yale if that's what we need, but their undergrad theater program isn't a conservatory program."

I arch an eyebrow at him.

"My dad has tried everything to get me to go to Yale." Cam smirks. "I pretty much know their curriculum backward and forward."

I walk over to him and sit on his lap. "You're smart enough to go to Yale. There will be parties there too. But stop selling yourself short. You don't need to go to Yale for your father, but you can choose to go to it to be with us. If Damon gets on the hockey team."

I lift my gaze to Damon. "This doesn't work if it's not D1. I'm okay adjusting my dream, but we're not giving up on yours."

Damon leans against the row of chairs in front of us. "If you get that internship, you take it. I'm not standing in the way of your dream either."

My heart thumps because unless the stars align perfectly, we'll have to compromise somewhere.

And knowing how stubborn we all are, I could see us bending our desires just to cling to each other.

I need to say this. "If it comes down to one or the other—"

"No, goody." Cam draws my chin back his way. "Neither of you will give up on your dreams. Hawk and I can figure out our shit, but we're going to support both of you. Compromise isn't an option when it comes to your careers."

I search his eyes. Our dreams are so big. I push my hand through Cam's hair. "You get to dream big too."

He smirks and leans into my hand. "I've already got my dream. My best friends and the girl we love. What more could I want?"

Chapter 50

Cam

Evan is quiet as we shower. Just her and me. The others took quick ones, so I guess this counts as my alone time with our girl. I trail my hand down her arm. Her skin is so soft. Every inch of her is soft and pretty. It's easy to get addicted to her.

When she looks up at me, her blue eyes are wide and nervous. "Do you really think we can make this work?"

I pull her into me and rest my chin on her head. She wraps her arms around my waist. Even though we're naked, I just want to hold her close for a second while I really think over her question. Because it's not an easy one.

None of us has ever had a real relationship. Nothing we wanted to keep longer than a week or two, but Evan is different. Everything about how she makes me feel, makes us feel, is different. All I know is I'll do anything to keep her.

"I think Damon would stop the world to make this work." I breathe out and stare at the dark tile of Hawk's shower. "He won't give up on his dream, but that also means he won't let you give up on yours."

"What about your dreams or Hawk's?" She pulls away to search my eyes. "Your dreams matter too."

I chuckle and shake my head at her. "Dreams change, goody. This year Damon was supposed to be off living his dream. Hawk would have spent all his time working to prove to Columbia he's worthy. I was going to be alone. Getting drunk at parties and trying to convince my dad Yale won't have me."

She drags in a breath. Probably ready to defend me to myself again. I love that about her.

"Instead, Damon was forced to stay and decided to make this year interesting. I've spent more time with my boys than in previous years because of you. Yes, wrong reasons and all that, but fuck, you don't understand how much we need you. How much you make us whole. So, yeah, we could all go fuck off to whatever college and uncertain future that holds. Or we could cling to the one thing that makes everything make sense. You, Evan."

Her cheeks are flushed, and the corners of her lips turn down like she's trying to come up with another reason it won't work. I want to kiss her until she understands.

I cup her jaw and run my thumb over her cheekbone. "You're the future I see now. You, Hawk, and Damon. Fuck everyone else."

She rolls her eyes at that last bit. I chuckle but continue.

"When I'm with you or the guys, I feel like I belong. Like I'm part of something special. I'm not about to give that up. Whether we all go to Crowne Mawr, or Yale, or fuck, maybe you'll get that internship and Damon will go for a year in the USHL to find his place. If that happens, we'll take a gap year and spend our time with you two so Damon doesn't go fucking crazy with you gone."

Evan steps back. "It's not the way things are supposed to work. High school romances rarely last. We—" She presses her hand against my chest. "We didn't start out with the best intentions."

"Who cares about our intentions?" I laugh and hold her hand against my heart. "It doesn't matter how we started, goody. It matters what we do with what we found. I've never seen Damon or Hawk as devoted to one person as they are to you. And I get it, because I can't stand the thought of having to leave you guys in a year. Of going off by myself and trying to start over. Not when I could choose you. Let me choose you, Evan."

She searches my eyes like she'll find the lie, but this is my truth. Because if she lets me, I'll give it all to her.

"I'm not a big dream guy." I smirk. "I'm decent at school and good at hockey, but I'm not Damon or Hawk. Maybe I'll end up in politics because I know how to give a rousing speech." It's not something I haven't thought of, but it's not my goal. "What I do know is wherever we go will have what I need because all I need is you."

She glances toward the closed bathroom door before moving closer to me. Her voice is quiet, like she's telling me a secret. "What if we make all these plans and crash and burn? What if we don't work out?"

I brush her hair behind her ear and smile. "What if we do?"

Damon

"You think it was best leaving him to talk her into it?" I ask Hawk as he lies on the bed staring up at the ceiling. I sit against the headboard in my boxers. My fingers roll the small box in my lap. Maybe I should be in there, talking her into it. Showing her exactly how much I need her.

Hawk chuckles. "Your tactic wasn't going to work." He turns his head toward me with an arched eyebrow. "*I'll stalk you* is your best idea?"

I shrug. "She has to know I have those tendencies by now."

Hawk rolls his head to return his stare to the ceiling. "My dream is flexible, but Columbia has always been the goal. Yale would be comparable. But if it's me that has to travel to you guys…"

He makes a noncommittal noise. Like it doesn't really matter to him. But I know the way he is with Evan. None of us would make it a week without her. Even during the week, I'll wake up to one or the other in bed with Evan and me.

I stare at the door, wondering if Cam can convince her. He's the one who makes the grand speeches about togetherness and the future. If anyone can convince her, it's him.

I open the box in my hand. It's not a promise ring or anything romantic. Not really, but if she needs it to be...

The door opens, and Evan steps out in a Devil's t-shirt, her long legs bare and her blond hair damp around her shoulders. Her skin is flushed pink from the heat. My chest tightens. I can't lose her.

Cam comes out behind her as she crawls onto the bed. She pauses next to Hawk and leans down to kiss him. He smiles up at her before she moves over to me and sits beside me. Her gaze rests on the box.

"I don't need a proposal to follow you." She arches an eyebrow and gives me a cocky smile, like she doesn't honestly believe that's what this is. "It's a little early for that."

I hold the box out to her. "Honestly, I wanted something a little more permanent, but I was vetoed."

"You can't just put a tracker in a girl like she's your pet." Cam rolls his eyes as he sits on the end of the bed. "Go on, goody, open it."

Evan glances at each of us before opening the box. It's a simple gold band with little flowers carved into the surface. She lifts it out of the box and slides it onto her ring finger on her right hand.

Something possessive in me rears its head.

"Wrong hand," I say.

She shakes her head and laughs. "When we make vows to each other, I'll put it on the left hand."

She gives me the look like *try me*. Every inch of me wants to prove to her she's mine all over again. I want to argue until she succumbs to me, all soft and willing, but I need her to wear the damned thing.

I hold out my phone and show her the dot in Hawk's house. "If you're ever in danger, I'll be able to find you."

She rests her head against my shoulder and releases her breath. She holds her hand out in front of her, studying the ring. "Do you think someone is really going to try to take me?"

"No need to risk it." I slide my fingers against hers.

She sighs and tangles her fingers with mine and drops our joined hands onto her lap. "Is this really what you all want? To be together through college and beyond? What happens when our careers take off, and we have to make decisions about where we go? Who gets to win?"

"I imagine that will be decided on a case-by-case decision, Annie." Hawk rolls his head to look at her. "That's not something we need to decide now though. Right now, we just have to apply to similar schools and find out where we all get in and if we can make college work. Decisions for college don't have to be in until May. Signing for D1 is in November. So we have time."

"Except for the applications. Those take time and money." She nods and looks up at me. "Is Yale really a contender?"

I swallow. "I didn't think it was, but the coach definitely seems interested. My coach has feelers out too. So I'll talk to him at school Monday."

"I don't want to ruin anyone's opportunity." She sighs. "I don't want you to regret choosing me."

Cam shakes his head. "Not a chance of that happening."

Hawk chuckles. "Regrets are for losers. That's not who we are."

I squeeze her hand, and she looks up at me. Her eyes are a stormy sky, gray and blue mixed perfectly.

"Why would I ever give you up, little devil?" I lift her hand and kiss her ring. "We can make this work. I'll stand up to anyone who tries to get in our way."

She swallows. "Even our parents?"

I smile. "Especially our parents."

"My mom isn't as bad as you think she is." Evan shakes her head. "This is always how she is when she's in a new relationship."

"Negligent?" I arch an eyebrow.

"I spend most of my time at school or studying. There's no reason for her to worry about me." She looks over at Hawk. "She's there for the big moments. My plays and performances, she's always there. We have dinners together when our schedules line up. This has definitely been extraordinary circumstances. My mom loves me and would do anything for me."

"Evan—"

"No, Damon. You're basing this on the couple weeks you've been around us." Evan shifts onto her knees to glare at me. "All you've seen is her in the first flush of love. Not the years we've spent together. Yes, I took on a lot, but that doesn't mean she hasn't supported me. That she doesn't come and cheer me on. That she wouldn't step in if I'm in trouble."

My chest aches a little at that look in her eyes. Like I'm misunderstanding her on purpose. But I don't say anything because I believe Evan deserves more than bits and pieces of love.

"Do I think she might react really poorly to me fucking my future stepbrother and his friends?" She blows out a breath. "What mother wouldn't? She hasn't had to worry about me because I haven't given her anything to worry about. She knows I'll roll with the punches life sends me. But that doesn't mean she doesn't care. Just like your dad cares about you."

"I never said she didn't care."

"You implied it," she says a little less snippy, but still belligerent. Her blue eyes hold mine. "I love my mom. We have a relationship, and it might not be the type of relationship you're familiar with, but it's not bad."

"Then why haven't you told her about Chase? Do you think I enjoyed watching that asshole touch you because you were pretending to be his girlfriend?"

Evan opens her mouth, but nothing comes out.

"You didn't do that for him. You did that for her." I narrow my eyes. The others remain quiet, but this affects them too. "He used the fact you never told your mom about him ditching you out in the woods or him cheating on you. You need to come clean with her. I don't care if you don't want to tell her about us. About any of us. But you need to make sure Chase can't use it against you again."

She glances at the others and sits on the bed a little less proud. "I don't want things to change."

"They already have."

She shakes her head and when she lifts her face, there are tears swimming in her eyes. "I'm scared she'll take me away from you."

"I'd never let that happen." I brush my fingers over her jaw.

She scoffs and tips her head back to blink back the tears. "You can't know that. My mom moved us around until that apartment complex. She found our house for rent, and it's the first time I had a home since I was ten."

I touch her arm, needing that connection, our connection.

She laughs bitterly. "She's never settled for a guy longer than a few months. And then she pays attention to me. We'd spend almost every minute together until I was feeling antsy from all of her attention. Then she'd find a new boyfriend and things would go back to normal. Maybe I liked not having her focus. I didn't want to be her little project. To have her fix my hair or offer me makeup. Buy me clothes. I like being me."

I agree. I like Evan the way she is. Cam moves on the bed and sits behind her. She relaxes back against him as he wraps his arm around her center.

"It's uncomfortable," Hawk says.

We all turn to him. She reaches out toward him.

"When they finally focus on you, it's like suddenly you have to be everything they want you to be." Hawk turns and he meets Evan's eyes. Their fingers entwine. "It's not about us. We're their little brags to their friends. How much we do on our own. How we take care of ourselves. But when they want to be involved, it feels like them trying to shove the wrong puzzle piece into place."

"It's not that I don't love her." Evan's gaze returns to me. "I still need her. But right now, she's not trying to control my life and I'm okay with that."

My jaw clenches. I don't know if I'll ever get over how I feel about Heather intruding on my life and not paying attention to Evan's.

Evan sighs. "You have your reasons for not liking my mom, but don't let it color your view of her as my mom. She's always there when I need her."

I keep my mouth shut, but when Evan needed her, her mother wasn't there. When Jackson stole Evan's first kiss. To pick Evan up when she was abandoned in the woods. She didn't do enough to protect Evan from me. And now it's too late.

I won't let her take Evan away from me. She can try, but Evan is mine.

Evan frowns at whatever she sees on my face. She releases Hawk and moves away from Cam to come straddle my lap. She cups my jaw and searches my eyes intently.

"I'm yours and you're mine." She fits against me perfectly. "I don't need to proclaim it from the rooftops. But I don't like lying that it's just me and Hawk in this relationship."

"You're already lying about being with Chase," I offer. "And I wouldn't hate it if you told everyone I'm yours."

She breathes in and rests her forehead against mine. "I'll tell Mom about Chase."

"When?" Eventually, it will come out. It's better if it comes from her.

"Can I just savor the fact I have the best boyfriends and a world-famous director wants me to apply to her intern program for a few days?" Evan looks so fucking hopeful.

"Soon, Evan." I'm not letting her off that easy.

"Fine. Soon."

Chapter 51

Hawk

Annie is sprawled over me in sleep. Cam's hand hits my arm as he rolls next to me. I shake my head. Damon is on the other side of Annie. His hand is over her hip, possessive even in sleep. I breathe in this moment.

Do I want a future with this in it? Absolutely. But I need to reevaluate my priorities if this is what I want.

I roll with Annie so she's on the bed and slide out from beside her. After I use the bathroom, I walk through the bedroom. The three of them are asleep, so I head downstairs to the kitchen to start some coffee.

The weekends are the staff's days off. It doesn't make sense for them to keep up service just for me, when I'm rarely home on those days anyway. The chef always makes sure to prepare some easy-to-reheat meals in case I'm actually at home.

As I get to the bottom of the stairs, I hear some footsteps behind me and turn to see Annie walking down to me. Barefoot, with her legs bared. My shirt covers her. Her hair falls around her shoulders as if she ran her fingers through it.

She's absolutely gorgeous.

She smiles. "Morning."

"Morning." I lean on the newel post to wait for her, watching her descend the stairs. "What's got you out of bed?"

She shrugs and stops beside me to wrap her arms around my waist. "I figured since you were up, you were probably trying to find us breakfast. Thought you could use a hand."

I kiss her softly before leading her toward the kitchen.

"I can't promise much for breakfast. Coffee, maybe some muffins, pastries. There might be some bacon or sausage and some eggs."

Annie laughs. "So not much then?"

"Probably not enough to feed everyone." I grin as I back into the kitchen and the smell of coffee hits me.

"Good morning, Hawk." My dad's voice makes me freeze. But not until both Annie and I are in the kitchen. His green eyes flick to Annie. "And Hawk's friend."

Annie stops behind me. Her cheeks are flushed red, and her hands tug at the shirt that she's wearing over panties. It's long enough to cover everything, but it's also obvious she's not wearing much more.

"Good morning." Her voice is a little unsure.

Dad leans on the counter next to the coffee machine that is already brewing a pot. He turns and grabs a coffee mug to add to the two already waiting and then he adds another cup.

I swallow. "Mom's home."

It's rare for my dad to be home, but even more rare that they're both here. A stone falls in my stomach.

He nods and looks at Annie. "Do you need to take your friend home?"

He puts emphasis on *friend*. Fuck that. Annie doesn't need to be shamed about being here.

"This is my girlfriend, EvanAnn." I step closer to her.

The coffee finishes brewing. My dad's eyes remain blank and unimpressed.

"And do EvanAnn's parents know about her little sleepover?" Dad pours the coffee into a cup and holds it out to me.

I pass it to Annie. She mumbles a *thank you* before blowing gently on it. When Dad hands me another, I take it and set it on the island in front of me. He gives me the look that he's processing this and isn't happy with it. God forbid I have anything in my life that might derail my education.

"Her mother knows she's out." At least I assume Annie texted her mom like she normally does. This is the part that stings about my parents being home. Them finally wanting to know what I'm doing and having opinions about it. When they're gone, my life is my own.

Dad finishes pouring the cups and nods. "We need to have a conversation." He glances at Annie. "I hope to meet you when you're better prepared."

He lifts the cups, rounds the island, and leaves the kitchen.

"Should I leave?" Annie's voice is small.

I take the cup from her and set it next to mine, before I drag her into my body and hug her. "No, baby girl. Not yet. Let's go back to my room and make sure the others know. We'll get dressed and head out."

She glances over her shoulder before lifting her gaze to mine. "Don't you need to talk to your parents?"

I don't know what they need to talk to me about, but it can't be good. Normally, they aren't home at the same time. And even then, I have autonomy to come and go as I please. Unless this is finally when they tell me they're getting a divorce.

I clench my jaw, but then soften it when I focus on Annie. "We have rehearsal this afternoon. It can wait until dinner tonight."

***

EvanAnn

It really feels like a ride of shame this morning. I've never been caught with a boyfriend before. And definitely not when he's standing in only his boxers and I'm in one of his shirts. I always wondered what it would feel like.

Now that I know, it's not an experience I want to repeat. My blood felt like lava coursing through my veins. If I thought watching the video of me naked in front of the Devil's trio was humiliating, this was that times ten. I'm usually a favorite with parents. After all, I have perfect grades and, not to toot my own horn, but I'm kind of a big deal at Anteros.

We pull up to Damon's and my house and park in the garage.

The guys haven't said much, but the mood has been somber since Hawk said his parents are back in town. After we told the others, we got dressed and left.

Fortunately, we didn't run into Mr. or Mrs. Wilker on the way out. I don't know how Hawk would explain his friends staying over while he also had his girlfriend stay the night. It's not like Damon couldn't walk home from there if he were too drunk to ride.

When we get inside, it looks like our parents are both out. I release my held breath as we head upstairs to our rooms. I go into mine with Hawk and Cam following me, while Damon goes into his.

I take off my clothes, dropping them in the hamper, and go to the closet to find something to wear for today. Lots of coverage, whatever it is. My cheeks burn, thinking of what I must have looked like to Hawk's dad. Fortunately, my panties had been covered by the t-shirt. I don't mind the guys seeing me like that, but an adult? A shudder rolls through me.

"Are you angry at me, Annie?"

I turn to find Hawk leaning against the doorframe, watching me. I grab a sweatshirt and tug it on over my underwear.

"Why would I be angry?" I lift my hair from the shirt and grab a pair of jeans to pull on.

"Because I called you my girlfriend." He studies my face.

"Why would that make me angry?" I shrug. "I am your girlfriend. And it's better than being your *friend*."

I walk up to him and put my hand on his chest when he doesn't move out of the way. For a moment, I let his heat flow over me. Even though we've drunk our fill of each other, I still want more. I want to explore more with him.

When he goes to step back, I clench my hand in his shirt, holding him there. Our eyes lock and I arch an eyebrow. "Has your dad met a lot of your *friends?*"

"Jealous, baby girl?" His eyes darken as his hands go to my hips to pull me closer.

I roll my eyes, trying to play off the twist in my stomach. He's been with a lot of other girls and probably at his house. It must be convenient with his parents always gone.

I try not to let my jealousy leak through to my words and try for flippant. "Only of all the girls who got a tour of that movie theater."

He smirks. "Only you got the full tour. Including the bedroom."

Relief washes through me. I don't understand this need to be special. To have pieces of them no one else has had.

"Good." I pat his chest and give him a slight push to let me out.

He chuckles but releases me. He walks over to the bed to sit next to Cam while I head to my desk.

"I've got homework—"

"For fuck's sake." Cam blows out a breath. "No wonder you're top of our class. Do you do anything besides homework, goody?"

"Apparently I do you guys now too." I arch an eyebrow and turn to my desk. "We have rehearsal this afternoon. I need to stay ahead in my classes because, as the production gets closer, I'll have less time."

"Of course, director." Hawk stands and kisses my head, resting his hand on my shoulder. I love the weight of it there. Solid.

Hawk waits for me to look up at him. When I relent, he smirks and kisses me. A lingering kiss that leaves me breathless when he straightens.

"I should head home anyway." Cam stretches and as his shirt lifts, I catch a glimpse of his abs. I'm a very lucky girl. He smirks when he sees me looking. "I've got a test this week I should study for."

When he comes over, I tip my face up for him, and he kisses me. I grab his shirt and pull him back down for a second kiss.

"What's that for?" he asks, tucking a strand of hair behind my ear, sending a shiver down my spine.

"I'm proud of you for studying. Without me telling you to."

He chuckles. "What else am I supposed to do with you working?"

"It's still a choice, Cam."

They head out, stopping in Damon's room to say goodbye. If the guys have their way, in the future, we won't have to say goodbye. We can all live together during college and see each other when we can. Though I'm not sure if Mom will be okay with that. We've never really discussed whether or not I should live with someone. But it's not really her choice after this year.

"I'm going to go work out." Damon's voice makes me turn my chair around to see him in shorts and a t-shirt. "Wait for Hawk to take you to rehearsal."

I roll my eyes. "There hasn't been anything new from the unknown number. I really think it was someone trying to scare me."

Damon crosses the room to kneel next to me so I don't have to stretch my neck to meet his gaze. He lifts my chin. "You need to be careful. Just because he hasn't escalated doesn't mean he isn't waiting for an opportunity."

I want to argue with him. "Fine. But if Hawk isn't here on time, I'm leaving without him."

"He will be." Damon kisses me soundly before standing and leaving. I stare at the door for a moment after he closes it.

I've gotten so used to driving Damon's car that it hasn't occurred to me to ask about my car. No one's mentioned it at dinner. Surely, it's done by now.

ME:

Hey, what's the deal with my car?

I send the message to Mom and set down my phone, figuring it will take her a while to get back to me. My phone buzzes.

MOM:

> There were too many issues with it

> We sold it and put the money in your
> savings account

> You can keep driving Damon's car or we
> can get you a new one

My first response is nearly *you sold my car?!* But I don't send it, sitting with this information first and letting it digest. The car wasn't anything special to me. Great Aunt Maude had it in her garage, and since she couldn't see well enough to drive anymore, she passed it on to me.

It's not even that it's gone that bothers me. The thing that really got to me is that she's willing to buy me another. Not with her money, because I know she doesn't have the money for it, but definitely with Adam's. I love my mom, but honestly, looking at this from Damon's point of view, she comes off as a gold digger.

Moving in here. Her new outfits. The clothes she bought me. Offering to buy me a car?

ME:

> I'll make do with what I have

> I wish you would have asked before selling
> the car

I set my phone to the side and look around my room. This is just the place I keep my stuff. At night I sleep with Damon. The only thing I need money for is college. And it's not like Mom's going to make Adam pay for that.

My academic record and my directing should help me get into almost any school, but it won't mean I can afford any school. Yes, I can get scholarships, but I'll need living expenses too. The guys all have the means to go to any school they want. What happens when I get in and then can't afford to go to the school with them?

That's the compromise I'm worried about. I may have to compromise location to go to a school that's good for directing and acting, plus one I can afford. What if that limits Damon's dream? Or Hawk's? Or Cam's?

I don't want to be responsible for limiting their futures. My battle was always going to be an uphill struggle. Any money my parents might have put away went to my father's treatment. After that, money was always tight.

But I don't have time to think about that right now. I have homework I need to focus on and a rehearsal to lead.

I glance at my phone. Fuck it. I can at least do one thing the guys want me to do. It makes sense. I can't just let Chase keep using me.

ME:

Chase and I broke up

I wait a minute or two, staring at the conversation with my mom. Maybe she only had a few minutes to text earlier, and she's busy now. Maybe her phone ran out of charge. A small part of me whispers that maybe Damon's right and she just doesn't care.

Chapter 52

EvanAnn

"Let's take it from the top of the scene." I turn and look at Keira. She gives me a thumbs up from the back of the theater.

Mr. Watson sits to the side working on grading homework. After the first few rehearsals where Chase behaved himself, Mr. Watson's been less vigilant. But he still shows up to make sure things go smoothly, which I'm thankful for.

I don't need another *whore* incident.

The actors take their places. It's a scene with Chase and Hawk. Chase keeps messing up his line. It's supposed to go *Well, happiness to their sheets!*, but he keeps saying *Well, happiness is to their sheets!*. If he doesn't get it this time, we'll have to keep going to get through the entire play today.

"Your line is *Well, happiness to their sheets!*" I look at Chase. It throws off the cadence of the words when he messes up, and the rest of the speech gets muddied. Practice is the time to get this right.

Chase glares at me. "I know my fucking line."

"Then say it correctly this time so we can move on," I say sweetly, like it isn't a problem. I glance at Mr. Watson. Chase's frustration is normal during a play. But it's pissing me off today, and I'm trying not to show it. It doesn't help that Chase came in with a smug smile on his face after the party yesterday.

The guys were right. I should have ended the charade then and there. Tom and Jessica have always been nice to me. They might have still introduced me to Sandra Cox. After all, Adam and Mom were there. It's not like I came alone as Chase's girlfriend.

I rub the bridge of my nose. "All right, let's do it again."

Hawk and Chase begin their back and forth as Cassio and Iago. Iago wants Cassio to drink more so he'll get in a fight.

They get to the line Chase has been messing up and he does it again. He flinches as he realizes it.

"Keep going. We'll work on it in Tuesday's rehearsal."

Chase bites his way through his next lines. Mr. Watson has stopped grading and is watching the play now. When we finish the act, I call for a break.

"EvanAnn," Mr. Watson calls and gestures for me to come over.

Everyone heads to their drinks or out to use the restroom as I sit in the chair beside Mr. Watson.

"Is he always so belligerent?" he asks softly.

This is part of student directing. Sometimes my actors are assholes with big egos. Honestly, most times. After all, we're all here because we're the most talented of the students who applied.

"He gets frustrated when he keeps tripping over the same line." I hate making excuses for him, but this is acting. "We're just starting to come off script. Everyone's a little shaky with their lines. I don't think he's doing it intentionally."

Mr. Watson nods. "I'll be at practice for another week. Just until things smooth out."

"Thank you."

"You're doing well, EvanAnn."

I straighten at the praise and thank him again before heading to my desk. There's a single red rose laid across the pages of my script. I've gotten used to finding red paper flowers everywhere I go.

Maybe Hawk thought I could use a flower instead of a drink

today. I glance around, but I don't see Hawk anywhere. Who else would leave me a rose? I rode with Hawk, and he didn't have a bag. I guess it could have been in his saddlebag.

When I lift it to set it aside to get to my pages, something pricks my fingers. I drop the rose and look at my hand. For a second, I'm shocked at the blood welling, but then burning pain tears at my fingers. I suck in my breath.

"You're bleeding," Keira says as she sets her script down. She grabs a tissue, but the burning pain grows even more intense, like it's flaying me from the inside. It's too intense. I can't hold back my cry of pain.

Hawk

"Doing great in there," I say to Chase as I pass him in the hallway.

"Fuck off," he mutters before turning his attention back to Sofia, the junior who plays my mistress. He leans over her with a cocky smile. She plays with her hair as she looks up at him through her lashes.

"Did you get rid of that jock itch problem?" I look pointedly at his crotch.

Sofia looks down at his crotch with worry before she walks away. Chase snarls, but I ignore him.

As I approach the doors, a scream shakes my bones. I've heard it before. Annie!

I hurry into the room and Annie is curled in on herself near the table. Blood drips onto the floor beside her as she rocks. Everything in me goes cold.

Fuck. I'm at Annie's side in a second.

"I've got you," I say. I kneel beside her and reach for her, afraid to touch her somewhere that's in pain. "What happened?"

Her teary eyes lift to mine.

"It burns." Her voice is rough, like she's holding back from screaming.

What the fuck happened?

"Where's Mr. Watson?" I ask Keira.

"Bathroom." Her eyes are wide. "I think it's her hand."

I grab Annie's wrist and draw it away from her body. She whimpers. So much blood. I grab a bottle of water off the table and pour it over her hand. She screams. There are a few cuts, red and angry with blisters forming around them. What the fuck.

"Get him!"

Keira races off.

I lift her into my arms. All I know is I need to protect her. I hold her close to me as she cries.

Annie keeps muttering something under her breath as she cries. I lean in to hear it.

"It burns. It burns. It burns."

Finish the journey in Dark Tangled Truths

Meet C.S. Berry

C.S. Berry is a combination of my love for writing and my love for reading. She began as an experiment and took off into something I absolutely adore. It's not often you can do what you love and it works as a career. As for me, I love reading and romance and heroines seriously getting railed. I assume since you've read my books, you do too.

If you want to discuss books or anything with me, come join my Facebook group, C.S. Berry's Spicy Executive Suite. And you can always catch me on Instagram @csberry.

Oh and me, I have a lovely family who aren't allowed to read my books. But are so proud, they keep leaking my pen name. My dog and cats don't care about my writing as long as I sit still long enough for them to snuggle.

XOXOXO,

C.S. Berry

Keep up with C.S. Berry

View the shop: csberrybooks.com

View the Patreon: patreon.com/csberry

Join her Newsletter on her website

Join the Facebook Group:

https://www.facebook.com/groups/csberryreaders

Checkout her Website: csberry.com